OXFORD WORLD'S CLASSICS

SILAS MARNER

GEORGE ELIOT was born Mary Anne Evans on 22 November 1819 near Nuneaton, Warwickshire, on the Arbury estate of the Newdigate family, of which her father was agent. At the age of 9 she was imbued with an intense Evangelicalism that dominated her life until she was 22. Removing to Coventry with her father in 1841, she became acquainted with the family of Charles Bray, a free-thinker, and was persuaded to translate Strauss's *Life of Jesus* (3 vols., 1846). After her father's death in 1849 she spent six months in Geneva, reading widely. On her return she lived in London in the house of the publisher John Chapman, editing the *Westminster Review*. At the focus of many radical ideas here she met George Henry Lewes, a versatile journalist, whose marriage was irretrievably ruined. Although divorce was impossible, in 1854 she went to Germany with him, and for twenty-four years lived openly with him as his wife until his death in 1878. Through his encouragement at the age of 37 she began to write fiction. *Scenes of Clerical Life*, serialized in *Blackwood's Magazine*, and reprinted (1858) under the *nom de plume* George Eliot, was an instant success. *Adam Bede* (1859) became a bestseller; *The Times* declared that 'its author takes rank at once among the masters of the art'. In *The Mill on the Floss* (1860) and the five novels that followed George Eliot, with increasing skill, continued the subtle probing of human motive that leads many modern critics to regard her as the greatest novelist of the nineteenth century. Lewes's death was a devastating blow that ended her writing career. On 6 May 1880 she married John Walter Cross, a banker twenty years her junior, and on 22 December died at 4 Cheyne Walk, London.

JULIETTE ATKINSON is a Lecturer in English at University College London. Her publications include *Victorian Biography Reconsidered: A Study of Nineteenth-Century 'Hidden' Lives* (2010) and *French Novels and the Victorians* (2017). She has also contributed essays to *George Eliot in Context* (2013) and regularly reviews for the *George Eliot Review*. She has introduced and annotated George Eliot, *The Mill on the Floss* (2015) for Oxford World's Classics.

OXFORD WORLD'S CLASSICS

For over 100 years Oxford World's Classics have brought readers closer to the world's great literature. Now with over 700 titles—from the 4,000-year-old myths of Mesopotamia to the twentieth century's greatest novels—the series makes available lesser-known as well as celebrated writing.

The pocket-sized hardbacks of the early years contained introductions by Virginia Woolf, T. S. Eliot, Graham Greene, and other literary figures which enriched the experience of reading. Today the series is recognized for its fine scholarship and reliability in texts that span world literature, drama and poetry, religion, philosophy and politics. Each edition includes perceptive commentary and essential background information to meet the changing needs of readers.

OXFORD WORLD'S CLASSICS

GEORGE ELIOT

Silas Marner:
The Weaver of Raveloe

Edited with an Introduction and Notes by
JULIETTE ATKINSON

UNIVERSITY PRESS

OXFORD
UNIVERSITY PRESS

Great Clarendon Street, Oxford, OX2 6DP
United Kingdom

Oxford University Press is a department of the University of Oxford.
It furthers the University's objective of excellence in research, scholarship,
and education by publishing worldwide. Oxford is a registered trade mark of
Oxford University Press in the UK and in certain other countries

First published as a World's Classics paperback 1996
Reissued as an Oxford World's Classics paperback 1998
New edition 2017

Impression: 2

Published in the United States of America by Oxford University Press
198 Madison Avenue, New York, NY 10016, United States of America

British Library Cataloguing in Publication Data
Data available

Library of Congress Control Number: 2016951440

ISBN 978–0–19–872464–3

Printed in Great Britain by
Clays Ltd, St Ives plc

CONTENTS

INTRODUCTION

Readers who do not wish to learn details of the plot will prefer to read the Introduction as an Afterword

In July 1859, the writer George Henry Lewes travelled to his sons' boarding school in Switzerland to inform the three boys that henceforth there would be a new mother in their lives. Lewes had long since separated from, but not divorced, Agnes Jervis Lewes, and the boys were to welcome into their family Marian Evans, already famous as George Eliot, author of the celebrated novel *Adam Bede* (1859). (It was a summer of revelations for Eliot: her pseudonym had been lifted only days earlier, in June.) Sixteen-year-old Charles dutifully addressed a letter to his 'Dear Mother', thanking her for the watch she had sent him; Eliot in return wrote of the 'great comfort to your father and me' that Charles had been working hard at school, adding: 'you are always giving a pleasure when you write to your loving mother'.[1] The following summer, Lewes and Eliot fetched Charles from his Hofwyl school (leaving his younger brothers Thornton and Herbert temporarily behind) so that he could join them in England. The couple soon left their Wandsworth home to establish residency in central London, 'in order to be *nearer* town for Charley's sake, who has an appointment in the Post Office'.[2] To a friend, Eliot painted the change as bittersweet: 'we are preparing to renounce the delights of roving and settle down quietly, as old folks should do, for the benefit of the young ones'.[3] It was in the midst of these domestic upheavals that *Silas Marner* (1861), Eliot's third novel, was begun. Eliot was in her early forties when she became a stepmother, roughly the same age as the weaver Silas when the golden-haired child Eppie unexpectedly crosses his threshold.

[1] Charles Lee Lewes to Marian Evans, 24 July 1859, quoted in Rosemarie Bodenheimer, *The Real Life of Mary Ann Evans: George Eliot, Her Letters and Fiction* (Ithaca, NY: Cornell University Press, 1994), 190–1; George Eliot to Charles Lee Lewes, 30 July 1859, in *The George Eliot Letters*, ed. Gordon S. Haight, 9 vols. (New Haven: Yale University Press, 1854–78), iii. 125–7.

[2] GE to Sara Sophia Hennell, 27–8 August 1860, *George Eliot Letters*, iii. 337.

[3] GE to Barbara Bodichon, 5 September 1860, *George Eliot Letters*, iii. 342.

Confiding to another friend nearly a decade later, George Eliot stated: 'I profoundly rejoice that I never brought a child into the world.'[4] The role of stepmother, however, was one she took to heart. In the midst of writing *Silas Marner*, Eliot wrote to her French translator: 'I begin, you know, to consider myself an experienced matron, knowing a great deal about parental joys and anxieties'; with her freethinking correspondent Cara Bray, she shared that 'Our big boy is a great delight to us and makes our home doubly cheery. It is very sweet as one gets old to have some young life about one.'[5] Nonetheless, just as Eppie gets in the way of Silas's weaving, the responsibilities of motherhood were disruptive. In January 1861, Eliot informed her publisher John Blackwood about the 'story of old-fashioned village life' she was busy writing, and worried in the same breath that 'I think I get slower and more timid in my writing, but perhaps worry about houses and servants and boys, with want of bodily strength, may have had something to do with that.'[6]

From the Italian orphan Caterina in 'Mr Gilfil's Love Story' (1857) to Daniel Deronda, raised by a man he mistakenly believes to be his father, George Eliot's fiction teems with reconstituted families and foster-parents. Parenthood, and the reinvigorating presence of 'young life', are also at the heart of *Silas Marner.* Although he has spent fifteen years in the village of Raveloe, after having abandoned the manufacturing town in which a severe religious community had falsely accused him of theft, Silas remains estranged from his neighbours. The weaver's solitary ways and the disquieting cataleptic seizures to which he is prone provoke gossip and suspicions, and his only companions are the gold coins he slowly accumulates. Across the village, 26-year-old Godfrey bitterly regrets his secret marriage to an alcoholic barmaid, which exposes him to his brother's blackmail and stands in the way of his union with the charming Nancy Lammeter. One winter, Silas's beloved coins are stolen and, shortly afterwards, a golden-haired child crawls across the weaver's threshold; Silas's decision to raise Eppie and Godfrey's resolve to keep his paternity concealed have a profound impact on their lives. While it contemplates

[4] GE to Emilia Patterson, 10 August 1869, *George Eliot Letters*, v. 52.

[5] GE to François d'Albert-Durade, 29 January 1861, *George Eliot Letters*, iii. 373; GE to Cara Bray, 18 September 1860, *George Eliot Letters*, iii. 346.

[6] GE to John Blackwood, 12 January 1861, *George Eliot Letters*, iii. 371–2.

these two unconventional forms of fatherhood, the novel is full of mothers who have passed away: Silas's father is not mentioned but we are told about his mother's death, and attention is drawn to the death of Nancy's and Priscilla's mother, as well as that of Godfrey and Dunstan Cass. The central event on which the plot turns, Eppie's arrival, hinges on the death of her mother in the snow, while the second part of the novel dwells on Nancy's painful exclusion from the joys of motherhood. The only strong maternal presence in the novel is that of Dolly Winthrop, and it is with this neighbour that Silas develops the closest relations. In combining the attributes of a father with qualities presented as maternal, Silas recalls another literary father, Wordsworth's 'Michael', the vigorous shepherd who, with his wife, raises his son Luke, for whom he does 'female service [. . .] with patient mind enforc'd | To acts of tenderness; and he had rock'd | His cradle with a woman's gentle hand'.[7]

'Michael', which appeared in the 1800 edition of *Lyrical Ballads*, provides *Silas Marner* with its epigraph: 'A child, more than all other gifts | That earth can offer to declining man, | Brings hope with it, and forward-looking thoughts.' The conclusion of Wordsworth's poem and Eliot's story are different: far from being a comfort to his ageing parents, Luke is sent to the city to help recover the family's fortunes but instead sinks into dissipation. Eppie, in contrast, becomes a welcome substitute for the theft of the reclusive Silas's cherished gold and restores his bonds with the community. Nonetheless, the affinity between Wordsworth's poetry and Eliot's fiction are profound. Eliot 'felt all through as if the story would have lent itself best to metrical rather than prose fiction', were it not for her desire to introduce elements of humour which she deemed better adapted to prose. Writing to John Blackwood, she speculated that Wordsworth (who had died a little over a decade earlier) would have been the reader most likely to feel an attraction to her story, which is indeed rich with Wordsworthian touches, from its setting amongst humble rural lives to its interest in childhood.[8]

The epigraph emphasizes 'forward-looking thoughts', but *Silas Marner* is also profoundly Wordsworthian in suggesting that a

[7] William Wordsworth, 'Michael' (1800), in Wordsworth and Coleridge, *Lyrical Ballads*, ed. Fiona Stafford (Oxford: Oxford World's Classics, 2013), 289.

[8] GE to John Blackwood, 24 February 1861, *George Eliot Letters*, iii. 382.

productive engagement with the present and future can only exist through a connection with one's past. Forgetfulness, like the attempt to bury the past, is often problematic in Eliot's novels. Godfrey takes 'draughts of forgetfulness' (p. 96) just as his first wife drinks the black liquid laudanum that confers 'oblivion' (p. 97). She is destroyed by it while he, less violently but nonetheless painfully, is rewarded with a lifetime of regret. After his false accusation Silas, too, lapses into a numbing state of forgetfulness, heightened by his cataleptic seizures, until Eppie folds him back into the community. The narrator notes that, 'As the child's mind was growing into knowledge, his mind was growing into memory: as her life unfolded, his soul, long stupefied in a cold narrow prison, was unfolding too, and trembling gradually into full consciousness' (p. 114). Underscoring this idea, the narrator later adds that caring for Eppie enables the weaver to recover 'a consciousness of unity between his past and present' (p. 126). It is striking, indeed, that even before Eppie regenerates her foster-father, the rare moments in which Silas engages empathetically with another being are immediately linked to his past: in one instance, the 'possibility of some fellowship with his neighbours' opens up when he treats an ailing cobbler's wife, whose suffering recalls his own mother's pain, triggering 'a rush of pity at the mingled sight and remembrance' (p. 15). Similarly, remorse that he has falsely accused Jem of stealing his gold evokes his own false accusation, as 'Memory was not so utterly torpid in Silas that it could not be wakened by these words' (p. 51). Again, Silas's discovery of Eppie in front of the hearth immediately brings to mind his little sister, 'whom he had carried about in his arms for a year before she died, when he was a small boy' (p. 99), and about whom the narrative had until then been silent. Healthy social bonds are repeatedly portrayed as growing out of older experiences and relationships, and the child in *Silas Marner* repairs the broken links between past, present, and future.

The theme of parents and children suggests another parallel, drawn this time not from Romantic poetry but from Shakespearean romance. *The Winter's Tale* (1610–11) includes the loss of a daughter, Perdita, who is abandoned in a hostile landscape before being found and raised by a shepherd; she is restored, sixteen years later, to her royal parents. At the end of the play King Leontes is in his forties, as is Eppie's father Godfrey at the end of the novel; the coldness of the scenes set in Sicily is replaced by the lush fertility of Perdita's life in Bohemia, much as winter gives way to spring in Eliot's work. There is something of the fairy tale about both works. *Silas Marner*, however, complicates the pastoral motif of an abandoned high-born child raised in humble life and later restored to her natural parents: when, after a sixteen-year gap, Godfrey comes to claim his daughter, Eppie chooses her foster-father and, with him, humble life. The scene opens up a debate about who has the stronger claims on Eppie, and whether blood or love should prevail. The novel, throughout, expresses a certain scepticism about rigid interpretations of what constitutes a family: it pokes fun, for example, at the villagers who welcome Doctor Kimble 'as a doctor by hereditary right' (p. 88), Squire Cass enjoys fulfilling 'the hereditary duty of being noisily jovial and patronising' (pp. 86–7) and Godfrey's cowardly behaviour towards his first wife is partly dictated by a reluctance to 'turn his back on that hereditary ease and dignity which, after all, was a sort of reason for living' (p. 28).[9] Nancy, too, holds narrow views on family, forcing her sister to dress like her and, later in life, resisting adoption on the grounds that the child 'would be a curse to those who had wilfully and rebelliously sought what it was clear that, for some high reason, they were better without' (p. 139). In choosing Silas (and, with him, marriage to the gardener Aaron rather than a match better suited to her station as the Casses' daughter), Eppie reaffirms the importance of love over law, and of preserving continuity between past and present. It is a measure of Eliot's achievement that the scene in which Silas's emotional claims are vindicated does not feel sentimental, and that the disappointments of the Casses are poignantly conveyed.

A 'Legendary Tale' Combined with 'Lifelike Reality'

Although the critical response to *Silas Marner* was not unanimously positive, the substantial admiration it has always provoked may have something to do with the circumstances of its creation. The novel provided respite from the longer, more laboured novel that Eliot had already embarked on. Having completed *The Mill on the Floss* on 21 March 1860, Eliot and Lewes travelled to Italy, where Eliot began to

[9] See Marianne Novy, 'Adoption in *Silas Marner* and *Daniel Deronda*', in Novy (ed.), *Imagining Adoption: Essays on Literature and Culture* (Ann Arbor: University of Michigan Press, 2001; repr. 2004), 35–56.

elaborate plans for *Romola*, eventually serialized in 1862–3. Set in fifteenth-century Florence and featuring historical figures such as Savonarola and Machiavelli, the novel required substantial research and proved enormously taxing. She interrupted the work a first time with the uncharacteristically sarcastic short story 'Brother Jacob' (published only in 1864), and soon followed this with another welcome diversion. In a diary entry for 28 November 1860, Eliot wrote: 'I am engaged now in writing a story, the idea of which came to me after our arrival in this house, and which has thrust itself between me and the other book I was meditating.'[10] This was *Silas Marner*, which she finished on 10 March 1861, shortly before setting off for a second trip to Florence. Although less autobiographical than her previous novel, the work was prompted by her 'recollection of having once, in early childhood, seen a linen-weaver with a bag on his back', and she chose to set the novel once more in a landscape evocative of her Warwickshire youth.[11] Indeed, the impulse to step back from Renaissance Florence and return to the early nineteenth-century English countryside may have stemmed not simply from her awareness that this had been the foundation of her critical and popular success, but also from her own recent move to central London. As she wrote in her journal during a moment of depression, 'the loss of the country has seemed very bitter to me'.[12]

Critics, on the whole, paid tribute to the artistic mastery displayed in the short novel. Many admitted a preference for her first novel, *Adam Bede*, but in many ways *Silas Marner* felt more controlled and mature: as the critic for the *Saturday Review* concluded, 'in combining the display of the author's characteristic excellences with freedom from blemishes and defects', it was 'perhaps superior' to Eliot's first full-length effort. The *Westminster Review* shared the widely held view that 'the stream of thought runs clearer, the structure of the story is more compact, while the philosophical insight is deeper and more penetrating than in any of her former productions'. For Henry James, writing in 1866, it 'holds a higher place than any of the author's works. It is more nearly a masterpiece; it has more of that simple, rounded,

[10] *The Journals of George Eliot*, ed. Margaret Harris and Judith Johnston (Cambridge: Cambridge University Press, 1998), 87.

[11] GE to John Blackwood, 24 February 1861, *George Eliot Letters*, iii. 382.

[12] GE, 28 November 1860, *Journals of George Eliot*, 86–7.

consummate aspect, that absence of loose ends and gaping issues, which marks a classical work.'[13]

Indeed, there is an undeniable clarity to the structure, which is the first of Eliot's novels to use the motif, hinted at in earlier works, of the double plot that eventually collides, as with the treatment of Lydgate and Dorothea in *Middlemarch* (1871–2), and Daniel and Gwendolen in *Daniel Deronda* (1876). There are several echoes between the trajectories of Silas and Godfrey, which Jenny Uglow has helpfully summarized: both 'are at the mercy of tyrannical father-figures—one religious, the other secular. Both are accused of misappropriating their "father's" money [. . .] Both, we are told, were originally warm, affectionate men, but by the time the story opens they are inward-looking and embittered, trapped by their own pasts [. . .] and both are deceived by "brothers" they trust.'[14] Both, one might add, also find that they cannot fix the past: Silas returns to Lantern Yard only to find that it has disappeared, and Godfrey's attempt to recover his child fails. The clarity of structure is also conveyed by Silas himself. Although the two events are not, in fact, connected, Silas links the theft of his gold to Eppie's arrival: 'he could only have said that the child was come instead of the gold—that the gold had turned into the child' (p. 110). This apparent simplicity, coupled with the romance elements traced above, confers a fable-like quality on the novel. In her letters to John Blackwood, Eliot referred to *Silas Marner* as a 'story' and as 'a sort of legendary tale'.[15] Others have described it as a fairy tale, which partly explains its enduring popularity as a children's book. There are also, in places, suggestions of allegory: here, as in so many of her works, the profound influence of Bunyan's *Pilgrim's Progress* (1678–84) is evident, and comes through in the symbolically named Lantern Yard, Prison Street, and the convivial Rainbow.

The more fable-like elements of the novel effortlessly coexist, however, with Eliot's realism. It was the faculty of conveying 'a lifelike reality' that, above all, held the attention of her reviewers.[16] It is hard

[13] [Unsigned], *Saturday Review* (April 1861) and [Unsigned], *Westminster Review* (July 1861), both in David Carroll (ed.), *George Eliot: The Critical Heritage* (London: Routledge and Kegan Paul, 1971; repr. 2000), 174 and 186 respectively. [Henry James], 'The Novels of George Eliot', *Atlantic Monthly*, 18 (October 1866), 482.

[14] Jenny Uglow, *George Eliot* (London: Virago, 1987; repr. 2008), 189–90.

[15] GE to John Blackwood, 24 February 1861, *George Eliot Letters*, iii. 382.

[16] *Saturday Review*, in Carroll (ed.), *George Eliot: Critical Heritage*, 173.

to convey quite how startlingly authentic Eliot's depiction of humble, rural life felt to her first readers. By the time of this, her third novel, it was evident to many that 'It is in the portraiture of the poor, and of what it is now fashionable to call "the lower middle class," that this writer is without a rival'; her 'gift' was so 'special' that her works 'come on us as a new revelation of what society in quiet English parishes really is and has been'.[17] E. S. Dallas agreed that she 'has given dignity to the life of boors and peasants in some of our bucolic districts, and this not by any concealment of their ignorance, follies, and frailties'. Neither Scott nor Dickens, who in their different ways had also broken new ground in the representation of the poor, came close to her level of 'truthfulness'.[18] The language of Eliot's detractors provides, if anything, more vivid evidence of how unusual this kind of literary realism felt: for the *Dublin University Magazine*, the characters in *Silas Marner* were 'dull clowns', 'Mean, boorish, heavy-witted'; 'What good', the irritated critic demanded, 'can any one gain by reading page after page of the boorish twaddle kept up by the folk who spend their evenings, with the help of pipes and beer, in the "Rainbow" parlour?'[19]

The good, Eliot might have answered, was as much ethical as it was aesthetic. As she declared in her first published work of fiction, the short story 'The Sad Fortunes of the Reverend Amos Barton' (1857), 'you would gain unspeakably if you would learn with me to see some of the poetry and the pathos, the tragedy and the comedy, lying in the experience of a human soul that looks out through dull grey eyes, and that speaks in a voice of quite ordinary tones'.[20] In *Silas Marner*, the invitation to engage empathetically with tragicomic humble life is achieved with a lighter, less didactic, touch. Eliot comes closest to drifting from her realist ideals, perhaps, when dealing in the second part of the novel with the 'blond dimpled girl of eighteen' (p. 122), surrounded by pets and dreaming over her garden. In a curious passage, the narrator draws attention to this by explaining the cause of Eppie's improbable loveliness. The 'peculiar love' with which Silas had raised her,

[17] *Saturday Review*, in Carroll (ed.), *George Eliot: Critical Heritage*, 170–1.

[18] [E. S. Dallas], *The Times* (April 1861), in Carroll (ed.), *George Eliot: Critical Heritage*, 179.

[19] [Unsigned], *Dublin University Magazine* (April 1862), in Carroll (ed.), *George Eliot: Critical Heritage*, 190–1.

[20] George Eliot, 'The Sad Fortunes of the Reverend Amos Barton' (1857), in *Scenes of Clerical Life* (1858), ed. Thomas A. Noble (Oxford: Oxford World's Classics, 2015), 39.

aided by the seclusion of their dwelling, had preserved her from the lowering influences of the village talk and habits, and had kept her mind in that freshness which is sometimes falsely supposed to be an invariable attribute of rusticity. Perfect love has a breath of poetry which can exalt the relations of the least-instructed human beings [. . .] so that it is not surprising if, in other things beside her delicate prettiness, she was not quite a common village maiden, but had a touch of refinement and fervour which came from no other teaching than that of tenderly-nurtured unvitiated feeling. (p. 130)

In her important essay 'The Natural History of German Life' (1856), which reads almost as a manifesto for the kind of fiction she would go on to write, Eliot had attacked the qualities painters and writers falsely attributed to rustic life: the 'notion that peasants are joyous [. . .] and village children necessarily rosy and merry, are prejudices difficult to dislodge from the artistic mind [. . .] But no one who has seen much of actual ploughmen thinks them jocund.'[21] Yet here, the narrator tells us, Eppie comes close to this idealized picture due to the manner in which she has been reared. The second sentence shines a light on the dual fable-like and realist impulses of the novel: the adopted girl, 'not quite a common village maiden', fits the pattern of fairy tale and romance princesses, like Perdita, whose royal blood cannot be suppressed. However, the language in which it is couched—the expression of faith in the ethical dimensions of love, the interest in causation, and the hint of intellectualism in the choice of the word 'unvitiated'—is characteristic of Eliot's vision.

Eppie's 'delicate prettiness' stands out in a novel in which the romanticization of pastoral life is resisted; for all its charm, *Silas Marner* is not the nostalgic vision of early nineteenth-century rural England that some have labelled it. The relief that a number of Eliot's critics appear to have felt when they realized that *Silas Marner* had largely eschewed the bitterness and psychosexual drama of the latter parts of *The Mill on the Floss* led them, and some later readers, to underplay the darker currents running through the novel. Eliot paints a community in which a regularly inebriated and idle Squire feeds his dog with 'enough bits of beef to make a poor man's holiday dinner' (p. 61), in which a weak-willed gentleman's son is ashamed of his connection with a drug-addicted barmaid who dies in the snow, in which

[21] [George Eliot], 'The Natural History of German Life' (1856), in Eliot, *Selected Critical Writings*, ed. Rosemary Ashton (Oxford: Oxford World's Classics, 1992), 261–2.

bad farming practices are endemic, landlords wish for the continuation of the war that brings them profit, and a gardener protests that 'there need nobody run short o' victuals if the land was made the most on' (p. 124). The novel may, as James put it, seem 'simple', but it is never simplistic.

A World 'At Once Occult and Familiar'

'One of the most striking features in this striking tale is the strong intellectual impress which the author contrives to give to a story of which the main elements are altogether unintellectual, without the smallest injury to the verisimilitude of the tale.'[22] Richard Holt Hutton, in his review, expresses the overall effect of Eliot's tale perfectly. While critics of Eliot's later novels regularly accused her of indulging in a kind of 'intellectual slang', the same cannot be said here, despite the fact that the novel enacts some of the debates discussed, as Hutton put it, 'in modern times by the educated classes'.[23] How people interpret the world around them is one of the central concerns of the novel. The Dissenting community in Lantern Yard is busy searching for evidence of their assured election, and Silas's cataleptic fits are interpreted with equal conviction, and equal misguidedness, as signs of his salvation and damnation. Nancy's eagerness to submit to what she understands to be God's will creates an alertness to Providential signs that is little other than superstition: 'She would have given up making a purchase at a particular place if, on three successive times, rain, or some other cause of Heaven's sending, had formed an obstacle' (p. 139). The most sustained attention to the question of interpretation takes place, of course, in the Rainbow. There, the villagers tackle four subjects of contention: whether the cow driven in by the butcher was the same cow the farrier had previously treated for disease, whether Mr Tookey can sing, whether an error in the Lammeters' marriage ceremony has undermined the legality of their union, and whether there are ghosts in Mr Lammeter's stables. The landlord acts as mediator, but also insists on the possibility that competing claims can

[22] [Richard Holt Hutton], *The Economist* (April 1861), in Carroll (ed.), *George Eliot: Critical Heritage*, 176.

[23] [Sidney Colvin, review of *Middlemarch*], *Fortnightly Review* (January 1873), in Carroll (ed.), *George Eliot: Critical Heritage*, 335; [Hutton], in Carroll (ed.), *George Eliot: Critical Heritage*, 176.

be equally valid: 'The truth lies atween you: you're both right and both wrong, as I allays say' (p. 41).

The narrator explains how, 'To the peasants of old times, the world outside their own direct experience was a region of vagueness and mystery' (p. 3), but even their everyday lives are pregnant with a sense of mystery. Characters feel caught in a dreamlike state: for individuals such as Silas, the present 'is dreamy because it is linked with no memories' (p. 13), and when Eppie arrives in his cottage, he wonders, '*Was* it a dream?' (p. 99). But even the more prosaic Dunstan Cass experiences a 'bewildering dreamy sense of unwontedness' (p. 32) after killing his horse and being forced to walk home. Exceptional occurrences are, understandably, described as mysteries. Silas's catalepsy is a 'mysterious rigidity' (p. 7), the theft of the gold is an 'impenetrable mystery' (p. 67), and there is a 'sense of mystery in the child's sudden presence' (p. 100). However, so are more familiar ones: Raveloe boys feel awe 'at the mysterious action of the loom' (p. 4), gout and apoplexy are 'things that ran mysteriously in respectable families' (p. 20), Eppie is 'occupied with the primary mystery of her own toes' (p. 100), Silas is 'initiated in the mysteries' (p. 110) of dressing a child by Dolly, and he understands the concept of money itself as 'mysterious' (p. 15). In Eliot's preceding novel, *The Mill on the Floss*, the miller Mr Tulliver laboured under a 'painful sense of the complicated puzzling nature of human affairs'; the feeling of incomprehension is replaced in *Silas Marner* by a feeling, on the whole less tormented, of an enigmatic universe.[24] The willingness of Raveloe's inhabitants to submit to the riddle, rather than rigidly interpret them as the Lantern Yard brethren do, produces a greater feeling of harmony. A church service brings 'a vague exulting sense [. . .] that something great and mysterious had been done for them' (p. 77), and they have made a space for mystery in their daily lives, much like Dolly Winthrop, who continues to stamp the letters I. H. S. on her lard-cakes without understanding their significance. Life in Raveloe is 'at once occult and familiar' (p. 13).

Silas's powerful attachment to material objects is another way in which the everyday gains mystical qualities. Silas fetishizes not only his gold, but also his 'brown earthenware pot' that, once broken, he sticks together and preserves as a 'memorial' (p. 18). His 'old brick

[24] George Eliot, *The Mill on the Floss* (1860), ed. Gordon Haight (Oxford: Oxford World's Classics, 2015), 72.

hearth' provokes a similar affection. The narrator notes that the 'gods of the hearth exist for us still; and let all new faith be tolerant of that fetishism, lest it bruise its own roots' (p. 126), a comment that provides further evidence of the novel's 'intellectual impress' by exhibiting Eliot's engagement with contemporary philosophy. The French positivist philosopher Auguste Comte (1798–1857), who had found a keen supporter in Lewes decades earlier, and with whose works Eliot was highly familiar, outlined three stages in mankind's world view. From an initial theological stage (in which phenomena are attributed to a personified God or gods), mankind progressed through a metaphysical one (in which God becomes an abstract concept) before reaching the final, positivist, stage, in which the world is explained by empirical, scientific means. Fetishism occurred in the first stage. Echoing Comte, for whom fetishism provided a necessary step on the path towards a more enlightened positivism and celebration of humanity, Eliot laments Silas's emotional sterility but defends his deification of pots, hearths, and gold as a step in his ability to forge non-material, human bonds.[25] Eliot also drew on her interest in the works of Ludwig Feuerbach (1804–72), whose 1841 work *Das Wesen des Christentums* she translated as *The Essence of Christianity* in 1854. For Feuerbach, religion issued from man's projection of his own needs onto a non-human being; '*Man feels nothing towards God which he does not also feel towards man*'.[26] Eliot's depiction of the fanatical Lantern Yard sect is in many ways a Feuerbachian and Comtian critique of a religion that has left the human dimension far behind.

The parish clerk Mr Macey resents attempts to explain the theft of Silas's gold by physical evidence and what he sees as a mistaken belief 'that everything must be done by human hands' (p. 54). In *Silas Marner*, however, an enormous amount *is* accomplished with hands: the novel focuses almost obsessively on hands and the sense of touch, as if feeling the world provides a compensation for the inability to seize it intellectually. Like many Victorian novelists, such as Dickens, Eliot was keenly alert to hands as a social marker: Silas's hand is 'a weaver's hand, with a palm and finger-tips that were sensitive to such pressure' (p. 153),

[25] See James McLaverty, 'Comtean Fetishism in *Silas Marner*', *Nineteenth-Century Fiction*, 36/3 (December 1981), 318–36.

[26] Ludwig Feuerbach, *The Essence of Christianity*, trans. Marian Evans (London: John Chapman, 1854), 275.

while Nancy has the coarse hand (p. 82) of a woman used to making butter and cheese—a hand, perhaps, not unlike Eliot's own. Hands are, however, made to do a lot more work in the novel. Characters fetishize not only what they can touch, but also what they can hold: the pleasure Silas takes in his earthenware pot lies in the 'impress of its handle on his palm' (p. 18), and Dunstan takes an almost fetishistic pleasure in the golden handle of Godfrey's whip that becomes the means by which he is later identified. Money in the novel is associated not with wealth but with what can be grasped: Silas is focused on the money that customers 'would put into his hand' (p. 14), and his representation as a miser is founded on the delight he takes in handling the money—he 'bathed his hands in them' (p. 19). (Nancy, too, struggles with the abstract concept of money, and is only able to count 'by removing visible metallic shillings and sixpences from a visible metallic total' (p. 83).[27]) It is appropriate, therefore, that when money is stolen both in Lantern Yard and in Raveloe, Silas's only image of the thief is as someone with hands: 'Some hand had removed that bag' (p. 10), and it was a 'robber with hands, who could be reached by hands' (p. 38).

The narrator makes a point of Silas's short-sightedness, and hands come to replace not only his sight but also his voice, offering his best means of expression. The reader is informed seven times that, during moments of emotional turmoil, Silas either lifts his hands to his head or presses his head between his hands. Silas *becomes* his hands, which take on a mind of their own: 'Silas's hand satisfied itself with throwing the shuttle' (p. 14), the narrator comments, and his bent shape even 'produced the same sort of impression as a handle' (p. 18). During the fraught confrontation with the Casses, when Silas is again suffocated with anguish, Eppie communicates with Silas through their hands, holding his own, resting hers on his head, and then grasping his more firmly. Indeed, their first contact, when Eppie was yet a baby, occurred when 'his fingers encountered soft warm curls' (p. 99), and the regeneration that Eppie brings to him is compared to the biblical image of angels 'who came and took men by the hand' (p. 119). Less obtrusively, and perhaps more movingly, a similar pattern of human connection is at work between Godfrey and Nancy. As Godfrey dreams of uniting with

[27] See Ilana Blumberg, 'Stealing the "Parson's Surplice"/the Person's Surplus: Narratives of Abstraction and Exchange in *Silas Marner*', *Nineteenth-Century Literature*, 67/4 (March 2013), 490–519.

Nancy, he already seems to feel 'her hand in mine' (p. 79). Yet, in married life, Nancy is shown three times with her hands tightly clasped, and it is only when they have overcome the trial of Godfrey's revelations and failed bid to gain Eppie, and experience a new-found closeness, that Godfrey is shown enjoying the long-imagined touch: 'he put out his hand' and 'Nancy placed hers within it' (p. 154). The consecration of Silas's acceptance by the community is, at the very end of the novel, again signalled by touch, as he and the wedding party see Mr Macey sitting outside his door, and stop 'to shake hands with the old man' (p. 160). Eliot's subtle use of hands throughout moves from a search for causality in a destabilizing world to an indication of strengthened human bonds.

Other characters stray from a Comtian 'religion of humanity' by clinging to the notion that their life is governed by luck. Eliot is always uneasy with the egotism implied in the conviction that the world is arranged according to one's desires—an egotism that the two Cass brothers are guilty of. Dunstan doggedly believes in his own luck, be it with the weather, the expectation that he will find buyers for Godfrey's horse ('he was such a lucky fellow' (p. 30)), or the lack of encounters on the road ('part of his usual good luck' (p. 32)). Godfrey, meanwhile, is associated with chance. He believes that 'The longer the interval, the more chance there was of deliverance from some, at least, of the hateful consequences to which he had sold himself' (p. 28), and the narrator later comments on 'the old disposition to rely on chances which might be favourable to him' (p. 59). Such a reliance is often, in Eliot's fiction, linked to moral cowardice. In *Adam Bede*, for example, the irresponsible Arthur Donnithorne 'told himself, he did not deserve that things should turn out badly [. . .] There was a sort of implicit confidence in him that he was really such a good fellow at bottom, Providence would not treat him harshly.'[28] Ideas of luck and chance are often paradoxical, as the different definitions of the word 'lot' highlight. A 'lot' can mean an object used, as with the brethren's determination of Silas's guilt, 'in methods of random selection to secure a decision' but one's 'lot' can also describe a destiny that, far from random, has 'been allotted by fate or divine providence'.[29] An important difference between Silas and the

[28] George Eliot, *Adam Bede* (1859), ed. Carol A. Martin (Oxford: Oxford World's Classics, 2001; repr. 2008), 284–5.

[29] *Oxford English Dictionary* (*OED*). Further references will be given in the text.

Cass brothers is that whereas they expect good fortune, he simply accepts luck, whether it works to his advantage (as with the return of the gold) or not.[30] Silas's catalepsy, unpredictable and unaccountable, represents his susceptibility to events he cannot control.

The novel's attitude towards causes and consequences adds further layers to its treatment of individual destinies. Many of the characters in *Silas Marner* make predictions which turn out to be correct: Dunstan speculates that Molly could die of an overdose, Godfrey warns that Dunstan may drink and injure his horse, and Macey interprets Silas's generosity as a 'sign that his money would come to light again' (p. 125). While the characters understand events in the light of their own interpretative frameworks—as evidence of luck, Providence, or faith—the narrative presents matters differently. In 1851, Eliot had reviewed Mackay's *The Progress of the Intellect* (1850) and commented on the 'invariability of sequence which is acknowledged to be the basis of physical science' and 'which alone can give value to experience and render education in the true sense possible'. Eliot stated her belief in the 'inexorable law of consequences', adding that 'human duty is comprised in the earnest study of this law'.[31] The novel makes the similar point that moral choices, not chance, shape lives. Godfrey's insight that 'Everything comes to light, Nancy, sooner or later' (p. 144) is experienced in religious terms, but the novel frames it in secular ones. For all that, the novel refuses to neatly dole out rewards and punishment according to what might seem the characters' just deserts: Silas's accuser William Dane is never located, Silas is never able to prove his innocence, and Nancy is condemned to a childless future. As critics have often noted, there is a duality running through Eliot's fiction, in which 'individual powerlessness' coexists with a vigorous defence of 'individual responsibility', and in which 'life as a kind of muddling through' sits alongside 'the need to discover a world where motives are, however briefly, distinct and direct and acted upon'.[32]

[30] See Peter New, 'Chance, Providence and Destiny in George Eliot's Fiction', *English*, 34/150 (1985), 191–208.

[31] [George Eliot], 'R. W. Mackay's *The Progress of the Intellect* (1851)', in Eliot, *Selected Critical Writings*, 21.

[32] Sally Shuttleworth, *George Eliot and Nineteenth-Century Science: The Make-Believe of a Beginning* (Cambridge: Cambridge University Press, 1984; repr. 1986), 83; David Carroll, *George Eliot and the Conflict of Interpretations: A Reading of the Novels* (Cambridge: Cambridge University Press, 1992), 140.

Habits and Variety

George Eliot's novels are, famously, profoundly concerned with historical change, and *Silas Marner* is no exception, with its detailed attention to fluctuations in the weaving industry, the impact of war on ordinary lives, and evolutions in fashion. It is also, more strikingly, a novel preoccupied with personal change. In Silas, Eliot offers a psychologically rich picture of habit and compulsion. Silas at first falls into repetitive behaviour through his work: 'The livelong day he sat in his loom, his ear filled with its monotony, his eyes bent close down on the slow growth of sameness in the brownish web, his muscles moving with such even repetition that their pause seemed almost as much a constraint as the holding of his breath' (p. 18). Absorption with his gold at first appears to promise respite (or 'revelry') but in fact creates another kind of repetition. Counting the coins, and arranging them into squares, become ends in themselves; as the narrator probes, 'Do we not wile away moments of inanity or fatigued waiting by repeating some trivial movement or sound, until the repetition has bred a want, which is incipient habit?' (p. 17). The emphasis on repetitive behaviour rather than greed distinguishes Silas from many literary misers, including Eliot's own Featherstone in *Middlemarch*. Silas's coins offer substitutes for human contact—they are 'his familiars' (p. 17)—but although the coins he has yet to earn are compared to 'unborn children' (p. 19), his behaviour is anything but fertile: the 'gold had kept his thoughts in an ever-repeated circle'. When the gold is stolen, Silas falls into yet another form of repetitive behaviour by continuously standing at his open door. In representing 'an object compacted of changes and hopes' (p. 113), Eppie disrupts such circularity, and by the end of the novel it is Silas himself who advocates change, reassuring Eppie, who would like to remain for 'a long, long while, just as we are', that 'things *will* change, whether we like it or no' (p. 133).

Although the novel's double plot suggests parallels between Godfrey and Silas, it is in many ways with Nancy that Silas has most in common. Silas has the memory of losing his little sister, while Nancy has suffered the death of her own child; Silas's weaving helps clothe women such as Nancy, who owns a drawer 'filled with the neat work of her hands' (p. 138), unworn by her lost infant. Nancy, like Silas, both avoids and is shut out from variety, and is given to mindless patterns: her person displays 'perfect unvarying neatness', and 'the very pins on her pincushion were stuck in after a pattern from which she was careful to allow no aberration' (p. 82). Her view of the world is correspondingly strict, and she is given to 'rigid principles' (p. 139)—something which, in Eliot's fiction, is always questionable even when, as is the case here, those principles are 'unvaryingly simple and truthful' (p. 141). Both Silas and Nancy are confined to their domestic space: Silas is shut in with his loom and his gold; Nancy, like 'the women of her generation', is 'not given to much walking beyond [her] own house and garden, finding sufficient exercise in domestic duties' (p. 136). Whereas Silas's isolation is presented as an anomaly, Nancy's is painted as all-too-sadly typical. As in *The Mill on the Floss*, in which Maggie Tulliver protests to her brother that, being a man, he has 'power, and can do something in the world' while she has little to relieve the monotony of domestic life, Nancy acquires a morbid turn of mind.[33] Unlike Silas, whose mindless habits cordon him off from the past, Nancy's repetitive behaviour has been interiorized: 'Her mind not being courted by a great variety of subjects, she filled the vacant moments by living inwardly, again and again, through all her remembered experience', indulging in 'excessive rumination and self-questioning' (p. 137).

Whereas clinging to narrow, repetitive acts clearly does not bode well for individuals, it is less clear what to make of the rituals and habits indulged in by communities. Conversation and personal interactions seem as carefully regulated as Nancy's pincushions: at Squire Cass's home, 'the annual Christmas talk was carried through without any omissions' (p. 77); during the New Year's Eve party, Nancy and her aunt go through a long-established series of polite questions and answers, and the Squire's guests offer up 'safe, well-tested personalities' (p. 90). Conversations at the Rainbow are equally ritualistic: when Mr Macey launches on the story of Mr Lammeter's marriage, 'Every one of Mr Macey's audience had heard this story many times, but it was listened to as if it had been a favourite tune' (p. 45). Once Mr Snell has developed his story about the suspicious pedlar, it becomes a similarly favourite tune, 'frequently repeated' (p. 56). Earlier in the novel, the narrator imagines the 'lives of those rural forefathers' who in their old age had little left except 'to drink and get merry, or to drink and get angry, so that they might be independent of variety, and

[33] Eliot, *The Mill on the Floss*,322.

say over again with eager emphasis the things they had said already any time that twelvemonth' (p. 27). Habits, here, retain their numbing and narrowing qualities but, because they are experienced communally, also provide sources of comfort and pleasure, much like the familiar songs with which they are often linked. There is a sense that religion, in Raveloe, accomplishes a similar function, with the minister handling 'the book in a long-accustomed manner' (p. 13)—the theological sophistication might be questioned, but the ritual brings the community together.

Even so, Raveloe itself, the novel makes clear, would benefit from a greater tolerance for change. As a number of critics have noted, *Silas Marner* contains many door frames and break-ins, from Eppie crawling over Silas's door frame, to Silas bursting into the Rainbow, and later Squire Cass's home; even Dunstan's burglary of Silas's home, while initially devastating, strengthens Silas's relationship with his neighbours.[34] It is also a novel full of strangers: Silas is, of course, the most prominent alien in the eyes of his community, but the story of Nancy's grandfather who, like Silas, 'came from a bit north'ard' (p. 43), and who used to remind his son that, like the song, he came 'from over the hills and far away' (p. 90), offers the promise that Silas will become accepted by the Raveloe community as the Lammeters have. While the general xenophobia provokes wild speculation about the pedlar, Silas and Godfrey are both betrayed not by strangers but by the men closest to them. Pauline Nestor has recently argued that the 'ethical challenge' that Eliot proposes in *Sila Marner* goes beyond mere sympathy, and asks us 'to embrace what is not known or like', much as Dolly and Silas accept without quite understanding each other.[35] George Eliot was fascinated by the effect that strangers have on close-knit communities, as in 'Brother Jacob', in which a confectioner steals money and attempts to rebuild his life under a new identity, or in the trajectory of Doctor Lydgate in *Middlemarch*. *Silas Marner* skilfully combines this interest with a study of the consequences of personal obsessive behaviour, and argues for the ethical and psychological value of variety—even men's stomachs, Dolly concedes, 'want a change' (p. 72). Novels too, it might be added, are reliant on change

[34] See e.g. David Sonstroem, 'The Breaks in *Silas Marner*', *Journal of English and Germanic Philology*, 97/4 (October 1998), 545–67.

[35] Pauline Nestor, *George Eliot* (Basingstoke: Palgrave, 2002), 84.

and incident; sameness and repetition threaten not only happiness but also storytelling.

Threads and Weaving

Repetition and storytelling are bound in the novel's representation of weaving, a theme that exemplifies the manner in which *Silas Marner* deftly moves between fable and realism. Classical mythology and fairy tales are crowded with weavers. Silas's insect-like activity (he is reduced 'to the unquestioning activity of a spinning insect' and 'seemed to weave, like the spider, from pure impulse, without reflection' (p. 14)) calls to mind the myth of Arachne, who boldly challenged a goddess to a weaving contest. In the version given by Ovid in *Metamorphoses*, the goddess Athena recognizes Arachne's superior skill but, enraged, transforms her into a spider. The myth presents Arachne's weaving as a source of tremendous artistic power, but other tales underscore the confinement of weaving: in the fairy tale of Rumpelstiltskin, for example, a miller's daughter is imprisoned and forced to spin straw into gold after her father's careless boast. In Tennyson's 'The Lady of Shalott', published in 1832, both creativity and imprisonment are suggested by the mysterious figure who 'weaves by night and day'.[36] Eliot was sufficiently intrigued by such tales to compose, sometime between 1873 and 1876, the elegiac poem 'Erinna' about the Greek poetess who, at the age of 19, supposedly died after having been chained by her mother to a spinning wheel. Here, too, the weaver is condemned 'to spin the byssus drearily | In insect labour'; unlike Silas, however, 'the passion in her eyes | Changes to melodic cries'.[37] Erinna develops a creative vision in spite of, not thanks to, the weaving.

Although Silas's weaving provides him with a numbing occupation rather than a creative vision, the novel nonetheless plays with the many affinities between weaving and writing, anticipating the narrator who, in *Middlemarch*, has 'so much to do in unraveling certain human lots, and seeing how they were woven and interwoven'.[38] The

[36] Alfred Tennyson, 'The Lady of Shalott' (1832), in *Alfred Tennyson: The Major Works*, ed. Adam Roberts (Oxford: Oxford World's Classics, 2000; repr. 2009), 22.

[37] George Eliot, 'Erinna', in *The Complete Shorter Poetry of George Eliot*, ed. Antoine Gerard van den Broek (London: Pickering & Chatto, 2005), ii. 114.

[38] George Eliot, *Middlemarch*, ed. David Carroll (Oxford: Oxford World's Classics, 1986; repr. 2008), 116.

Latin etymology of the word 'text', *textus*, evokes 'that which is woven, web, texture' (*OED*). The language of storytelling is replete with similar associations, as indicated by Silas who recognizes that the Lantern Yard brethren have 'woven a plot to lay the sin' at his door (p. 11), or the farrier who, in the Rainbow, is shown 'taking up the thread of discourse' (p. 40). The narrator's comment on 'the only clew' that Silas's 'bewildered mind could hold by' (p. 126) evokes the dual significance of 'clew': a solution, but also a 'ball of thread or yarn', like that with which Ariadne leads Theseus out of the Minotaur's labyrinth (*OED*). There are similarly suggestive links between storytelling and counting. To 'tell' is to narrate, but it is also to enumerate or count—Silas, for example, works 'far on into the night to finish the tale of Mrs Osgood's table-linen' (p. 14). The unproductive, materialistic 'telling' of Silas's coins contrasts with Eliot's view of storytelling as an outward-looking mode that sheds light on the web-like nature of society and produces sympathetic ties. *Silas Marner* is interested in the slippage between the figurative and the literal; Silas loses his heap of coins, but Eppie becomes a far more valued 'new treasure' (p. 121). As Mary Poovey explores, in this work 'metaphor trumps such literalness', just as the bonds Eppie forges with Silas make him more of a father to her than her 'literal' parent Godfrey.[39]

The fairy-tale and mythical affinities of Silas's weaving are counterbalanced by a far more realist preoccupation with weaving. The Raveloe community attaches mysterious powers to string, and compares Silas to the Wise Woman of Tarley who 'tied a bit of red thread round the child's toe' to 'keep off water in the head' (p. 16). But Silas, whose livelihood depends on thread, has much more practical uses for it: his door closes with a latch-string, and in order to cook a piece of pork he ties it with string passed through a door-key. He relies on cloth as a child-rearing method, attaching Eppie to his loom with an umbilical-like 'broad strip of linen' (p. 115) that Eppie cuts. This attention to detail reflects Eliot's careful rendering of the lives and economic status of weavers at the turn of the nineteenth century. The novel's depiction of Silas's labour echoes a number of nineteenth-century studies, such as Philip Gaskell's *The Manufacturing Population*

[39] See Mary Poovey, *Genres of the Credit Economy: Mediating Value in Eighteenth- and Nineteenth-Century Britain* (Chicago: University of Chicago Press, 2008), 383.

of England (1833), which describes the period between 1760 and 1800 as the heyday of domestic manufacture, when 'the cottage every where resounded with the clack of the hand-loom', a carefully tended garden was 'an invariable adjunct to the cottage of the hand-loom weaver', and the labour was deemed respectable and both financially and physically comfortable.[40] In 1841, the report of the *Royal Commission on the Condition of the Handloom Weavers* lamented the degraded condition of handloom weavers who by then were in decline, and contrasted it with that of an older, happier, generation.[41]

Eliot puts the language of weaving and threads to still further use by drawing upon it to explore the emotional lives of her characters. Silas's personality is one that seeks attachments: his life as a miser 'had been a clinging life; and though the object round which its fibres had clung was a dead disrupted thing, it satisfied the need for clinging' (p. 67). This need finds a more rewarding outlet in Eppie, and Eliot returns to the language of fibres to trace this new connection, as her presence 'stirred fibres that had never been moved' (p. 100); he is later compared to an 'affectionate Goliath' who has got 'himself tied to a small tender thing, dreading to hurt it by pulling, and dreading still more to snap the cord' (pp. 114–15). In contrast, Godfrey is presented as a character who strains against personal ties, and finds the 'chain' of his wife Molly 'all the more galling'. Nancy offers the promise of healthier bonds, but 'Instead of keeping fast hold of the strong silken rope by which Nancy would have drawn him safe to the green banks where it was easy to step firmly, he had let himself be dragged back into mud and slime' (p. 28). It is singularly appropriate that, when Godfrey and Nancy are dancing at the ball, the Squire steps on her dress, 'so as to rend certain stitches at the waist' (p. 94)—precisely at the moment when Silas forges a new bond with Eppie, Godfrey's ties with Nancy threaten to become unravelled. When Silas interrupts the dance with Eppie, Godfrey hears his child and 'felt the cry as if some fibre were drawn tight within him' (p. 104). Unlike Silas, however, Godfrey represses the impulse so that, many years later, childlessness remains the 'one main thread of painful experience in Nancy's

[40] Philip Gaskell, *The Manufacturing Population of England* (London: Baldwin and Cradock, 1833), 16–17.

[41] See John Holloway, 'Introduction', in Eliot, *Silas Marner* (London: Everyman's Library, 1977), p. x.

married life' (p. 137). Such imagery is not applied rigidly or obtrusively, but on the contrary quietly brings together the different facets—mythical, social, and psychological—of this deceptively simple novel, revealing the profound artistry of a work as touching to discover as it is endlessly rewarding to revisit.

NOTE ON THE TEXT

On 28 November 1860, a little over a month after having moved to a new house in Marylebone, George Eliot updated her journal as follows:

I am engaged now in writing a story, the idea of which came to me after our arrival in this house, and which has thrust itself between me and the other book I was meditating [*Romola*]. It is 'Silas Marner, the weaver of Raveloe.' I am still only at about the 62nd page, for I have written slowly and interruptedly of late.

On 10 March 1861, she exclaimed: 'Finished "Silas Marner", and sent off the last 30pp. to Edinburgh. Magnificat anima mea!'[1] The neatly written manuscript of the novel held by the British Library (Add. MS 34026) shows comparatively few revisions, many of which are detailed in Selected Variants, pp. 163–81.

The first edition of *Silas Marner: The Weaver of Raveloe* appeared on 2 April 1861 and sold for 12 shillings. The initial impression counted 4,103 copies; five additional impressions soon raised the number to over 8,000, and plans were rapidly made for a new, corrected, edition. On 23 September 1861, Eliot noted in her journal: 'I have been unwell ever since we returned from Malvern, and have been disturbed from various causes in my work, so that I have scarcely done any thing except correct my own books for a new edition.' Six days later, she added: 'Finished Silas Marner. I have thus corrected all my books for a new and cheaper edition and feel my mind free for other work.'[2] Eliot's corrections, written inside a copy of the printed first edition, are preserved at the Harry Ransom Library in Austin, Texas. The changes Eliot made were, on the whole, small: they included the addition and removal of punctuation, and corrections of inconsistencies (a reference to twelve years Silas had spent in Raveloe was changed to fifteen). Speech was occasionally tweaked to convey a more natural, less polished air. The corrected 6-shilling edition duly appeared in December.

[1] George Eliot, 28 November 1860 and 10 March 1861, *The Journals of George Eliot*, ed. Margaret Harris and Judith Johnston (Cambridge: Cambridge University Press, 1998), 87 and 89.

[2] George Eliot, 23 and 28 September 1861, *Journals*, 101–2.

Blackwood and Eliot also had plans to publish *Scenes of Clerical Life* and *Silas Marner* together in a single, 6-shilling edition, alongside the rest of 'The Works of George Eliot'. In January 1862, Eliot expressed a hope that the volume might appear at Easter, but the following January the matter was still under discussion.[3] John Blackwood checked whether Eliot had any further corrections to make, but she replied: 'I corrected Silas carefully for the last edition, so that the reprint may be made from that without any need for my revision.'[4] The volume appeared in April 1863. Sales proved disappointing; in November, Blackwood regretted that he had no good news to offer, and that the 'failure of this 6/ edition is very annoying'.[5]

Blackwood later entered into negotiations with Eliot regarding a further edition. In December 1866, he suggested the following: 'the opinion we have formed here is that the best plan will be to try the cheap illustrated edition of your Novels in sixpenny numbers of which Adam, The Mill, Scenes, Silas, and Felix would make 30, ultimately to make four volumes selling at 3/6 each [. . .] We would use the stereotype plates of the present 6/- edition of Adam, The Mill, Clerical Scenes, and Silas.'[6] The stereotyped edition, made from the plates of the 1863 (third) edition, appeared in 1868, without Eliot having made additional changes to the text.

In 1877, Eliot and Blackwood completed arrangements for the Cabinet Edition of her works; this was initially composed of ten titles, but with the addition of essays and John Walter Cross's biography of his wife the collection, completed posthumously, came to encompass thirteen titles spread out across twenty-four volumes. Eliot undertook further revisions for the Cabinet Edition, and her notes are again preserved in the Harry Ransom Library. The changes were, once more, comparatively minor. She removed a significant number of commas, corrected typographical errors, slightly rephrased a few sentences and clarified others. Speech patterns were again made more colloquial, and, intriguingly, this affected principally Godfrey's speech, which became less formal during his confrontation with Silas over Eppie's fate. The first titles of the Cabinet Edition, including *Silas Marner*,

[3] GE to John Blackwood, 12 January 1862, *The George Eliot Letters*, ed. Gordon S. Haight (New Haven: Yale University Press, 1954–78), iv. 6.

[4] GE to John Blackwood, 6 February 1863, *George Eliot Letters*, iv. 76.

[5] John Blackwood to GE, 10 November 1863, *George Eliot Letters*, iv. 113.

[6] John Blackwood to GE, 21 December 1866, *George Eliot Letters*, iv. 320.

appeared in 1878. Blackwood had argued for publishing *Silas Marner* on its own ('Silas Marner is such a perfect thing that I incline to keep it a small volume by itself'), but Eliot's plea that the volume be expanded to include *The Lifted Veil* and *Brother Jacob* prevailed.[7]

As the 1878 Cabinet Edition incorporates Eliot's final revisions of *Silas Marner*, it is the basis for this Oxford World's Classics edition. This edition follows the Cabinet closely, and has not, for example, regularized Eliot's inconsistent spelling of O/Oh. However, five corrections have been made:

page 106 the child could make no visible [or] audible claim on its father: *all editions overseen by Eliot give the clause as* the child could make no visible audible claim on its father.

page 109 afore it's time to go about the victual: *the Cabinet Edition reads* afore its time to go about the victual.

page 124 *the Cabinet Edition omitted the following opening quotation marks*: ["]but you'll make yourself fine and beholden to Aaron."

page 142 *the Cabinet Edition added a misplaced quotation mark at the end of the following*: said Jane, not altogether despising a hypothesis which covered a few imaginary calamities."

page 145 *the Cabinet Edition added a misplaced quotation mark as follows*: There was a faint sad smile on Nancy's face as she said the last words."

In addition, although the editions published in Eliot's lifetime used double quotation marks, these have been replaced here with single quotation marks, in keeping with the practice of Oxford World's Classics.

[7] John Blackwood to George Eliot, 8 February 1877, *George Eliot Letters*, vi. 340.

SELECT BIBLIOGRAPHY

Principal Editions Published in England during Eliot's Lifetime

Silas Marner: The Weaver of Raveloe (Edinburgh and London: William Blackwood and Sons, 1861). [First edition, sold for 12 shillings; published in one volume in April.]

Silas Marner: The Weaver of Raveloe (Edinburgh and London: William Blackwood and Sons, 1861). [6-shilling edition, including Eliot's corrections to the first edition; published in December.]

Scenes of Clerical Life and Silas Marner (Edinburgh and London: William Blackwood and Sons, 1863). [6-shilling edition, published in April. Volume iii of the three-volume 'Cheap Edition' of 'The Works of George Eliot'.]

Silas Marner: The Weaver of Raveloe (Edinburgh and London: William Blackwood and Sons, 1868). [Stereotyped edition, with illustrations. Volume iii of *Novels of George Eliot*.]

The Works of George Eliot: Silas Marner, The Lifted Veil, Brother Jacob (Edinburgh and London: William Blackwood and Sons, 1878) ['Cabinet' Edition, including Eliot's corrections; published in February. 5 shillings.]

Letters, Essays, and Journals

Essays of George Eliot, ed. Thomas Pinney (New York: Columbia University Press, 1963).

The George Eliot Letters, ed. Gordon S. Haight (New Haven, CT: Yale University Press, 1954–78), 9 vols.

The Journals of George Eliot, ed. Margaret Harris and Judith Johnston (Cambridge: Cambridge University Press, 1998).

George Eliot: Selected Critical Writings, ed. Rosemary Ashton (Oxford: Oxford World's Classics, 1992).

Select Biographies and Reference Works

Ashton, Rosemary, *George Eliot: A Life* (London: Hamish Hamilton, 1996).

Baker, William, and Ross, John C., *George Eliot: A Bibliographical History* (New Castle, DE: Oak Knoll, 2002).

Bodenheimer, Rosemarie, *The Real Life of Mary Ann Evans: George Eliot, Her Letters and Fiction* (Ithaca, NY: Cornell University Press, 1994).

Cross, J. W., *George Eliot's Life as Related in Her Letters and Journals* (Edinburgh: William Blackwood and Sons, 1885), 3 vols.

Haight, Gordon, *George Eliot: A Biography* (Oxford: Clarendon Press, 1968).

Hands, Timothy, *A George Eliot Chronology* (London: Macmillan Press, 1989).
Henry, Nancy, *The Life of George Eliot: A Critical Biography* (Oxford: Wiley-Blackwell, 2012).
Hughes, Kathryn, *George Eliot: The Last Victorian* (London: Fourth Estate, 1998).
Rignall, John (ed.), *Oxford Reader's Companion to George Eliot* (Oxford: Oxford University Press, 2000).
Uglow, Jenny, *George Eliot* (London: Virago, 1987; repr. 2008).

Criticism: General Studies on Eliot Including Discussions of Silas Marner

Anderson, Amanda, and Harry E. Shaw (eds.), *A Companion to George Eliot* (Oxford: Wiley-Blackwell, 2013; repr. 2016).
Ashton, Rosemary, *Past Masters: George Eliot* (Oxford: Oxford University Press, 1983).
Beer, Gillian, *George Eliot* (Brighton: Harvester Press, 1986).
Carroll, David (ed.), *George Eliot: The Critical Heritage* (London: Routledge and Kegan Paul, 1971; repr. 2000).
Carroll, David, *George Eliot and the Conflict of Interpretations* (Cambridge: Cambridge University Press, 1992).
Dolin, Tim, *Authors in Context: George Eliot* (Oxford: Oxford World's Classics, 2005).
Haight, Gordon (ed.), *A Century of George Eliot Criticism* (London: Methuen, 1966).
Hardy, Barbara, *The Novels of George Eliot: A Study in Form* (London: Athlone Press, 1959; repr. 1994).
Harris, Margaret (ed.), *George Eliot in Context* (Cambridge: Cambridge University Press, 2013).
Hutchinson, Stuart (ed.), *George Eliot: Critical Assessments*, 4 vols. (Mountfield: Helm, 1996).
Leavis, F. R., *The Great Tradition: George Eliot, Henry James, and Joseph Conrad* (London: Chatto and Windus, 1948).
Levine, George (ed.), *The Cambridge Companion to George Eliot* (Cambridge: Cambridge University Press, 2001).
Nestor, Pauline, *Critical Issues: George Eliot* (Basingstoke: Palgrave, 2002).
Raines, Melissa, *George Eliot's Grammar of Being* (London: Anthem, 2011; repr. 2013).
Rignall, John, *George Eliot, European Novelist* (Farnham: Ashgate, 2011).
Shuttleworth, Sally, *George Eliot and Nineteenth-Century Science: The Make-Believe of a Beginning* (Cambridge: Cambridge University Press, 1984; repr. 1986).

Criticism: Individual Works on Silas Marner

Blumberg, Ilana M., 'Stealing the "Parson's Surplice"/ the Person's Surplus: Narratives of Abstraction and Exchange in *Silas Marner*', *Nineteenth-Century Literature*, 67/4 (March 2013), 490–519.

Bowlby, Rachel, 'Finding a Life: George Eliot's *Silas Marner*', in Bowlby, *A Child of One's Own* (Oxford: Oxford University Press, 2013), 132–47.

Burton, Marianne, '"There is no such thing as natural barrenness in natural women": Childless Marriages in *Silas Marner* and *The Lifted Veil*', *George Eliot Review*, 43 (2012), 31–8.

Davis, Jen, '*Silas Marner*: George Eliot's Most Coleridgean Work?', *George Eliot Review*, 46 (2015), 8–14.

Draper, R. P. (ed.), *George Eliot,* The Mill on the Floss *and* Silas Marner*: A Casebook* (London: Macmillan, 1977).

Durham, Robert H., '*Silas Marner* and the Wordsworthian Child', *Studies in English Literature*, 26 (1976), 645–59.

Gill, Stephen, 'Wordsworth at Full Length: George Eliot', in Gill, *Wordsworth and the Victorians* (Oxford: Clarendon Press, 1998), 145–67.

Hardy, Barbara, 'Politics and Pastoral in *Silas Marner*', *George Eliot Review*, 45 (2014), 17–21.

Koepp, Robert C., 'Mode of Belief or Evidence of Doubt? George Eliot and the "Religion of Favourable Chance"', in Alisa Clapp-Intyre and Julie Melnyk (eds.), *'Perplext in Faith': Essays on Victorian Beliefs and Doubts* (Newcastle upon Tyne: Cambridge Scholars, 2015), 304–26.

Levine, George, 'Determinism and Responsibility in the Works of George Eliot', *PMLA*, 77/3 (June 1962), 268–79.

Levine, George, 'The Protestant Ethic and the "Spirit" of Money: Max Weber, *Silas Marner*, and the Victorian Novel', in Lisa Rodensky (ed.), *The Oxford Handbook of the Victorian Novel* (Oxford: Oxford University Press, 2013), 376–96.

McLaverty, James, 'Comtean Fetishism in *Silas Marner*', *Nineteenth-Century Fiction*, 36/3 (December 1981), 318–36.

Mazaheri, J. H., *George Eliot's Spiritual Quest in* Silas Marner (Newcastle upon Tyne: Cambridge Scholars, 2012).

New, Peter, 'Chance, Providence and Destiny in George Eliot's Fiction', *English*, 34/150 (1985), 191–208.

Novy, Marianne, 'Adoption in *Silas Marner* and *Daniel Deronda*', in Novy (ed.), *Imagining Adoption: Essays on Literature and Culture* (Ann Arbor: University of Michigan Press, 2001; repr. 2004), 35–56.

Pond, Kristen, 'Bearing Witness in *Silas Marner*: George Eliot's Experiment in Sympathy', *Victorian Literature and Culture*, 41/4 (December 2013), 691–709.

Poovey, Mary, 'From Gesture to Formalism: *Little Dorrit* and *Silas Marner*', in Poovey, *Genres of the Credit Economy: Mediating Value in Eighteenth- and Nineteenth-Century Britain* (Chicago: University of Chicago Press, 2008), 373–83.

Sicher, Efraim, 'George Eliot's 'Glue Test': Language, Law, and Legitimacy in *Silas Marner*', *Modern Language Review*, 94/1 (1999), 11–21.

Sonstroem, David, 'The Breaks in *Silas Marner*', *Journal of English and Germanic Philology*, 97/4 (October 1998), 545–67.

Swinden, Patrick, *Silas Marner: Memory and Salvation* (New York: Twayne, 1992).

Willis, Martin, '*Silas Marner,* Catalepsy, and Mid-Victorian Medicine: George Eliot's Ethics of Care', *Journal of Victorian Culture*, 20/3 (2015), 326–40.

Wolf, Peter, 'Epilepsy and Catalepsy in Anglo-American Literature between Romanticism and Realism: Tennyson, Poe, Eliot and Collins', *Journal of the History of the Neurosciences*, 9/3 (2000), 286–93.

Yousaf, Nahem, and Andrew Maunders (eds.), *New Casebooks:* The Mill on the Floss *and* Silas Marner (Basingstoke: Palgrave Macmillan, 2002).

Further Reading in Oxford World's Classics

Eliot, George, *Adam Bede*, ed. Carol A. Martin.

Eliot, George, *Daniel Deronda*, ed. Graham Handley, introduction by K. M. Newton.

Eliot, George, *The Lifted Veil and Brother Jacob*, ed. Helen Small.

Eliot, George, *Middlemarch*, ed. David Carroll, introduction by Felicia Bonaparte.

Eliot, George, *The Mill on the Floss*, ed. Gordon S. Haight, introduction by Juliette Atkinson.

Eliot, George, *Scenes of Clerical Life*, ed. Thomas A. Noble, introduction by Josie Billington.

A CHRONOLOGY OF GEORGE ELIOT

	Life	*Cultural and Historical Background*
1819	Born, 22 November, at South Farm, Arbury, nr Nuneaton, Warwickshire, the youngest of the three children of Robert Evans and his second wife Christiana Pearson. Christened Mary Anne Evans, 29 November.	Birth of Victoria. Scott, *The Bride of Lammermoor*, *Ivanhoe*
1820	Evans family moves to Griff House, Arbury, where Robert Evans is agent for Francis Newdigate's estate.	Death of George III; accession of George IV. Keats, *Lamia, . . . and other Poems* Shelley, *Prometheus Unbound*
1824–7	Boarder at Miss Lathom's School in nearby Attleborough, with her sister Chrissey.	
1828–32	At Mrs Wallington's boarding-school, Nuneaton, where she becomes friendly with Miss Lewis, the principal governess and a strong evangelical.	1829: Catholic Emancipation Act. 1830: Death of George IV; accession of William IV. Tennyson, *Poems, Chiefly Lyrical* 1830–3: Charles Lyell, *Principles of Geology*
1832–5	At the Miss Franklins' School, Coventry, run by the daughters of a Baptist minister. Leaves school finally at Christmas.	1832: First Reform Act. 1833: First Factory Act. 1835: David Friedrich Strauss, *Das Leben Jesu*
1836	Mother dies 3 February. After Chrissey marries, in May 1837, GE takes charge of her father's household. Learns Italian and Greek from a Coventry teacher, and reads Greek and Latin with the headmaster of Coventry Grammar School. Changes her name to Mary Ann.	

	Life	*Cultural and Historical Background*
1837–9	Reads widely, especially in theology, the history of religion and Romanticism, including Wordsworth, Coleridge, Southey, and Scott (her favourite novelist).	1837: Death of William IV; accession of Victoria. Carlyle, *The French Revolution* Dickens, *Pickwick Papers* 1838: Anti Corn Law League founded; London–Birmingham railway opened. 1839: Chartists demand suffrage. Charles Hennell, *An Inquiry into the Origins of Christianity*
1840	Her first publication, a religious poem, appears in the *Christian Observer* in January.	Penny Post established; Victoria marries Prince Albert.
1841	Brother, Isaac, marries and takes over the house at Griff. GE moves with father to Coventry. Introduced to Charles Bray and his wife Caroline (Cara), Coventry freethinkers through whom she makes contact with Charles Hennell. Reads Hennell's *Inquiry* and finds her religious faith challenged.	Robert Peel becomes Prime Minister. Carlyle, *Heroes and Hero Worship*
1842	Refuses to attend church with her father, January–May, but finally agrees to accompany him at the end of what she calls their 'Holy War'. Meets and begins corresponding with Charles Hennell's sister Sara.	Chartist riots; child and female underground labour becomes illegal. Act for inspection of asylums. Browning, *Dramatic Lyrics* Comte, *Cours de philosophie positive* Macaulay, *Lays of Ancient Rome* Tennyson, *Poems*
1843	In November visits Dr Brabant of Devizes, father of Charles Hennell's wife who had undertaken a translation of Strauss's *Das Leben Jesu* but, on marrying, discontinued it.	Thames Tunnel opened. Carlyle, *Past and Present* Ruskin, *Modern Painters* begins publication. Wordsworth, *Poems*
1844	Takes over the translation of *Das Leben Jesu*.	Robert Chambers, *Vestiges of Creation* (published anonymously).
1845	In March declines a proposal of marriage. Meets Harriet Martineau. In October visits Scotland with the Brays, and visits Scott's home, Abbotsford.	Newman received into the Catholic Church; Irish potato crop fails. Disraeli, *Sybil; or, The Two Nations*

	Life	*Cultural and Historical Background*
1846	The *Life of Jesus* published in 3 vols. in June after much labour and many complaints of being 'Strauss-sick'.	Repeal of the Corn Laws; Irish famine. Ruskin, *Modern Painters* II
1847	Nurses her father.	James Simpson discovers the anaesthetic properties of chloroform. 'Currer Bell', *Jane Eyre* 'Ellis Bell', *Wuthering Heights* Thackeray, *Vanity Fair* Dickens, *Dombey and Son*
1848	Meets Emerson; reads Sand and Scott. Nurses her father.	Revolutions in Europe; Disraeli becomes leader of the Tory party in the House of Commons. Elizabeth Gaskell, *Mary Barton*
1849	Reviews J. A. Froude's *Nemesis of Faith* favourably for the Coventry *Herald*. Begins translation of Spinoza's *Tractatus theologico-politicus*. Father dies on 31 May. In June leaves for France, Italy, and Switzerland with the Brays; winters alone in Geneva. Begins *Journal*.	Cholera epidemic in England; Bedford College for Women founded. Henry Mayhew's 'London Labour and the London Poor' articles begin publication in the *Morning Chronicle*.
1850	Returns, unhappily, to Coventry and lives with the Brays for seven months. Adopts the French spelling of her name, Marian, in preference to Mary Ann. Decides to earn her living by writing. Lodges with John Chapman in London for two weeks in November.	Death of Wordsworth. *The Prelude* published posthumously. Spencer, *Social Statics* Dickens, *David Copperfield*
1851	Reviews Mackay's *The Progress of the Intellect* for the January number of Chapman's *Westminster Review* and moves to Chapman's home, 142 Strand, but in March is driven away by the jealousy of his wife and his mistress. Returns in September to become, in all but name, the editor of the *Westminster Review*.	Great Exhibition opens at the Crystal Palace.

	Life	*Cultural and Historical Background*
1852	Friendship with Herbert Spencer leads to rumours of an engagement. Through him she meets George Henry Lewes, arts editor of the *Leader*.	Death of the Duke of Wellington, 14 September; Kings Cross station completed.
1853	Heavily involved with the *Westminster Review*. Reads Gaskell's *Ruth*, Brontë's *Villette*, Goethe, Schiller, Lessing, and Hegel. Resigns editorship of *Westminster Review* at the end of the year.	Harriet Martineau's translation of Comte, *Positive Philosophy* Dickens, *Bleak House* Charlotte Brontë, *Villette* Elizabeth Gaskell, *Ruth* and *Cranford*
1854	Her translation of Ludwig Feuerbach's radical critique of orthodox belief, *The Essence of Christianity*, is published in July. In the same month she travels to Germany with Lewes, first visiting Weimar then wintering in Berlin, causing scandal back in Britain. Lewes unable to obtain a divorce because he had condoned his wife's adultery. Assists Lewes in the research and writing of his biography of Goethe and in November begins a translation of Spinoza's *Ethics* (unpublished until 1981).	Crimean War begins.
1855	Returns to England in March and sets up house with Lewes in Richmond. Writes regularly for the *Leader* and *Westminster Review*. In November Lewes's *Life and Work of Goethe* is published to general and lasting acclaim.	Gaskell, *North and South* Turgenev, *Russian Life*, trans. by James D. Meiklejohn
1856	Visits Ilfracombe, May–June, for Lewes's research into marine biology (later published as *Sea-Side Studies*, 1858), then Tenby in Wales, July–early August where she conceives the idea of writing 'The Sad Fortunes of the Reverend Amos Barton'. Begins writing in September, and the story is	Crimean War ends 29 April; public celebrations of the peace with Russia are held across Britain on 29 May. Meredith, *The Shaving of Shagpat*

	Life	*Cultural and Historical Background*
	accepted by *Blackwood's Edinburgh Magazine*. Her review of Riehl's *The Natural History of German Life* appears in the *Westminster Review* in July, and 'Silly Novels by Lady Novelists' in October. Begins writing 'Mr Gilfil's Love-Story' on Christmas Day.	
1857	In January Part I of 'Amos Barton' appears in *Blackwood's* and her last major article in the *Westminster Review*. Assumes the pseudonym 'George Eliot'. In March travels with Lewes to Scilly Isles where she completes 'Mr Gilfil's Love-Story' for the June issue of *Blackwood's*. Tells her brother, Isaac, about her relationship and he insists her family break off all communication with her. 'Janet's Repentance' finished 30 May on Jersey, where GE and Lewes stay until late July. Begins writing *Adam Bede* in October.	Indian Mutiny. Flaubert, *Madame Bovary* Gaskell, *The Life of Charlotte Brontë* Dickens, *Little Dorrit*
1858	*Scenes of Clerical Life* published in 2 vols. in January. Dickens writes praising the book, and convinced the author must be a woman. In April GE and Lewes travel via Nuremberg to Munich, remaining there until 6 July when they make their way via Salzburg, Vienna, and Prague to Dresden. Work on *Adam Bede* proceeds quickly. They return to England in September, and the novel is completed on 16 November.	Government of India Act transferring British power over India from the East India Co. to the Crown; Burton and Speke discover source of the Nile; Bessie Parkes and Barbara Bodichon found the *English Woman's Journal* which campaigns for married women's property rights and higher education for women.
1859	*Adam Bede* published in 3 vols. in February to critical acclaim; 16,000 copies sold in the first year. In February they settle at Holly Lodge, Wandsworth, where GE forms a close	Charles Darwin, *The Origin of Species* J. S. Mill, *On Liberty* Tennyson, *Idylls of the King* *Macmillan's Magazine* launched in November.

	Life	*Cultural and Historical Background*
	friendship with the positivists, Mr and Mrs Richard Congreve. Sister Chrissey dies of consumption in March. Work on *The Mill on the Floss* is slow, and she breaks off to write 'The Lifted Veil' (finished in April and published in *Blackwood's* in July). In July, under pressure, the secrecy of the pseudonym is relinquished. Dickens visits in November and invites her to contribute to *All the Year Round*.	
1860	*The Mill on the Floss* finished on 22 March and published in 3 vols. on 4 April. GE and Lewes leave for a holiday in Italy where, in May, GE conceives the idea for a historical novel based on the life of Savonarola. They return to England via Switzerland, bringing Lewes's eldest son Charles back with them. GE writes 'Brother Jacob'; begins *Silas Marner*. With Charles they move house twice, settling in December at 16 Blandford Square, off Regent's Park.	Unification of Italy. *Cornhill Magazine* founded.
1861	*Silas Marner* published in April; they revisit Florence where GE collects more material, and she begins writing *Romola* in October.	American Civil War begins.
1862	Smith, Elder offer the unprecedented sum of £10,000 for *Romola* (GE eventually accepts £7,000) which begins serialization in the *Cornhill Magazine* in July. As part of her research for the book reads Elizabeth Barrett Browning's *Casa Guidi Windows*.	

	Life	*Cultural and Historical Background*
1863	*Romola* published in 3 vols. in July and finishes serialization in the *Cornhill* in August: 'I began it as a young woman,—I finished it an old woman.' In August they move to The Priory, Regent's Park, the house associated with GE's most famous years.	Thackeray dies suddenly on Christmas Eve; over 1,000 people attend the funeral. Elizabeth Gaskell, *Sylvia's Lovers*
1864	They visit Italy in May. In June GE begins research for *The Spanish Gypsy*, a tragic play in blank verse. Starts writing in October. Reading includes Newman's *Apologia pro Vita Sua*.	Dickens, *Our Mutual Friend* begins publication.
1865	Work on *The Spanish Gypsy* proves so stressful that Lewes insists she abandon it in February. Begins *Felix Holt* in March. Lewes becomes editor of the *Fortnightly Review* and GE contributes a review of Lecky.	Abraham Lincoln assassinated, 14 April; American Civil War ends in May; death of Palmerston in October; Russell succeeds him as leader of the House of Commons. *Fortnightly Review* founded. Walter Bagehot, *The English Constitution* serialized. Lecky, *History of . . . Rationalism in Europe*
1866	*Felix Holt* completed in May and published in 3 vols. in June but sales disappoint. Eliot and Lewes visit the Low Countries and Germany, and in August GE resumes work on *The Spanish Gypsy*. In December they set off for the South of France.	Russell's 1st Reform Bill defeated; in April Gladstone tells the House: 'You cannot fight against the future. Time is on our side'; rioting in Hyde Park on 23 July after the resignation of Russell's ministry; Austria and Prussia at war.
1867	In January they extend their trip to Spain so that GE can collect material. On 22 February they visit gypsies living in holes in the mountains above Granada. Return on 16 March.	2nd Reform Bill introduced by Disraeli; 20 May John Stuart Mill moves to amend the new Reform Bill to include women. Turgenev, *Fathers and Sons*, trans. E. Schuyler.
1868	Gives £50 'from the author of *Romola*' to the foundation of what would become Girton College, Cambridge. *The Spanish Gypsy* finished 29 April and published in June.	Browning, *The Ring and the Book* begins publication.

	Life	*Cultural and Historical Background*
1869	Writes 'Address to Working Men, by Felix Holt', for publication in *Blackwood's* in January. Writes some short poems early in the year. March and April in Italy. In Rome GE meets the stockbroker John Walter Cross for the first time. Henry James visits in May. GE intermittently researches a long poem to be called 'Timoleon', but abandons the project in September. Begins writing 'Middlemarch' (the Featherstone–Vincy part) in August. Lewes's second son, Thornton (Thornie), returns from Natal in May with spinal tuberculosis and dies in October. GE writes the poems eventually published as *The Legend of Jubal and Other Poems* (1874).	Hitchin College opens in May (becomes Girton College in 1873). J. S. Mill, *The Subjection of Women* Arnold, *Culture and Anarchy* (book form).
1870	Puts aside 'Middlemarch' in despair, and in December begins a new story, 'Miss Brooke', which develops rapidly. Corresponds with Harriet Beecher Stowe. Combines the two narratives early in the year to create the first section of *Middlemarch*, to be published in 8 parts.	Franco-Prussian War begins. Death of Dickens. Married Women's Property Act. Elementary Education Act.
1871	Book I of *Middlemarch* published in December.	Franco-Prussian War ends.
1872	'Simmering towards a new book', November. Final part of *Middlemarch* published in December; the whole published in 4 vols.	Le Fanu, *In a Glass Darkly*
1873	Begins 'Sketches towards Daniel Deronda', January. July–August visits France and Germany to research the novel.	Pater, *Studies in the History of the Renaissance*

	Life	*Cultural and Historical Background*
1874	*The Legend of Jubal and Other Poems* published, including the 'Brother and Sister sonnets'. Suffers a first attack of kidney stone in February. Begins writing *Daniel Deronda* in the late autumn, but progress is slow due to ill health. Vol. I of Lewes's *Problems of Life and Mind* published in November.	Disraeli becomes Prime Minister. Hardy, *Far from the Madding Crowd*
1875	Writing *Daniel Deronda*. Vol. II of Lewes's *Problems of Life and Mind* published.	Death of Kingsley. Trollope, *The Way We Live Now*
1876	*Daniel Deronda* begins publication in 8 parts in February, the last part appearing in September. Richard Wagner and his wife visit in May. June–September travelling in France, Germany, Switzerland. In December they buy The Heights at Witley in Surrey as a summer residence.	Alexander Graham Bell patents the telephone. James, *Roderick Hudson*
1878	Writes *Impressions of Theophrastus Such*. Lewes dies on 30 November. GE refuses to see anyone for several weeks and occupies herself in completing and preparing the last two volumes of his major philosophical work, *Problems of Life and Mind*, for the press.	London University becomes the first to offer degrees to women. Gilbert and Sullivan, *HMS Pinafore*
1879	Agrees to see Cross in February, and helps him to learn Italian. *Impressions of Theophrastus Such* published in May. Gives £5,000 to fund a Studentship in Physiology at Cambridge in Lewes's name, the first Student being appointed in October. For legal reasons changes her name by deed poll to Mary Ann Evans Lewes.	Ibsen, *A Doll's House* James, *Daisy Miller*

	Life	*Cultural and Historical Background*
1880	In April agrees to marry Cross. Married on 6 May, upon which her brother Isaac writes to congratulate her after 23 years of estrangement. Honeymoons in France and Italy, principally Venice, returning to England via Austria and Germany in late July. Moves to 4 Cheyne Walk on 3 December. Catches cold at a concert and dies on 22 December aged 61, her death probably in part the result of kidney disease. Buried in Highgate Cemetery on 29 December.	Elementary education becomes compulsory in England and Wales; Parnell demands Home Rule for Ireland. Tennyson, *Ballads and Other Poems* Gissing, *Workers in the Dawn*

THE WORKS

OF

GEORGE ELIOT

SILAS MARNER
THE LIFTED VEIL
BROTHER JACOB

WILLIAM BLACKWOOD AND SONS
ENDINBURGH AND LONDON
MDCCCLXXVIII

Facsimile title-page of the 1878 Cabinet Edition

'A child, more than all other gifts
That earth can offer to declining man,
Brings hope with it, and forward-looking thoughts.'

— Wordsworth.*

PART ONE

CHAPTER I

In the days when the spinning-wheels hummed busily in the farm-houses—and even great ladies, clothed in silk and thread-lace,* had their toy spinning-wheels of polished oak—there might be seen in districts far away among the lanes, or deep in the bosom of the hills, certain pallid undersized men, who, by the side of the brawny country-folk, looked like the remnants of a disinherited race. The shepherd's dog barked fiercely when one of these alien-looking men* appeared on the upland, dark against the early winter sunset; for what dog likes a figure bent under a heavy bag?—and these pale men rarely stirred abroad without that mysterious burden. The shepherd himself, though he had good reason to believe that the bag held nothing but flaxen thread, or else the long rolls of strong linen spun from that thread, was not quite sure that this trade of weaving, indispensable though it was, could be carried on entirely without the help of the Evil One. In that far-off time superstition clung easily round every person or thing that was at all unwonted, or even intermittent and occasional merely, like the visits of the pedlar or the knife-grinder. No one knew where wandering men had their homes or their origin; and how was a man to be explained unless you at least knew somebody who knew his father and mother? To the peasants of old times, the world outside their own direct experience was a region of vagueness and mystery: to their untravelled thought a state of wandering was a conception as dim as the winter life of the swallows that came back with the spring; and even a settler, if he came from distant parts, hardly ever ceased to be viewed with a remnant of distrust, which would have prevented any surprise if a long course of inoffensive conduct on his part had ended in the commission of a crime; especially if he had any reputation for knowledge, or showed any skill in handicraft. All cleverness, whether in the rapid use of that difficult instrument the tongue, or in some other art unfamiliar to villagers, was in itself suspicious: honest folk, born and bred in a visible manner, were mostly not overwise or clever—at least, not beyond such a matter as knowing the signs of the weather; and the process by which rapidity and dexterity of any kind were acquired was so wholly hidden, that they partook of the nature of conjuring. In this way it came to pass that those scattered linen-weavers—emigrants from the town into the country—were to the last regarded as aliens by their rustic neighbours, and usually contracted the eccentric habits which belong to a state of loneliness.

In the early years of this century,* such a linen-weaver, named Silas Marner, worked at his vocation in a stone cottage that stood among the nutty hedgerows near the village of Raveloe,* and not far from the edge of a deserted stone-pit. The questionable sound of Silas's loom, so unlike the natural cheerful trotting of the winnowing-machine, or the simpler rhythm of the flail,* had a half-fearful fascination for the Raveloe boys, who would often leave off their nutting or birds'-nesting to peep in at the window of the stone cottage, counterbalancing a certain awe at the mysterious action of the loom, by a pleasant sense of scornful superiority, drawn from the mockery of its alternating noises, along with the bent, tread-mill attitude of the weaver. But sometimes it happened that Marner, pausing to adjust an irregularity in his thread, became aware of the small scoundrels, and, though chary of his time, he liked their intrusion so ill that he would descend from his loom, and, opening the door, would fix on them a gaze that was always enough to make them take to their legs in terror. For how was it possible to believe that those large brown protuberant eyes in Silas Marner's pale face really saw nothing very distinctly that was not close to them, and not rather that their dreadful stare could dart cramp, or rickets, or a wry mouth* at any boy who happened to be in the rear? They had, perhaps, heard their fathers and mothers hint that Silas Marner could cure folk's rheumatism if he had a mind, and add, still more darkly, that if you could only speak the devil fair enough, he might save you the cost of the doctor. Such strange lingering echoes of the old demon-worship might perhaps even now be caught by the diligent listener among the grey-haired peasantry; for the rude mind with difficulty associates the ideas of power and benignity. A shadowy conception of power that by much persuasion can be induced to refrain from inflicting harm, is the shape most easily taken by the sense of the Invisible in the minds of men who have always been pressed close by primitive wants, and to whom a life of hard toil has never been illuminated by any enthusiastic religious faith. To them pain and mishap present a far wider range of possibilities than gladness and enjoyment: their imagination is almost barren of the images that feed desire and hope, but is all overgrown by recollections that are a perpetual pasture to fear. 'Is there anything you can fancy that you would like to eat?' I once said to an old labouring man, who was in his last illness, and who had refused all the food his wife had offered him. 'No,' he answered, 'I've never been used to nothing but common victual, and I can't eat that.' Experience had bred no fancies in him that could raise the phantasm of appetite.

And Raveloe was a village where many of the old echoes lingered, undrowned by new voices. Not that it was one of those barren parishes lying on the outskirts of civilisation—inhabited by meagre sheep and thinly-scattered shepherds: on the contrary, it lay in the rich central plain of what we are pleased to call Merry England, and held farms which, speaking from a spiritual point of view, paid highly-desirable tithes.* But it was nestled in a snug well-wooded hollow, quite an hour's journey on horseback from any turnpike, where it was never reached by the vibrations of the coach-horn, or of public opinion. It was an important-looking village, with a fine old church and large churchyard in the heart of it, and two or three large brick-and-stone homesteads, with well-walled orchards and ornamental weather-cocks, standing close upon the road, and lifting more imposing fronts than the rectory, which peeped from among the trees on the other side of the churchyard:—a village which showed at once the summits of its social life, and told the practised eye that there was no great park and manor-house in the vicinity, but that there were several chiefs in Raveloe who could farm badly quite at their ease, drawing enough money from their bad farming, in those war times,* to live in a rollicking fashion, and keep a jolly Christmas, Whitsun,* and Easter tide.

It was fifteen years since Silas Marner had first come to Raveloe; he was then simply a pallid young man, with prominent short-sighted brown eyes, whose appearance would have had nothing strange for people of average culture and experience, but for the villagers near whom he had come to settle it had mysterious peculiarities which corresponded with the exceptional nature of his occupation, and his advent from an unknown region called 'North'ard.' So had his way of life:—he invited no comer to step across his door-sill, and he never strolled into the village to drink a pint at the Rainbow, or to gossip at the wheelwright's:* he sought no man or woman, save for the purposes of his calling, or in order to supply himself with necessaries; and it was soon clear to the Raveloe lasses that he would never urge one of them to accept him against her will—quite as if he had heard them declare that they would never marry a dead man come to life again. This view of Marner's personality was not without another ground than his pale face and unexampled* eyes; for Jem Rodney, the mole-catcher, averred that one evening as he was returning homeward he saw Silas Marner leaning against a stile with a heavy bag on his back,* instead of resting the bag on the stile as a man in his senses would have done; and that, on coming up to him, he saw that Marner's eyes were set like a dead man's, and he spoke to him, and shook him, and his limbs were stiff, and his hands clutched the bag as if they'd been made of iron; but just as he had made up his mind that the weaver was dead, he came all right again, like, as you might say, in the winking of an eye, and said 'Good night,' and walked off. All this Jem swore he had seen, more by token that it was the very day he had been mole-catching on Squire Cass's land, down by the old saw-pit. Some said Marner must have been in a 'fit,'* a word which seemed to explain things otherwise incredible; but the argumentative Mr Macey, clerk of the parish, shook his head, and asked if anybody was ever known to go off in a fit and not fall down. A fit was a stroke, wasn't it? and it was in the nature of a stroke to partly take away the use of a man's limbs and throw him on the parish,* if he'd got no children to look to. No, no; it was no stroke that would let a man stand on his legs, like a horse between the shafts, and then walk off as soon as you can say 'Gee!' But there might be such a thing as a man's soul being loose from his body, and going out and in, like a bird out of its nest and back; and that was how folks got over-wise, for they went to school in this shell-less state to those who could teach them more than their neighbours could learn with their five senses and the parson. And where did Master Marner get his knowledge of herbs from—and charms too, if he liked to give them away? Jem Rodney's story was no more than what might have been expected by anybody who had seen how Marner had cured Sally Oates, and made her sleep like a baby, when her heart had been beating enough to burst her body, for two months and more, while she had been under the doctor's care. He might cure more folks if he would; but he was worth speaking fair, if it was only to keep him from doing you a mischief.

It was partly to this vague fear that Marner was indebted for protecting him from the persecution that his singularities might have drawn upon him, but still more to the fact that, the old linen-weaver in the neighbouring parish of Tarley being dead, his handicraft made him a highly welcome settler to the richer housewives of the district, and even to the more provident cottagers, who had their little stock of yarn at the year's end. Their sense of his usefulness would have counteracted any repugnance or suspicion which was not confirmed by a deficiency in the quality or the tale* of the cloth he wove for them. And the years had rolled on without producing any change in the impressions of the neighbours concerning Marner, except the change from novelty to habit. At the end of fifteen years the Raveloe men said just the same things about Silas Marner as at the beginning: they did not say them quite so often, but they believed them much more strongly when they did say them. There was only one important addition which the years had brought: it was, that Master Marner had laid by a fine sight of money somewhere, and that he could buy up 'bigger men' than himself.

But while opinion concerning him had remained nearly stationary, and his daily habits had presented scarcely any visible change, Marner's inward life had been a history and a metamorphosis, as that of every fervid nature must be when it has fled, or been condemned to solitude. His life, before he came to Raveloe, had been filled with the movement, the mental activity, and the close fellowship, which, in that day as in this, marked the life of an artisan early incorporated in a narrow religious sect,* where the poorest layman has the chance of distinguishing himself by gifts of speech, and has, at the very least, the weight of a silent voter in the government of his community. Marner was highly thought of in that little hidden world, known to itself as the church assembling in Lantern Yard; he was believed to be a young man of exemplary life and ardent faith; and a peculiar interest had been centred in him ever since he had fallen, at a prayer-meeting, into a mysterious rigidity and suspension of consciousness, which, lasting for an hour or more, had been mistaken for death. To have sought a medical explanation for this phenomenon would have been held by Silas himself, as well as by his minister and fellow-members, a wilful self-exclusion from the spiritual significance that might lie therein. Silas was evidently a brother selected for a peculiar discipline; and though the effort to interpret this discipline was discouraged by the absence, on his part, of any spiritual vision during his outward trance, yet it was believed by himself and others that its effect was seen in an accession of light and fervour. A less truthful man than he might have been tempted into the subsequent creation of a vision in the form of resurgent memory; a less sane man might have believed in such a creation; but Silas was both sane and honest, though, as with many honest and fervent men, culture had not defined any channels for his sense of mystery, and so it spread itself over the proper pathway of inquiry and knowledge. He had inherited from his mother some acquaintance with medicinal herbs and their preparation—a little store of wisdom which she had imparted to him as a solemn bequest—but of late years he had had doubts about the lawfulness of applying this knowledge, believing that herbs could have no efficacy without prayer, and that prayer might suffice without herbs; so that his inherited delight to wander through the fields in search of foxglove and dandelion and coltsfoot, began to wear to him the character of a temptation.

Among the members of his church there was one young man, a little older than himself, with whom he had long lived in such close friendship that it was the custom of their Lantern Yard brethren to call them David and Jonathan.* The real name of the friend was William Dane, and he, too, was regarded as a shining instance of youthful piety, though somewhat given to over-severity towards weaker brethren, and to be so dazzled by his own light as to hold himself wiser than his teachers. But whatever blemishes others might discern in William, to his friend's mind he was faultless; for Marner had one of those impressible self-doubting natures which, at an inexperienced age, admire imperativeness and lean on contradiction. The expression of trusting simplicity in Marner's face, heightened by that absence of special observation, that defenceless, deer-like gaze which belongs to large prominent eyes, was strongly contrasted by the self-complacent suppression of inward triumph that lurked in the narrow slanting eyes and compressed lips of William Dane. One of the most frequent topics of conversation between the two friends was Assurance of salvation:* Silas confessed that he could never arrive at anything higher than hope mingled with fear, and listened with longing wonder when William declared that he had possessed unshaken assurance ever since, in the period of his conversion, he had dreamed that he saw the words 'calling and election sure'* standing by themselves on a white page in the open Bible. Such colloquies have occupied many a pair of pale-faced weavers, whose unnurtured souls have been like young winged things, fluttering forsaken in the twilight.

It had seemed to the unsuspecting Silas that the friendship had suffered no chill even from his formation of another attachment of a closer kind. For some months he had been engaged to a young servant-woman, waiting only for a little increase to their mutual savings in order to their marriage;* and it was a great delight to him that Sarah did not object to William's occasional presence in their Sunday interviews. It was at this point in their history that Silas's cataleptic fit* occurred during the prayer-meeting; and amidst the various queries and expressions of interest addressed to him by his fellow-members, William's suggestion alone jarred with the general sympathy towards a brother thus singled out for special dealings. He observed that, to him, this trance looked more like a visitation of Satan than a proof of divine favour, and exhorted his friend to see that he hid no accursed thing within his soul. Silas, feeling bound to accept rebuke and admonition as a brotherly office, felt no resentment, but only pain, at his friend's doubts concerning him; and to this was soon added some anxiety at the perception that Sarah's manner towards him began to exhibit a strange fluctuation between an effort at an increased manifestation of regard and involuntary signs of shrinking and dislike. He asked her if she wished to break off their engagement; but she denied this: their engagement was known to the church, and had been recognised in the prayer-meetings; it could not be broken off without strict investigation, and Sarah could render no reason that would be sanctioned by the feeling of the community. At this time the senior deacon* was taken dangerously ill, and, being a childless widower, he was tended night and day by some of the younger brethren or sisters. Silas frequently took his turn in the night-watching with William, the one relieving the other at two in the morning. The old man, contrary to expectation, seemed to be on the way to recovery, when one night Silas, sitting up by his bedside, observed that his usual audible breathing had ceased. The candle was burning low, and he had to lift it to see the patient's face distinctly. Examination convinced him that the deacon was dead—had been dead some time, for the limbs were rigid. Silas asked himself if he had been asleep, and looked at the clock: it was already four in the morning. How was it that William had not come? In much anxiety he went to seek for help, and soon there were several friends assembled in the house, the minister among them, while Silas went away to his work, wishing he could have met William to know the reason of his non-appearance. But at six o'clock, as he was thinking of going to seek his friend, William came, and with him the minister. They came to summon him to Lantern Yard, to meet the church members there; and to his inquiry concerning the cause of the summons the only reply was, 'You will hear.' Nothing further was said until Silas was seated in the vestry, in front of the minister, with the eyes of those who to him represented God's people fixed solemnly upon him. Then the minister, taking out a pocket-knife, showed it to Silas, and asked him if he knew where he had left that knife? Silas said, he did not know that he had left it anywhere out of his own pocket—but he was trembling at this strange interrogation. He was then exhorted not to hide his sin, but to confess and repent. The knife had been found in the bureau by the departed deacon's bedside—found in the place where the little bag of church money had lain, which the minister himself had seen the day before. Some hand had removed that bag; and whose hand could it be, if not that of the man to whom the knife belonged? For some time Silas was mute with astonishment: then he said, 'God will clear me: I know nothing about the knife being there, or the money being gone. Search me and my dwelling; you will find nothing but three pound five of my own savings, which William Dane knows I have had these six months.' At this William groaned, but the minister said, 'The proof is heavy against you, brother Marner. The money was taken in the night last past, and no man was with our departed brother but you, for William Dane declares to us that he was hindered by sudden sickness from going to take his place as usual, and you yourself said that he had not come; and, moreover, you neglected the dead body.'

'I must have slept,' said Silas. Then after a pause, he added, 'Or I must have had another visitation like that which you have all seen me under, so that the thief must have come and gone while I was not in the body, but out of the body.* But, I say again, search me and my dwelling, for I have been nowhere else.'

The search was made, and it ended—in William Dane's finding the well-known bag, empty, tucked behind the chest of drawers in Silas's chamber! On this William exhorted his friend to confess, and not to hide his sin any longer. Silas turned a look of keen reproach on him, and said, 'William, for nine years that we have gone in and out together, have you ever known me tell a lie? But God will clear me.'

'Brother,' said William, 'how do I know what you may have done in the secret chambers of your heart, to give Satan an advantage over you?'

Silas was still looking at his friend. Suddenly a deep flush came over his face, and he was about to speak impetuously, when he seemed checked again by some inward shock, that sent the flush back and made him tremble. But at last he spoke feebly, looking at William.

'I remember now—the knife wasn't in my pocket.'

William said, 'I know nothing of what you mean.' The other persons present, however, began to inquire where Silas meant to say that the knife was, but he would give no further explanation: he only said, 'I am sore stricken; I can say nothing. God will clear me.'

On their return to the vestry there was further deliberation. Any resort to legal measures for ascertaining the culprit was contrary to the principles of the church in Lantern Yard, according to which prosecution was forbidden to Christians,* even had the case held less scandal to the community. But the members were bound to take other measures for finding out the truth, and they resolved on praying and drawing lots.* This resolution can be a ground of surprise only to those who are unacquainted with that obscure religious life which has gone on in the alleys of our towns. Silas knelt with his brethren, relying on his own innocence being certified by immediate divine interference, but feeling that there was sorrow and mourning behind for him even then—that his trust in man had been cruelly bruised. *The lots declared that Silas Marner was guilty.* He was solemnly suspended from church-membership, and called upon to render up the stolen money: only on confession, as the sign of repentance, could he be received once more within the folds of the church. Marner listened in silence. At last, when everyone rose to depart, he went towards William Dane and said, in a voice shaken by agitation—

'The last time I remember using my knife, was when I took it out to cut a strap for you. I don't remember putting it in my pocket again. *You* stole the money, and you have woven a plot to lay the sin at my door. But you may prosper, for all that: there is no just God that governs the earth righteously, but a God of lies, that bears witness against the innocent.'

There was a general shudder at this blasphemy.

William said meekly, 'I leave our brethren to judge whether this is the voice of Satan or not. I can do nothing but pray for you, Silas.'

Poor Marner went out with that despair in his soul—that shaken trust in God and man, which is little short of madness to a loving nature. In the bitterness of his wounded spirit, he said to himself, '*She* will cast me off too.' And he reflected that, if she did not believe the testimony against him, her whole faith must be upset as his was. To people accustomed to reason about the forms in which their religious feeling has incorporated itself, it is difficult to enter into that simple, untaught state of mind in which the form and the feeling have never been severed by an act of reflection. We are apt to think it inevitable that a man in Marner's position should have begun to question the validity of an appeal to the divine judgment by drawing lots; but to him this would have been an effort of independent thought such as he had never known; and he must have made the effort at a moment when all his energies were turned into the anguish of disappointed faith. If there is an angel who records the sorrows of men as well as their sins, he knows how many and deep are the sorrows that spring from false ideas for which no man is culpable.

Marner went home, and for a whole day sat alone, stunned by despair, without any impulse to go to Sarah and attempt to win her belief in his innocence. The second day he took refuge from benumbing unbelief, by getting into his loom and working away as usual; and before many hours were past, the minister and one of the deacons came to him with the message from Sarah, that she held her engagement to him at an end. Silas received the message mutely, and then turned away from the messengers to work at his loom again. In little more than a month from that time, Sarah was married to William Dane; and not long afterwards it was known to the brethren in Lantern Yard that Silas Marner had departed from the town.

CHAPTER II

EVEN people whose lives have been made various by learning,* sometimes find it hard to keep a fast hold on their habitual views of life, on their faith in the Invisible, nay, on the sense that their past joys and sorrows are a real experience, when they are suddenly transported to a new land, where the beings around them know nothing of their history, and share none of their ideas—where their mother earth shows another lap, and human life has other forms than those on which their souls have been nourished. Minds that have been unhinged from their old faith and love, have perhaps sought this Lethean* influence of exile, in which the past becomes dreamy because its symbols have all vanished, and the present too is dreamy because it is linked with no memories. But even *their* experience may hardly enable them thoroughly to imagine what was the effect on a simple weaver like Silas Marner, when he left his own country and people and came to settle in Raveloe. Nothing could be more unlike his native town, set within sight of the widespread hillsides, than this low, wooded region, where he felt hidden even from the heavens by the screening trees and hedgerows. There was nothing here, when he rose in the deep morning quiet and looked out on the dewy brambles and rank tufted grass, that seemed to have any relation with that life centring in Lantern Yard, which had once been to him the altar-place of high dispensations. The whitewashed walls; the little pews where well-known figures entered with a subdued rustling, and where first one well-known voice and then another, pitched in a peculiar key of petition,* uttered phrases at once occult and familiar, like the amulet* worn on the heart; the pulpit where the minister delivered unquestioned doctrine, and swayed to and fro, and handled the book in a long-accustomed manner; the very pauses between the couplets of the hymn, as it was given out, and the recurrent swell of voices in song: these things had been the channel of divine influences to Marner—they were the fostering home of his religious emotions—they were Christianity and God's kingdom upon earth. A weaver who finds hard words in his hymn-book knows nothing of abstractions; as the little child knows nothing of parental love, but only knows one face and one lap towards which it stretches its arms for refuge and nurture.

And what could be more unlike that Lantern Yard world than the world in Raveloe?—orchards looking lazy with neglected plenty; the large church in the wide churchyard, which men gazed at lounging at their own doors in service-time; the purple-faced farmers jogging along the lanes or turning in at the Rainbow; homesteads, where men supped heavily and slept in the light of the evening hearth, and where women seemed to be laying up a stock of linen for the life to come. There were no lips in Raveloe from which a word could fall that would stir Silas Marner's benumbed faith to a sense of pain. In the early ages of the world, we know, it was believed that each territory was inhabited and ruled by its own divinities,* so that a man could cross the bordering heights and be out of the reach of his native gods, whose presence was confined to the streams and the groves and the hills among which he had lived from his birth. And poor Silas was vaguely conscious of something not unlike the feeling of primitive men, when they fled thus, in fear or in sullenness, from the face of an unpropitious deity. It seemed to him that the Power he had vainly trusted in among the streets and at the prayer-meetings, was very far away from this land in which he had taken refuge, where men lived in careless abundance, knowing and needing nothing of that trust, which, for him, had been turned to bitterness. The little light he possessed spread its beams so narrowly, that frustrated belief was a curtain broad enough to create for him the blackness of night.

His first movement after the shock had been to work in his loom; and he went on with this unremittingly, never asking himself why, now he was come to Raveloe, he worked far on into the night to finish the tale of Mrs Osgood's table-linen sooner than she expected—without contemplating beforehand the money she would put into his hand for the work. He seemed to weave, like the spider, from pure impulse, without reflection. Every man's work, pursued steadily, tends in this way to become an end in itself, and so to bridge over the loveless chasms of his life. Silas's hand satisfied itself with throwing the shuttle, and his eye with seeing the little squares in the cloth complete themselves under his effort. Then there were the calls of hunger; and Silas, in his solitude, had to provide his own breakfast, dinner, and supper, to fetch his own water from the well, and put his own kettle on the fire; and all these immediate promptings helped, along with the weaving, to reduce his life to the unquestioning activity of a spinning insect. He hated the thought of the past; there was nothing that called out his love and fellowship toward the strangers he had come amongst; and the future was all dark, for there was no Unseen Love that cared for him. Thought was arrested by utter bewilderment, now its old narrow pathway was closed, and affection seemed to have died under the bruise that had fallen on its keenest nerves.

But at last Mrs Osgood's table-linen was finished, and Silas was paid in gold. His earnings in his native town, where he worked for a wholesale dealer, had been after a lower rate; he had been paid weekly, and of his weekly earnings a large proportion had gone to objects of piety and charity. Now, for the first time in his life, he had five bright guineas put into his hand;* no man expected a share of them, and he loved no man that he should offer him a share. But what were the guineas to him who saw no vista beyond countless days of weaving? It was needless for him to ask that, for it was pleasant to him to feel them in his palm, and look at their bright faces, which were all his own: it was another element of life, like the weaving and the satisfaction of hunger, subsisting quite aloof from the life of belief and love from which he had been cut off. The weaver's hand had known the touch of hard-won money even before the palm had grown to its full breadth; for twenty years, mysterious money had stood to him as the symbol of earthly good, and the immediate object of toil. He had seemed to love it little in the years when every penny had its purpose for him; for he loved the *purpose* then. But now, when all purpose was gone, that habit of looking towards the money and grasping it with a sense of fulfilled effort made a loam* that was deep enough for the seeds of desire; and as Silas walked homeward across the fields in the twilight, he drew out the money and thought it was brighter in the gathering gloom.

About this time an incident happened which seemed to open a possibility of some fellowship with his neighbours. One day, taking a pair of shoes to be mended, he saw the cobbler's wife seated by the fire, suffering from the terrible symptoms of heart-disease and dropsy,* which he had witnessed as the precursors of his mother's death. He felt a rush of pity at the mingled sight and remembrance, and, recalling the relief his mother had found from a simple preparation of foxglove, he promised Sally Oates to bring her something that would ease her, since the doctor did her no good. In this office of charity, Silas felt, for the first time since he had come to Raveloe, a sense of unity between his past and present life, which might have been the beginning of his rescue from the insect-like existence into which his nature had shrunk. But Sally Oates's disease had raised her into a personage of much interest and importance among the neighbours, and the fact of her having found relief from drinking Silas Marner's 'stuff' became a matter of general discourse. When Doctor Kimble gave physic, it was natural that it should have an effect; but when a weaver, who came from nobody knew where, worked wonders with a bottle of brown waters, the occult character of the process was evident. Such a sort of thing had not been known since the Wise Woman at Tarley died; and she had charms as well as 'stuff:' everybody went to her when their children had fits. Silas Marner must be a person of the same sort, for how did he know what would bring back Sally

Oates's breath, if he didn't know a fine sight more than that? The Wise Woman had words that she muttered to herself, so that you couldn't hear what they were, and if she tied a bit of red thread round the child's toe the while, it would keep off the water in the head.* There were women in Raveloe, at that present time, who had worn one of the Wise Woman's little bags round their necks, and, in consequence, had never had an idiot child, as Ann Coulter had. Silas Marner could very likely do as much, and more; and now it was all clear how he should have come from unknown parts, and be so 'comical-looking.' But Sally Oates must mind and not tell the doctor, for he would be sure to set his face against Marner: he was always angry about the Wise Woman, and used to threaten those who went to her that they should have none of his help any more.

Silas now found himself and his cottage suddenly beset by mothers who wanted him to charm away the hooping-cough, or bring back the milk, and by men who wanted stuff against the rheumatics or the knots in the hands; and, to secure themselves against a refusal, the applicants brought silver in their palms. Silas might have driven a profitable trade in charms as well as in his small list of drugs; but money on this condition was no temptation to him: he had never known an impulse towards falsity, and he drove one after another away with growing irritation, for the news of him as a wise man had spread even to Tarley, and it was long before people ceased to take long walks for the sake of asking his aid. But the hope in his wisdom was at length changed into dread, for no one believed him when he said he knew no charms and could work no cures, and every man and woman who had an accident or a new attack after applying to him, set the misfortune down to Master Marner's ill-will and irritated glances. Thus it came to pass that his movement of pity towards Sally Oates, which had given him a transient sense of brotherhood, heightened the repulsion between him and his neighbours, and made his isolation more complete.

Gradually the guineas, the crowns, and the half-crowns, grew to a heap, and Marner drew less and less for his own wants, trying to solve the problem of keeping himself strong enough to work sixteen hours a-day on as small an outlay as possible. Have not men, shut up in solitary imprisonment, found an interest in marking the moments by straight strokes of a certain length on the wall, until the growth of the sum of straight strokes, arranged, in triangles, has become a mastering purpose? Do we not wile away moments of inanity or fatigued waiting by repeating some trivial movement or sound, until the repetition has bred a want, which is incipient habit? That will help us to understand how the love of accumulating money grows an absorbing passion in men whose imaginations, even in the very beginning of their hoard, showed them no purpose beyond it. Marner wanted the heaps of ten to grow into a square, and then into a larger square; and every added guinea, while it was itself a satisfaction, bred a new desire. In this strange world, made a hopeless riddle to him, he might, if he had had a less intense nature, have sat weaving, weaving—looking towards the end of his pattern, or towards the end of his web, till he forgot the riddle, and everything else but his immediate sensations; but the money had come to mark off his weaving into periods, and the money not only grew, but it remained with him. He began to think it was conscious of him, as his loom was, and he would on no account have exchanged those coins, which had become his familiars, for other coins with unknown faces. He handled them, he counted them, till their form and colour were like the satisfaction of a thirst to him; but it was only in the night, when his work was done, that he drew them out to enjoy their companionship. He had taken up some bricks in his floor underneath his loom, and here he had made a hole in which he set the iron pot that contained his guineas and silver coins, covering the bricks with sand whenever he replaced them. Not that the idea of being robbed presented itself often or strongly to his mind: hoarding was common in country districts in those days; there were old labourers in the parish of Raveloe who were known to have their savings by them, probably inside their flock-beds;* but their rustic neighbours, though not all of them as honest as their ancestors in the days of King Alfred,* had not imaginations bold enough to lay a plan of burglary. How could they have spent the money in their own village without betraying themselves? They would be obliged to 'run away'—a course as dark and dubious as a balloon journey.*

So, year after year, Silas Marner had lived in this solitude, his guineas rising in the iron pot, and his life narrowing and hardening itself more and more into a mere pulsation of desire and satisfaction that had no relation to any other being. His life had reduced itself to the functions of weaving and hoarding, without any contemplation of an end towards which the functions tended. The same sort of process has perhaps been undergone by wiser men, when they have been cut off from faith and love—only, instead of a loom and a heap of guineas, they have had some erudite research, some ingenious project, or some well-knit theory. Strangely Marner's face and figure shrank and bent themselves into a constant mechanical relation to the objects of his life, so that he produced the same sort of impression as a handle or a crooked tube, which has no meaning standing apart. The prominent eyes that used to look trusting and dreamy, now looked as if they had been made to see only one kind of thing that was very small, like tiny grain, for which they hunted everywhere: and he was so withered and yellow, that, though he was not yet forty, the children always called him 'Old Master Marner.'

Yet even in this stage of withering a little incident happened, which showed that the sap of affection was not all gone. It was one of his daily tasks to fetch his water from a well a couple of fields off, and for this purpose, ever since he came to Raveloe, he had had a brown earthenware pot, which he held as his most precious utensil* among the very few conveniences he had granted himself. It had been his companion for twelve years, always standing on the same spot, always lending its handle to him in the early morning, so that its form had an expression for him of willing helpfulness, and the impress of its handle on his palm gave a satisfaction mingled with that of having the fresh clear water. One day as he was returning from the well, he stumbled against the step of the stile, and his brown pot, falling with force against the stones that overarched the ditch below him, was broken in three pieces. Silas picked up the pieces and carried them home with grief in his heart. The brown pot could never be of use to him any more, but he stuck the bits together and propped the ruin in its old place for a memorial.

This is the history of Silas Marner, until the fifteenth year after he came to Raveloe. The livelong day he sat in his loom, his ear filled with its monotony, his eyes bent close down on the slow growth of sameness in the brownish web, his muscles moving with such even repetition that their pause seemed almost as much a constraint as the holding of his breath. But at night came his revelry: at night he closed his shutters, and made fast his doors, and drew forth his gold. Long ago the heap of coins had become too large for the iron pot to hold them, and he had made for them two thick leather bags, which wasted no room in their resting-place, but lent themselves flexibly to every corner. How the guineas shone as they came pouring out of the dark leather mouths! The silver bore no large proportion in amount to the gold, because the long pieces of linen which formed his chief work were always partly paid for in gold, and out of the silver he supplied his own bodily wants, choosing always the shillings and sixpences to spend in this way. He loved the guineas best, but he would not change the silver—the crowns and half-crowns that were his own earnings, begotten by his labour; he loved them all. He spread them out in heaps and bathed his hands in them; then he counted them and set them up in regular piles, and felt their rounded outline between his thumb and fingers, and thought fondly of the guineas that were only half earned by the work in his loom, as if they had been unborn children—thought of the guineas that were coming slowly through the coming years, through all his life, which spread far away before him, the end quite hidden by countless days of weaving. No wonder his thoughts were still with his loom and his money when he made his journeys through the fields and the lanes to fetch and carry home his work, so that his steps never wandered to the hedge-banks and the lane-side in search of the once familiar herbs: these too belonged to the past, from which his life had shrunk away, like a rivulet that has sunk far down from the grassy fringe of its old breadth into a little shivering thread, that cuts a groove for itself in the barren sand.

But about the Christmas of that fifteenth year, a second great change came over Marner's life, and his history became blent in a singular manner with the life of his neighbours.

CHAPTER III

THE greatest man in Raveloe was Squire Cass, who lived in the large red house with the handsome flight of stone steps in front and the high stables behind it, nearly opposite the church. He was only one among several landed parishioners, but he alone was honoured with the title of Squire;* for though Mr Osgood's family was also understood to be of timeless origin—the Raveloe imagination having never ventured back to that fearful blank when there were no Osgoods—still, he merely owned the farm he occupied; whereas Squire Cass had a tenant or two, who complained of the game to him quite as if he had been a lord.

It was still that glorious war-time which was felt to be a peculiar favour of Providence towards the landed interest, and the fall of prices had not yet come to carry the race of small squires and yeomen* down that road to ruin for which extravagant habits and bad husbandry were plentifully anointing their wheels. I am speaking now in relation to Raveloe and the parishes that resembled it; for our old-fashioned country life had many different aspects, as all life must have when it is spread over a various surface, and breathed on variously by multitudinous currents, from the winds of heaven to the thoughts of men, which are for ever moving and crossing each other with incalculable results. Raveloe lay low among the bushy trees and the rutted lanes, aloof from the currents of industrial energy and Puritan earnestness: the rich ate and drank freely, accepting gout and apoplexy as things that ran mysteriously in respectable families, and the poor thought that the rich were entirely in the right of it to lead a jolly life; besides, their feasting caused a multiplication of orts,* which were the heirlooms of the poor. Betty Jay scented the boiling of Squire Cass's hams, but her longing was arrested by the unctuous liquor in which they were boiled; and when the seasons brought round the great merry-makings, they were regarded on all hands as a fine thing for the poor. For the Raveloe feasts were like the rounds of beef and the barrels of ale—they were on a large scale, and lasted a good while, especially in the winter-time. After ladies had packed up their best gowns and top-knots in bandboxes, and had incurred the risk of fording streams on pillions* with the precious burden in rainy or snowy weather, when there was no knowing how high the water would rise, it was not to be supposed that they looked forward to a brief pleasure. On this ground it was always contrived in the dark seasons, when there was little work to be done, and the hours were long, that several neighbours should keep open house in succession. So soon as Squire Cass's standing dishes* diminished in plenty and freshness, his guests had nothing to do but to walk a little higher up the village to Mr Osgood's, at the Orchards, and they found hams and chines uncut,* pork-pies with the scent of the fire in them, spun butter* in all its freshness—everything, in fact, that appetites at leisure could desire, in perhaps greater perfection, though not in greater abundance, than at Squire Cass's.

For the Squire's wife had died long ago, and the Red House was without that presence of the wife and mother which is the fountain of wholesome love and fear in parlour and kitchen; and this helped to account not only for there being more profusion than finished excellence in the holiday provisions, but also for the frequency with which the proud Squire condescended to preside in the parlour of the Rainbow rather than under the shadow of his own dark wainscot; perhaps, also, for the fact that his sons had turned out rather ill. Raveloe was not a place where moral censure was severe, but it was thought a weakness in the Squire that he had kept all his sons at home in idleness; and though some licence was to be allowed to young men whose fathers could afford it, people shook their heads at the courses of the second son, Dunstan, commonly called Dunsey Cass, whose taste for swopping and betting might turn out to be a sowing of something worse than wild oats. To be sure, the neighbours said, it was no matter what became of Dunsey—a spiteful jeering fellow, who seemed to enjoy his drink the more when other people went dry—always provided that his doings did not bring trouble on a family like Squire Cass's, with a monument in the church, and tankards older than King George.* But it would be a thousand pities if Mr Godfrey, the eldest, a fine open-faced good-natured young man who was to come into the land some day, should take to going along the same road with his brother, as he had seemed to do of late. If he went on in that way, he would lose Miss Nancy Lammeter; for it was well known that she had looked very shyly on him ever since last Whitsuntide twelvemonth, when there was so much talk about his being away from home days and days together. There was something wrong, more than common—that was quite clear; for Mr Godfrey didn't look half so fresh-coloured and open as he used to do. At one time everybody was saying, What a handsome couple he and Miss Nancy Lammeter would make! and if she could come to be mistress at the Red House, there would be a fine change, for the Lammeters had been brought up in that way, that they never suffered a pinch of salt to be wasted, and yet everybody in their household had of the best, according to his place. Such a daughter-in-law would be a saving to the old Squire, if she never brought a penny to her fortune; for it was to be feared that, notwithstanding his incomings, there were more holes in his pocket than the one where he put his own hand in. But if Mr Godfrey didn't turn over a new leaf, he might say 'Good-bye' to Miss Nancy Lammeter.

It was the once hopeful Godfrey who was standing, with his hands in his side-pockets and his back to the fire, in the dark wainscoted parlour, one late November afternoon in that fifteenth year of Silas Marner's life at Raveloe. The fading grey light fell dimly on the walls decorated with guns, whips, and foxes' brushes,* on coats and hats flung on the chairs, on tankards sending forth a scent of flat ale, and on a half-choked fire, with pipes propped up in the chimney-corners: signs of a domestic life destitute of any hallowing charm, with which the look of gloomy vexation on Godfrey's blond face was in sad accordance. He seemed to be waiting and listening for some one's approach, and presently the sound of a heavy step, with an accompanying whistle, was heard across the large empty entrance-hall.

The door opened, and a thick-set, heavy-looking young man entered, with the flushed face and the gratuitously elated bearing which mark the first stage of intoxication. It was Dunsey, and at the sight of him Godfrey's face parted with some of its gloom to take on the more active expression of hatred. The handsome brown spaniel that lay on the hearth retreated under the chair in the chimney-corner.

'Well, Master Godfrey, what do you want with me?' said Dunsey, in a mocking tone. 'You're my elders and betters, you know; I was obliged to come when you sent for me.'

'Why, this is what I want—and just shake yourself sober and listen, will you?' said Godfrey, savagely. He had himself been drinking more than was good for him, trying to turn his gloom into uncalculating anger. 'I want to tell you, I must hand over that rent of Fowler's to the Squire, or else tell him I gave it you; for he's threatening to distrain* for it, and it'll all be out soon, whether I tell him or not. He said, just now, before he went out, he should send word to Cox to distrain, if Fowler didn't come and pay up his arrears this week. The Squire's short o' cash, and in no humour to stand any nonsense; and you know what he threatened, if ever he found you making away with his money again. So, see and get the money, and pretty quickly, will you?'

'Oh!' said Dunsey, sneeringly, coming nearer to his brother and looking in his face. 'Suppose, now, you get the money yourself, and save me the trouble, eh? Since you was so kind as to hand it over to me, you'll not refuse me the kindness to pay it back for me: it was your brotherly love made you do it, you know.'

Godfrey bit his lips and clenched his fist. 'Don't come near me with that look, else I'll knock you down.'

'Oh no, you won't,' said Dunsey, turning away on his heel, however. 'Because I'm such a good-natured brother, you know. I might get you turned out of house and home, and cut off with a shilling any day. I might tell the Squire how his handsome son was married to that nice young woman, Molly Farren, and was very unhappy because he couldn't live with his drunken wife, and I should slip into your place as comfortable as could be. But you see, I don't do it—I'm so easy and good-natured. You'll take any trouble for me. You'll get the hundred pounds for me—I know you will.'

'How can I get the money?' said Godfrey, quivering. 'I haven't a shilling to bless myself with. And it's a lie that you'd slip into my place: you'd get yourself turned out too, that's all. For if you begin telling tales, I'll follow. Bob's my father's favourite—you know that very well. He'd only think himself well rid of you.'

'Never mind,' said Dunsey, nodding his head sideways as he looked out of the window. 'It 'ud be very pleasant to me to go in your company—you're such a handsome brother, and we've always been so fond of quarrelling with one another, I shouldn't know what to do without you. But you'd like better for us both to stay at home together; I know you would. So you'll manage to get that little sum o' money, and I'll bid you good-bye, though I'm sorry to part.'

Dunstan was moving off, but Godfrey rushed after him and seized him by the arm, saying, with an oath—

'I tell you, I have no money: I can get no money.'

'Borrow of old Kimble.'

'I tell you, he won't lend me any more, and I shan't ask him.'

'Well, then, sell Wildfire.'

'Yes, that's easy talking. I must have the money directly.'

'Well, you've only got to ride him to the hunt to-morrow. There'll be Bryce and Keating there, for sure. You'll get more bids than one.'

'I daresay, and get back home at eight o'clock, splashed up to the chin. I'm going to Mrs Osgood's birthday dance.'

'Oho!' said Dunsey, turning his head on one side, and trying to speak in a small mincing treble. 'And there's sweet Miss Nancy coming; and we shall dance with her, and promise never to be naughty again, and be taken into favour, and——'

'Hold your tongue about Miss Nancy, you fool,' said Godfrey, turning red, 'else I'll throttle you.'

'What for?' said Dunsey, still in an artificial tone, but taking a whip from the table and beating the butt-end of it on his palm. 'You've a very good chance. I'd advise you to creep up her sleeve again: it 'ud be saving time, if Molly should happen to take a drop too much laudanum* some day, and make a widower of you. Miss Nancy wouldn't mind being a second, if she didn't know it. And you've got a good-natured brother, who'll keep your secret well, because you'll be so very obliging to him.'

'I'll tell you what it is,' said Godfrey, quivering, and pale again, 'my patience is pretty near at an end. If you'd a little more sharpness in you, you might know that you may urge a man a bit too far, and make one leap as easy as another. I don't know but what it is so now: I may as well tell the Squire everything myself—I should get you off my back, if I got nothing else. And, after all, he'll know some time. She's been threatening to come herself and tell him. So, don't flatter yourself that your secrecy's worth any price you choose to ask. You drain me of money till I have got nothing to pacify *her* with, and she'll do as she threatens some day. It's all one. I'll tell my father everything myself, and you may go to the devil.'

Dunsey perceived that he had overshot his mark, and that there was a point at which even the hesitating Godfrey might be driven into decision. But he said, with an air of unconcern—

'As you please; but I'll have a draught of ale first.' And ringing the bell, he threw himself across two chairs, and began to rap the window-seat with the handle of his whip.

Godfrey stood, still with his back to the fire, uneasily moving his fingers among the contents of his side-pockets, and looking at the floor. That big muscular frame of his held plenty of animal courage, but helped him to no decision when the dangers to be braved were such as could neither be knocked down nor throttled. His natural irresolution and moral cowardice were exaggerated by a position in which dreaded consequences seemed to press equally on all sides, and his irritation had no sooner provoked him to defy Dunstan and anticipate all possible betrayals, than the miseries he must bring on himself by such a step seemed more unendurable to him than the present evil. The results of confession were not contingent, they were certain; whereas betrayal was not certain. From the near vision of that certainty he fell back on suspense and vacillation with a sense of repose. The disinherited son of a small squire, equally disinclined to dig and to beg,* was almost as helpless as an uprooted tree, which, by the favour of earth and sky, has grown to a handsome bulk on the spot where it first shot upward. Perhaps it would have been possible to think of digging with some cheerfulness if Nancy Lammeter were to be won on those terms; but, since he must irrevocably lose *her* as well as the inheritance, and must break every tie but the one that degraded him and left him without motive for trying to recover his better self, he could imagine no future for himself on the other side of confession but that of ''listing for a soldier'*—the most desperate step, short of suicide, in the eyes of respectable families. No! he would rather trust to casualties than to his own resolve—rather go on sitting at the feast, and sipping the wine he loved, though with the sword hanging over him and terror in his heart, than rush away into the cold darkness where there was no pleasure left. The utmost concession to Dunstan about the horse began to seem easy, compared with the fulfilment of his own threat. But his pride would not let him recommence the conversation otherwise than by continuing the quarrel. Dunstan was waiting for this, and took his ale in shorter draughts than usual.

'It's just like you,' Godfrey burst out, in a bitter tone, 'to talk about my selling Wildfire in that cool way—the last thing I've got to call my own, and the best bit of horse-flesh I ever had in my life. And if you'd got a spark of pride in you, you'd be ashamed to see the stables emptied, and everybody sneering about it. But it's my belief you'd sell yourself, if it was only for the pleasure of making somebody feel he'd got a bad bargain.'

'Ay, ay,' said Dunstan, very placably, 'you do me justice, I see. You know I'm a jewel for 'ticing people into bargains. For which reason I advise you to let *me* sell Wildfire. I'd ride him to the hunt to-morrow for you, with pleasure. I shouldn't look so handsome as you in the saddle, but it's the horse they'll bid for, and not the rider.'

'Yes, I daresay—trust my horse to you!'

'As you please,' said Dunstan, rapping the window-seat again with an air of great unconcern. 'It's *you* have got to pay Fowler's money; it's none of my business. You received the money from him when you went to Bramcote, and *you* told the Squire it wasn't paid. I'd nothing to do with that; you chose to be so obliging as to give it me, that was all. If you don't want to pay the money, let it alone; it's all one to me. But I was willing to accommodate you by undertaking to sell the horse, seeing it's not convenient to you to go so far to-morrow.'

Godfrey was silent for some moments. He would have liked to spring on Dunstan, wrench the whip from his hand, and flog him to within an inch of his life; and no bodily fear could have deterred him; but he was mastered by another sort of fear, which was fed by feelings stronger even than his resentment. When he spoke again it was in a half-conciliatory tone.

'Well, you mean no nonsense about the horse, eh? You'll sell him all fair, and hand over the money? If you don't, you know, everything 'ull go to smash, for I've got nothing else to trust to. And you'll have less pleasure in pulling the house over my head, when your own skull's to be broken too.'

'Ay, ay,' said Dunstan, rising; 'all right. I thought you'd come round. I'm the fellow to bring old Bryce up to the scratch. I'll get you a hundred and twenty for him, if I get you a penny.'

'But it'll perhaps rain cats and dogs to-morrow, as it did yesterday, and then you can't go,' said Godfrey, hardly knowing whether he wished for that obstacle or not.

'Not *it*,' said Dunstan. 'I'm always lucky in my weather. It might rain if you wanted to go yourself. You never hold trumps,* you know—I always do. You've got the beauty, you see, and I've got the luck, so you must keep me by you for your crooked sixpence;* you'll *ne*-ver get along without me.'

'Confound you, hold your tongue!' said Godfrey, impetuously. 'And take care to keep sober to-morrow, else you'll get pitched on your head coming home, and Wildfire might be the worse for it.'

'Make your tender heart easy,' said Dunstan, opening the door. 'You never knew me see double when I'd got a bargain to make; it 'ud spoil the fun. Besides, whenever I fall, I'm warranted to fall on my legs.'

With that, Dunstan slammed the door behind him, and left Godfrey to that bitter rumination on his personal circumstances which was now unbroken from day to day save by the excitement of sporting, drinking, card-playing, or the rarer and less oblivious pleasure of seeing Miss Nancy Lammeter. The subtle and varied pains springing from the higher sensibility that accompanies higher culture, are perhaps less pitiable than that dreary absence of impersonal enjoyment and consolation which leaves ruder minds to the perpetual urgent companionship of their own griefs and discontents. The lives of those rural forefathers, whom we are apt to think very prosaic figures—men whose only work was to ride round their land, getting heavier and heavier in their saddles, and who passed the rest of their days in the half-listless gratification of senses dulled by monotony—had a certain pathos in them nevertheless. Calamities came to *them* too, and their early errors carried hard consequences: perhaps the love of some sweet maiden, the image of purity, order, and calm, had opened their eyes to the vision of a life in which the days would not seem too long, even without rioting;* but the maiden was lost, and the vision passed away, and then what was left to them, especially when they had become too heavy for the hunt, or for carrying a gun over the furrows, but to drink and get merry, or to drink and get angry, so that they might be independent of variety, and say over again with eager emphasis the things they had said already any time that twelvemonth? Assuredly, among these flushed and dull-eyed men there were some whom—thanks to their native human-kindness—even riot could never drive into brutality; men who, when their cheeks were fresh, had felt the keen point of sorrow or remorse, had been pierced by the reeds they leaned on,* or had lightly put their limbs in fetters from which no struggle could loose them; and under these sad circumstances, common to us all, their thoughts could find no resting-place outside the ever-trodden round of their own petty history.

That, at least, was the condition of Godfrey Cass in this six-and-twentieth year of his life. A movement of compunction, helped by those small indefinable influences which every personal relation exerts on a pliant nature, had urged him into a secret marriage, which was a blight on his life. It was an ugly story of low passion, delusion, and waking from delusion, which needs not to be dragged from the privacy of Godfrey's bitter memory. He had long known that the delusion was partly due to a trap laid for him by Dunstan, who saw in his brother's degrading marriage the means of gratifying at once his jealous hate and his cupidity. And if Godfrey could have felt himself simply a victim, the iron bit that destiny had put into his mouth would have chafed him less intolerably. If the curses he muttered half aloud when he was alone had had no other object than Dunstan's diabolical cunning, he might have shrunk less from the consequences of avowal. But he had something else to curse—his own vicious folly, which now seemed as mad and unaccountable to him as almost all our follies and vices do when their promptings have long passed away. For four years he had thought of Nancy Lammeter, and wooed her with tacit patient worship, as the woman who made him think of the future with joy: she would be his wife, and would make home lovely to him, as his father's home had never been; and it would be easy, when she was always near, to shake off those foolish habits that were no pleasures, but only a feverish way of annulling vacancy. Godfrey's was an essentially domestic nature, bred up in a home where the hearth had no smiles, and where the daily habits were not chastised by the presence of household order. His easy disposition made him fall in unresistingly with the family courses, but the need of some tender permanent affection, the longing for some influence that would make the good he preferred easy to pursue, caused the neatness, purity, and liberal orderliness of the Lammeter household, sunned by the smile of Nancy, to seem like those fresh bright hours of the morning when temptations go to sleep and leave the ear open to the voice of the good angel, inviting to industry, sobriety, and peace. And yet the hope of this paradise had not been enough to save him from a course which shut him out of it for ever. Instead of keeping fast hold of the strong silken rope by which Nancy would have drawn him safe to the green banks where it was easy to step firmly, he had let himself be dragged back into mud and slime, in which it was useless to struggle. He had made ties for himself which robbed him of all wholesome motive and were a constant exasperation.

Still, there was one position worse than the present: it was the position he would be in when the ugly secret was disclosed; and the desire that continually triumphed over every other was that of warding off the evil day, when he would have to bear the consequences of his father's violent resentment for the wound inflicted on his family pride—would have, perhaps, to turn his back on that hereditary ease and dignity which, after all, was a sort of reason for living, and would carry with him the certainty that he was banished for ever from the sight and esteem of Nancy Lammeter. The longer the interval, the more chance there was of deliverance from some, at least, of the hateful consequences to which he had sold himself; the more opportunities remained for him to snatch the strange gratification of seeing Nancy, and gathering some faint indications of her lingering regard. Towards this gratification he was impelled, fitfully, every now and then, after having passed weeks in which he had avoided her as the far-off bright-winged prize that only made him spring forward and find his chain all the more galling. One of those fits of yearning was on him now, and it would have been strong enough to have persuaded him to trust Wildfire to Dunstan rather than disappoint the yearning, even if he had not had another reason for his disinclination towards the morrow's hunt. That other reason was the fact that the morning's meet was near Batherley, the market-town where the unhappy woman lived, whose image became more odious to him every day; and to his thought the whole vicinage was haunted by her. The yoke a man creates for himself by wrong-doing will breed hate in the kindliest nature; and the good-humoured, affectionate-hearted Godfrey Cass was fast becoming a bitter man, visited by cruel wishes, that seemed to enter, and depart, and enter again, like demons who had found in him a ready-garnished home.*

What was he to do this evening to pass the time? He might as well go to the Rainbow, and hear the talk about the cock-fighting:* everybody was there, and what else was there to be done? Though, for his own part, he did not care a button for cock-fighting. Snuff, the brown spaniel, who had placed herself in front of him, and had been watching him for some time, now jumped up in impatience for the expected caress. But Godfrey thrust her away without looking at her, and left the room, followed humbly by the unresenting Snuff—perhaps because she saw no other career open to her.

CHAPTER IV

DUNSTAN CASS, setting off in the raw morning, at the judiciously quiet pace of a man who is obliged to ride to cover* on his hunter, had to take his way along the lane which, at its farther extremity, passed by the piece of unenclosed ground called the Stone-pit, where stood the cottage, once a stone-cutter's shed, now for fifteen years inhabited by Silas Marner. The spot looked very dreary at this season, with the moist trodden clay about it, and the red, muddy water high up in the deserted quarry. That was Dunstan's first thought as he approached it; the second was, that the old fool of a weaver, whose loom he heard rattling already, had a great deal of money hidden somewhere. How was it that he, Dunstan Cass, who had often heard talk of Marner's miserliness, had never thought of suggesting to Godfrey that he should frighten or persuade the old fellow into lending the money on the excellent security of the young Squire's prospects? The resource occurred to him now as so easy and agreeable, especially as Marner's hoard was likely to be large enough to leave Godfrey a handsome surplus beyond his immediate needs, and enable him to accommodate his faithful brother, that he had almost turned the horse's head towards home again. Godfrey would be ready enough to accept the suggestion: he would snatch eagerly at a plan that might save him from parting with Wildfire. But when Dunstan's meditation reached this point, the inclination to go on grew strong and prevailed. He didn't want to give Godfrey that pleasure: he preferred that Master Godfrey should be vexed. Moreover, Dunstan enjoyed the self-important consciousness of having a horse to sell, and the opportunity of driving a bargain, swaggering, and possibly taking somebody in. He might have all the satisfaction attendant on selling his brother's horse, and not the less have the further satisfaction of setting Godfrey to borrow Marner's money. So he rode on to cover.

Bryce and Keating were there, as Dunstan was quite sure they would be—he was such a lucky fellow.

'Heyday!' said Bryce, who had long had his eye on Wildfire, 'you're on your brother's horse to-day: how's that?'

'Oh, I've swopped with him,' said Dunstan, whose delight in lying, grandly independent of utility, was not to be diminished by the likelihood that his hearer would not believe him—'Wildfire's mine now.'

'What! has he swopped with you for that big-boned hack of yours?' said Bryce, quite aware that he should get another lie in answer.

'Oh, there was a little account between us,' said Dunsey, carelessly, 'and Wildfire made it even. I accommodated him by taking the horse, though it was against my will, for I'd got an itch for a mare o' Jortin's—as rare a bit o' blood as ever you threw your leg across. But I shall keep Wildfire, now I've got him, though I'd a bid of a hundred and fifty for him the other day, from a man over at Flitton—he's buying for Lord Cromleck—a fellow with a cast in his eye, and a green waistcoat. But I mean to stick to Wildfire: I shan't get a better at a fence in a hurry. The mare's got more blood, but she's a bit too weak in the hind-quarters.'

Bryce of course divined that Dunstan wanted to sell the horse, and Dunstan knew that he divined it (horse-dealing is only one of many human transactions carried on in this ingenious manner); and they both considered that the bargain was in its first stage, when Bryce replied, ironically—

'I wonder at that now; I wonder you mean to keep him; for I never heard of a man who didn't want to sell his horse getting a bid of half as much again as the horse was worth. You'll be lucky if you get a hundred.'

Keating rode up now, and the transaction became more complicated. It ended in the purchase of the horse by Bryce for a hundred and twenty, to be paid on the delivery of Wildfire, safe and sound, at the Batherley stables. It did occur to Dunsey that it might be wise for him to give up the day's hunting, proceed at once to Batherley, and, having waited for Bryce's return, hire a horse to carry him home with the money in his pocket. But the inclination for a run, encouraged by confidence in his luck, and by a draught of brandy from his pocket-pistol* at the conclusion of the bargain, was not easy to overcome, especially with a horse under him that would take the fences to the admiration of the field. Dunstan, however, took one fence too many, and got his horse pierced with a hedge-stake. His own ill-favoured person, which was quite unmarketable, escaped without injury; but poor Wildfire, unconscious of his price, turned on his flank and painfully panted his last. It happened that Dunstan, a short time before, having had to get down to arrange his stirrup, had muttered a good many curses at this interruption, which had thrown him in the rear of the hunt near the moment of glory, and under this exasperation had taken the fences more blindly. He would soon have been up with the hounds again, when the fatal accident happened; and hence he was between eager riders in advance, not troubling themselves about what happened behind them, and far-off stragglers, who were as likely as not to pass quite aloof from the line of road in which Wildfire had fallen. Dunstan, whose nature it was to care more for immediate annoyances than for remote consequences, no sooner recovered his legs, and saw that it was all over with Wildfire, than he felt a satisfaction at the absence of witnesses to a position which no swaggering could make enviable. Reinforcing himself, after his shake, with a little brandy and much swearing, he walked as fast as he could to a coppice on his right hand, through which it occurred to him that he could make his way to Batherley without danger of encountering any member of the hunt. His first intention was to hire a horse there and ride home forthwith, for to walk many miles without a gun in his hand and along an ordinary road, was as much out of the question to him as to other spirited young men of his kind. He did not much mind about taking the bad news to Godfrey, for he had to offer him at the same time the resource of Marner's money; and if Godfrey kicked, as he always did, at the notion of making a fresh debt from which he himself got the smallest share of advantage, why, he wouldn't kick long: Dunstan felt sure he could worry Godfrey into anything. The idea of Marner's money kept growing in vividness, now the want of it had become immediate;

the prospect of having to make his appearance with the muddy boots of a pedestrian at Batherley, and to encounter the grinning queries of stablemen, stood unpleasantly in the way of his impatience to be back at Raveloe and carry out his felicitous plan; and a casual visitation of his waistcoat-pocket, as he was ruminating, awakened his memory to the fact that the two or three small coins his fore-finger encountered there, were of too pale a colour to cover that small debt, without payment of which the stable-keeper had declared he would never do any more business with Dunsey Cass. After all, according to the direction in which the run had brought him, he was not so very much farther from home than he was from Batherley; but Dunsey, not being remarkable for clearness of head, was only led to this conclusion by the gradual perception that there were other reasons for choosing the unprecedented course of walking home. It was now nearly four o'clock, and a mist was gathering: the sooner he got into the road the better. He remembered having crossed the road and seen the finger-post only a little while before Wildfire broke down; so, buttoning his coat, twisting the lash of his hunting-whip compactly round the handle, and rapping the tops of his boots with a self-possessed air, as if to assure himself that he was not at all taken by surprise, he set off with the sense that he was undertaking a remarkable feat of bodily exertion, which somehow and at some time he should be able to dress up and magnify to the admiration of a select circle at the Rainbow. When a young gentleman like Dunsey is reduced to so exceptional a mode of locomotion as walking, a whip in his hand is a desirable corrective to a too bewildering dreamy sense of unwontedness in his position; and Dunstan, as he went along through the gathering mist, was always rapping his whip somewhere. It was Godfrey's whip, which he had chosen to take without leave because it had a gold handle; of course no one could see, when Dunstan held it, that the name *Godfrey Cass* was cut in deep letters on that gold handle—they could only see that it was a very handsome whip. Dunsey was not without fear that he might meet some acquaintance in whose eyes he would cut a pitiable figure, for mist is no screen when people get close to each other; but when he at last found himself in the well-known Raveloe lanes without having met a soul, he silently remarked that that was part of his usual good luck. But now the mist, helped by the evening darkness, was more of a screen than he desired, for it hid the ruts into which his feet were liable to slip—hid everything, so that he had to guide his steps by dragging his whip along the low bushes in advance of the hedgerow. He must soon, he thought, be getting near the opening at the Stone-pits: he should find it out by the break in the hedgerow. He found it out, however, by another circumstance which he had not expected—namely, by certain gleams of light, which he presently guessed to proceed from Silas Marner's cottage. That cottage and the money hidden within it had been in his mind continually during his walk, and he had been imagining ways of cajoling and tempting the weaver to part with the immediate possession of his money for the sake of receiving interest. Dunstan felt as if there must be a little frightening added to the cajolery, for his own arithmetical convictions were not clear enough to afford him any forcible demonstration as to the advantages of interest; and as for security, he regarded it vaguely as a means of cheating a man by making him believe that he would be paid. Altogether, the operation on the miser's mind was a task that Godfrey would be sure to hand over to his more daring and cunning brother: Dunstan had made up his mind to that; and by the time he saw the light gleaming through the chinks of Marner's shutters, the idea of a dialogue with the weaver had become so familiar to him, that it occurred to him as quite a natural thing to make the acquaintance forthwith. There might be several conveniences attending this course: the weaver had possibly got a lantern, and Dunstan was tired of feeling his way. He was still nearly three-quarters of a mile from home, and the lane was becoming unpleasantly slippery, for the mist was passing into rain. He turned up the bank, not without some fear lest he might miss the right way, since he was not certain whether the light were in front or on the side of the cottage. But he felt the ground before him cautiously with his whip-handle, and at last arrived safely at the door. He knocked loudly, rather enjoying the idea that the old fellow would be frightened at the sudden noise. He heard no movement in reply: all was silence in the cottage. Was the weaver gone to bed, then? If so, why had he left a light? That was a strange forgetfulness in a miser. Dunstan knocked still more loudly, and, without pausing for a reply, pushed his fingers through the latch-hole, intending to shake the door and pull the latch-string up and down, not doubting that the door was fastened. But, to his surprise, at this double motion the door opened, and he found himself in front of a bright fire which lit up every corner of the cottage—the bed, the loom, the three chairs, and the table—and showed him that Marner was not there.

Nothing at that moment could be much more inviting to Dunsey than the bright fire on the brick hearth: he walked in and seated himself by it at once. There was something in front of the fire, too, that would have been inviting to a hungry man, if it had been in a different stage of cooking. It was a small bit of pork suspended from the kettle-hanger by a string passed through a large door-key, in a way known to primitive housekeepers unpossessed of jacks.* But the pork had been hung at the farthest extremity of the hanger, apparently to prevent the roasting from proceeding too rapidly during the owner's absence. The old staring simpleton had hot meat for his supper, then? thought Dunstan. People had always said he lived on mouldy bread, on purpose to check his appetite. But where could he be at this time, and on such an evening, leaving his supper in this stage of preparation, and his door unfastened? Dunstan's own recent difficulty in making his way suggested to him that the weaver had perhaps gone outside his cottage to fetch in fuel, or for some such brief purpose, and had slipped into the Stone-pit. That was an interesting idea to Dunstan, carrying consequences of entire novelty. If the weaver was dead, who had a right to his money? Who would know where his money was hidden? *Who would know that anybody had come to take it away?* He went no farther into the subtleties of evidence: the pressing question, 'Where *is* the money?' now took such entire possession of him as to make him quite forget that the weaver's death was not a certainty. A dull mind, once arriving at an inference that flatters a desire, is rarely able to retain the impression that the notion from which the inference started was purely problematic. And Dunstan's mind was as dull as the mind of a possible felon usually is. There were only three hiding-places where he had ever heard of cottagers' hoards being found: the thatch, the bed, and a hole in the floor. Marner's cottage had no thatch; and Dunstan's first act, after a train of thought made rapid by the stimulus of cupidity, was to go up to the bed; but while he did so, his eyes travelled eagerly over the floor, where the bricks, distinct in the fire-light, were discernible under the sprinkling of sand. But not everywhere; for there was one spot, and one only, which was quite covered with sand, and sand showing the marks of fingers, which had apparently been careful to spread it over a given space. It was near the treddles of the loom.* In an instant Dunstan darted to that spot, swept away the sand with his whip, and, inserting the thin end of the hook between the bricks, found that they were loose. In haste he lifted up two bricks, and saw what he had no doubt was the object of his search; for what could there be but money in those two leathern bags? And, from their weight, they must be filled with guineas. Dunstan felt round the hole, to be certain that it held no more; then hastily replaced the bricks, and spread the sand over them. Hardly more than five minutes had passed since he entered the cottage, but it seemed to Dunstan like a long while; and though he was without any distinct recognition of the possibility that Marner might be alive, and might re-enter the cottage at any moment, he felt an undefinable dread laying hold on him, as he rose to his feet with the bags in his hand. He would hasten out into the darkness, and then consider what he should do with the bags. He closed the door behind him immediately, that he might shut in the stream of light: a few steps would be enough to carry him beyond betrayal by the gleams from the shutter-chinks and the latch-hole. The rain and darkness had got thicker, and he was glad of it; though it was awkward walking with both hands filled, so that it was as much as he could do to grasp his whip along with one of the bags. But when he had gone a yard or two, he might take his time. So he stepped forward into the darkness.

CHAPTER V

When Dunstan Cass turned his back on the cottage, Silas Marner was not more than a hundred yards away from it, plodding along from the village with a sack thrown round his shoulders as an over-coat, and with a horn lantern* in his hand. His legs were weary, but his mind was at ease, free from the presentiment of change. The sense of security more frequently springs from habit than from conviction, and for this reason it often subsists after such a change in the conditions as might have been expected to suggest alarm. The lapse of time during which a given event has not happened, is, in this logic of habit, constantly alleged as a reason why the event should never happen, even when the lapse of time is precisely the added condition which makes the event imminent. A man will tell you that he has worked in a mine for forty years unhurt by an accident as a reason why he should apprehend no danger, though the roof is beginning to sink; and it is often observable, that the older a man gets, the more difficult it is to him to retain a believing conception of his own death. This influence of habit was necessarily strong in a man whose life was so monotonous as Marner's—who saw no new people and heard of no new events to keep alive in him the idea of the unexpected and the changeful; and it explains simply enough, why his mind could be at ease, though he had left his house and his treasure more defenceless than usual. Silas was thinking with double complacency of his supper: first, because it would be hot and savoury; and secondly, because it would cost him nothing. For the little bit of pork was a present from that excellent housewife, Miss Priscilla Lammeter, to whom he had this day carried home a handsome piece of linen; and it was only on occasion of a present like this, that Silas indulged himself with roast-meat. Supper was his favourite meal, because it came at his time of revelry, when his heart warmed over his gold; whenever he had roast-meat, he always chose to have it for supper. But this evening, he had no sooner ingeniously knotted his string fast round his bit of pork, twisted the string according to rule over his door-key, passed it through the handle, and made it fast on the hanger, than he remembered that a piece of very fine twine was indispensable to his 'setting up' a new piece of work in his loom early in the morning. It had slipped his memory, because, in coming from Mr Lammeter's, he had not had to pass through the village; but to lose time by going on errands in the morning was out of the question. It was a nasty fog to turn out into, but there were things Silas loved better than his own comfort; so, drawing his pork to the extremity of the hanger, and arming himself with his lantern and his old sack, he set out on what, in ordinary weather, would have been a twenty minutes' errand. He could not have locked his door without undoing his well-knotted string and retarding his supper; it was not worth his while to make that sacrifice. What thief would find his way to the Stone-pits on such a night as this? and why should he come on this particular night, when he had never come through all the fifteen years before? These questions were not distinctly present in Silas's mind; they merely serve to represent the vaguely-felt foundation of his freedom from anxiety.

He reached his door in much satisfaction that his errand was done: he opened it, and to his short-sighted eyes everything remained as he had left it, except that the fire sent out a welcome increase of heat. He trod about the floor while putting by his lantern and throwing aside his hat and sack, so as to merge the marks of Dunstan's feet on the sand in the marks of his own nailed boots. Then he moved his pork nearer to the fire, and sat down to the agreeable business of tending the meat and warming himself at the same time.

Any one who had looked at him as the red light shone upon his pale face, strange straining eyes, and meagre form, would perhaps have understood the mixture of contemptuous pity, dread, and suspicion with which he was regarded by his neighbours in Raveloe. Yet few men could be more harmless than poor Marner. In his truthful simple soul, not even the growing greed and worship of gold could beget any vice directly injurious to others. The light of his faith quite put out, and his affections made desolate, he had clung with all the force of his nature to his work and his money; and like all objects to which a man devotes himself, they had fashioned him into correspondence with themselves. His loom, as he wrought in it without ceasing, had in its turn wrought on him, and confirmed more and more the monotonous craving for its monotonous response. His gold, as he hung over it and saw it grow, gathered his power of loving together into a hard isolation like its own.

As soon as he was warm he began to think it would be a long while to wait till after supper before he drew out his guineas, and it would be pleasant to see them on the table before him as he ate his unwonted feast. For joy is the best of wine, and Silas's guineas were a golden wine of that sort.

He rose and placed his candle unsuspectingly on the floor near his loom, swept away the sand without noticing any change, and removed the bricks. The sight of the empty hole made his heart leap violently, but the belief that his gold was gone could not come at once—only terror, and the eager effort to put an end to the terror. He passed his trembling hand all about the hole, trying to think it possible that his eyes had deceived him; then he held the candle in the hole and examined it curiously, trembling more and more. At last he shook so violently that he let fall the candle, and lifted his hands to his head, trying to steady himself, that he might think. Had he put his gold somewhere else, by a sudden resolution last night, and then forgotten it? A man falling into dark waters seeks a momentary footing even on sliding stones; and Silas, by acting as if he believed in false hopes, warded off the moment of despair. He searched in every corner, he turned his bed over, and shook it, and kneaded it; he looked in his brick oven where he laid his sticks. When there was no other place to be searched, he kneeled down again and felt once more all round the hole. There was no untried refuge left for a moment's shelter from the terrible truth.

Yes, there was a sort of refuge which always comes with the prostration of thought under an overpowering passion: it was that expectation of impossibilities, that belief in contradictory images, which is still distinct from madness, because it is capable of being dissipated by the external fact. Silas got up from his knees trembling, and looked round at the table: didn't the gold lie there after all? The table was bare. Then he turned and looked behind him—looked all round his dwelling, seeming to strain his brown eyes after some possible appearance of the bags where he had already sought them in vain. He could see every object in his cottage—and his gold was not there.

Again he put his trembling hands to his head, and gave a wild ringing scream, the cry of desolation. For a few moments after, he stood motionless; but the cry had relieved him from the first maddening pressure of the truth. He turned, and tottered towards his loom, and got into the seat where he worked, instinctively seeking this as the strongest assurance of reality.

And now that all the false hopes had vanished, and the first shock of certainty was past, the idea of a thief began to present itself, and he entertained it eagerly, because a thief might be caught and made to restore the gold. The thought brought some new strength with it, and he started from his loom to the door. As he opened it the rain beat in upon him, for it was falling more and more heavily. There were no footsteps to be tracked on such a night—footsteps? When had the thief come? During Silas's absence in the daytime the door had been locked, and there had been no marks of any inroad on his return by daylight. And in the evening, too, he said to himself, everything was the same as when he had left it. The sand and bricks looked as if they had not been moved. *Was* it a thief who had taken the bags? or was it a cruel power that no hands could reach which had delighted in making him a second time desolate? He shrank from this vaguer dread, and fixed his mind with struggling effort on the robber with hands, who could be reached by hands. His thoughts glanced at all the neighbours who had made any remarks, or asked any questions which he might now regard as a ground of suspicion. There was Jem Rodney, a known poacher, and otherwise disreputable: he had often met Marner in his journeys across the fields, and had said something jestingly about the weaver's money; nay, he had once irritated Marner, by lingering at the fire when he called to light his pipe, instead of going about his business. Jem Rodney was the man—there was ease in the thought. Jem could be found and made to restore the money: Marner did not want to punish him, but only to get back his gold which had gone from him, and left his soul like a forlorn traveller on an unknown desert. The robber must be laid hold of. Marner's ideas of legal authority were confused, but he felt that he must go and proclaim his loss; and the great people in the village—the clergyman, the constable, and Squire Cass—would make Jem Rodney, or somebody else, deliver up the stolen money. He rushed out in the rain, under the stimulus of this hope, forgetting to cover his head, not caring to fasten his door; for he felt as if he had nothing left to lose. He ran swiftly, till want of breath compelled him to slacken his pace as he was entering the village at the turning close to the Rainbow.

The Rainbow, in Marner's view, was a place of luxurious resort for rich and stout husbands, whose wives had superfluous stores of linen; it was the place where he was likely to find the powers and dignities of Raveloe, and where he could most speedily make his loss public. He lifted the latch, and turned into the bright bar or kitchen on the right hand, where the less lofty customers of the house were in the habit of assembling, the parlour on the left being reserved for the more select society in which Squire Cass frequently enjoyed the double pleasure of conviviality and condescension. But the parlour was dark to-night, the chief personages who ornamented its circle being all at Mrs Osgood's birthday dance, as Godfrey Cass was. And in consequence of this, the party on the high-screened seats in the kitchen was more numerous than usual; several personages, who would otherwise have been admitted into the parlour and enlarged the opportunity of hectoring and condescension for their betters, being content this evening to vary their enjoyment by taking their spirits-and-water where they could themselves hector and condescend in company that called for beer.

CHAPTER VI

THE conversation, which was at a high pitch of animation when Silas approached the door of the Rainbow, had, as usual, been slow and intermittent when the company first assembled. The pipes began to be puffed in a silence which had an air of severity; the more important customers, who drank spirits and sat nearest the fire, staring at each other as if a bet were depending on the first man who winked; while the beer-drinkers, chiefly men in fustian jackets and smock-frocks,* kept their eyelids down and rubbed their hands across their mouths, as if their draughts of beer were a funereal duty attended with embarrassing sadness. At last, Mr Snell, the landlord, a man of a neutral disposition, accustomed to stand aloof from human differences as those of beings who were all alike in need of liquor, broke silence, by saying in a doubtful tone to his cousin the butcher—

'Some folks 'ud say that was a fine beast you druv in yesterday, Bob?'

The butcher, a jolly, smiling, red-haired man, was not disposed to answer rashly. He gave a few puffs before he spat and replied, 'And they wouldn't be fur wrong, John.'

After this feeble delusive thaw, the silence set in as severely as before.

'Was it a red Durham?'* said the farrier,* taking up the thread of discourse after the lapse of a few minutes.

The farrier looked at the landlord, and the landlord looked at the butcher, as the person who must take the responsibility of answering.

'Red it was,' said the butcher, in his good-humoured husky treble—'and a Durham it was.'

'Then you needn't tell *me* who you bought it of,' said the farrier, looking round with some triumph; 'I know who it is has got the red Durhams o' this country-side. And she'd a white star on her brow, I'll bet a penny?' The farrier leaned forward with his hands on his knees as he put this question, and his eyes twinkled knowingly.

'Well; yes—she might,' said the butcher, slowly, considering that he was giving a decided affirmative. 'I don't say contrairy.'

'I knew that very well,' said the farrier, throwing himself backward again, and speaking defiantly; 'if *I* don't know Mr Lammeter's cows, I should like to know who does—that's all. And as for the cow you've bought, bargain or no bargain, I've been at the drenching* of her—contradick me who will.'

The farrier looked fierce, and the mild butcher's conversational spirit was roused a little.

'I'm not for contradicking no man,' he said; 'I'm for peace and quietness. Some are for cutting long ribs—I'm for cutting 'em short myself; but *I* don't quarrel with 'em. All I say is, it's a lovely carkiss—and anybody as was reasonable, it 'ud bring tears into their eyes to look at it.'

'Well, it's the cow as I drenched, whatever it is,' pursued the farrier, angrily; 'and it was Mr Lammeter's cow, else you told a lie when you said it was a red Durham.'

'I tell no lies,' said the butcher, with the same mild huskiness as before, 'and I contradick none—not if a man was to swear himself black: he's no meat o' mine, nor none o' my bargains. All I say is, it's a lovely carkiss. And what I say, I'll stick to; but I'll quarrel wi' no man.'

'No,' said the farrier, with bitter sarcasm, looking at the company generally; 'and p'rhaps you arn't pig-headed; and p'rhaps you didn't say the cow was a red Durham; and p'rhaps you didn't say she'd got a star on her brow—stick to that, now you're at it.'

'Come, come,' said the landlord; 'let the cow alone. The truth lies atween you: you're both right and both wrong, as I allays say. And as for the cow's being Mr Lammeter's, I say nothing to that; but this I say, as the Rainbow's the Rainbow. And for the matter o' that, if the talk is to be o' the Lammeters, *you* know the most upo' that head, eh, Mr Macey? You remember when first Mr Lammeter's father come into these parts, and took the Warrens?'

Mr Macey, tailor and parish-clerk, the latter of which functions rheumatism had of late obliged him to share with a small-featured young man who sat opposite him, held his white head on one side, and twirled his thumbs with an air of complacency, slightly seasoned with criticism. He smiled pityingly, in answer to the landlord's appeal, and said—

'Ay, ay; I know, I know; but I let other folks talk. I've laid by now, and gev up to the young uns. Ask them as have been to school at Tarley: they've learnt pernouncing; that's come up since my day.'

'If you're pointing at me, Mr Macey,' said the deputy-clerk with an air of anxious propriety, 'I'm nowise a man to speak out of my place. As the psalm says—

"I know what's right, nor only so,
But also practise what I know." '*

'Well, then, I wish you'd keep hold o' the tune, when it's set for you; if you're for prac*tis*ing, I wish you'd prac*tise* that,' said a large jocose-looking man, an excellent wheelwright in his week-day capacity, but on Sundays leader of the choir. He winked, as he spoke, at two of the company, who were known officially as the 'bassoon' and the 'key-bugle,'* in the confidence that he was expressing the sense of the musical profession in Raveloe.

Mr Tookey, the deputy-clerk, who shared the unpopularity common to deputies, turned very red, but replied, with careful moderation—'Mr Winthrop, if you'll bring me any proof as I'm in the wrong, I'm not the man to say I won't alter. But there's people set up their own ears for a standard, and expect the whole choir to follow 'em. There may be two opinions, I hope.'

'Ay, ay,' said Mr Macey, who felt very well satisfied with this attack on youthful presumption; 'you're right there, Tookey: there's allays two 'pinions; there's the 'pinion a man has of himsen, and there's the 'pinion other folks have on him. There'd be two 'pinions about a cracked bell, if the bell could hear itself.'

'Well, Mr Macey,' said poor Tookey, serious amidst the general laughter, 'I undertook to partially fill up the office of parish-clerk by Mr Crackenthorp's desire, whenever your infirmities should make you unfitting; and it's one of the rights thereof to sing in the choir—else why have you done the same yourself?'

'Ah! but the old gentleman and you are two folks,' said Ben Winthrop. 'The old gentleman's got a gift. Why, the Squire used to invite him to take a glass, only to hear him sing the "Red Rovier";* didn't he, Mr Macey? It's a nat'ral gift. There's my little lad Aaron, he's got a gift—he can sing a tune off straight, like a throstle. But as for you, Master Tookey, you'd better stick to your "Amens": your voice is well enough when you keep it up in your nose. It's your inside as isn't right made for music: it's no better nor a hollow stalk.'

This kind of unflinching frankness was the most piquant form of joke to the company at the Rainbow, and Ben Winthrop's insult was felt by everybody to have capped Mr Macey's epigram.

'I see what it is plain enough,' said Mr Tookey, unable to keep cool any longer. 'There's a consperacy to turn me out o' the choir, as I shouldn't share the Christmas money—that's where it is. But I shall speak to Mr Crackenthorp; I'll not be put upon by no man.'

'Nay, nay, Tookey,' said Ben Winthrop. 'We'll pay you your share to keep out of it—that's what we'll do. There's things folks 'ud pay to be rid on, besides varmin.'

'Come, come,' said the landlord, who felt that paying people for their absence was a principle dangerous to society; 'a joke's a joke. We're all good friends here, I hope. We must give and take. You're both right and you're both wrong, as I say. I agree wi' Mr Macey here, as there's two opinions; and if mine was asked, I should say they're both right. Tookey's right and Winthrop's right, and they've only got to split the difference and make themselves even.'

The farrier was puffing his pipe rather fiercely, in some contempt at this trivial discussion. He had no ear for music himself, and never went to church, as being of the medical profession, and likely to be in requisition for delicate cows. But the butcher, having music in his soul, had listened with a divided desire for Tookey's defeat and for the preservation of the peace.

'To be sure,' he said, following up the landlord's conciliatory view, 'we're fond of our old clerk; it's nat'ral, and him used to be such a singer, and got a brother as is known for the first fiddler in this country-side. Eh, it's a pity but what Solomon lived in our village, and could give us a tune when we liked; eh, Mr Macey? I'd keep him in liver and lights* for nothing—that I would.'

'Ay, ay,' said Mr Macey, in the height of complacency; 'our family's been known for musicianers as far back as anybody can tell. But them things are dying out, as I tell Solomon every time he comes round; there's no voices like what there used to be, and there's nobody remembers what we remember, if it isn't the old crows.'

'Ay, you remember when first Mr Lammeter's father come into these parts, don't you, Mr Macey?' said the landlord.

'I should think I did,' said the old man, who had now gone through that complimentary process necessary to bring him up to the point of narration; 'and a fine old gentleman he was—as fine, and finer nor the Mr Lammeter as now is. He came from a bit north'ard, so far as I could ever make out. But there's nobody rightly knows about those parts: only it couldn't be far north'ard, nor much different from this country, for he brought a fine breed o' sheep with him, so there must be pastures there, and everything reasonable. We heared tell as he'd sold his own land to come and take the Warrens, and that seemed odd for a man as had land of his own, to come and rent a farm in a strange place. But they said it was along of his wife's dying; though there's reasons in things as nobody knows on—that's pretty much what I've made out; yet some folks are so wise, they'll find you fifty reasons straight off, and all the while the real reason's winking at 'em in the corner, and they niver see't. Howsomever, it was soon seen as we'd got a new parish'ner as know'd the rights and customs o' things, and kep a good house, and was well looked on by everybody. And the young man—that's the Mr Lammeter as now is, for he'd niver a sister—soon begun to court Miss Osgood, that's the sister o' the Mr Osgood as now is, and a fine handsome lass she was—eh, you can't think—they pretend this young lass is like her, but that's the way wi' people as don't know what come before 'em. *I* should know, for I helped the old rector, Mr Drumlow as was, I helped him marry 'em.'

Here Mr Macey paused; he always gave his narrative in instalments, expecting to be questioned according to precedent.

'Ay, and a partic'lar thing happened, didn't it, Mr Macey, so as you were likely to remember that marriage?' said the landlord, in a congratulatory tone.

'I should think there did—a *very* partic'lar thing,' said Mr Macey, nodding sideways. 'For Mr Drumlow—poor old gentleman, I was fond on him, though he'd got a bit confused in his head, what wi' age and wi' taking a drop o' summat warm when the service come of a cold morning. And young Mr Lammeter he'd have no way but he must be married in Janiwary, which, to be sure, 's a unreasonable time to be married in, for it isn't like a christening or a burying, as you can't help; and so Mr Drumlow—poor old gentleman, I was fond on him—but when he come to put the questions, he put 'em by the rule o' contrairy, like, and he says, "Wilt thou have this man to thy wedded wife?" says he, and then he says, "Wilt thou have this woman to thy wedded husband?" says he. But the partic'larest thing of all is, as nobody took any notice on it but me, and they answered straight off "yes," like as if it had been me saying "Amen" i' the right place, without listening to what went before.'

'But *you* knew what was going on well enough, didn't you, Mr Macey? You were live enough, eh?' said the butcher.

'Lor bless you!' said Mr Macey, pausing, and smiling in pity at the impotence of his hearer's imagination—'why, I was all of a tremble: it was as if I'd been a coat pulled by the two tails, like; for I couldn't stop the parson, I couldn't take upon me to do that; and yet I said to myself, I says, "Suppose they shouldn't be fast married, 'cause the words are contrairy?" and my head went working like a mill, for I was allays uncommon for turning things over and seeing all round 'em; and I says to myself, "Is't the meanin' or the words as makes folks fast i' wedlock?" For the parson meant right, and the bride and bridegroom meant right. But then, when I come to think on it, meanin' goes but a little way i' most things, for you may mean to stick things together and your glue may be bad, and then where are you? And so I says to mysen, "It isn't the meanin', it's the glue." And I was worreted as if I'd got three bells to pull at once, when we went into the vestry, and they begun to sign their names. But where's the use o' talking?—you can't think what goes on in a 'cute* man's inside.'

'But you held in for all that, didn't you, Mr Macey?' said the landlord.

'Ay, I held in tight till I was by mysen wi' Mr Drumlow, and then I out wi' everything, but respectful, as I allays did. And he made light on it, and he says, "Pooh, pooh, Macey, make yourself easy," he says; "it's neither the meaning nor the words—it's the re*ges*ter does it—that's the glue." So you see he settled it easy; for parsons and doctors know everything by heart, like, so as they aren't worreted wi' thinking what's the rights and wrongs o' things, as I'n been many and many's the time. And sure enough the wedding turned out all right, on'y poor Mrs Lammeter—that's Miss Osgood as was—died afore the lasses was growed up; but for prosperity and everything respectable, there's no family more looked on.'

Every one of Mr Macey's audience had heard this story many times, but it was listened to as if it had been a favourite tune, and at certain points the puffing of the pipes was momentarily suspended, that the listeners might give their whole minds to the expected words. But there was more to come; and Mr Snell, the landlord, duly put the leading question.

'Why, old Mr Lammeter had a pretty fortin, didn't they say, when he come into these parts?'

'Well, yes,' said Mr Macey; 'but I daresay it's as much as this Mr Lammeter's done to keep it whole. For there was allays a talk as nobody could get rich on the Warrens: though he holds it cheap, for it's what they call Charity Land.'

'Ay, and there's few folks know so well as you how it come to be Charity Land, eh, Mr Macey?' said the butcher.

'How should they?' said the old clerk, with some contempt. 'Why, my grandfather made the grooms' livery for that Mr Cliff as came and built the big stables at the Warrens. Why, they're stables four times as big as Squire Cass's, for he thought o' nothing but hosses and hunting, Cliff didn't—a Lunnon tailor, some folks said, as had gone mad wi' cheating. For he couldn't ride; lor bless you! they said he'd got no more grip o' the hoss than if his legs had been cross-sticks: my grandfather heared old Squire Cass say so many and many a time. But ride he would as if Old Harry* had been a-driving him; and he'd a son, a lad o' sixteen; and nothing would his father have him do, but he must ride and ride—though the lad was frighted, they said. And it was a common saying as the father wanted to ride the tailor out o' the lad, and make a gentleman on him—not but what I'm a tailor myself, but in respect as God made me such, I'm proud on it, for "Macey, tailor," 's been wrote up over our door since afore the Queen's heads went out on the shillings.* But Cliff, he was ashamed o' being called a tailor, and he was sore vexed as his riding was laughed at, and nobody o' the gentlefolks hereabout could abide him. Howsomever, the poor lad got sickly and died, and the father didn't live long after him, for he got queerer nor ever, and they said he used to go out i' the dead o' the night, wi' a lantern in his hand, to the stables, and set a lot o' lights burning, for he got as he couldn't sleep; and there he'd stand, cracking his whip and looking at his hosses; and they said it was a mercy as the stables didn't get burnt down wi' the poor dumb creaturs in 'em. But at last he died raving, and they found as he'd left all his property, Warrens and all, to a Lunnon Charity, and that's how the Warrens come to be Charity Land; though, as for the stables, Mr Lammeter never uses 'em—they're out o' all charicter—lor bless you! if you was to set the doors a-banging in 'em, it 'ud sound like thunder half o'er the parish.'

'Ay, but there's more going on in the stables than what folks see by daylight, eh, Mr Macey?' said the landlord.

'Ay, ay; go that way of a dark night, that's all,' said Mr Macey, winking mysteriously, 'and then make believe, if you like, as you didn't see lights i' the stables, nor hear the stamping o' the hosses, nor the cracking o' the whips, and howling, too, if it's tow'rt daybreak. "Cliff's Holiday" has been the name of it ever sin' I were a boy; that's to say, some said as it was the holiday Old Harry gev him from roasting, like. That's what my father told me, and he was a reasonable man, though there's folks nowadays know what happened afore they were born better nor they know their own business.'

'What do you say to that, eh, Dowlas?' said the landlord, turning to the farrier, who was swelling with impatience for his cue. 'There's a nut for *you* to crack.'

Mr Dowlas was the negative spirit in the company, and was proud of his position.

'Say? I say what a man *should* say as doesn't shut his eyes to look at a finger-post. I say, as I'm ready to wager any man ten pound, if he'll stand out wi' me any dry night in the pasture before the Warren stables, as we shall neither see lights nor hear noises, if it isn't the blowing of our own noses. That's what I say, and I've said it many a time; but there's nobody 'ull ventur a ten-pun' note on their ghos'es as they make so sure of.'

'Why, Dowlas, that's easy betting, that is,' said Ben Winthrop. 'You might as well bet a man as he wouldn't catch the rheumatise if he stood up to's neck in the pool of a frosty night. It 'ud be fine fun for a man to win his bet as he'd catch the rheumatise. Folks as believe in Cliff's Holiday aren't agoing to ventur near it for a matter o' ten pound.'

'If Master Dowlas wants to know the truth on it,' said Mr Macey, with a sarcastic smile, tapping his thumbs together, 'he's no call to lay any bet—let him go and stan' by himself—there's nobody 'ull hinder him; and then he can let the parish'ners know if they're wrong.'

'Thank you! I'm obliged to you,' said the farrier, with a snort of scorn. 'If folks are fools, it's no business o' mine. *I* don't want to make out the truth about ghos'es: I know it a'ready. But I'm not against a bet—everything fair and open. Let any man bet me ten pound as I shall see Cliff's Holiday, and I'll go and stand by myself. I want no company. I'd as lief* do it as I'd fill this pipe.'

'Ah, but who's to watch you, Dowlas, and see you do it? That's no fair bet,' said the butcher.

'No fair bet?' replied Mr Dowlas, angrily. 'I should like to hear any man stand up and say I want to bet unfair. Come now, Master Lundy, I should like to hear you say it.'

'Very like you would,' said the butcher. 'But it's no business o' mine. You're none o' my bargains, and I aren't a-going to try and 'bate* your price. If anybody 'll bid for you at your own vallying, let him. I'm for peace and quietness, I am.'

'Yes, that's what every yapping cur is, when you hold a stick up at him,' said the farrier. 'But I'm afraid o' neither man nor ghost, and I'm ready to lay a fair bet. *I* aren't a turn-tail cur.'

'Ay, but there's this in it, Dowlas,' said the landlord, speaking in a tone of much candour and tolerance. 'There's folks, i' my opinion, they can't see ghos'es, not if they stood as plain as a pike-staff* before 'em. And there's reason i' that. For there's my wife, now, can't smell, not if she'd the strongest o' cheese under her nose. I never see'd a ghost myself; but then I says to myself, "Very like I haven't got the smell for 'em." I mean, putting a ghost for a smell, or else contrairiways. And so, I'm for holding with both sides; for, as I say, the truth lies between 'em. And if Dowlas was to go and stand, and say he'd never seen a wink o' Cliff's Holiday all the night through, I'd back him; and if anybody said as Cliff's Holiday was certain sure, for all that, I'd back *him* too. For the smell's what I go by.'

The landlord's analogical argument was not well received by the farrier—a man intensely opposed to compromise.

'Tut, tut,' he said, setting down his glass with refreshed irritation; 'what's the smell got to do with it? Did ever a ghost give a man a black eye? That's what I should like to know. If ghos'es want me to believe in 'em, let 'em leave off skulking i' the dark and i' lone places—let 'em come where there's company and candles.'

'As if ghos'es 'ud want to be believed in by anybody so ignirant!' said Mr Macey, in deep disgust at the farrier's crass incompetence to apprehend the conditions of ghostly phenomena.

CHAPTER VII

YET the next moment there seemed to be some evidence that ghosts had a more condescending disposition than Mr Macey attributed to them; for the pale thin figure of Silas Marner was suddenly seen standing in the warm light, uttering no word, but looking round at the company with his strange unearthly eyes. The long pipes gave a simultaneous movement, like the antennæ of startled insects, and every man present, not excepting even the sceptical farrier, had an impression that he saw, not Silas Marner in the flesh, but an apparition; for the door by which Silas had entered was hidden by the high-screened seats, and no one had noticed his approach. Mr Macey, sitting a long way off the ghost, might be supposed to have felt an argumentative triumph, which would tend to neutralise his share of the general alarm. Had he not always said that when Silas Marner was in that strange trance of his, his soul went loose from his body? Here was the demonstration: nevertheless, on the whole, he would have been as well contented without it. For a few moments there was a dead silence, Marner's want of breath and agitation not allowing him to speak. The landlord, under the habitual sense that he was bound to keep his house open to all company, and confident in the protection of his unbroken neutrality, at last took on himself the task of adjuring the ghost.

'Master Marner,' he said, in a conciliatory tone, 'what's lacking to you? What's your business here?'

'Robbed!' said Silas, gaspingly. 'I've been robbed! I want the constable—and the Justice*—and Squire Cass—and Mr Crackenthorp.'

'Lay hold on him, Jem Rodney,' said the landlord, the idea of a ghost subsiding; 'he's off his head, I doubt. He's wet through.'

Jem Rodney was the outermost man, and sat conveniently near Marner's standing-place; but he declined to give his services.

'Come and lay hold on him yourself, Mr Snell, if you've a mind,' said Jem, rather sullenly. 'He's been robbed, and murdered too, for what I know,' he added, in a muttering tone.

'Jem Rodney!' said Silas, turning and fixing his strange eyes on the suspected man.

'Ay, Master Marner, what do ye want wi' me?' said Jem, trembling a little, and seizing his drinking-can as a defensive weapon.

'If it was you stole my money,' said Silas, clasping his hands entreatingly, and raising his voice to a cry, 'give it me back,—and I won't meddle with you. I won't set the constable on you. Give it me back, and I'll let you—I'll let you have a guinea.'

'Me stole your money!' said Jem, angrily. 'I'll pitch this can at your eye if you talk o' *my* stealing your money.'

'Come, come, Master Marner,' said the landlord, now rising resolutely, and seizing Marner by the shoulder, 'if you've got any information to lay, speak it out sensible, and show as you're in your right mind, if you expect anybody to listen to you. You're as wet as a drownded rat. Sit down and dry yourself, and speak straight forrard.'

'Ah, to be sure, man,' said the farrier, who began to feel that he had not been quite on a par with himself and the occasion. 'Let's have no more staring and screaming, else we'll have you strapped for a madman. That was why I didn't speak at the first—thinks I, the man's run mad.'

'Ay, ay, make him sit down,' said several voices at once, well pleased that the reality of ghosts remained still an open question.

The landlord forced Marner to take off his coat, and then to sit down on a chair aloof from every one else, in the centre of the circle and in the direct rays of the fire. The weaver, too feeble to have any distinct purpose beyond that of getting help to recover his money, submitted unresistingly. The transient fears of the company were now forgotten in their strong curiosity, and all faces were turned towards Silas, when the landlord, having seated himself again, said—

'Now then, Master Marner, what's this you've got to say—as you've been robbed? Speak out.'

'He'd better not say again as it was me robbed him,' cried Jem Rodney, hastily. 'What could I ha' done with his money? I could as easy steal the parson's surplice, and wear it.'

'Hold your tongue, Jem, and let's hear what he's got to say,' said the landlord. 'Now then, Master Marner.'

Silas now told his story, under frequent questioning as the mysterious character of the robbery became evident.

This strangely novel situation of opening his trouble to his Raveloe neighbours, of sitting in the warmth of a hearth not his own, and feeling the presence of faces and voices which were his nearest promise of help, had doubtless its influence on Marner, in spite of his passionate preoccupation with his loss. Our consciousness rarely registers the beginning of a growth within us any more than without us: there have been many circulations of the sap before we detect the smallest sign of the bud.

The slight suspicion with which his hearers at first listened to him, gradually melted away before the convincing simplicity of his distress: it was impossible for the neighbours to doubt that Marner was telling the truth, not because they were capable of arguing at once from the nature of his statements to the absence of any motive for making them falsely, but because, as Mr Macey observed, 'Folks as had the devil to back 'em were not likely to be so mushed'* as poor Silas was. Rather, from the strange fact that the robber had left no traces, and had happened to know the nick of time, utterly incalculable by mortal agents, when Silas would go away from home without locking his door, the more probable conclusion seemed to be, that his disreputable intimacy in that quarter, if it ever existed, had been broken up, and that, in consequence, this ill turn had been done to Marner by somebody it was quite in vain to set the constable after. Why this preternatural felon should be obliged to wait till the door was left unlocked, was a question which did not present itself.

'It isn't Jem Rodney as has done this work, Master Marner,' said the landlord. 'You mustn't be a-casting your eye at poor Jem. There may be a bit of a reckoning against Jem for the matter of a hare or so, if anybody was bound to keep their eyes staring open, and niver to wink; but Jem's been a-sitting here drinking his can, like the decentest man i' the parish, since before you left your house, Master Marner, by your own account.'

'Ay, ay,' said Mr Macey; 'let's have no accusing o' the innicent. That isn't the law. There must be folks to swear again' a man before he can be ta'en up. Let's have no accusing o' the innicent, Master Marner.'

Memory was not so utterly torpid in Silas that it could not be wakened by these words. With a movement of compunction as new and strange to him as everything else within the last hour, he started from his chair and went close up to Jem, looking at him as if he wanted to assure himself of the expression in his face.

'I was wrong,' he said—'yes, yes—I ought to have thought. There's nothing to witness against you, Jem. Only you'd been into my house oftener than anybody else, and so you came into my head. I don't accuse you—I won't accuse anybody—only,' he added, lifting up his hands to his head, and turning away with bewildered misery, 'I try—I try to think where my guineas can be.'

'Ay, ay, they're gone where it's hot enough to melt 'em, I doubt,' said Mr Macey.

'Tchuh!' said the farrier. And then he asked, with a cross-examining air, 'How much money might there be in the bags, Master Marner?'

'Two hundred and seventy-two pounds, twelve and sixpence, last night when I counted it,' said Silas, seating himself again, with a groan.

'Pooh! why, they'd be none so heavy to carry. Some tramp's been in, that's all; and as for the no footmarks, and the bricks and the sand being all right—why, your eyes are pretty much like a insect's, Master Marner; they're obliged to look so close, you can't see much at a time. It's my opinion as, if I'd been you, or you'd been me—for it comes to the same thing—you wouldn't have thought you'd found everything as you left it. But what I vote is, as two of the sensiblest o' the company should go with you to Master Kench, the constable's—he's ill i' bed, I know that much—and get him to appoint one of us his deppity; for that's the law, and I don't think anybody 'ull take upon him to contradick me there. It isn't much of a walk to Kench's; and then, if it's me as is deppity, I'll go back with you, Master Marner, and examine your premises; and if anybody's got any fault to find with that, I'll thank him to stand up and say it out like a man.'

By this pregnant speech the farrier had re-established his self-complacency, and waited with confidence to hear himself named as one of the superlatively sensible men.

'Let us see how the night is, though,' said the landlord, who also considered himself personally concerned in this proposition. 'Why, it rains heavy still,' he said, returning from the door.

'Well, I'm not the man to be afraid o' the rain,' said the farrier. 'For it'll look bad when Justice Malam hears as respectable men like us had a information laid before 'em and took no steps.'

The landlord agreed with this view, and after taking the sense of the company, and duly rehearsing a small ceremony known in high ecclesiastical life as the *nolo episcopari*,* he consented to take on himself the chill dignity of going to Kench's. But to the farrier's strong disgust, Mr Macey now started an objection to his proposing himself as a deputy-constable; for that oracular old gentleman, claiming to know the law, stated, as a fact delivered to him by his father, that no doctor could be a constable.

'And you're a doctor, I reckon, though you're only a cow-doctor—for a fly's a fly, though it may be a hoss-fly,' concluded Mr Macey, wondering a little at his own ''cuteness.'

There was a hot debate upon this, the farrier being of course indisposed to renounce the quality of doctor, but contending that a doctor could be a constable if he liked—the law meant, he needn't be one if he didn't like. Mr Macey thought this was nonsense, since the law was not likely to be fonder of doctors than of other folks. Moreover, if it was in the nature of doctors more than of other men not to like being constables, how came Mr Dowlas to be so eager to act in that capacity?

'*I* don't want to act the constable,' said the farrier, driven into a corner by this merciless reasoning; 'and there's no man can say it of me, if he'd tell the truth. But if there's to be any jealousy and en*vy*ing about going to Kench's in the rain, let them go as like it—you won't get me to go, I can tell you.'

By the landlord's intervention, however, the dispute was accommodated. Mr Dowlas consented to go as a second person disinclined to act officially; and so poor Silas, furnished with some old coverings, turned out with his two companions into the rain again, thinking of the long night-hours before him, not as those do who long to rest, but as those who expect to 'watch for the morning.'*

CHAPTER VIII

WHEN Godfrey Cass returned from Mrs Osgood's party at midnight, he was not much surprised to learn that Dunsey had not come home. Perhaps he had not sold Wildfire, and was waiting for another chance—perhaps, on that foggy afternoon, he had preferred housing himself at the Red Lion at Batherley for the night, if the run had kept him in that neighbourhood; for he was not likely to feel much concern about leaving his brother in suspense. Godfrey's mind was too full of Nancy Lammeter's looks and behaviour, too full of the exasperation against himself and his lot, which the sight of her always produced in him, for him to give much thought to Wildfire, or to the probabilities of Dunstan's conduct.

The next morning the whole village was excited by the story of the robbery, and Godfrey, like every one else, was occupied in gathering and discussing news about it, and in visiting the Stone-pits. The rain had washed away all possibility of distinguishing foot-marks, but a close investigation of the spot had disclosed, in the direction opposite to the village, a tinder-box, with a flint and steel, half sunk in the mud. It was not Silas's tinder-box, for the only one he had ever had was still standing on his shelf; and the inference generally accepted was, that the tinder-box in the ditch was somehow connected with the robbery. A small minority shook their heads, and intimated their opinion that it was not a robbery to have much light thrown on it by tinder-boxes, that Master Marner's tale had a queer look with it, and that such things had been known as a man's doing himself a mischief, and then setting the justice to look for the doer. But when questioned closely as to their grounds for this opinion, and what Master Marner had to gain by such false pretences, they only shook their heads as before, and observed that there was no knowing what some folks counted gain; moreover, that everybody had a right to their own opinions, grounds or no grounds, and that the weaver, as everybody knew, was partly crazy. Mr Macey, though he joined in the defence of Marner against all suspicions of deceit, also pooh-poohed the tinder-box;

indeed, repudiated it as a rather impious suggestion, tending to imply that everything must be done by human hands, and that there was no power which could make away with the guineas without moving the bricks. Nevertheless, he turned round rather sharply on Mr Tookey, when the zealous deputy, feeling that this was a view of the case peculiarly suited to a parish-clerk, carried it still farther, and doubted whether it was right to inquire into a robbery at all when the circumstances were so mysterious.

'As if,' concluded Mr Tookey—'as if there was nothing but what could be made out by justices and constables.'

'Now, don't you be for overshooting the mark, Tookey,' said Mr Macey, nodding his head aside admonishingly. 'That's what you're allays at; if I throw a stone and hit, you think there's summat better than hitting, and you try to throw a stone beyond. What I said was against the tinder-box: I said nothing against justices and constables, for they're o' King George's making,* and it 'ud be ill-becoming a man in a parish office to fly out again' King George.'

While these discussions were going on amongst the group outside the Rainbow, a higher consultation was being carried on within, under the presidency of Mr Crackenthorp, the rector, assisted by Squire Cass and other substantial parishioners. It had just occurred to Mr Snell, the landlord—he being, as he observed, a man accustomed to put two and two together—to connect with the tinder-box, which, as deputy-constable, he himself had had the honourable distinction of finding, certain recollections of a pedlar who had called to drink at the house about a month before, and had actually stated that he carried a tinder-box about with him to light his pipe. Here, surely, was a clue to be followed out. And as memory, when duly impregnated with ascertained facts, is sometimes surprisingly fertile, Mr Snell gradually recovered a vivid impression of the effect produced on him by the pedlar's countenance and conversation. He had a 'look with his eye' which fell unpleasantly on Mr Snell's sensitive organism. To be sure, he didn't say anything particular—no, except that about the tinder-box—but it isn't what a man says, it's the way he says it. Moreover, he had a swarthy foreignness of complexion which boded little honesty.

'Did he wear ear-rings?' Mr Crackenthorp wished to know, having some acquaintance with foreign customs.

'Well—stay—let me see,' said Mr Snell, like a docile clairvoyante, who would really not make a mistake if she could help it. After stretching the corners of his mouth and contracting his eyes, as if he were trying to see the ear-rings, he appeared to give up the effort, and said, 'Well, he'd got ear-rings in his box to sell, so it's nat'ral to suppose he might wear 'em. But he called at every house, a'most, in the village; there's somebody else, mayhap, saw 'em in his ears, though I can't take upon me rightly to say.'

Mr Snell was correct in his surmise, that somebody else would remember the pedlar's ear-rings. For on the spread of inquiry among the villagers it was stated with gathering emphasis, that the parson had wanted to know whether the pedlar wore ear-rings in his ears, and an impression was created that a great deal depended on the eliciting of this fact. Of course, every one who heard the question, not having any distinct image of the pedlar as *without* ear-rings, immediately had an image of him *with* ear-rings, larger or smaller, as the case might be; and the image was presently taken for a vivid recollection, so that the glazier's wife, a well-intentioned woman, not given to lying, and whose house was among the cleanest in the village, was ready to declare, as sure as ever she meant to take the sacrament* the very next Christmas that was ever coming, that she had seen big ear-rings, in the shape of the young moon, in the pedlar's two ears; while Jinny Oates, the cobbler's daughter, being a more imaginative person, stated not only that she had seen them too, but that they had made her blood creep, as it did at that very moment while there she stood.

Also, by way of throwing further light on this clue of the tinderbox, a collection was made of all the articles purchased from the pedlar at various houses, and carried to the Rainbow to be exhibited there. In fact, there was a general feeling in the village, that for the clearing-up of this robbery there must be a great deal done at the Rainbow, and that no man need offer his wife an excuse for going there while it was the scene of severe public duties.

Some disappointment was felt, and perhaps a little indignation also, when it became known that Silas Marner, on being questioned by the Squire and the parson, had retained no other recollection of the pedlar than that he had called at his door, but had not entered his house, having turned away at once when Silas, holding the door ajar, had said that he wanted nothing. This had been Silas's testimony, though he clutched strongly at the idea of the pedlar's being the culprit, if only because it gave him a definite image of a whereabout for his gold after it had been taken away from its hiding-place: he could see it now in the pedlar's box. But it was observed with some irritation in the village, that anybody but a 'blind creatur' like Marner would have seen the man prowling about, for how came he to leave his tinder-box in the ditch close by, if he hadn't been lingering there? Doubtless, he had made his observations when he saw Marner at the door. Anybody might know—and only look at him—that the weaver was a half-crazy miser. It was a wonder the pedlar hadn't murdered him; men of that sort, with rings in their ears, had been known for murderers often and often; there had been one tried at the 'sizes,* not so long ago but what there were people living who remembered it.

Godfrey Cass, indeed, entering the Rainbow during one of Mr Snell's frequently repeated recitals of his testimony, had treated it lightly, stating that he himself had bought a pen-knife of the pedlar, and thought him a merry grinning fellow enough; it was all nonsense, he said, about the man's evil looks. But this was spoken of in the village as the random talk of youth, 'as if it was only Mr Snell who had seen something odd about the pedlar!' On the contrary, there were at least half-a-dozen who were ready to go before Justice Malam, and give in much more striking testimony than any the landlord could furnish. It was to be hoped Mr Godfrey would not go to Tarley and throw cold water on what Mr Snell said there, and so prevent the justice from drawing up a warrant. He was suspected of intending this, when, after mid-day, he was seen setting off on horseback in the direction of Tarley.

But by this time Godfrey's interest in the robbery had faded before his growing anxiety about Dunstan and Wildfire, and he was going, not to Tarley, but to Batherley, unable to rest in uncertainty about them any longer. The possibility that Dunstan had played him the ugly trick of riding away with Wildfire, to return at the end of a month, when he had gambled away or otherwise squandered the price of the horse, was a fear that urged itself upon him more, even, than the thought of an accidental injury; and now that the dance at Mrs Osgood's was past, he was irritated with himself that he had trusted his horse to Dunstan. Instead of trying to still his fears he encouraged them, with that superstitious impression which clings to us all, that if we expect evil very strongly it is the less likely to come; and when he heard a horse approaching at a trot, and saw a hat rising above a hedge beyond an angle of the lane, he felt as if his conjuration had succeeded. But no sooner did the horse come within sight, than his heart sank again. It was not Wildfire; and in a few moments more he discerned that the rider was not Dunstan, but Bryce, who pulled up to speak, with a face that implied something disagreeable.

'Well, Mr Godfrey, that's a lucky brother of yours, that Master Dunsey, isn't he?'

'What do you mean?' said Godfrey, hastily.

'Why, hasn't he been home yet?' said Bryce.

'Home? no. What has happened? Be quick. What has he done with my horse?'

'Ah, I thought it was yours, though he pretended you had parted with it to him.'

'Has he thrown him down and broken his knees?' said Godfrey, flushed with exasperation.

'Worse than that,' said Bryce. 'You see, I'd made a bargain with him to buy the horse for a hundred and twenty—a swinging* price, but I always liked the horse. And what does he do but go and stake him—fly at a hedge with stakes in it, atop of a bank with a ditch before it. The horse had been dead a pretty good while when he was found. So he hasn't been home since, has he?'

'Home? no,' said Godfrey, 'and he'd better keep away. Confound me for a fool! I might have known this would be the end of it.'

'Well, to tell you the truth,' said Bryce, 'after I'd bargained for the horse, it did come into my head that he might be riding and selling the horse without your knowledge, for I didn't believe it was his own. I knew Master Dunsey was up to his tricks sometimes. But where can he be gone? He's never been seen at Batherley. He couldn't have been hurt, for he must have walked off.'

'Hurt?' said Godfrey, bitterly. 'He'll never be hurt—he's made to hurt other people.'

'And so you *did* give him leave to sell the horse, eh?' said Bryce.

'Yes; I wanted to part with the horse—he was always a little too hard in the mouth for me,' said Godfrey; his pride making him wince under the idea that Bryce guessed the sale to be a matter of necessity. 'I was going to see after him—I thought some mischief had happened. I'll go back now,' he added, turning the horse's head, and wishing he could get rid of Bryce; for he felt that the long-dreaded crisis in his life was close upon him. 'You're coming on to Raveloe, aren't you?'

'Well, no, not now,' said Bryce. 'I *was* coming round there, for I had to go to Flitton, and I thought I might as well take you in my way, and just let you know all I knew myself about the horse. I suppose Master Dunsey didn't like to show himself till the ill news had blown over a bit. He's perhaps gone to pay a visit at the Three Crowns, by Whitbridge—I know he's fond of the house.'

'Perhaps he is,' said Godfrey, rather absently. Then rousing himself, he said, with an effort at carelessness, 'We shall hear of him soon enough, I'll be bound.'

'Well, here's my turning,' said Bryce, not surprised to perceive that Godfrey was rather 'down;' 'so I'll bid you good-day, and wish I may bring you better news another time.'

Godfrey rode along slowly, representing to himself the scene of confession to his father from which he felt that there was now no longer any escape. The revelation about the money must be made the very next morning; and if he withheld the rest, Dunstan would be sure to come back shortly, and, finding that he must bear the brunt of his father's anger, would tell the whole story out of spite, even though he had nothing to gain by it. There was one step, perhaps, by which he might still win Dunstan's silence and put off the evil day: he might tell his father that he had himself spent the money paid to him by Fowler; and as he had never been guilty of such an offence before, the affair would blow over after a little storming. But Godfrey could not bend himself to this. He felt that in letting Dunstan have the money, he had already been guilty of a breach of trust hardly less culpable than that of spending the money directly for his own behoof; and yet there was a distinction between the two acts which made him feel that the one was so much more blackening than the other as to be intolerable to him.

'I don't pretend to be a good fellow,' he said to himself; 'but I'm not a scoundrel—at least, I'll stop short somewhere. I'll bear the consequences of what I *have* done sooner than make believe I've done what I never would have done. I'd never have spent the money for my own pleasure—I was tortured into it.'

Through the remainder of this day Godfrey, with only occasional fluctuations, kept his will bent in the direction of a complete avowal to his father, and he withheld the story of Wildfire's loss till the next morning, that it might serve him as an introduction to heavier matter. The old Squire was accustomed to his son's frequent absence from home, and thought neither Dunstan's nor Wildfire's non-appearance a matter calling for remark. Godfrey said to himself again and again, that if he let slip this one opportunity of confession, he might never have another; the revelation might be made even in a more odious way than by Dunstan's malignity: *she* might come as she had threatened to do. And then he tried to make the scene easier to himself by rehearsal: he made up his mind how he would pass from the admission of his weakness in letting Dunstan have the money to the fact that Dunstan had a hold on him which he had been unable to shake off, and how he would work up his father to expect something very bad before he told him the fact. The old Squire was an implacable man: he made resolutions in violent anger, and he was not to be moved from them after his anger had subsided—as fiery volcanic matters cool and harden into rock. Like many violent and implacable men, he allowed evils to grow under favour of his own heedlessness, till they pressed upon him with exasperating force, and then he turned round with fierce severity and became unrelentingly hard. This was his system with his tenants: he allowed them to get into arrears, neglect their fences, reduce their stock, sell their straw, and otherwise go the wrong way,—and then, when he became short of money in consequence of this indulgence, he took the hardest measures and would listen to no appeal. Godfrey knew all this, and felt it with the greater force because he had constantly suffered annoyance from witnessing his father's sudden fits of unrelentingness, for which his own habitual irresolution deprived him of all sympathy. (He was not critical on the faulty indulgence which preceded these fits; *that* seemed to him natural enough.) Still there was just the chance, Godfrey thought, that his father's pride might see this marriage in a light that would induce him to hush it up, rather than turn his son out and make the family the talk of the country for ten miles round.

This was the view of the case that Godfrey managed to keep before him pretty closely till midnight, and he went to sleep thinking that he had done with inward debating. But when he awoke in the still morning darkness he found it impossible to reawaken his evening thoughts; it was as if they had been tired out and were not to be roused to further work. Instead of arguments for confession, he could now feel the presence of nothing but its evil consequences: the old dread of disgrace came back—the old shrinking from the thought of raising a hopeless barrier between himself and Nancy—the old disposition to rely on chances which might be favourable to him, and save him from betrayal. Why, after all, should he cut off the hope of them by his own act? He had seen the matter in a wrong light yesterday. He had been in a rage with Dunstan, and had thought of nothing but a thorough break-up of their mutual understanding; but what it would be really wisest for him to do, was to try and soften his father's anger against Dunsey, and keep things as nearly as possible in their old condition. If Dunsey did not come back for a few days (and Godfrey did not know but that the rascal had enough money in his pocket to enable him to keep away still longer), everything might blow over.

CHAPTER IX

GODFREY rose and took his own breakfast earlier than usual, but lingered in the wainscoted parlour till his younger brothers had finished their meal and gone out; awaiting his father, who always took a walk with his managing-man* before breakfast. Every one breakfasted at a different hour in the Red House, and the Squire was always the latest, giving a long chance to a rather feeble morning appetite before he tried it. The table had been spread with substantial eatables nearly two hours before he presented himself—a tall, stout man of sixty, with a face in which the knit brow and rather hard glance seemed contradicted by the slack and feeble mouth. His person showed marks of habitual neglect, his dress was slovenly; and yet there was something in the presence of the old Squire distinguishable from that of the ordinary farmers in the parish, who were perhaps every whit as refined as he, but, having slouched their way through life with a consciousness of being in the vicinity of their 'betters,' wanted that self-possession and authoritativeness of voice and carriage which belonged to a man who thought of superiors as remote existences with whom he had personally little more to do than with America or the stars. The Squire had been used to parish homage all his life, used to the presupposition that his family, his tankards, and everything that was his, were the oldest and best; and as he never associated with any gentry higher than himself, his opinion was not disturbed by comparison.

He glanced at his son as he entered the room, and said, 'What, sir! haven't *you* had your breakfast yet?' but there was no pleasant morning greeting between them; not because of any unfriendliness, but because the sweet flower of courtesy is not a growth of such homes as the Red House.

'Yes, sir,' said Godfrey, 'I've had my breakfast, but I was waiting to speak to you.'

'Ah! well,' said the Squire, throwing himself indifferently into his chair, and speaking in a ponderous coughing fashion, which was felt in Raveloe to be a sort of privilege of his rank, while he cut a piece of beef, and held it up before the deer-hound that had come in with him. 'Ring the bell for my ale, will you? You youngsters' business is your own pleasure, mostly. There's no hurry about it for anybody but yourselves.'

The Squire's life was quite as idle as his sons', but it was a fiction kept up by himself and his contemporaries in Raveloe that youth was exclusively the period of folly, and that their aged wisdom was constantly in a state of endurance mitigated by sarcasm. Godfrey waited, before he spoke again, until the ale had been brought and the door closed—an interval during which Fleet, the deer-hound, had consumed enough bits of beef to make a poor man's holiday dinner.

'There's been a cursed piece of ill-luck with Wildfire,' he began; 'happened the day before yesterday.'

'What! broke his knees?' said the Squire, after taking a draught of ale. 'I thought you knew how to ride better than that, sir. I never threw a horse down in my life. If I had, I might ha' whistled for another, for *my* father wasn't quite so ready to unstring* as some other fathers I know of. But they must turn over a new leaf—*they* must. What with mortgages and arrears, I'm as short o' cash as a roadside pauper. And that fool Kimble says the newspaper's talking about peace. Why, the country wouldn't have a leg to stand on. Prices 'ud run down like a jack, and I should never get my arrears, not if I sold all the fellows up. And there's that damned Fowler, I won't put up with him any longer; I've told Winthrop to go to Cox this very day. The lying scoundrel told me he'd be sure to pay me a hundred last month. He takes advantage because he's on that outlying farm, and thinks I shall forget him.'

The Squire had delivered this speech in a coughing and interrupted manner, but with no pause long enough for Godfrey to make it a pretext for taking up the word again. He felt that his father meant to ward off any request for money on the ground of the misfortune with Wildfire, and that the emphasis he had thus been led to lay on his shortness of cash and his arrears was likely to produce an attitude of mind the utmost unfavourable for his own disclosure. But he must go on, now he had begun.

'It's worse than breaking the horse's knees—he's been staked and killed,' he said, as soon as his father was silent, and had begun to cut his meat. 'But I wasn't thinking of asking you to buy me another horse; I was only thinking I'd lost the means of paying you with the price of Wildfire, as I'd meant to do. Dunsey took him to the hunt to sell him for me the other day, and after he'd made a bargain for a hundred and twenty with Bryce, he went after the hounds, and took some fool's leap or other that did for the horse at once. If it hadn't been for that, I should have paid you a hundred pounds this morning.'

The Squire had laid down his knife and fork, and was staring at his son in amazement, not being sufficiently quick of brain to form a probable guess as to what could have caused so strange an inversion of the paternal and filial relations as this proposition of his son to pay him a hundred pounds.

'The truth is, sir—I'm very sorry—I was quite to blame,' said Godfrey. 'Fowler did pay that hundred pounds. He paid it to me, when I was over there one day last month. And Dunsey bothered me for the money, and I let him have it, because I hoped I should be able to pay it you before this.'

The Squire was purple with anger before his son had done speaking, and found utterance difficult. 'You let Dunsey have it, sir? And how long have you been so thick with Dunsey that you must *collogue** with him to embezzle my money? Are you turning out a scamp? I tell you I won't have it. I'll turn the whole pack of you out of the house together, and marry again. I'd have you to remember, sir, my property's got no entail* on it;—since my grandfather's time the Casses can do as they like with their land. Remember that, sir. Let Dunsey have the money! Why should you let Dunsey have the money? There's some lie at the bottom of it.'

'There's no lie, sir,' said Godfrey. 'I wouldn't have spent the money myself, but Dunsey bothered me, and I was a fool, and let him have it. But I meant to pay it, whether he did or not. That's the whole story. I never meant to embezzle money, and I'm not the man to do it. You never knew me do a dishonest trick, sir.'

'Where's Dunsey, then? What do you stand talking there for? Go and fetch Dunsey, as I tell you, and let him give account of what he wanted the money for, and what he's done with it. He shall repent it. I'll turn him out. I said I would, and I'll do it. He shan't brave me. Go and fetch him.'

'Dunsey isn't come back, sir.'

'What! did he break his own neck, then?' said the Squire, with some disgust at the idea that, in that case, he could not fulfil his threat.

'No, he wasn't hurt, I believe, for the horse was found dead, and Dunsey must have walked off. I daresay we shall see him again by-and-by. I don't know where he is.'

'And what must you be letting him have my money for? Answer me that,' said the Squire, attacking Godfrey again, since Dunsey was not within reach.

'Well, sir, I don't know,' said Godfrey, hesitatingly. That was a feeble evasion, but Godfrey was not fond of lying, and, not being sufficiently aware that no sort of duplicity can long flourish without the help of vocal falsehoods, he was quite unprepared with invented motives.

'You don't know? I tell you what it is, sir. You've been up to some trick, and you've been bribing him not to tell,' said the Squire, with a sudden acuteness which startled Godfrey, who felt his heart beat violently at the nearness of his father's guess. The sudden alarm pushed him on to take the next step—a very slight impulse suffices for that on a downward road.

'Why, sir,' he said, trying to speak with careless ease, 'it was a little affair between me and Dunsey; it's no matter to anybody else. It's hardly worth while to pry into young men's fooleries: it wouldn't have made any difference to you, sir, if I'd not had the bad luck to lose Wildfire. I should have paid you the money.'

'Fooleries! Pshaw! it's time you'd done with fooleries. And I'd have you know, sir, you *must* ha' done with 'em,' said the Squire, frowning and casting an angry glance at his son. 'Your goings-on are not what I shall find money for any longer. There's my grandfather had his stables full o' horses, and kept a good house, too, and in worse times, by what I can make out; and so might I, if I hadn't four good-for-nothing fellows to hang on me like horse-leeches. I've been too good a father to you all—that's what it is. But I shall pull up, sir.'

Godfrey was silent. He was not likely to be very penetrating in his judgments, but he had always had a sense that his father's indulgence had not been kindness, and had had a vague longing for some discipline that would have checked his own errant weakness and helped his better will. The Squire ate his bread and meat hastily, took a deep draught of ale, then turned his chair from the table, and began to speak again.

'It'll be all the worse for you, you know—you'd need try and help me keep things together.'

'Well, sir, I've often offered to take the management of things, but you know you've taken it ill always, and seemed to think I wanted to push you out of your place.'

'I know nothing o' your offering or o' my taking it ill,' said the Squire, whose memory consisted in certain strong impressions unmodified by detail; 'but I know, one while you seemed to be thinking o' marrying, and I didn't offer to put any obstacles in your way, as some fathers would. I'd as lieve you married Lammeter's daughter as anybody. I suppose, if I'd said you nay, you'd ha' kept on with it; but, for want o' contradiction, you've changed your mind. You're a shilly-shally* fellow: you take after your poor mother. She never had a will of her own; a woman has no call for one, if she's got a proper man for her husband. But *your* wife had need have one, for you hardly know your own mind enough to make both your legs walk one way. The lass hasn't said downright she won't have you, has she?'

'No,' said Godfrey, feeling very hot and uncomfortable; 'but I don't think she will.'

'Think! why haven't you the courage to ask her? Do you stick to it, you want to have *her*—that's the thing?'

'There's no other woman I want to marry,' said Godfrey, evasively.

'Well, then, let me make the offer for you, that's all, if you haven't the pluck to do it yourself. Lammeter isn't likely to be loath for his daughter to marry into *my* family, I should think. And as for the pretty lass, she wouldn't have her cousin—and there's nobody else, as I see, could ha' stood in your way.'

'I'd rather let it be, please sir, at present,' said Godfrey, in alarm. 'I think she's a little offended with me just now, and I should like to speak for myself. A man must manage these things for himself.'

'Well, speak, then, and manage it, and see if you can't turn over a new leaf. That's what a man must do when he thinks o' marrying.'

'I don't see how I can think of it at present, sir. You wouldn't like to settle me on one of the farms, I suppose, and I don't think she'd come to live in this house with all my brothers. It's a different sort of life to what she's been used to.'

'Not come to live in this house? Don't tell me. You ask her, that's all,' said the Squire, with a short, scornful laugh.

'I'd rather let the thing be, at present, sir,' said Godfrey. 'I hope you won't try to hurry it on by saying anything.'

'I shall do what I choose,' said the Squire, 'and I shall let you know

I'm master; else you may turn out, and find an estate to drop into somewhere else. Go out and tell Winthrop not to go to Cox's, but wait for me. And tell 'em to get my horse saddled. And stop: look out and get that hack o' Dunsey's sold, and hand me the money, will you? He'll keep no more hacks at my expense. And if you know where he's sneaking—I daresay you do—you may tell him to spare himself the journey o' coming back home. Let him turn ostler, and keep himself. He shan't hang on me any more.'

'I don't know where he is; and if I did, it isn't my place to tell him to keep away,' said Godfrey, moving towards the door.

'Confound it, sir, don't stay arguing, but go and order my horse,' said the Squire, taking up a pipe.

Godfrey left the room, hardly knowing whether he were more relieved by the sense that the interview was ended without having made any change in his position, or more uneasy that he had entangled himself still further in prevarication and deceit. What had passed about his proposing to Nancy had raised a new alarm, lest by some after-dinner words of his father's to Mr Lammeter he should be thrown into the embarrassment of being obliged absolutely to decline her when she seemed to be within his reach. He fled to his usual refuge, that of hoping for some unforeseen turn of fortune, some favourable chance which would save him from unpleasant consequences—perhaps even justify his insincerity by manifesting its prudence.

In this point of trusting to some throw of fortune's dice, Godfrey can hardly be called old-fashioned. Favourable Chance is the god of all men who follow their own devices instead of obeying a law they believe in. Let even a polished man of these days get into a position he is ashamed to avow, and his mind will be bent on all the possible issues that may deliver him from the calculable results of that position. Let him live outside his income, or shirk the resolute honest work that brings wages, and he will presently find himself dreaming of a possible benefactor, a possible simpleton who may be cajoled into using his interest, a possible state of mind in some possible person not yet forthcoming. Let him neglect the responsibilities of his office, and he will inevitably anchor himself on the chance, that the thing left undone may turn out not to be of the supposed importance. Let him betray his friend's confidence, and he will adore that same cunning complexity called Chance, which gives him the hope that his friend will never know. Let him forsake a decent craft that he may pursue the gentilities of a profession to which nature never called him, and his religion will infallibly be the worship of blessed Chance, which he will believe in as the mighty creator of success. The evil principle deprecated in that religion, is the orderly sequence by which the seed brings forth a crop after its kind.*

CHAPTER X

JUSTICE MALAM was naturally regarded in Tarley and Raveloe as a man of capacious mind, seeing that he could draw much wider conclusions without evidence than could be expected of his neighbours who were not on the Commission of the Peace.* Such a man was not likely to neglect the clue of the tinder-box, and an inquiry was set on foot concerning a pedlar, name unknown, with curly black hair and a foreign complexion, carrying a box of cutlery and jewellery, and wearing large rings in his ears. But either because inquiry was too slow-footed to overtake him, or because the description applied to so many pedlars that inquiry did not know how to choose among them, weeks passed away, and there was no other result concerning the robbery than a gradual cessation of the excitement it had caused in Raveloe. Dunstan Cass's absence was hardly a subject of remark: he had once before had a quarrel with his father, and had gone off, nobody knew whither, to return at the end of six weeks, take up his old quarters unforbidden and swagger as usual. His own family, who equally expected this issue, with the sole difference that the Squire was determined this time to forbid him the old quarters, never mentioned his absence; and when his uncle Kimble or Mr Osgood noticed it, the story of his having killed Wildfire and committed some offence against his father was enough to prevent surprise. To connect the fact of Dunsey's disappearance with that of the robbery occurring on the same day, lay quite away from the track of every one's thought—even Godfrey's, who had better reason than any one else to know what his brother was capable of. He remembered no mention of the weaver between them since the time, twelve years ago, when it was their boyish sport to deride him; and, besides, his imagination constantly created an *alibi* for Dunstan: he saw him continually in some congenial haunt, to which he had walked off on leaving Wildfire—saw him sponging on chance acquaintances, and meditating a return home to the old amusement of tormenting his elder brother. Even if any brain in Raveloe had put the said two facts together, I doubt whether a combination so injurious to the prescriptive respectability of a family with a mural monument* and venerable tankards, would not have been suppressed as of unsound tendency. But Christmas puddings, brawn,* and abundance of spirituous liquors, throwing the mental originality into the channel of nightmare, are great preservatives against a dangerous spontaneity of waking thought.

When the robbery was talked of at the Rainbow and elsewhere, in good company, the balance continued to waver between the rational explanation founded on the tinder-box, and the theory of an impenetrable mystery that mocked investigation. The advocates of the tinder-box-and-pedlar view considered the other side a muddle-headed and credulous set, who, because they themselves were wall-eyed, supposed everybody else to have the same blank outlook; and the adherents of the inexplicable more than hinted that their antagonists were animals inclined to crow before they had found any corn—mere skimming-dishes* in point of depth—whose clear-sightedness consisted in supposing there was nothing behind a barn-door because they couldn't see through it; so that, though their controversy did not serve to elicit the fact concerning the robbery, it elicited some true opinions of collateral importance.

But while poor Silas's loss served thus to brush the slow current of Raveloe conversation, Silas himself was feeling the withering desolation of that bereavement about which his neighbours were arguing at their ease. To any one who had observed him before he lost his gold, it might have seemed that so withered and shrunken a life as his could hardly be susceptible of a bruise, could hardly endure any subtraction but such as would put an end to it altogether. But in reality it had been an eager life, filled with immediate purpose which fenced him in from the wide, cheerless unknown. It had been a clinging life; and though the object round which its fibres had clung was a dead disrupted thing, it satisfied the need for clinging. But now the fence was broken down—the support was snatched away. Marner's thoughts could no longer move in their old round, and were baffled by a blank like that which meets a plodding ant when the earth has broken away on its homeward path. The loom was there, and the weaving, and the growing pattern in the cloth; but the bright treasure in the hole under his feet was gone; the prospect of handling and counting it was gone:

the evening had no phantasm of delight to still the poor soul's craving. The thought of the money he would get by his actual work could bring no joy, for its meagre image was only a fresh reminder of his loss; and hope was too heavily crushed by the sudden blow, for his imagination to dwell on the growth of a new hoard from that small beginning.

He filled up the blank with grief. As he sat weaving, he every now and then moaned low, like one in pain: it was the sign that his thoughts had come round again to the sudden chasm—to the empty evening time. And all the evening, as he sat in his loneliness by his dull fire, he leaned his elbows on his knees, and clasped his head with his hands, and moaned very low—not as one who seeks to be heard.

And yet he was not utterly forsaken in his trouble. The repulsion Marner had always created in his neighbours was partly dissipated by the new light in which this misfortune had shown him. Instead of a man who had more cunning than honest folks could come by, and, what was worse, had not the inclination to use that cunning in a neighbourly way, it was now apparent that Silas had not cunning enough to keep his own. He was generally spoken of as a 'poor mushed creatur;' and that avoidance of his neighbours, which had before been referred to his ill-will and to a probable addiction to worse company, was now considered mere craziness.

This change to a kindlier feeling was shown in various ways. The odour of Christmas cooking being on the wind, it was the season when superfluous pork and black puddings are suggestive of charity in well-to-do families; and Silas's misfortune had brought him uppermost in the memory of housekeepers like Mrs Osgood. Mr Crackenthorp, too, while he admonished Silas that his money had probably been taken from him because he thought too much of it and never came to church, enforced the doctrine by a present of pigs' pettitoes,* well calculated to dissipate unfounded prejudices against the clerical character. Neighbours who had nothing but verbal consolation to give showed a disposition not only to greet Silas and discuss his misfortune at some length when they encountered him in the village, but also to take the trouble of calling at his cottage and getting him to repeat all the details on the very spot; and then they would try to cheer him by saying, 'Well, Master Marner, you're no worse off nor other poor folks, after all; and if you was to be crippled, the parish 'ud give you a 'lowance.'

I suppose one reason why we are seldom able to comfort our neighbours with our words is that our goodwill gets adulterated, in spite of ourselves, before it can pass our lips. We can send black puddings and pettitoes without giving them a flavour of our own egoism; but language is a stream that is almost sure to smack of a mingled soil. There was a fair proportion of kindness in Raveloe; but it was often of a beery and bungling sort, and took the shape least allied to the complimentary and hypocritical.

Mr Macey, for example, coming one evening expressly to let Silas know that recent events had given him the advantage of standing more favourably in the opinion of a man whose judgment was not formed lightly, opened the conversation by saying, as soon as he had seated himself and adjusted his thumbs—

'Come, Master Marner, why, you've no call to sit a-moaning. You're a deal better off to ha' lost your money, nor to ha' kep it by foul means. I used to think, when you first come into these parts, as you were no better nor you should be; you were younger a deal than what you are now; but you were allays a staring, white-faced creatur, partly like a bald-faced calf, as I may say. But there's no knowing: it isn't every queer-looksed thing as Old Harry's had the making of—I mean, speaking o' toads and such; for they're often harmless, like, and useful against varmin. And it's pretty much the same wi' you, as fur as I can see. Though as to the yarbs and stuff to cure the breathing, if you brought that sort o' knowledge from distant parts, you might ha' been a bit freer of it. And if the knowledge wasn't well come by, why, you might ha' made up for it by coming to church reg'lar; for as for the children as the Wise Woman charmed, I've been at the christening of 'em again and again, and they took the water just as well. And that's reasonable; for if Old Harry's a mind to do a bit o' kindness for a holiday, like, who's got anything against it? That's my thinking; and I've been clerk o' this parish forty year, and I know, when the parson and me does the cussing of a Ash Wednesday,* there's no cussing o' folks as have a mind to be cured without a doctor, let Kimble say what he will. And so, Master Marner, as I was saying—for there's windings i' things as they may carry you to the fur end o' the prayer-book afore you get back to 'em—my advice is, as you keep up your sperrits; for as for thinking you're a deep un, and ha' got more inside you nor 'ull bear daylight, I'm not o' that opinion at all, and so I tell the neighbours. For, says I, you talk o' Master Marner making out a tale—why, it's nonsense, that is: it 'ud take a 'cute man to make a tale like that; and, says I, he looked as scared as a rabbit.'

During this discursive address Silas had continued motionless in his previous attitude, leaning his elbows on his knees, and pressing his hands against his head. Mr Macey, not doubting that he had been listened to, paused, in the expectation of some appreciatory reply, but Marner remained silent. He had a sense that the old man meant to be good-natured and neighbourly; but the kindness fell on him as sunshine falls on the wretched—he had no heart to taste it, and felt that it was very far off him.

'Come, Master Marner, have you got nothing to say to that?' said Mr Macey at last, with a slight accent of impatience.

'Oh,' said Marner, slowly, shaking his head between his hands, 'I thank you—thank you—kindly.'

'Ay, ay, to be sure: I thought you would,' said Mr Macey; 'and my advice is—have you got a Sunday suit?'

'No,' said Marner.

'I doubted it was so,' said Mr Macey. 'Now, let me advise you to get a Sunday suit: there's Tookey, he's a poor creatur, but he's got my tailoring business, and some o' my money in it, and he shall make a suit at a low price, and give you trust,* and then you can come to church, and be a bit neighbourly. Why, you've never heared me say "Amen" since you come into these parts, and I recommend you to lose no time, for it'll be poor work when Tookey has it all to himself, for I mayn't be equil to stand i' the desk at all, come another winter.' Here Mr Macey paused, perhaps expecting some sign of emotion in his hearer; but not observing any, he went on. 'And as for the money for the suit o' clothes, why, you get a matter of a pound a-week at your weaving, Master Marner, and you're a young man, eh, for all you look so mushed. Why, you couldn't ha' been five-and-twenty when you come into these parts, eh?'

Silas started a little at the change to a questioning tone, and answered mildly, 'I don't know; I can't rightly say—it's a long while since.'

After receiving such an answer as this, it is not surprising that Mr Macey observed, later on in the evening at the Rainbow, that Marner's head was 'all of a muddle,' and that it was to be doubted if he ever knew when Sunday came round, which showed him a worse heathen than many a dog.

Another of Silas's comforters,* besides Mr Macey, came to him with a mind highly charged on the same topic. This was Mrs Winthrop, the wheelwright's wife. The inhabitants of Raveloe were not severely regular in their church-going, and perhaps there was hardly a person in the parish who would not have held that to go to church every Sunday in the calendar would have shown a greedy desire to stand well with Heaven, and get an undue advantage over their neighbours—a wish to be better than the 'common run,' that would have implied a reflection on those who had had godfathers and godmothers as well as themselves, and had an equal right to the burying-service. At the same time, it was understood to be requisite for all who were not household servants, or young men, to take the sacrament at one of the great festivals: Squire Cass himself took it on Christmas-day; while those who were held to be 'good livers' went to church with greater, though still with moderate, frequency.

Mrs Winthrop was one of these: she was in all respects a woman of scrupulous conscience, so eager for duties that life seemed to offer them too scantily unless she rose at half-past four, though this threw a scarcity of work over the more advanced hours of the morning, which it was a constant problem with her to remove. Yet she had not the vixenish temper which is sometimes supposed to be a necessary condition of such habits: she was a very mild, patient woman, whose nature it was to seek out all the sadder and more serious elements of life, and pasture her mind upon them. She was the person always first thought of in Raveloe when there was illness or death in a family, when leeches were to be applied, or there was a sudden disappointment in a monthly nurse.* She was a 'comfortable woman'—good-looking, fresh-complexioned, having her lips always slightly screwed, as if she felt herself in a sick-room with the doctor or the clergyman present. But she was never whimpering; no one had seen her shed tears; she was simply grave and inclined to shake her head and sigh, almost imperceptibly, like a funereal mourner who is not a relation. It seemed surprising that Ben Winthrop, who loved his quart-pot and his joke, got along so well with Dolly; but she took her husband's jokes and joviality as patiently as everything else, considering that 'men *would* be so,' and viewing the stronger sex in the light of animals whom it had pleased Heaven to make naturally troublesome, like bulls and turkey-cocks.

This good wholesome woman could hardly fail to have her mind drawn strongly towards Silas Marner, now that he appeared in the light of a sufferer; and one Sunday afternoon she took her little boy

Aaron with her, and went to call on Silas, carrying in her hand some small lard-cakes,* flat paste-like articles much esteemed in Raveloe. Aaron, an apple-cheeked youngster of seven, with a clean starched frill which looked like a plate for the apples, needed all his adventurous curiosity to embolden him against the possibility that the big-eyed weaver might do him some bodily injury; and his dubiety was much increased when, on arriving at the Stone-pits, they heard the mysterious sound of the loom.

'Ah, it is as I thought,' said Mrs Winthrop, sadly.

They had to knock loudly before Silas heard them; but when he did come to the door he showed no impatience, as he would once have done, at a visit that had been unasked for and unexpected. Formerly, his heart had been as a locked casket with its treasure inside; but now the casket was empty, and the lock was broken. Left groping in darkness, with his prop utterly gone, Silas had inevitably a sense, though a dull and half-despairing one, that if any help came to him it must come from without; and there was a slight stirring of expectation at the sight of his fellow-men, a faint consciousness of dependence on their goodwill. He opened the door wide to admit Dolly, but without otherwise returning her greeting than by moving the armchair a few inches as a sign that she was to sit down in it. Dolly, as soon as she was seated, removed the white cloth that covered her lard-cakes, and said in her gravest way—

'I'd a baking yisterday, Master Marner, and the lard-cakes turned out better nor common, and I'd ha' asked you to accept some, if you'd thought well. I don't eat such things myself, for a bit o' bread's what I like from one year's end to the other; but men's stomichs are made so comical, they want a change—they do, I know, God help 'em.'

Dolly sighed gently as she held out the cakes to Silas, who thanked her kindly and looked very close at them, absently, being accustomed to look so at everything he took into his hand—eyed all the while by the wondering bright orbs of the small Aaron, who had made an outwork of his mother's chair, and was peeping round from behind it.

'There's letters pricked on 'em,' said Dolly. 'I can't read 'em myself, and there's nobody, not Mr Macey himself, rightly knows what they mean; but they've a good meaning, for they're the same as is on the pulpit-cloth at church. What are they, Aaron, my dear?'

Aaron retreated completely behind his outwork.

'Oh go, that's naughty,' said his mother, mildly. 'Well, whativer the letters are, they've a good meaning; and it's a stamp as has been in our house, Ben says, ever since he was a little un, and his mother used to put it on the cakes, and I've allays put it on too; for if there's any good, we've need of it i' this world.'

'It's I. H. S.,'* said Silas, at which proof of learning Aaron peeped round the chair again.

'Well, to be sure, you can read 'em off,' said Dolly. 'Ben's read 'em to me many and many a time, but they slip out o' my mind again; the more's the pity, for they're good letters, else they wouldn't be in the church; and so I prick 'em on all the loaves and all the cakes, though sometimes they won't hold, because o' the rising—for, as I said, if there's any good to be got we've need of it i' this world—that we have; and I hope they'll bring good to you, Master Marner, for it's wi' that will I brought you the cakes; and you see the letters have held better nor common.'

Silas was as unable to interpret the letters as Dolly, but there was no possibility of misunderstanding the desire to give comfort that made itself heard in her quiet tones. He said, with more feeling than before—'Thank you—thank you kindly.' But he laid down the cakes and seated himself absently—drearily unconscious of any distinct benefit towards which the cakes and the letters, or even Dolly's kindness, could tend for him.

'Ah, if there's good anywhere, we've need of it,' repeated Dolly, who did not lightly forsake a serviceable phrase. She looked at Silas pityingly as she went on. 'But you didn't hear the church-bells this morning, Master Marner? I doubt you didn't know it was Sunday. Living so lone here, you lose your count, I daresay; and then, when your loom makes a noise, you can't hear the bells, more partic'lar now the frost kills the sound.'

'Yes, I did; I heard 'em,' said Silas, to whom Sunday bells were a mere accident of the day, and not part of its sacredness. There had been no bells in Lantern Yard.

'Dear heart!' said Dolly, pausing before she spoke again. 'But what a pity it is you should work of a Sunday, and not clean yourself—if you *didn't* go to church; for if you'd a roasting bit, it might be as you couldn't leave it, being a lone man. But there's the bakehus,* if you could make up your mind to spend a twopence on the oven now and then,—not every week, in course—I shouldn't like to do that myself,—you might carry your bit o' dinner there, for it's nothing but right to have a bit o' summat hot of a Sunday, and not to make it as you can't know your dinner from Saturday. But now, upo' Christmas-day, this blessed Christmas as is ever coming, if you was to take your dinner to the bakehus, and go to church, and see the holly and the yew, and hear the anthim, and then take the sacramen', you'd be a deal the better, and you'd know which end you stood on, and you could put your trust i' Them as knows better nor we do, seein' you'd ha' done what it lies on us all to do.'

Dolly's exhortation, which was an unusually long effort of speech for her, was uttered in the soothing persuasive tone with which she would have tried to prevail on a sick man to take his medicine, or a basin of gruel for which he had no appetite. Silas had never before been closely urged on the point of his absence from church, which had only been thought of as a part of his general queerness; and he was too direct and simple to evade Dolly's appeal.

'Nay, nay,' he said, 'I know nothing o' church. I've never been to church.'

'No!' said Dolly, in a low tone of wonderment. Then bethinking herself of Silas's advent from an unknown country, she said, 'Could it ha' been as they'd no church where you was born?'

'Oh yes,' said Silas, meditatively, sitting in his usual posture of leaning on his knees, and supporting his head. 'There was churches—a many—it was a big town. But I knew nothing of 'em—I went to chapel.'*

Dolly was much puzzled at this new word, but she was rather afraid of inquiring further, lest 'chapel' might mean some haunt of wickedness. After a little thought, she said—

'Well, Master Marner, it's niver too late to turn over a new leaf, and if you've niver had no church, there's no telling the good it'll do you. For I feel so set up and comfortable as niver was, when I've been and heard the prayers, and the singing to the praise and glory o' God, as Mr Macey gives out—and Mr Crackenthorp saying good words, and more partic'lar on Sacramen' Day; and if a bit o' trouble comes, I feel as I can put up wi' it, for I've looked for help i' the right quarter, and gev myself up to Them as we must all give ourselves up to at the last; and if we'n done our part, it isn't to be believed as Them as are above us 'ull be worse nor we are, and come short o' Their'n.'

Poor Dolly's exposition of her simple Raveloe theology fell rather unmeaningly on Silas's ears, for there was no word in it that could rouse a memory of what he had known as religion, and his comprehension was quite baffled by the plural pronoun, which was no heresy of Dolly's, but only her way of avoiding a presumptuous familiarity. He remained silent, not feeling inclined to assent to the part of Dolly's speech which he fully understood—her recommendation that he should go to church. Indeed, Silas was so unaccustomed to talk beyond the brief questions and answers necessary for the transaction of his simple business, that words did not easily come to him without the urgency of a distinct purpose.

But now, little Aaron, having become used to the weaver's awful presence, had advanced to his mother's side, and Silas, seeming to notice him for the first time, tried to return Dolly's signs of goodwill by offering the lad a bit of lard-cake. Aaron shrank back a little, and rubbed his head against his mother's shoulder, but still thought the piece of cake worth the risk of putting his hand out for it.

'Oh, for shame, Aaron,' said his mother, taking him on her lap, however; 'why, you don't want cake again yet awhile. He's wonderful hearty,' she went on, with a little sigh—'that he is, God knows. He's my youngest, and we spoil him sadly, for either me or the father must allays hev him in our sight—that we must.'

She stroked Aaron's brown head, and thought it must do Master Marner good to see such a 'pictur of a child.' But Marner, on the other side of the hearth, saw the neat-featured rosy face as a mere dim round, with two dark spots in it.

'And he's got a voice like a bird—you wouldn't think,' Dolly went on; 'he can sing a Christmas carril as his father's taught him; and I take it for a token as he'll come to good, as he can learn the good tunes so quick. Come, Aaron, stan' up and sing the carril to Master Marner, come.'

Aaron replied by rubbing his forehead against his mother's shoulder.

'Oh, that's naughty,' said Dolly, gently. 'Stan' up, when mother tells you, and let me hold the cake till you've done.'

Aaron was not indisposed to display his talents, even to an ogre, under protecting circumstances; and after a few more signs of coyness, consisting chiefly in rubbing the backs of his hands over his eyes, and then peeping between them at Master Marner, to see if he looked anxious for the 'carril,' he at length allowed his head to be duly adjusted, and standing behind the table, which let him appear above it only as far as his broad frill, so that he looked like a cherubic head untroubled with a body, he began with a clear chirp, and in a melody that had the rhythm of an industrious hammer—

> 'God rest you, merry gentlemen,
> Let nothing you dismay,
> For Jesus Christ our Saviour
> Was born on Christmas-day.'*

Dolly listened with a devout look, glancing at Marner in some confidence that this strain would help to allure him to church.

'That's Christmas music,' she said, when Aaron had ended, and had secured his piece of cake again. 'There's no other music equil to the Christmas music—"Hark the erol angils sing."* And you may judge what it is at church, Master Marner, with the bassoon and the voices, as you can't help thinking you've got to a better place a'ready—for I wouldn't speak ill o' this world, seeing as Them put us in it as knows best—but what wi' the drink, and the quarrelling, and the bad illnesses, and the hard dying, as I've seen times and times, one's thankful to hear of a better. The boy sings pretty, don't he, Master Marner?'

'Yes,' said Silas, absently, 'very pretty.'

The Christmas carol, with its hammer-like rhythm, had fallen on his ears as strange music, quite unlike a hymn, and could have none of the effect Dolly contemplated. But he wanted to show her that he was grateful, and the only mode that occurred to him was to offer Aaron a bit more cake.

'Oh no, thank you, Master Marner,' said Dolly, holding down Aaron's willing hands. 'We must be going home now. And so I wish you good-bye, Master Marner; and if you ever feel anyways bad in your inside, as you can't fend for yourself, I'll come and clean up for you, and get you a bit o' victual, and willing. But I beg and pray of you to leave off weaving of a Sunday, for it's bad for soul and body—and the money as comes i' that way 'ull be a bad bed to lie down on at the last, if it doesn't fly away, nobody knows where, like the white frost. And you'll excuse me being that free with you, Master Marner, for I wish you well—I do. Make your bow, Aaron.'

Silas said 'Good-bye, and thank you kindly,' as he opened the door for Dolly, but he couldn't help feeling relieved when she was gone—relieved that he might weave again and moan at his ease. Her simple view of life and its comforts, by which she had tried to cheer him, was only like a report of unknown objects, which his imagination could not fashion. The fountains of human love and of faith in a divine love had not yet been unlocked, and his soul was still the shrunken rivulet, with only this difference, that its little groove of sand was blocked up, and it wandered confusedly against dark obstruction.

And so, notwithstanding the honest persuasions of Mr Macey and Dolly Winthrop, Silas spent his Christmas-day in loneliness, eating his meat in sadness of heart, though the meat had come to him as a neighbourly present. In the morning he looked out on the black frost that seemed to press cruelly on every blade of grass, while the half-icy red pool shivered under the bitter wind; but towards evening the snow began to fall, and curtained from him even that dreary outlook, shutting him close up with his narrow grief. And he sat in his robbed home through the livelong evening, not caring to close his shutters or lock his door, pressing his head between his hands and moaning, till the cold grasped him and told him that his fire was grey.

Nobody in this world but himself knew that he was the same Silas Marner who had once loved his fellow with tender love, and trusted in an unseen goodness. Even to himself that past experience had become dim.

But in Raveloe village the bells rang merrily, and the church was fuller than all through the rest of the year, with red faces among the abundant dark-green boughs—faces prepared for a longer service than usual by an odorous breakfast of toast and ale. Those green boughs, the hymn and anthem never heard but at Christmas—even the Athanasian Creed,* which was discriminated from the others only as being longer and of exceptional virtue, since it was only read on rare occasions—brought a vague exulting sense, for which the grown men could as little have found words as the children, that something great and mysterious had been done for them in heaven above and in earth below, which they were appropriating by their presence. And then the red faces made their way through the black biting frost to their own homes, feeling themselves free for the rest of the day to eat, drink, and be merry, and using that Christian freedom without diffidence.

At Squire Cass's family party that day nobody mentioned Dunstan—nobody was sorry for his absence, or feared it would be too long. The doctor and his wife, uncle and aunt Kimble, were there, and the annual Christmas talk was carried through without any omissions, rising to the climax of Mr Kimble's experience when he walked the London hospitals thirty years back, together with striking professional anecdotes then gathered. Whereupon cards followed, with aunt Kimble's annual failure to follow suit, and uncle Kimble's irascibility concerning the odd trick which was rarely explicable to him, when it was not on his side, without a general visitation of tricks to see that they were formed on sound principles: the whole being accompanied by a strong steaming odour of spirits-and-water.

But the party on Christmas-day, being a strictly family party, was not the pre-eminently brilliant celebration of the season at the Red House. It was the great dance on New Year's Eve that made the glory of Squire Cass's hospitality, as of his forefathers', time out of mind. This was the occasion when all the society of Raveloe and Tarley, whether old acquaintances separated by long rutty distances, or cooled acquaintances separated by misunderstandings concerning runaway calves, or acquaintances founded on intermittent condescension, counted on meeting and on comporting themselves with mutual appropriateness. This was the occasion on which fair dames who came on pillions sent their bandboxes before them, supplied with more than their evening costume; for the feast was not to end with a single evening, like a paltry town entertainment, where the whole supply of eatables is put on the table at once, and bedding is scanty. The Red House was provisioned as if for a siege; and as for the spare feather-beds ready to be laid on floors, they were as plentiful as might naturally be expected in a family that had killed its own geese for many generations.

Godfrey Cass was looking forward to this New Year's Eve with a foolish reckless longing, that made him half deaf to his importunate companion, Anxiety.

'Dunsey will be coming home soon: there will be a great blow-up, and how will you bribe his spite to silence?' said Anxiety.

'Oh, he won't come home before New Year's Eve, perhaps,' said Godfrey; 'and I shall sit by Nancy then, and dance with her, and get a kind look from her in spite of herself.'

'But money is wanted in another quarter,' said Anxiety, in a louder voice, 'and how will you get it without selling your mother's diamond pin? And if you don't get it . . . ?'

'Well, but something may happen to make things easier. At any rate, there's one pleasure for me close at hand: Nancy is coming.'

'Yes, and suppose your father should bring matters to a pass that will oblige you to decline marrying her—and to give your reasons?'

'Hold your tongue, and don't worry me. I can see Nancy's eyes, just as they will look at me, and feel her hand in mine already.'

But Anxiety went on, though in noisy Christmas company; refusing to be utterly quieted even by much drinking.

CHAPTER XI

SOME women, I grant, would not appear to advantage seated on a pillion, and attired in a drab joseph* and a drab beaver-bonnet, with a crown resembling a small stew-pan; for a garment suggesting a coachman's greatcoat, cut out under an exiguity of cloth that would only allow of miniature capes, is not well adapted to conceal deficiencies of contour, nor is drab a colour that will throw sallow cheeks into lively contrast. It was all the greater triumph to Miss Nancy Lammeter's beauty that she looked thoroughly bewitching in that costume, as, seated on the pillion behind her tall, erect father, she held one arm round him, and looked down, with open-eyed anxiety, at the treacherous snow-covered pools and puddles, which sent up formidable splashings of mud under the stamp of Dobbin's foot. A painter would, perhaps, have preferred her in those moments when she was free from self-consciousness; but certainly the bloom on her cheeks was at its highest point of contrast with the surrounding drab when she arrived at the door of the Red House, and saw Mr Godfrey Cass ready to lift her from the pillion. She wished her sister Priscilla had come up at the same time behind the servant, for then she would have contrived that Mr Godfrey should have lifted off Priscilla first, and, in the meantime, she would have persuaded her father to go round to the horse-block* instead of alighting at the door-steps. It was very painful, when you had made it quite clear to a young man that you were determined not to marry him, however much he might wish it, that he would still continue to pay you marked attentions; besides, why didn't he always show the same attentions, if he meant them sincerely, instead of being so strange as Mr Godfrey Cass was, sometimes behaving as if he didn't want to speak to her, and taking no notice of her for weeks and weeks, and then, all on a sudden, almost making love again? Moreover, it was quite plain he had no real love for her, else he would not let people have *that* to say of him which they did say. Did he suppose that Miss Nancy Lammeter was to be won by any man, squire or no squire, who led a bad life? That was not what she had been used to see in her own father, who was the soberest and best man in that country-side, only a little hot and hasty now and then, if things were not done to the minute.

All these thoughts rushed through Miss Nancy's mind, in their habitual succession, in the moments between her first sight of Mr Godfrey Cass standing at the door and her own arrival there. Happily, the Squire came out too and gave a loud greeting to her father, so that, somehow, under cover of this noise she seemed to find concealment for her confusion and neglect of any suitably formal behaviour, while she was being lifted from the pillion by strong arms which seemed to find her ridiculously small and light. And there was the best reason for hastening into the house at once, since the snow was beginning to fall again, threatening an unpleasant journey for such guests as were still on the road. These were a small minority; for already the afternoon was beginning to decline, and there would not be too much time for the ladies who came from a distance to attire themselves in readiness for the early tea which was to inspirit them for the dance.

There was a buzz of voices through the house, as Miss Nancy entered, mingled with the scrape of a fiddle preluding in the kitchen; but the Lammeters were guests whose arrival had evidently been thought of so much that it had been watched for from the windows, for Mrs Kimble, who did the honours at the Red House on these great occasions, came forward to meet Miss Nancy in the hall, and conduct her up-stairs. Mrs Kimble was the Squire's sister, as well as the doctor's wife—a double dignity, with which her diameter was in direct proportion; so that, a journey up-stairs being rather fatiguing to her, she did not oppose Miss Nancy's request to be allowed to find her way alone to the Blue Room, where the Miss Lammeters' band-boxes had been deposited on their arrival in the morning.

There was hardly a bedroom in the house where feminine compliments were not passing and feminine toilettes going forward, in various stages, in space made scanty by extra beds spread upon the floor; and Miss Nancy, as she entered the Blue Room, had to make her little formal curtsy to a group of six. On the one hand, there were ladies no less important than the two Miss Gunns, the wine merchant's daughters from Lytherly, dressed in the height of fashion, with the tightest skirts and the shortest waists, and gazed at by Miss Ladbrook (of the Old Pastures) with a shyness not unsustained by inward criticism.

Partly, Miss Ladbrook felt that her own skirt must be regarded as unduly lax by the Miss Gunns, and partly, that it was a pity the Miss Gunns did not show that judgment which she herself would show if she were in their place, by stopping a little on this side of the fashion. On the other hand, Mrs Ladbrook was standing in skullcap and front, with her turban* in her hand, curtsying and smiling blandly and saying, 'After you, ma'am,' to another lady in similar circumstances, who had politely offered the precedence at the looking-glass.

But Miss Nancy had no sooner made her curtsy than an elderly lady came forward, whose full white muslin kerchief, and mob-cap* round her curls of smooth grey hair, were in daring contrast with the puffed yellow satins and top-knotted caps of her neighbours. She approached Miss Nancy with much primness, and said, with a slow, treble suavity—

'Niece, I hope I see you well in health.' Miss Nancy kissed her aunt's cheek dutifully, and answered, with the same sort of amiable primness, 'Quite well, I thank you, aunt; and I hope I see you the same.'

'Thank you, niece; I keep my health for the present. And how is my brother-in-law?'

These dutiful questions and answers were continued until it was ascertained in detail that the Lammeters were all as well as usual, and the Osgoods likewise, also that niece Priscilla must certainly arrive shortly, and that travelling on pillions in snowy weather was unpleasant, though a joseph was a great protection. Then Nancy was formally introduced to her aunt's visitors, the Miss Gunns, as being the daughters of a mother known to *their* mother, though now for the first time induced to make a journey into these parts; and these ladies were so taken by surprise at finding such a lovely face and figure in an out-of-the-way country place, that they began to feel some curiosity about the dress she would put on when she took off her joseph. Miss Nancy, whose thoughts were always conducted with the propriety and moderation conspicuous in her manners, remarked to herself that the Miss Gunns were rather hard-featured than otherwise, and that such very low dresses as they wore might have been attributed to vanity if their shoulders had been pretty, but that, being as they were, it was not reasonable to suppose that they showed their necks from a love of display, but rather from some obligation not inconsistent with sense and modesty. She felt convinced, as she opened her box, that this must be her aunt Osgood's opinion, for Miss Nancy's mind resembled her aunt's to a degree that everybody said was surprising, considering the kinship was on Mr Osgood's side; and though you might not have supposed it from the formality of their greeting, there was a devoted attachment and mutual admiration between aunt and niece. Even Miss Nancy's refusal of her cousin Gilbert Osgood (on the ground solely that he was her cousin), though it had grieved her aunt greatly, had not in the least cooled the preference which had determined her to leave Nancy several of her hereditary ornaments, let Gilbert's future wife be whom she might.

Three of the ladies quickly retired, but the Miss Gunns were quite content that Mrs Osgood's inclination to remain with her niece gave them also a reason for staying to see the rustic beauty's toilette. And it was really a pleasure—from the first opening of the bandbox, where everything smelt of lavender and rose-leaves, to the clasping of the small coral necklace that fitted closely round her little white neck. Everything belonging to Miss Nancy was of delicate purity and nattiness:* not a crease was where it had no business to be, not a bit of her linen professed whiteness without fulfilling its profession; the very pins on her pincushion were stuck in after a pattern from which she was careful to allow no aberration; and as for her own person, it gave the same idea of perfect unvarying neatness as the body of a little bird. It is true that her light-brown hair was cropped behind like a boy's, and was dressed in front in a number of flat rings, that lay quite away from her face; but there was no sort of coiffure that could make Miss Nancy's cheek and neck look otherwise than pretty; and when at last she stood complete in her silvery twilled silk, her lace tucker,* her coral necklace, and coral ear-drops, the Miss Gunns could see nothing to criticise except her hands, which bore the traces of butter-making, cheese-crushing, and even still coarser work.* But Miss Nancy was not ashamed of that, for while she was dressing she narrated to her aunt how she and Priscilla had packed their boxes yesterday, because this morning was baking morning, and since they were leaving home, it was desirable to make a good supply of meat-pies for the kitchen; and as she concluded this judicious remark, she turned to the Miss Gunns that she might not commit the rudeness of not including them in the conversation. The Miss Gunns smiled stiffly, and thought what a pity it was that these rich country people, who could afford to buy such good clothes (really Miss Nancy's lace and silk were very costly), should be brought up in utter ignorance and vulgarity. She actually said 'mate' for 'meat,' ''appen' for 'perhaps,' and 'oss' for 'horse,' which, to young ladies living in good Lytherly society, who habitually said 'orse, even in domestic privacy, and only said 'appen on the right occasions, was necessarily shocking. Miss Nancy, indeed, had never been to any school higher than Dame Tedman's:* her acquaintance with profane literature hardly went beyond the rhymes she had worked in her large sampler under the lamb and the shepherdess; and in order to balance an account, she was obliged to effect her subtraction by removing visible metallic shillings and sixpences from a visible metallic total. There is hardly a servant-maid in these days who is not better informed than Miss Nancy; yet she had the essential attributes of a lady—high veracity, delicate honour in her dealings, deference to others, and refined personal habits,—and lest these should not suffice to convince grammatical fair ones that her feelings can at all resemble theirs, I will add that she was slightly proud and exacting, and as constant in her affection towards a baseless opinion as towards an erring lover.

The anxiety about sister Priscilla, which had grown rather active by the time the coral necklace was clasped, was happily ended by the entrance of that cheerful-looking lady herself, with a face made blowsy by cold and damp. After the first questions and greetings, she turned to Nancy, and surveyed her from head to foot—then wheeled her round, to ascertain that the back view was equally faultless.

'What do you think o' *these* gowns, aunt Osgood?' said Priscilla, while Nancy helped her to unrobe.

'Very handsome indeed, niece,' said Mrs Osgood, with a slight increase of formality. She always thought niece Priscilla too rough.

'I'm obliged to have the same as Nancy, you know, for all I'm five years older, and it makes me look yallow; for she never *will* have anything without I have mine just like it, because she wants us to look like sisters. And I tell her, folks 'ull think it's my weakness makes me fancy as I shall look pretty in what she looks pretty in. For I *am* ugly—there's no denying that: I feature my father's family. But, law! I don't mind, do you?' Priscilla here turned to the Miss Gunns, rattling on in too much preoccupation with the delight of talking, to notice that her candour was not appreciated. 'The pretty uns do for fly-catchers—they keep the men off us. I've no opinion o' the men, Miss Gunn—I don't know what *you* have. And as for fretting and stewing about what *they*'ll think of you from morning till night, and making your life uneasy about what they're doing when they're out o' your sight—as I tell Nancy, it's a folly no woman need be guilty of, if she's got a good father and a good home: let her leave it to them as have got no fortin, and can't help themselves. As I say, Mr Have-your-own-way is the best husband, and the only one I'd ever promise to obey. I know it isn't pleasant, when you've been used to living in a big way, and managing hogsheads* and all that, to go and put your nose in by somebody else's fireside, or to sit down by yourself to a scrag or a knuckle;* but, thank God! my father's a sober man and likely to live; and if you've got a man by the chimney-corner, it doesn't matter if he's childish—the business needn't be broke up.'

The delicate process of getting her narrow gown over her head without injury to her smooth curls, obliged Miss Priscilla to pause in this rapid survey of life, and Mrs Osgood seized the opportunity of rising and saying—

'Well, niece, you'll follow us. The Miss Gunns will like to go down.'

'Sister,' said Nancy, when they were alone, 'you've offended the Miss Gunns, I'm sure.'

'What have I done, child?' said Priscilla, in some alarm.

'Why, you asked them if they minded about being ugly—you're so very blunt.'

'Law, did I? Well, it popped out: it's a mercy I said no more, for I'm a bad un to live with folks when they don't like the truth. But as for being ugly, look at me, child, in this silver-coloured silk—I told you how it 'ud be—I look as yallow as a daffadil. Anybody 'ud say you wanted to make a mawkin* of me.'

'No, Priscy, don't say so. I begged and prayed of you not to let us have this silk if you'd like another better. I was willing to have *your* choice, you know I was,' said Nancy, in anxious self-vindication.

'Nonsense, child! you know you'd set your heart on this; and reason good, for you're the colour o' cream. It 'ud be fine doings for you to dress yourself to suit *my* skin. What I find fault with, is that notion o' yours as I must dress myself just like you. But you do as you like with me—you always did, from when first you begun to walk. If you wanted to go the field's length, the field's length you'd go; and there was no whipping you, for you looked as prim and innicent as a daisy all the while.'

'Priscy,' said Nancy, gently, as she fastened a coral necklace, exactly like her own, round Priscilla's neck, which was very far from being like her own, 'I'm sure I'm willing to give way as far as is right, but who shouldn't dress alike if it isn't sisters? Would you have us go about looking as if we were no kin to one another—us that have got no mother and not another sister in the world? I'd do what was right, if I dressed in a gown dyed with cheese-colouring; and I'd rather you'd choose, and let me wear what pleases you.'

'There you go again! You'd come round to the same thing if one talked to you from Saturday night till Saturday morning. It'll be fine fun to see how you'll master your husband and never raise your voice above the singing o' the kettle all the while. I like to see the men mastered!'

'Don't talk *so*, Priscy,' said Nancy, blushing. 'You know I don't mean ever to be married.'

'Oh, you never mean a fiddlestick's end!' said Priscilla, as she arranged her discarded dress, and closed her bandbox. 'Who shall *I* have to work for when father's gone, if you are to go and take notions in your head and be an old maid, because some folks are no better than they should be? I haven't a bit o' patience with you—sitting on an addled egg* for ever, as if there was never a fresh un in the world. One old maid's enough out o' two sisters; and I shall do credit to a single life, for God A'mighty meant me for it. Come, we can go down now. I'm as ready as a mawkin *can* be—there's nothing awanting to frighten the crows, now I've got my ear-droppers* in.'

As the two Miss Lammeters walked into the large parlour together, any one who did not know the character of both might certainly have supposed that the reason why the square-shouldered, clumsy, high-featured Priscilla wore a dress the facsimile of her pretty sister's, was either the mistaken vanity of the one, or the malicious contrivance of the other in order to set off her own rare beauty. But the good-natured self-forgetful cheeriness and common-sense of Priscilla would soon have dissipated the one suspicion; and the modest calm of Nancy's speech and manners told clearly of a mind free from all disavowed devices.

Places of honour had been kept for the Miss Lammeters near the head of the principal tea-table in the wainscoted parlour, now looking fresh and pleasant with handsome branches of holly, yew, and laurel, from the abundant growths of the old garden; and Nancy felt an inward flutter, that no firmness of purpose could prevent, when she saw Mr Godfrey Cass advancing to lead her to a seat between himself and Mr Crackenthorp, while Priscilla was called to the opposite side between her father and the Squire. It certainly did make some difference to Nancy that the lover she had given up was the young man of quite the highest consequence in the parish—at home in a venerable and unique parlour, which was the extremity of grandeur in her experience, a parlour where *she* might one day have been mistress, with the consciousness that she was spoken of as 'Madam Cass,' the Squire's wife. These circumstances exalted her inward drama in her own eyes, and deepened the emphasis with which she declared to herself that not the most dazzling rank should induce her to marry a man whose conduct showed him careless of his character, but that, 'love once, love always,' was the motto of a true and pure woman, and no man should ever have any right over her which would be a call on her to destroy the dried flowers that she treasured, and always would treasure, for Godfrey Cass's sake. And Nancy was capable of keeping her word to herself under very trying conditions. Nothing but a becoming blush betrayed the moving thoughts that urged themselves upon her as she accepted the seat next to Mr Crackenthorp; for she was so instinctively neat and adroit in all her actions, and her pretty lips met each other with such quiet firmness, that it would have been difficult for her to appear agitated.

It was not the Rector's practice to let a charming blush pass without an appropriate compliment. He was not in the least lofty or aristocratic, but simply a merry-eyed, small-featured, grey-haired man, with his chin propped by an ample many-creased white neckcloth which seemed to predominate over every other point in his person, and somehow to impress its peculiar character on his remarks; so that to have considered his amenities apart from his cravat would have been a severe, and perhaps a dangerous, effort of abstraction.

'Ha, Miss Nancy,' he said, turning his head within his cravat and smiling down pleasantly upon her, 'when anybody pretends this has been a severe winter, I shall tell them I saw the roses blooming on New Year's Eve—eh, Godfrey, what do *you* say?'

Godfrey made no reply, and avoided looking at Nancy very markedly; for though these complimentary personalities* were held to be in excellent taste in old-fashioned Raveloe society, reverent love has a politeness of its own which it teaches to men otherwise of small schooling. But the Squire was rather impatient at Godfrey's showing himself a dull spark in this way. By this advanced hour of the day, the Squire was always in higher spirits than we have seen him in at the breakfast-table, and felt it quite pleasant to fulfil the hereditary duty of being noisily jovial and patronising: the large silver snuff-box was in active service and was offered without fail to all neighbours from time to time, however often they might have declined the favour. At present, the Squire had only given an express welcome to the heads of families as they appeared; but always as the evening deepened, his hospitality rayed out more widely, till he had tapped the youngest guests on the back and shown a peculiar fondness for their presence, in the full belief that they must feel their lives made happy by their belonging to a parish where there was such a hearty man as Squire Cass to invite them and wish them well. Even in this early stage of the jovial mood, it was natural that he should wish to supply his son's deficiencies by looking and speaking for him.

'Ay, ay,' he began, offering his snuff-box to Mr Lammeter, who for the second time bowed his head and waved his hand in stiff rejection of the offer, 'us old fellows may wish ourselves young to-night, when we see the mistletoe-bough in the White Parlour. It's true, most things are gone back'ard in these last thirty years—the country's going down since the old king fell ill.* But when I look at Miss Nancy here, I begin to think the lasses keep up their quality;—ding me if I remember a sample to match her, not when I was a fine young fellow, and thought a deal about my pigtail. No offence to you, madam,' he added, bending to Mrs Crackenthorp, who sat by him, 'I didn't know *you* when you were as young as Miss Nancy here.'

Mrs Crackenthorp—a small blinking woman, who fidgeted incessantly with her lace, ribbons, and gold chain, turning her head about and making subdued noises, very much like a guinea-pig that twitches its nose and soliloquises in all company indiscriminately—now blinked and fidgeted towards the Squire, and said, 'Oh, no—no offence.'

This emphatic compliment of the Squire's to Nancy was felt by others besides Godfrey to have a diplomatic significance; and her father gave a slight additional erectness to his back, as he looked across the table at her with complacent gravity. That grave and orderly senior was not going to bate a jot of his dignity by seeming elated at the notion of a match between his family and the Squire's: he was gratified by any honour paid to his daughter; but he must see an alteration in several ways before his consent would be vouchsafed. His spare but healthy person, and high-featured firm face, that looked as if it had never been flushed by excess, was in strong contrast, not only with the Squire's, but with the appearance of the Raveloe farmers generally—in accordance with a favourite saying of his own, that 'breed was stronger than pasture.'

'Miss Nancy's wonderful like what her mother was, though; isn't she, Kimble?' said the stout lady of that name, looking round for her husband.

But Doctor Kimble (country apothecaries in old days enjoyed that title without authority of diploma*), being a thin and agile man, was flitting about the room with his hands in his pockets, making himself agreeable to his feminine patients, with medical impartiality, and being welcomed everywhere as a doctor by hereditary right—not one of those miserable apothecaries who canvass for practice in strange neighbourhoods, and spend all their income in starving their one horse, but a man of substance, able to keep an extravagant table like the best of his patients. Time out of mind the Raveloe doctor had been a Kimble; Kimble was inherently a doctor's name; and it was difficult to contemplate firmly the melancholy fact that the actual Kimble had no son, so that his practice might one day be handed over to a successor with the incongruous name of Taylor or Johnson. But in that case the wiser people in Raveloe would employ Dr Blick of Flitton—as less unnatural.

'Did you speak to me, my dear?' said the authentic doctor, coming quickly to his wife's side; but, as if foreseeing that she would be too much out of breath to repeat her remark, he went on immediately—'Ha, Miss Priscilla, the sight of you revives the taste of that super-excellent pork-pie. I hope the batch isn't near an end.'

'Yes, indeed, it is, doctor,' said Priscilla; 'but I'll answer for it the next shall be as good. My pork-pies don't turn out well by chance.'

'Not as your doctoring does, eh, Kimble?—because folks forget to take your physic, eh?' said the Squire, who regarded physic and doctors as many loyal churchmen regard the church and the clergy—tasting a joke against them when he was in health, but impatiently eager for their aid when anything was the matter with him. He tapped his box, and looked round with a triumphant laugh.

'Ah, she has a quick wit, my friend Priscilla has,' said the doctor, choosing to attribute the epigram to a lady rather than allow a brother-in-law that advantage over him. 'She saves a little pepper to sprinkle over her talk—that's the reason why she never puts too much into her pies. There's my wife now, she never has an answer at her tongue's end; but if I offend her, she's sure to scarify my throat with black pepper the next day, or else give me the colic with watery greens. That's an awful tit-for-tat.' Here the vivacious doctor made a pathetic grimace.

'Did you ever hear the like?' said Mrs Kimble, laughing above her double chin with much good-humour, aside to Mrs Crackenthorp, who blinked and nodded, and amiably intended to smile, but the intention lost itself in small twitchings and noises.

'I suppose that's the sort of tit-for-tat adopted in your profession, Kimble, if you've a grudge against a patient,' said the rector.

'Never do have a grudge against our patients,' said Mr Kimble, 'except when they leave us: and then, you see, we haven't the chance of prescribing for 'em. Ha, Miss Nancy,' he continued, suddenly skipping to Nancy's side, 'you won't forget your promise? You're to save a dance for me, you know.'

'Come, come, Kimble, don't you be too for'ard,' said the Squire. 'Give the young uns fair-play. There's my son Godfrey 'll be wanting to have a round with you if you run off with Miss Nancy. He's bespoke her for the first dance, I'll be bound. Eh, sir! what do you say?' he continued, throwing himself backward, and looking at Godfrey. 'Haven't you asked Miss Nancy to open the dance with you?'

Godfrey, sorely uncomfortable under this significant insistence about Nancy, and afraid to think where it would end by the time his father had set his usual hospitable example of drinking before and after supper, saw no course open but to turn to Nancy and say, with as little awkwardness as possible—

'No; I've not asked her yet, but I hope she'll consent—if somebody else hasn't been before me.'

'No, I've not engaged myself,' said Nancy, quietly, though blushingly. (If Mr Godfrey founded any hopes on her consenting to dance with him, he would soon be undeceived; but there was no need for her to be uncivil.)

'Then I hope you've no objections to dancing with me,' said Godfrey, beginning to lose the sense that there was anything uncomfortable in this arrangement.

'No, no objections,' said Nancy, in a cold tone.

'Ah, well, you're a lucky fellow, Godfrey,' said uncle Kimble; 'but you're my godson, so I won't stand in your way. Else I'm not so very old, eh, my dear?' he went on, skipping to his wife's side again. 'You wouldn't mind my having a second after you were gone—not if I cried a good deal first?'

'Come, come, take a cup o' tea and stop your tongue, do,' said good-humoured Mrs Kimble, feeling some pride in a husband who must be regarded as so clever and amusing by the company generally. If he had only not been irritable at cards!

While safe, well-tested personalities were enlivening the tea in this way, the sound of the fiddle approaching within a distance at which it could be heard distinctly, made the young people look at each other with sympathetic impatience for the end of the meal.

'Why, there's Solomon in the hall,' said the Squire, 'and playing my fav'rite tune, *I* believe—"The flaxen-headed ploughboy"*—he's for giving us a hint as we aren't enough in a hurry to hear him play. Bob,' he called out to his third long-legged son, who was at the other end of the room, 'open the door, and tell Solomon to come in. He shall give us a tune here.'

Bob obeyed, and Solomon walked in, fiddling as he walked, for he would on no account break off in the middle of a tune.

'Here, Solomon,' said the Squire, with loud patronage. 'Round here, my man. Ah, I knew it was "The flaxen-headed ploughboy:" there's no finer tune.'

Solomon Macey, a small hale old man, with an abundant crop of long white hair reaching nearly to his shoulders, advanced to the indicated spot, bowing reverently while he fiddled, as much as to say that he respected the company though he respected the key-note more. As soon as he had repeated the tune and lowered his fiddle, he bowed again to the Squire and the Rector, and said, 'I hope I see your honour and your reverence well, and wishing you health and long life and a happy New Year. And wishing the same to you, Mr Lammeter, sir; and to the other gentlemen, and the madams, and the young lasses.'

As Solomon uttered the last words, he bowed in all directions solicitously, lest he should be wanting in due respect. But thereupon he immediately began to prelude, and fell into the tune which he knew would be taken as a special compliment by Mr Lammeter.

'Thank ye, Solomon, thank ye,' said Mr Lammeter when the fiddle paused again. 'That's "Over the hills and far away,"* that is. My father used to say to me, whenever we heard that tune, "Ah, lad, *I* come from over the hills and far away." There's a many tunes I don't make head or tail of; but that speaks to me like the blackbird's whistle. I suppose it's the name: there's a deal in the name of a tune.'

But Solomon was already impatient to prelude again, and presently broke with much spirit into 'Sir Roger de Coverley,'* at which there was a sound of chairs pushed back, and laughing voices.

'Ay, ay, Solomon, we know what that means,' said the Squire, rising. 'It's time to begin the dance, eh? Lead the way, then, and we'll all follow you.'

So Solomon, holding his white head on one side, and playing vigorously, marched forward at the head of the gay procession into the White Parlour, where the mistletoe-bough was hung, and multitudinous tallow candles made rather a brilliant effect, gleaming from among the berried holly-boughs, and reflected in the old-fashioned oval mirrors fastened in the panels of the white wainscot. A quaint procession! Old Solomon, in his seedy clothes and long white locks, seemed to be luring that decent company by the magic scream of his fiddle—luring discreet matrons in turban-shaped caps, nay, Mrs Crackenthorp herself, the summit of whose perpendicular feather was on a level with the Squire's shoulder—luring fair lasses complacently conscious of very short waists and skirts blameless of front-folds—luring burly fathers in large variegated waistcoats, and ruddy sons, for the most part shy and sheepish, in short nether garments and very long coat-tails.

Already Mr Macey and a few other privileged villagers, who were allowed to be spectators on these great occasions, were seated on benches placed for them near the door; and great was the admiration and satisfaction in that quarter when the couples had formed themselves for the dance, and the Squire led off with Mrs Crackenthorp, joining hands with the Rector and Mrs Osgood. That was as it should be—that was what everybody had been used to—and the charter of Raveloe seemed to be renewed by the ceremony. It was not thought of as an unbecoming levity for the old and middle-aged people to dance a little before sitting down to cards, but rather as part of their social duties. For what were these if not to be merry at appropriate times, interchanging visits and poultry with due frequency, paying each other old-established compliments in sound traditional phrases, passing well-tried personal jokes, urging your guests to eat and drink too much out of hospitality, and eating and drinking too much in your neighbour's house to show that you liked your cheer? And the parson naturally set an example in these social duties. For it would not have been possible for the Raveloe mind, without a peculiar revelation, to know that a clergyman should be a pale-faced memento of solemnities, instead of a reasonably faulty man whose exclusive authority to read prayers and preach, to christen, marry, and bury you, necessarily coexisted with the right to sell you the ground to be buried in and to take tithe in kind;* on which last point, of course, there was a little grumbling, but not to the extent of irreligion—not of deeper significance than the grumbling at the rain, which was by no means accompanied with a spirit of impious defiance, but with a desire that the prayer for fine weather might be read forthwith.

There was no reason, then, why the rector's dancing should not be received as part of the fitness of things quite as much as the Squire's, or why, on the other hand, Mr Macey's official respect should restrain him from subjecting the parson's performance to that criticism with which minds of extraordinary acuteness must necessarily contemplate the doings of their fallible fellow-men.

'The Squire's pretty springe,* considering his weight,' said Mr Macey, 'and he stamps uncommon well. But Mr Lammeter beats 'em all for shapes: you see he holds his head like a sodger,* and he isn't so cushiony as most o' the oldish gentlefolks—they run fat in general; and he's got a fine leg. The parson's nimble enough, but he hasn't got much of a leg: it's a bit too thick down'ard, and his knees might be a bit nearer wi'out damage; but he might do worse, he might do worse. Though he hasn't that grand way o' waving his hand as the Squire has.'

'Talk o' nimbleness, look at Mrs Osgood,' said Ben Winthrop, who was holding his son Aaron between his knees. 'She trips along with her little steps, so as nobody can see how she goes—it's like as if she had little wheels to her feet. She doesn't look a day older nor last year: she's the finest-made woman as is, let the next be where she will.'

'I don't heed how the women are made,' said Mr Macey, with some contempt. 'They wear nayther coat nor breeches: you can't make much out o' their shapes.'

'Fayder,' said Aaron, whose feet were busy beating out the tune, 'how does that big cock's-feather stick in Mrs Crackenthorp's yead? Is there a little hole for it, like in my shuttle-cock?'

'Hush, lad, hush; that's the way the ladies dress theirselves, that is,' said the father, adding, however, in an under-tone to Mr Macey, 'It does make her look funny, though—partly like a short-necked bottle wi' a long quill in it. Hey, by jingo, there's the young Squire leading off now, wi' Miss Nancy for partners! There's a lass for you!—like a pink-and-white posy—there's nobody 'ud think as anybody could be so pritty. I shouldn't wonder if she's Madam Cass some day, arter all—and nobody more rightfuller, for they'd make a fine match. You can find nothing against Master Godfrey's shapes, Macey, *I*'ll bet a penny.'

Mr Macey screwed up his mouth, leaned his head further on one side, and twirled his thumbs with a presto movement as his eyes followed Godfrey up the dance. At last he summed up his opinion.

'Pretty well down'ard, but a bit too round i' the shoulder-blades. And as for them coats as he gets from the Flitton tailor, they're a poor cut to pay double money for.'

'Ah, Mr Macey, you and me are two folks,' said Ben, slightly indignant at this carping. 'When I've got a pot o' good ale, I like to swaller it, and do my inside good, i'stead o' smelling and staring at it to see if I can't find faut wi' the brewing. I should like you to pick me out a finer-limbed young fellow nor Master Godfrey—one as 'ud knock you down easier, or 's more pleasanter looksed when he's piert* and merry.'

'Tchuh!' said Mr Macey, provoked to increased severity, 'he isn't come to his right colour yet: he's partly like a slack-baked pie.* And I doubt he's got a soft place in his head, else why should he be turned round the finger by that offal Dunsey as nobody's seen o' late, and let him kill that fine hunting hoss as was the talk o' the country? And one while he was allays after Miss Nancy, and then it all went off again, like a smell o' hot porridge, as I may say. That wasn't my way when *I* went a-coorting.'

'Ah, but mayhap Miss Nancy hung off, like, and your lass didn't,' said Ben.

'I should say she didn't,' said Mr Macey, significantly. 'Before I said "sniff," I took care to know as she'd say "snaff,"* and pretty quick too. I wasn't a-going to open *my* mouth, like a dog at a fly, and snap it to again, wi' nothing to swaller.'

'Well, I think Miss Nancy's a-coming round again,' said Ben, 'for Master Godfrey doesn't look so down-hearted to-night. And I see he's for taking her away to sit down, now they're at the end o' the dance: that looks like sweethearting, that does.'

The reason why Godfrey and Nancy had left the dance was not so tender as Ben imagined. In the close press of couples a slight accident had happened to Nancy's dress, which, while it was short enough to show her neat ankle in front, was long enough behind to be caught under the stately stamp of the Squire's foot, so as to rend certain stitches at the waist, and cause much sisterly agitation in Priscilla's mind, as well as serious concern in Nancy's. One's thoughts may be much occupied with love-struggles, but hardly so as to be insensible to a disorder in the general framework of things. Nancy had no sooner completed her duty in the figure they were dancing than she said to Godfrey, with a deep blush, that she must go and sit down till Priscilla could come to her; for the sisters had already exchanged a short whisper and an open-eyed glance full of meaning. No reason less urgent than this could have prevailed on Nancy to give Godfrey this opportunity of sitting apart with her. As for Godfrey, he was feeling so happy and oblivious under the long charm of the country-dance with Nancy, that he got rather bold on the strength of her confusion, and was capable of leading her straight away, without leave asked, into the adjoining small parlour, where the card-tables were set.

'O no, thank you,' said Nancy, coldly, as soon as she perceived where he was going, 'not in there. I'll wait here till Priscilla's ready to come to me. I'm sorry to bring you out of the dance and make myself troublesome.'

'Why, you'll be more comfortable here by yourself,' said the artful Godfrey: 'I'll leave you here till your sister can come.' He spoke in an indifferent tone.

That was an agreeable proposition, and just what Nancy desired; why, then, was she a little hurt that Mr Godfrey should make it? They entered, and she seated herself on a chair against one of the card-tables, as the stiffest and most unapproachable position she could choose.

'Thank you, sir,' she said immediately. 'I needn't give you any more trouble. I'm sorry you've had such an unlucky partner.'

'That's very ill-natured of you,' said Godfrey, standing by her without any sign of intended departure, 'to be sorry you've danced with me.'

'Oh no, sir, I don't mean to say what's ill-natured at all,' said Nancy, looking distractingly prim and pretty. 'When gentlemen have so many pleasures, one dance can matter but very little.'

'You know that isn't true. You know one dance with you matters more to me than all the other pleasures in the world.'

It was a long, long while since Godfrey had said anything so direct as that, and Nancy was startled. But her instinctive dignity and repugnance to any show of emotion made her sit perfectly still, and only throw a little more decision into her voice, as she said—

'No, indeed, Mr Godfrey, that's not known to me, and I have very good reasons for thinking different. But if it's true, I don't wish to hear it.'

'Would you never forgive me, then, Nancy—never think well of me, let what would happen—would you never think the present made amends for the past? Not if I turned a good fellow, and gave up everything you didn't like?'

Godfrey was half conscious that this sudden opportunity of speaking to Nancy alone had driven him beside himself; but blind feeling had got the mastery of his tongue. Nancy really felt much agitated by the possibility Godfrey's words suggested, but this very pressure of emotion that she was in danger of finding too strong for her roused all her power of self-command.

'I should be glad to see a good change in anybody, Mr Godfrey,' she answered, with the slightest discernible difference of tone, 'but it 'ud be better if no change was wanted.'

'You're very hard-hearted, Nancy,' said Godfrey, pettishly. 'You might encourage me to be a better fellow. I'm very miserable—but you've no feeling.'

'I think those have the least feeling that act wrong to begin with,' said Nancy, sending out a flash in spite of herself. Godfrey was delighted with that little flash, and would have liked to go on and make her quarrel with him; Nancy was so exasperatingly quiet and firm. But she was not indifferent to him *yet*.

The entrance of Priscilla, bustling forward and saying, 'Dear heart alive, child, let us look at this gown,' cut off Godfrey's hopes of a quarrel.

'I suppose I must go now,' he said to Priscilla.

'It's no matter to me whether you go or stay,' said that frank lady, searching for something in her pocket, with a preoccupied brow.

'Do *you* want me to go?' said Godfrey, looking at Nancy, who was now standing up by Priscilla's order.

'As you like,' said Nancy, trying to recover all her former coldness, and looking down carefully at the hem of her gown.

'Then I like to stay,' said Godfrey, with a reckless determination to get as much of this joy as he could to-night, and think nothing of the morrow.

CHAPTER XII

WHILE Godfrey Cass was taking draughts of forgetfulness from the sweet presence of Nancy, willingly losing all sense of that hidden bond which at other moments galled and fretted him so as to mingle irritation with the very sunshine, Godfrey's wife was walking with slow uncertain steps through the snow-covered Raveloe lanes, carrying her child in her arms.

This journey on New Year's Eve was a premeditated act of vengeance which she had kept in her heart ever since Godfrey, in a fit of passion, had told her he would sooner die than acknowledge her as his wife. There would be a great party at the Red House on New Year's Eve, she knew: her husband would be smiling and smiled upon, hiding *her* existence in the darkest corner of his heart. But she would mar his pleasure: she would go in her dingy rags, with her faded face, once as handsome as the best, with her little child that had its father's hair and eyes, and disclose herself to the Squire as his eldest son's wife. It is seldom that the miserable can help regarding their misery as a wrong inflicted by those who are less miserable. Molly knew that the cause of her dingy rags was not her husband's neglect, but the demon Opium* to whom she was enslaved, body and soul, except in the lingering mother's tenderness that refused to give him her hungry child. She knew this well; and yet, in the moments of wretched unbenumbed consciousness, the sense of her want and degradation transformed itself continually into bitterness towards Godfrey. *He* was well off; and if she had her rights she would be well off too. The belief that he repented his marriage, and suffered from it, only aggravated her vindictiveness. Just and self-reproving thoughts do not come to us too thickly, even in the purest air and with the best lessons of heaven and earth; how should those white-winged delicate messengers make their way to Molly's poisoned chamber, inhabited by no higher memories than those of a barmaid's paradise of pink ribbons and gentlemen's jokes?

She had set out at an early hour, but had lingered on the road, inclined by her indolence to believe that if she waited under a warm shed the snow would cease to fall. She had waited longer than she knew, and now that she found herself belated in the snow-hidden ruggedness of the long lanes, even the animation of a vindictive purpose could not keep her spirit from failing. It was seven o'clock, and by this time she was not very far from Raveloe, but she was not familiar enough with those monotonous lanes to know how near she was to her journey's end. She needed comfort, and she knew but one comforter—the familiar demon in her bosom; but she hesitated a moment, after drawing out the black remnant, before she raised it to her lips. In that moment the mother's love pleaded for painful consciousness rather than oblivion—pleaded to be left in aching weariness, rather than to have the encircling arms benumbed so that they could not feel the dear burden. In another moment Molly had flung something away, but it was not the black remnant—it was an empty phial. And she walked on again under the breaking cloud, from which there came now and then the light of a quickly veiled star, for a freezing wind had sprung up since the snowing had ceased. But she walked always more and more drowsily, and clutched more and more automatically the sleeping child at her bosom.

Slowly the demon was working his will, and cold and weariness were his helpers. Soon she felt nothing but a supreme immediate longing that curtained off all futurity—the longing to lie down and sleep. She had arrived at a spot where her footsteps were no longer checked by a hedgerow, and she had wandered vaguely, unable to distinguish any objects, notwithstanding the wide whiteness around her, and the growing starlight. She sank down against a straggling furze bush,* an easy pillow enough; and the bed of snow, too, was soft. She did not feel that the bed was cold, and did not heed whether the child would wake and cry for her. But her arms had not yet relaxed their instinctive clutch; and the little one slumbered on as gently as if it had been rocked in a lace-trimmed cradle.

But the complete torpor came at last: the fingers lost their tension, the arms unbent; then the little head fell away from the bosom, and the blue eyes opened wide on the cold starlight. At first there was a little peevish cry of 'mammy,' and an effort to regain the pillowing arm and bosom; but mammy's ear was deaf, and the pillow seemed to be slipping away backward. Suddenly, as the child rolled downward on its mother's knees, all wet with snow, its eyes were caught by a bright glancing light on the white ground, and, with the ready transition of infancy, it was immediately absorbed in watching the bright living thing running towards it, yet never arriving. That bright living thing must be caught; and in an instant the child had slipped on all fours, and held out one little hand to catch the gleam. But the gleam would not be caught in that way, and now the head was held up to see where the cunning gleam came from. It came from a very bright place; and the little one, rising on its legs, toddled through the snow, the old grimy shawl in which it was wrapped trailing behind it, and the queer little bonnet dangling at its back—toddled on to the open door of Silas Marner's cottage, and right up to the warm hearth, where there was a bright fire of logs and sticks, which had thoroughly warmed the old sack (Silas's greatcoat) spread out on the bricks to dry. The little one, accustomed to be left to itself for long hours without notice from its mother, squatted down on the sack, and spread its tiny hands towards the blaze, in perfect contentment, gurgling and making many inarticulate communications to the cheerful fire, like a new-hatched gosling beginning to find itself comfortable. But presently the warmth had a lulling effect, and the little golden head sank down on the old sack, and the blue eyes were veiled by their delicate half-transparent lids.

But where was Silas Marner while this strange visitor had come to his hearth? He was in the cottage, but he did not see the child. During the last few weeks, since he had lost his money, he had contracted the habit of opening his door and looking out from time to time, as if he thought that his money might be somehow coming back to him, or that some trace, some news of it, might be mysteriously on the road, and be caught by the listening ear or the straining eye. It was chiefly at night, when he was not occupied in his loom, that he fell into this repetition of an act for which he could have assigned no definite purpose, and which can hardly be understood except by those who have undergone a bewildering separation from a supremely loved object. In the evening twilight, and later whenever the night was not dark, Silas looked out on that narrow prospect round the Stone-pits, listening and gazing, not with hope, but with mere yearning and unrest.

This morning he had been told by some of his neighbours that it was New Year's Eve, and that he must sit up and hear the old year rung out and the new rung in, because that was good luck, and might bring his money back again. This was only a friendly Raveloe-way of jesting with the half-crazy oddities of a miser, but it had perhaps helped to throw Silas into a more than usually excited state. Since the on-coming of twilight he had opened his door again and again, though only to shut it immediately at seeing all distance veiled by the falling snow. But the last time he opened it the snow had ceased, and the clouds were parting here and there. He stood and listened, and gazed for a long while—there was really something on the road coming towards him then, but he caught no sign of it; and the stillness and the wide trackless snow seemed to narrow his solitude, and touched his yearning with the chill of despair. He went in again, and put his right hand on the latch of the door to close it—but he did not close it: he was arrested, as he had been already since his loss, by the invisible wand of catalepsy, and stood like a graven image, with wide but sightless eyes, holding open his door, powerless to resist either the good or the evil that might enter there.

When Marner's sensibility returned, he continued the action which had been arrested, and closed his door, unaware of the chasm in his consciousness, unaware of any intermediate change, except that the light had grown dim, and that he was chilled and faint. He thought he had been too long standing at the door and looking out. Turning towards the hearth, where the two logs had fallen apart, and sent forth only a red uncertain glimmer, he seated himself on his fireside chair, and was stooping to push his logs together, when, to his blurred vision, it seemed as if there were gold on the floor in front of the hearth. Gold!—his own gold—brought back to him as mysteriously as it had been taken away! He felt his heart begin to beat violently, and for a few moments he was unable to stretch out his hand and grasp the restored treasure. The heap of gold seemed to glow and get larger beneath his agitated gaze. He leaned forward at last, and stretched forth his hand; but instead of the hard coin with the familiar resisting outline, his fingers encountered soft warm curls. In utter amazement, Silas fell on his knees and bent his head low to examine the marvel: it was a sleeping child—a round, fair thing, with soft yellow rings all over its head. Could this be his little sister come back to him in a dream—his little sister whom he had carried about in his arms for a year before she died, when he was a small boy without shoes or stockings? That was the first thought that darted across Silas's blank wonderment. *Was* it a dream? He rose to his feet again, pushed his logs together, and, throwing on some dried leaves and sticks, raised a flame; but the flame did not disperse the vision—it only lit up more distinctly the little round form of the child, and its shabby clothing. It was very much like his little sister. Silas sank into his chair powerless, under the double presence of an inexplicable surprise and a hurrying influx of memories. How and when had the child come in without his knowledge? He had never been beyond the door. But along with that question, and almost thrusting it away, there was a vision of the old home and the old streets leading to Lantern Yard—and within that vision another, of the thoughts which had been present with him in those far-off scenes. The thoughts were strange to him now, like old friendships impossible to revive; and yet he had a dreamy feeling that this child was somehow a message come to him from that far-off life: it stirred fibres that had never been moved in Raveloe—old quiverings of tenderness—old impressions of awe at the presentiment of some Power presiding over his life; for his imagination had not yet extricated itself from the sense of mystery in the child's sudden presence, and had formed no conjectures of ordinary natural means by which the event could have been brought about.

But there was a cry on the hearth: the child had awaked, and Marner stooped to lift it on his knee. It clung round his neck, and burst louder and louder into that mingling of inarticulate cries with 'mammy' by which little children express the bewilderment of waking. Silas pressed it to him, and almost unconsciously uttered sounds of hushing tenderness, while he bethought himself that some of his porridge, which had got cool by the dying fire, would do to feed the child with if it were only warmed up a little.

He had plenty to do through the next hour. The porridge, sweetened with some dry brown sugar from an old store which he had refrained from using for himself, stopped the cries of the little one, and made her lift her blue eyes with a wide quiet gaze at Silas, as he put the spoon into her mouth. Presently she slipped from his knee and began to toddle about, but with a pretty stagger that made Silas jump up and follow her lest she should fall against anything that would hurt her. But she only fell in a sitting posture on the ground, and began to pull at her boots, looking up at him with a crying face as if the boots hurt her. He took her on his knee again, but it was some time before it occurred to Silas's dull bachelor mind that the wet boots were the grievance, pressing on her warm ankles. He got them off with difficulty, and baby was at once happily occupied with the primary mystery of her own toes, inviting Silas, with much chuckling, to consider the mystery too. But the wet boots had at last suggested to Silas that the child had been walking on the snow, and this roused him from his entire oblivion of any ordinary means by which it could have entered or been brought into his house. Under the prompting of this new idea, and without waiting to form conjectures, he raised the child in his arms, and went to the door. As soon as he had opened it, there was the cry of 'mammy' again, which Silas had not heard since the child's first hungry waking. Bending forward, he could just discern the marks made by the little feet on the virgin snow, and he followed their track to the furze bushes. 'Mammy!' the little one cried again and again, stretching itself forward so as almost to escape from Silas's arms, before he himself was aware that there was something more than the bush before him—that there was a human body, with the head sunk low in the furze, and half-covered with the shaken snow.

CHAPTER XIII

It was after the early supper-time at the Red House, and the entertainment was in that stage when bashfulness itself had passed into easy jollity, when gentlemen, conscious of unusual accomplishments, could at length be prevailed on to dance a hornpipe, and when the Squire preferred talking loudly, scattering snuff, and patting his visitors' backs, to sitting longer at the whist-table—a choice exasperating to uncle Kimble, who, being always volatile in sober business hours, became intense and bitter over cards and brandy, shuffled before his adversary's deal with a glare of suspicion, and turned up a mean trump-card with an air of inexpressible disgust, as if in a world where such things could happen one might as well enter on a course of reckless profligacy. When the evening had advanced to this pitch of freedom and enjoyment, it was usual for the servants, the heavy duties of supper being well over, to get their share of amusement by coming to look on at the dancing; so that the back regions of the house were left in solitude.

There were two doors by which the White Parlour was entered from the hall, and they were both standing open for the sake of air; but the lower one was crowded with the servants and villagers, and only the upper doorway was left free. Bob Cass was figuring in a hornpipe, and his father, very proud of this lithe son, whom he repeatedly declared to be just like himself in his young days in a tone that implied this to be the very highest stamp of juvenile merit, was the centre of a group who had placed themselves opposite the performer, not far from the upper door. Godfrey was standing a little way off, not to admire his brother's dancing, but to keep sight of Nancy, who was seated in the group, near her father. He stood aloof, because he wished to avoid suggesting himself as a subject for the Squire's fatherly jokes in connection with matrimony and Miss Nancy Lammeter's beauty, which were likely to become more and more explicit. But he had the prospect of dancing with her again when the hornpipe was concluded, and in the meanwhile it was very pleasant to get long glances at her quite unobserved.

But when Godfrey was lifting his eyes from one of those long glances, they encountered an object as startling to him at that moment as if it had been an apparition from the dead. It *was* an apparition from that hidden life which lies, like a dark by-street, behind the goodly ornamented façade that meets the sunlight and the gaze of respectable admirers. It was his own child carried in Silas Marner's arms. That was his instantaneous impression, unaccompanied by doubt, though he had not seen the child for months past; and when the hope was rising that he might possibly be mistaken, Mr Crackenthorp and Mr Lammeter had already advanced to Silas, in astonishment at this strange advent. Godfrey joined them immediately, unable to rest without hearing every word—trying to control himself, but conscious that if any one noticed him, they must see that he was white-lipped and trembling.

But now all eyes at that end of the room were bent on Silas Marner; the Squire himself had risen, and asked angrily, 'How's this?—what's this?—what do you do coming in here in this way?'

'I'm come for the doctor—I want the doctor,' Silas had said, in the first moment, to Mr Crackenthorp.

'Why, what's the matter, Marner?' said the rector. 'The doctor's here; but say quietly what you want him for.'

'It's a woman,' said Silas, speaking low, and half-breathlessly, just as Godfrey came up. 'She's dead, I think—dead in the snow at the Stone-pits—not far from my door.'

Godfrey felt a great throb: there was one terror in his mind at that moment: it was, that the woman might *not* be dead. That was an evil terror—an ugly inmate to have found a nestling-place in Godfrey's kindly disposition; but no disposition is a security from evil wishes to a man whose happiness hangs on duplicity.

'Hush, hush!' said Mr Crackenthorp. 'Go out into the hall there. I'll fetch the doctor to you. Found a woman in the snow—and thinks she's dead,' he added, speaking low, to the Squire. 'Better say as little about it as possible: it will shock the ladies. Just tell them a poor woman is ill from cold and hunger. I'll go and fetch Kimble.'

By this time, however, the ladies had pressed forward, curious to know what could have brought the solitary linen-weaver there under such strange circumstances, and interested in the pretty child, who, half alarmed and half attracted by the brightness and the numerous company, now frowned and hid her face, now lifted up her head again and looked round placably, until a touch or a coaxing word brought back the frown, and made her bury her face with new determination.

'What child is it?' said several ladies at once, and, among the rest, Nancy Lammeter, addressing Godfrey.

'I don't know—some poor woman's who has been found in the snow, I believe,' was the answer Godfrey wrung from himself with a terrible effort. ('After all, *am* I certain?' he hastened to add, in anticipation of his own conscience.)

'Why, you'd better leave the child here, then, Master Marner,' said good-natured Mrs Kimble, hesitating, however, to take those dingy clothes into contact with her own ornamented satin boddice. 'I'll tell one o' the girls to fetch it.'

'No—no—I can't part with it, I can't let it go,' said Silas, abruptly. 'It's come to me—I've a right to keep it.'

The proposition to take the child from him had come to Silas quite unexpectedly, and his speech, uttered under a strong sudden impulse, was almost like a revelation to himself: a minute before, he had no distinct intention about the child.

'Did you ever hear the like?' said Mrs Kimble, in mild surprise, to her neighbour.

'Now, ladies, I must trouble you to stand aside,' said Mr Kimble, coming from the card-room, in some bitterness at the interruption, but drilled by the long habit of his profession into obedience to unpleasant calls, even when he was hardly sober.

'It's a nasty business turning out now, eh, Kimble?' said the Squire. 'He might ha' gone for your young fellow—the 'prentice, there—what's his name?'

'Might? ay—what's the use of talking about might?' growled uncle Kimble, hastening out with Marner, and followed by Mr Crackenthorp and Godfrey. 'Get me a pair of thick boots, Godfrey, will you? And stay, let somebody run to Winthrop's and fetch Dolly—she's the best woman to get. Ben was here himself before supper; is he gone?'

'Yes, sir, I met him,' said Marner; 'but I couldn't stop to tell him anything, only I said I was going for the doctor, and he said the doctor was at the Squire's. And I made haste and ran, and there was nobody to be seen at the back o' the house, and so I went in to where the company was.'

The child, no longer distracted by the bright light and the smiling women's faces, began to cry and call for 'mammy,' though always clinging to Marner, who had apparently won her thorough confidence. Godfrey had come back with the boots, and felt the cry as if some fibre were drawn tight within him.

'I'll go,' he said, hastily, eager for some movement; 'I'll go and fetch the woman—Mrs Winthrop.'

'O, pooh—send somebody else,' said uncle Kimble, hurrying away with Marner.

'You'll let me know if I can be of any use, Kimble,' said Mr Crackenthorp. But the doctor was out of hearing.

Godfrey, too, had disappeared: he was gone to snatch his hat and coat, having just reflection enough to remember that he must not look like a madman; but he rushed out of the house into the snow without heeding his thin shoes.

In a few minutes he was on his rapid way to the Stone-pits by the side of Dolly, who, though feeling that she was entirely in her place in encountering cold and snow on an errand of mercy, was much concerned at a young gentleman's getting his feet wet under a like impulse.

'You'd a deal better go back, sir,' said Dolly, with respectful compassion. 'You've no call to catch cold; and I'd ask you if you'd be so good as tell my husband to come, on your way back—he's at the Rainbow, I doubt—if you found him anyway sober enough to be o' use. Or else, there's Mrs Snell 'ud happen send the boy up to fetch and carry, for there may be things wanted from the doctor's.'

'No, I'll stay, now I'm once out—I'll stay outside here,' said Godfrey, when they came opposite Marner's cottage. 'You can come and tell me if I can do anything.'

'Well, sir, you're very good: you've a tender heart,' said Dolly, going to the door.

Godfrey was too painfully preoccupied to feel a twinge of self-reproach at this undeserved praise. He walked up and down, unconscious that he was plunging ankle-deep in snow, unconscious of everything but trembling suspense about what was going on in the cottage, and the effect of each alternative on his future lot. No, not quite unconscious of everything else. Deeper down, and half-smothered by passionate desire and dread, there was the sense that he ought not to be waiting on these alternatives; that he ought to accept the consequences of his deeds, own the miserable wife, and fulfil the claims of the helpless child. But he had not moral courage enough to contemplate that active renunciation of Nancy as possible for him: he had only conscience and heart enough to make him for ever uneasy under the weakness that forbade the renunciation. And at this moment his mind leaped away from all restraint toward the sudden prospect of deliverance from his long bondage.

'Is she dead?' said the voice that predominated over every other within him. 'If she is, I may marry Nancy; and then I shall be a good fellow in future, and have no secrets, and the child—shall be taken care of somehow.' But across that vision came the other possibility—'She may live, and then it's all up with me.'

Godfrey never knew how long it was before the door of the cottage opened and Mr Kimble came out. He went forward to meet his uncle, prepared to suppress the agitation he must feel, whatever news he was to hear.

'I waited for you, as I'd come so far,' he said, speaking first.

'Pooh, it was nonsense for you to come out: why didn't you send one of the men? There's nothing to be done. She's dead—has been dead for hours, I should say.'

'What sort of woman is she?' said Godfrey, feeling the blood rush to his face.

'A young woman, but emaciated, with long black hair. Some vagrant—quite in rags. She's got a wedding-ring on, however. They must fetch her away to the workhouse* to-morrow. Come, come along.'

'I want to look at her,' said Godfrey. 'I think I saw such a woman yesterday. I'll overtake you in a minute or two.'

Mr Kimble went on, and Godfrey turned back to the cottage. He cast only one glance at the dead face on the pillow, which Dolly had smoothed with decent care; but he remembered that last look at his unhappy hated wife so well, that at the end of sixteen years every line in the worn face was present to him when he told the full story of this night.

He turned immediately towards the hearth, where Silas Marner sat lulling the child. She was perfectly quiet now, but not asleep—only soothed by sweet porridge and warmth into that wide-gazing calm which makes us older human beings, with our inward turmoil, feel a certain awe in the presence of a little child, such as we feel before some quiet majesty or beauty in the earth or sky—before a steady glowing planet, or a full-flowered eglantine, or the bending trees over a silent pathway. The wide-open blue eyes looked up at Godfrey's without any uneasiness or sign of recognition: the child could make no visible [or] audible claim on its father; and the father felt a strange mixture of feelings, a conflict of regret and joy, that the pulse of that little heart had no response for the half-jealous yearning in his own, when the blue eyes turned away from him slowly, and fixed themselves on the weaver's queer face, which was bent low down to look at them, while the small hand began to pull Marner's withered cheek with loving disfiguration.

'You'll take the child to the parish* to-morrow?' asked Godfrey, speaking as indifferently as he could.

'Who says so?' said Marner, sharply. 'Will they make me take her?'

'Why, you wouldn't like to keep her, should you—an old bachelor like you?'

'Till anybody shows they've a right to take her away from me,' said Marner. 'The mother's dead, and I reckon it's got no father: it's a lone thing—and I'm a lone thing. My money's gone, I don't know where—and this is come from I don't know where. I know nothing—I'm partly mazed.'

'Poor little thing!' said Godfrey. 'Let me give something towards finding it clothes.'

He had put his hand in his pocket and found half-a-guinea, and, thrusting it into Silas's hand, he hurried out of the cottage to overtake Mr Kimble.

'Ah, I see it's not the same woman I saw,' he said, as he came up. 'It's a pretty little child: the old fellow seems to want to keep it; that's strange for a miser like him. But I gave him a trifle to help him out: the parish isn't likely to quarrel with him for the right to keep the child.'

'No; but I've seen the time when I might have quarrelled with him for it myself. It's too late now, though. If the child ran into the fire, your aunt's too fat to overtake it: she could only sit and grunt like an alarmed sow. But what a fool you are, Godfrey, to come out in your dancing shoes and stockings in this way—and you one of the beaux of the evening, and at your own house! What do you mean by such freaks, young fellow? Has Miss Nancy been cruel, and do you want to spite her by spoiling your pumps?'

'O, everything has been disagreeable to-night. I was tired to death of jigging and gallanting, and that bother about the hornpipes. And I'd got to dance with the other Miss Gunn,' said Godfrey, glad of the subterfuge his uncle had suggested to him.

The prevarication and white lies which a mind that keeps itself ambitiously pure is as uneasy under as a great artist under the false touches that no eye detects but his own, are worn as lightly as mere trimmings when once the actions have become a lie.

Godfrey reappeared in the White Parlour with dry feet, and, since the truth must be told, with a sense of relief and gladness that was too strong for painful thoughts to struggle with. For could he not venture now, whenever opportunity offered, to say the tenderest things to Nancy Lammeter—to promise her and himself that he would always be just what she would desire to see him? There was no danger that his dead wife would be recognised: those were not days of active inquiry and wide report; and as for the registry of their marriage, that was a long way off, buried in unturned pages, away from every one's interest but his own. Dunsey might betray him if he came back; but Dunsey might be won to silence.

And when events turn out so much better for a man than he has had reason to dread, is it not a proof that his conduct has been less foolish and blameworthy than it might otherwise have appeared? When we are treated well, we naturally begin to think that we are not altogether unmeritorious, and that it is only just we should treat ourselves well, and not mar our own good fortune. Where, after all, would be the use of his confessing the past to Nancy Lammeter, and throwing away his happiness?—nay, hers? for he felt some confidence that she loved him. As for the child, he would see that it was cared for: he would never forsake it; he would do everything but own it. Perhaps it would be just as happy in life without being owned by its father, seeing that nobody could tell how things would turn out, and that—is there any other reason wanted?—well, then, that the father would be much happier without owning the child.

CHAPTER XIV

THERE was a pauper's burial that week in Raveloe, and up Kench Yard at Batherley it was known that the dark-haired woman with the fair child, who had lately come to lodge there, was gone away again. That was all the express note taken that Molly had disappeared from the eyes of men. But the unwept death which, to the general lot, seemed as trivial as the summer-shed leaf, was charged with the force of destiny to certain human lives that we know of, shaping their joys and sorrows even to the end.

Silas Marner's determination to keep the 'tramp's child' was matter of hardly less surprise and iterated talk in the village than the robbery of his money. That softening of feeling towards him which dated from his misfortune, that merging of suspicion and dislike in a rather contemptuous pity for him as lone and crazy, was now accompanied with a more active sympathy, especially amongst the women. Notable mothers, who knew what it was to keep children 'whole and sweet;' lazy mothers, who knew what it was to be interrupted in folding their arms and scratching their elbows by the mischievous propensities of children just firm on their legs, were equally interested in conjecturing how a lone man would manage with a two-year-old child on his hands, and were equally ready with their suggestions: the notable chiefly telling him what he had better do, and the lazy ones being emphatic in telling him what he would never be able to do.

Among the notable mothers, Dolly Winthrop was the one whose neighbourly offices were the most acceptable to Marner, for they were rendered without any show of bustling instruction. Silas had shown her the half-guinea given to him by Godfrey, and had asked her what he should do about getting some clothes for the child.

'Eh, Master Marner,' said Dolly, 'there's no call to buy, no more nor a pair o' shoes; for I've got the little petticoats as Aaron wore five years ago, and it's ill spending the money on them baby-clothes, for the child 'ull grow like grass i' May, bless it—that it will.'

And the same day Dolly brought her bundle, and displayed to Marner, one by one, the tiny garments in their due order of succession, most of them patched and darned, but clean and neat as fresh-sprung herbs. This was the introduction to a great ceremony with soap and water, from which baby came out in new beauty, and sat on Dolly's knee, handling her toes and chuckling and patting her palms together with an air of having made several discoveries about herself, which she communicated by alternate sounds of 'gug-gug-gug,' and 'mammy.' The 'mammy' was not a cry of need or uneasiness: Baby had been used to utter it without expecting either tender sound or touch to follow.

'Anybody 'ud think the angils in heaven couldn't be prettier,' said Dolly, rubbing the golden curls and kissing them. 'And to think of its being covered wi' them dirty rags—and the poor mother—froze to death; but there's Them as took care of it, and brought it to your door, Master Marner. The door was open, and it walked in over the snow, like as if it had been a little starved robin. Didn't you say the door was open?'

'Yes,' said Silas, meditatively. 'Yes—the door was open. The money's gone I don't know where, and this is come from I don't know where.'

He had not mentioned to any one his unconsciousness of the child's entrance, shrinking from questions which might lead to the fact he himself suspected—namely, that he had been in one of his trances.

'Ah,' said Dolly, with soothing gravity, 'it's like the night and the morning, and the sleeping and the waking, and the rain and the harvest*—one goes and the other comes, and we know nothing how nor where. We may strive and scrat* and fend, but it's little we can do arter all—the big things come and go wi' no striving o' our'n—they do, that they do; and I think you're in the right on it to keep the little un, Master Marner, seeing as it's been sent to you, though there's folks as thinks different. You'll happen be a bit moithered* with it while it's so little; but I'll come, and welcome, and see to it for you: I've a bit o' time to spare most days, for when one gets up betimes i' the morning, the clock seems to stan' still tow'rt ten, afore it's time to go about the victual. So, as I say, I'll come and see to the child for you, and welcome.'

'Thank you . . . kindly,' said Silas, hesitating a little. 'I'll be glad if you'll tell me things. But,' he added, uneasily, leaning forward to look at Baby with some jealousy, as she was resting her head backward against Dolly's arm, and eyeing him contentedly from a distance—'But I want to do things for it myself, else it may get fond o' somebody else, and not fond o' me. I've been used to fending for myself in the house—I can learn, I can learn.'

'Eh, to be sure,' said Dolly, gently. 'I've seen men as are wonderful handy wi' children. The men are awk'ard and contrairy mostly, God help 'em—but when the drink's out of 'em, they aren't unsensible, though they're bad for leeching and bandaging—so fiery and unpatient. You see this goes first, next the skin,' proceeded Dolly, taking up the little shirt, and putting it on.

'Yes,' said Marner, docilely, bringing his eyes very close, that they might be initiated in the mysteries; whereupon Baby seized his head with both her small arms, and put her lips against his face with purring noises.

'See there,' said Dolly, with a woman's tender tact, 'she's fondest o' you. She wants to go o' your lap, I'll be bound. Go, then: take her, Master Marner; you can put the things on, and then you can say as you've done for her from the first of her coming to you.'

Marner took her on his lap, trembling with an emotion mysterious to himself, at something unknown dawning on his life. Thought and feeling were so confused within him, that if he had tried to give them utterance, he could only have said that the child was come instead of the gold—that the gold had turned into the child. He took the garments from Dolly, and put them on under her teaching; interrupted, of course, by Baby's gymnastics.

'There, then! why, you take to it quite easy, Master Marner,' said Dolly; 'but what shall you do when you're forced to sit in your loom? For she'll get busier and mischievouser every day—she will, bless her. It's lucky as you've got that high hearth i'stead of a grate, for that keeps the fire more out of her reach: but if you've got anything as can be spilt or broke, or as is fit to cut her fingers off, she'll be at it—and it is but right you should know.'

Silas meditated a little while in some perplexity. 'I'll tie her to the leg o' the loom,' he said at last—'tie her with a good long strip o' something.'

'Well, mayhap that'll do, as it's a little gell, for they're easier persuaded to sit i' one place nor the lads. I know what the lads are; for I've had four—four I've had, God knows—and if you was to take and tie 'em up, they'd make a fighting and a crying as if you was ringing the pigs.* But I'll bring you my little chair, and some bits o' red rag and things for her to play wi'; an' she'll sit and chatter to 'em as if they was alive. Eh, if it wasn't a sin to the lads to wish 'em made different, bless 'em, I should ha' been glad for one of 'em to be a little gell; and to think as I could ha' taught her to scour, and mend, and the knitting, and everything. But I can teach 'em this little un, Master Marner, when she gets old enough.'

'But she'll be *my* little un,' said Marner, rather hastily. 'She'll be nobody else's.'

'No, to be sure; you'll have a right to her, if you're a father to her, and bring her up according. But,' added Dolly, coming to a point which she had determined beforehand to touch upon, 'you must bring her up like christened folks's children, and take her to church, and let her learn her catechise, as my little Aaron can say off—the "I believe," and everything, and "hurt nobody by word or deed,"*—as well as if he was the clerk. That's what you must do, Master Marner, if you'd do the right thing by the orphin child.'

Marner's pale face flushed suddenly under a new anxiety. His mind was too busy trying to give some definite bearing to Dolly's words for him to think of answering her.

'And it's my belief,' she went on, 'as the poor little creatur has never been christened, and it's nothing but right as the parson should be spoke to; and if you was noways unwilling, I'd talk to Mr Macey about it this very day. For if the child ever went anyways wrong, and you hadn't done your part by it, Master Marner—'noculation,* and everything to save it from harm—it 'ud be a thorn i' your bed for ever o' this side the grave; and I can't think as it 'ud be easy lying down for anybody when they'd got to another world, if they hadn't done their part by the helpless children as come wi'out their own asking.'

Dolly herself was disposed to be silent for some time now, for she had spoken from the depths of her own simple belief, and was much concerned to know whether her words would produce the desired effect on Silas. He was puzzled and anxious, for Dolly's word 'christened' conveyed no distinct meaning to him. He had only heard of baptism, and had only seen the baptism of grown-up men and women.*

'What is it as you mean by "christened"?' he said at last, timidly. 'Won't folks be good to her without it?'

'Dear, dear! Master Marner,' said Dolly, with gentle distress and compassion. 'Had you never no father nor mother as taught you to say your prayers, and as there's good words and good things to keep us from harm?'

'Yes,' said Silas, in a low voice; 'I know a deal about that—used to, used to. But your ways are different: my country was a good way off.' He paused a few moments, and then added, more decidedly, 'But I want to do everything as can be done for the child. And whatever's right for it i' this country, and you think 'ull do it good, I'll act according, if you'll tell me.'

'Well, then, Master Marner,' said Dolly, inwardly rejoiced, 'I'll ask Mr Macey to speak to the parson about it; and you must fix on a name for it, because it must have a name giv' it when it's christened.'

'My mother's name was Hephzibah,'* said Silas, 'and my little sister was named after her.'

'Eh, that's a hard name,' said Dolly. 'I partly think it isn't a christened name.'

'It's a Bible name,' said Silas, old ideas recurring.

'Then I've no call to speak again' it,' said Dolly, rather startled by Silas's knowledge on this head; 'but you see I'm no scholard, and I'm slow at catching the words. My husband says I'm allays like as if I was putting the haft for the handle*—that's what he says—for he's very sharp, God help him. But it was awk'ard calling your little sister by such a hard name, when you'd got nothing big to say, like—wasn't it, Master Marner?'

'We called her Eppie,' said Silas.

'Well, if it was noways wrong to shorten the name, it 'ud be a deal handier. And so I'll go now, Master Marner, and I'll speak about the christening afore dark; and I wish you the best o' luck, and it's my belief as it'll come to you, if you do what's right by the orphin child;—and there's the 'noculation to be seen to; and as to washing its bits o' things, you need look to nobody but me, for I can do 'em wi' one hand when I've got my suds about. Eh, the blessed angil! You'll let me bring my Aaron one o' these days, and he'll show her his little cart as his father's made for him, and the black-and-white pup as he's got a-rearing.'

Baby *was* christened, the rector deciding that a double baptism was the lesser risk to incur; and on this occasion Silas, making himself as clean and tidy as he could, appeared for the first time within the church, and shared in the observances held sacred by his neighbours. He was quite unable, by means of anything he heard or saw, to identify the Raveloe religion with his old faith; if he could at any time in his previous life have done so, it must have been by the aid of a strong feeling ready to vibrate with sympathy, rather than by a comparison of phrases and ideas: and now for long years that feeling had been dormant. He had no distinct idea about the baptism and the church-going, except that Dolly had said it was for the good of the child; and in this way, as the weeks grew to months, the child created fresh and fresh links between his life and the lives from which he had hitherto shrunk continually into narrower isolation. Unlike the gold which needed nothing, and must be worshipped in close-locked solitude—which was hidden away from the daylight, was deaf to the song of birds, and started to no human tones—Eppie was a creature of endless claims and ever-growing desires, seeking and loving sunshine, and living sounds, and living movements; making trial of everything, with trust in new joy, and stirring the human kindness in all eyes that looked on her. The gold had kept his thoughts in an ever-repeated circle, leading to nothing beyond itself; but Eppie was an object compacted of changes and hopes that forced his thoughts onward, and carried them far away from their old eager pacing towards the same blank limit—carried them away to the new things that would come with the coming years, when Eppie would have learned to understand how her father Silas cared for her; and made him look for images of that time in the ties and charities that bound together the families of his neighbours. The gold had asked that he should sit weaving longer and longer, deafened and blinded more and more to all things except the monotony of his loom and the repetition of his web; but Eppie called him away from his weaving, and made him think all its pauses a holiday, reawakening his senses with her fresh life, even to the old winter-flies that came crawling forth in the early spring sunshine, and warming him into joy because *she* had joy.

And when the sunshine grew strong and lasting, so that the buttercups were thick in the meadows, Silas might be seen in the sunny midday, or in the late afternoon when the shadows were lengthening under the hedgerows, strolling out with uncovered head to carry Eppie beyond the Stone-pits to where the flowers grew, till they reached some favourite bank where he could sit down, while Eppie toddled to pluck the flowers, and make remarks to the winged things that murmured happily above the bright petals, calling 'Dad-dad's' attention continually by bringing him the flowers. Then she would turn her ear to some sudden bird-note, and Silas learned to please her by making signs of hushed stillness, that they might listen for the note to come again: so that when it came, she set up her small back and laughed with gurgling triumph. Sitting on the banks in this way, Silas began to look for the once familiar herbs again; and as the leaves, with their unchanged outline and markings, lay on his palm, there was a sense of crowding remembrances from which he turned away timidly, taking refuge in Eppie's little world, that lay lightly on his enfeebled spirit.

As the child's mind was growing into knowledge, his mind was growing into memory: as her life unfolded, his soul, long stupefied in a cold narrow prison, was unfolding too, and trembling gradually into full consciousness.

It was an influence which must gather force with every new year: the tones that stirred Silas's heart grew articulate, and called for more distinct answers; shapes and sounds grew clearer for Eppie's eyes and ears, and there was more that 'Dad-dad' was imperatively required to notice and account for. Also, by the time Eppie was three years old, she developed a fine capacity for mischief, and for devising ingenious ways of being troublesome, which found much exercise, not only for Silas's patience, but for his watchfulness and penetration. Sorely was poor Silas puzzled on such occasions by the incompatible demands of love. Dolly Winthrop told him that punishment was good for Eppie, and that, as for rearing a child without making it tingle a little in soft and safe places now and then, it was not to be done.

'To be sure, there's another thing you might do, Master Marner,' added Dolly, meditatively: 'you might shut her up once i' the coal-hole. That was what I did wi' Aaron; for I was that silly wi' the youngest lad, as I could never bear to smack him. Not as I could find i' my heart to let him stay i' the coal-hole more nor a minute, but it was enough to colly* him all over, so as he must be new washed and dressed, and it was as good as a rod to him—that was. But I put it upo' your conscience, Master Marner, as there's one of 'em you must choose—ayther smacking or the coal-hole—else she'll get so masterful, there'll be no holding her.'

Silas was impressed with the melancholy truth of this last remark; but his force of mind failed before the only two penal methods open to him, not only because it was painful to him to hurt Eppie, but because he trembled at a moment's contention with her, lest she should love him the less for it. Let even an affectionate Goliath* get himself tied to a small tender thing, dreading to hurt it by pulling, and dreading still more to snap the cord, and which of the two, pray, will be master? It was clear that Eppie, with her short toddling steps, must lead father Silas a pretty dance on any fine morning when circumstances favoured mischief.

For example. He had wisely chosen a broad strip of linen as a means of fastening her to his loom when he was busy: it made a broad belt round her waist, and was long enough to allow of her reaching the truckle-bed* and sitting down on it, but not long enough for her to attempt any dangerous climbing. One bright summer's morning Silas had been more engrossed than usual in 'setting up' a new piece of work, an occasion on which his scissors were in requisition. These scissors, owing to an especial warning of Dolly's, had been kept carefully out of Eppie's reach; but the click of them had had a peculiar attraction for her ear, and watching the results of that click, she had derived the philosophic lesson that the same cause would produce the same effect. Silas had seated himself in his loom, and the noise of weaving had begun; but he had left his scissors on a ledge which Eppie's arm was long enough to reach; and now, like a small mouse, watching her opportunity, she stole quietly from her corner, secured the scissors, and toddled to the bed again, setting up her back as a mode of concealing the fact. She had a distinct intention as to the use of the scissors; and having cut the linen strip in a jagged but effectual manner, in two moments she had run out at the open door where the sunshine was inviting her, while poor Silas believed her to be a better child than usual. It was not until he happened to need his scissors that the terrible fact burst upon him: Eppie had run out by herself—had perhaps fallen into the Stone-pit. Silas, shaken by the worst fear that could have befallen him, rushed out, calling 'Eppie!' and ran eagerly about the unenclosed space, exploring the dry cavities into which she might have fallen, and then gazing with questioning dread at the smooth red surface of the water. The cold drops stood on his brow. How long had she been out? There was one hope—that she had crept through the stile and got into the fields, where he habitually took her to stroll. But the grass was high in the meadow, and there was no descrying her, if she were there, except by a close search that would be a trespass on Mr Osgood's crop. Still, that misdemeanour must be committed; and poor Silas, after peering all round the hedgerows, traversed the grass, beginning with perturbed vision to see Eppie behind every group of red sorrel, and to see her moving always farther off as he approached. The meadow was searched in vain; and he got over the stile into the next field, looking with dying hope towards a small pond which was now reduced to its summer shallowness, so as to leave a wide margin of good adhesive mud. Here, however, sat Eppie, discoursing cheerfully to her own small boot, which she was using as a bucket to convey the water into a deep hoof-mark, while her little naked foot was planted comfortably on a cushion of olive-green mud. A red-headed calf was observing her with alarmed doubt through the opposite hedge.

Here was clearly a case of aberration in a christened child which demanded severe treatment; but Silas, overcome with convulsive joy at finding his treasure again, could do nothing but snatch her up, and cover her with half-sobbing kisses. It was not until he had carried her home, and had begun to think of the necessary washing, that he recollected the need that he should punish Eppie, and 'make her remember.' The idea that she might run away again and come to harm, gave him unusual resolution, and for the first time he determined to try the coal-hole—a small closet near the hearth.

'Naughty, naughty Eppie,' he suddenly began, holding her on his knee, and pointing to her muddy feet and clothes—'naughty to cut with the scissors and run away. Eppie must go into the coal-hole for being naughty. Daddy must put her in the coal-hole.'

He half-expected that this would be shock enough, and that Eppie would begin to cry. But instead of that, she began to shake herself on his knee, as if the proposition opened a pleasing novelty. Seeing that he must proceed to extremities, he put her into the coal-hole, and held the door closed, with a trembling sense that he was using a strong measure. For a moment there was silence, but then came a little cry, 'Opy, opy!' and Silas let her out again, saying, 'Now Eppie 'ull never be naughty again, else she must go in the coal-hole—a black naughty place.'

The weaving must stand still a long while this morning, for now Eppie must be washed, and have clean clothes on; but it was to be hoped that this punishment would have a lasting effect, and save time in future—though, perhaps, it would have been better if Eppie had cried more.

In half an hour she was clean again, and Silas having turned his back to see what he could do with the linen band, threw it down again, with the reflection that Eppie would be good without fastening for the rest of the morning. He turned round again, and was going to place her in her little chair near the loom, when she peeped out at him with black face and hands again, and said, 'Eppie in de toal-hole!'

This total failure of the coal-hole discipline shook Silas's belief in the efficacy of punishment. 'She'd take it all for fun,' he observed to Dolly, 'if I didn't hurt her, and that I can't do, Mrs Winthrop. If she makes me a bit o' trouble, I can bear it. And she's got no tricks but what she'll grow out of.'

'Well, that's partly true, Master Marner,' said Dolly, sympathetically; 'and if you can't bring your mind to frighten her off touching things, you must do what you can to keep 'em out of her way. That's what I do wi' the pups as the lads are allays a-rearing. They *will* worry and gnaw—worry and gnaw they will, if it was one's Sunday cap as hung anywhere so as they could drag it. They know no difference, God help 'em: it's the pushing o' the teeth as sets 'em on, that's what it is.'

So Eppie was reared without punishment, the burden of her misdeeds being borne vicariously by father Silas. The stone hut was made a soft nest for her, lined with downy patience: and also in the world that lay beyond the stone hut she knew nothing of frowns and denials.

Notwithstanding the difficulty of carrying her and his yarn or linen at the same time, Silas took her with him in most of his journeys to the farm-houses, unwilling to leave her behind at Dolly Winthrop's, who was always ready to take care of her; and little curly-headed Eppie, the weaver's child, became an object of interest at several outlying homesteads, as well as in the village. Hitherto he had been treated very much as if he had been a useful gnome or brownie—a queer and unaccountable creature, who must necessarily be looked at with wondering curiosity and repulsion, and with whom one would be glad to make all greetings and bargains as brief as possible, but who must be dealt with in a propitiatory way, and occasionally have a present of pork or garden stuff to carry home with him, seeing that without him there was no getting the yarn woven. But now Silas met with open smiling faces and cheerful questioning, as a person whose satisfactions and difficulties could be understood. Everywhere he must sit a little and talk about the child, and words of interest were always ready for him: 'Ah, Master Marner, you'll be lucky if she takes the measles soon and easy!'—or, 'Why, there isn't many lone men 'ud ha' been wishing to take up with a little un like that: but I reckon the weaving makes you handier than men as do out-door work—you're partly as handy as a woman, for weaving comes next to spinning.' Elderly masters and mistresses, seated observantly in large kitchen arm-chairs, shook their heads over the difficulties attendant on rearing children, felt Eppie's round arms and legs, and pronounced them remarkably firm, and told Silas that, if she turned out well (which, however, there was no telling), it would be a fine thing for him to have a steady lass to do for him when he got helpless. Servant maidens were fond of carrying her out to look at the hens and chickens, or to see if any cherries could be shaken down in the orchard; and the small boys and girls approached her slowly, with cautious movement and steady gaze, like little dogs face to face with one of their own kind, till attraction had reached the point at which the soft lips were put out for a kiss. No child was afraid of approaching Silas when Eppie was near him: there was no repulsion around him now, either for young or old; for the little child had come to link him once more with the whole world. There was love between him and the child that blent them into one, and there was love between the child and the world—from men and women with parental looks and tones, to the red lady-birds and the round pebbles.

Silas began now to think of Raveloe life entirely in relation to Eppie: she must have everything that was a good in Raveloe; and he listened docilely, that he might come to understand better what this life was, from which, for fifteen years, he had stood aloof as from a strange thing, wherewith he could have no communion: as some man who has a precious plant to which he would give a nurturing home in a new soil, thinks of the rain, and the sunshine, and all influences, in relation to his nursling, and asks industriously for all knowledge that will help him to satisfy the wants of the searching roots, or to guard leaf and bud from invading harm. The disposition to hoard had been utterly crushed at the very first by the loss of his long-stored gold: the coins he earned afterwards seemed as irrelevant as stones brought to complete a house suddenly buried by an earthquake; the sense of bereavement was too heavy upon him for the old thrill of satisfaction to arise again at the touch of the newly-earned coin. And now something had come to replace his hoard which gave a growing purpose to the earnings, drawing his hope and joy continually onward beyond the money.

In old days there were angels who came and took men by the hand and led them away from the city of destruction.* We see no white-winged angels now. But yet men are led away from threatening destruction: a hand is put into theirs, which leads them forth gently towards a calm and bright land, so that they look no more backward; and the hand may be a little child's.

CHAPTER XV

THERE was one person, as you will believe, who watched with keener though more hidden interest than any other, the prosperous growth of Eppie under the weaver's care. He dared not do anything that would imply a stronger interest in a poor man's adopted child than could be expected from the kindliness of the young Squire, when a chance meeting suggested a little present to a simple old fellow whom others noticed with goodwill; but he told himself that the time would come when he might do something towards furthering the welfare of his daughter without incurring suspicion. Was he very uneasy in the meantime at his inability to give his daughter her birthright? I cannot say that he was. The child was being taken care of, and would very likely be happy, as people in humble stations often were—happier, perhaps, than those brought up in luxury.

That famous ring* that pricked its owner when he forgot duty and followed desire—I wonder if it pricked very hard when he set out on the chase, or whether it pricked but lightly then, and only pierced to the quick when the chase had long been ended, and hope, folding her wings, looked backward and became regret?

Godfrey Cass's cheek and eye were brighter than ever now. He was so undivided in his aims, that he seemed like a man of firmness. No Dunsey had come back: people had made up their minds that he was gone for a soldier, or gone 'out of the country,' and no one cared to be specific in their inquiries on a subject delicate to a respectable family. Godfrey had ceased to see the shadow of Dunsey across his path; and the path now lay straight forward to the accomplishment of his best, longest-cherished wishes. Everybody said Mr Godfrey had taken the right turn; and it was pretty clear what would be the end of things, for there were not many days in the week that he was not seen riding to the Warrens. Godfrey himself, when he was asked jocosely if the day had been fixed, smiled with the pleasant consciousness of a lover who could say 'yes,' if he liked. He felt a reformed man, delivered from temptation; and the vision of his future life seemed to him as a promised land for which he had no cause to fight. He saw himself with all his happiness centred on his own hearth, while Nancy would smile on him as he played with the children.

And that other child, not on the hearth—he would not forget it; he would see that it was well provided for. That was a father's duty.

PART TWO

CHAPTER XVI

It was a bright autumn Sunday, sixteen years after Silas Marner had found his new treasure on the hearth. The bells of the old Raveloe church were ringing the cheerful peal which told that the morning service was ended; and out of the arched doorway in the tower came slowly, retarded by friendly greetings and questions, the richer parishioners who had chosen this bright Sunday morning as eligible for church-going. It was the rural fashion of that time for the more important members of the congregation to depart first, while their humbler neighbours waited and looked on, stroking their bent heads or dropping their curtsies to any large ratepayer who turned to notice them.

Foremost among these advancing groups of well-clad people, there are some whom we shall recognise, in spite of Time, who has laid his hand on them all. The tall blond man of forty is not much changed in feature from the Godfrey Cass of six-and-twenty: he is only fuller in flesh, and has only lost the indefinable look of youth—a loss which is marked even when the eye is undulled and the wrinkles are not yet come. Perhaps the pretty woman, not much younger than he, who is leaning on his arm, is more changed than her husband: the lovely bloom that used to be always on her cheek now comes but fitfully, with the fresh morning air or with some strong surprise; yet to all who love human faces best for what they tell of human experience, Nancy's beauty has a heightened interest. Often the soul is ripened into fuller goodness while age has spread an ugly film, so that mere glances can never divine the preciousness of the fruit. But the years have not been so cruel to Nancy. The firm yet placid mouth, the clear veracious glance of the brown eyes, speak now of a nature that has been tested and has kept its highest qualities; and even the costume, with its dainty neatness and purity, has more significance now the coquetries of youth can have nothing to do with it.

Mr and Mrs Godfrey Cass (any higher title has died away from Raveloe lips since the old Squire was gathered to his fathers and his inheritance was divided) have turned round to look for the tall aged man and the plainly dressed woman who are a little behind—Nancy having observed that they must wait for 'father and Priscilla'—and now they all turn into a narrower path leading across the churchyard to a small gate opposite the Red House. We will not follow them now; for may there not be some others in this departing congregation whom we should like to see again—some of those who are not likely to be handsomely clad, and whom we may not recognise so easily as the master and mistress of the Red House?

But it is impossible to mistake Silas Marner. His large brown eyes seem to have gathered a longer vision, as is the way with eyes that have been short-sighted in early life, and they have a less vague, a more answering gaze; but in everything else one sees signs of a frame much enfeebled by the lapse of the sixteen years. The weaver's bent shoulders and white hair give him almost the look of advanced age, though he is not more than five-and-fifty; but there is the freshest blossom of youth close by his side—a blond dimpled girl of eighteen, who has vainly tried to chastise her curly auburn hair into smoothness under her brown bonnet: the hair ripples as obstinately as a brooklet under the March breeze, and the little ringlets burst away from the restraining comb behind and show themselves below the bonnet-crown. Eppie cannot help being rather vexed about her hair, for there is no other girl in Raveloe who has hair at all like it, and she thinks hair ought to be smooth. She does not like to be blameworthy even in small things: you see how neatly her prayer-book is folded in her spotted handkerchief.

That good-looking young fellow, in a new fustian suit, who walks behind her, is not quite sure upon the question of hair in the abstract, when Eppie puts it to him, and thinks that perhaps straight hair is the best in general, but he doesn't want Eppie's hair to be different. She surely divines that there is some one behind her who is thinking about her very particularly, and mustering courage to come to her side as soon as they are out in the lane, else why should she look rather shy, and take care not to turn away her head from her father Silas, to whom she keeps murmuring little sentences as to who was at church, and who was not at church, and how pretty the red mountain-ash is over the Rectory wall!

'I wish *we* had a little garden, father, with double daisies in, like Mrs Winthrop's,' said Eppie, when they were out in the lane; 'only they say it 'ud take a deal of digging and bringing fresh soil—and you couldn't do that, could you, father? Anyhow, I shouldn't like you to do it, for it 'ud be too hard work for you.'

'Yes, I could do it, child, if you want a bit o' garden: these long evenings, I could work at taking in a little bit o' the waste, just enough for a root or two o' flowers for you; and again, i' the morning, I could have a turn wi' the spade before I sat down to the loom. Why didn't you tell me before as you wanted a bit o' garden?'

'*I* can dig it for you, Master Marner,' said the young man in fustian, who was now by Eppie's side, entering into the conversation without the trouble of formalities. 'It'll be play to me after I've done my day's work, or any odd bits o' time when the work's slack. And I'll bring you some soil from Mr Cass's garden—he'll let me, and willing.'

'Eh, Aaron, my lad, are you there?' said Silas; 'I wasn't aware of you; for when Eppie's talking o' things, I see nothing but what she's a-saying. Well, if you could help me with the digging, we might get her a bit o' garden all the sooner.'

'Then, if you think well and good,' said Aaron, 'I'll come to the Stone-pits this afternoon, and we'll settle what land's to be taken in, and I'll get up an hour earlier i' the morning, and begin on it.'

'But not if you don't promise me not to work at the hard digging, father,' said Eppie. 'For I shouldn't ha' said anything about it,' she added, half-bashfully, half-roguishly, 'only Mrs Winthrop said as Aaron 'ud be so good, and——'

'And you might ha' known it without mother telling you,' said Aaron. 'And Master Marner knows too, I hope, as I'm able and willing to do a turn o' work for him, and he won't do me the unkindness to anyways take it out o' my hands.'

'There, now, father, you won't work in it till it's all easy,' said Eppie, 'and you and me can mark out the beds, and make holes and plant the roots. It'll be a deal livelier at the Stone-pits when we've got some flowers, for I always think the flowers can see us and know what we're talking about. And I'll have a bit o' rosemary, and bergamot, and thyme, because they're so sweet-smelling; but there's no lavender only in the gentlefolks' gardens, I think.'

'That's no reason why you shouldn't have some,' said Aaron, 'for I can bring you slips of anything; I'm forced to cut no end of 'em when I'm gardening, and throw 'em away mostly. There's a big bed o' lavender at the Red House: the missis is very fond of it.'

'Well,' said Silas, gravely, 'so as you don't make free for us, or ask for anything as is worth much at the Red House: for Mr Cass's been so good to us, and built us up the new end o' the cottage, and given us beds and things, as I couldn't abide to be imposin' for garden-stuff or anything else.'

'No, no, there's no imposin',' said Aaron; 'there's never a garden in all the parish but what there's endless waste in it for want o' somebody as could use everything up. It's what I think to myself sometimes, as there need nobody run short o' victuals if the land was made the most on, and there was never a morsel but what could find its way to a mouth. It sets one thinking o' that—gardening does. But I must go back now, else mother 'ull be in trouble as I aren't there.'

'Bring her with you this afternoon, Aaron,' said Eppie; 'I shouldn't like to fix about the garden, and her not know everything from the first—should *you*, father?'

'Ay, bring her if you can, Aaron,' said Silas; 'she's sure to have a word to say as 'll help us to set things on their right end.'

Aaron turned back up the village, while Silas and Eppie went on up the lonely sheltered lane.

'O daddy!' she began, when they were in privacy, clasping and squeezing Silas's arm, and skipping round to give him an energetic kiss. 'My little old daddy! I'm so glad. I don't think I shall want anything else when we've got a little garden; and I knew Aaron would dig it for us,' she went on with roguish triumph—'I knew that very well.'

'You're a deep little puss, you are,' said Silas, with the mild passive happiness of love-crowned age in his face; 'but you'll make yourself fine and beholden to Aaron.'

'O no, I shan't,' said Eppie, laughing and frisking; 'he likes it.'

'Come, come, let me carry your prayer-book, else you'll be dropping it, jumping i' that way.'

Eppie was now aware that her behaviour was under observation, but it was only the observation of a friendly donkey, browsing with a log fastened to his foot—a meek donkey, not scornfully critical of human trivialities, but thankful to share in them, if possible, by getting his nose scratched; and Eppie did not fail to gratify him with her usual notice, though it was attended with the inconvenience of his following them, painfully, up to the very door of their home.

But the sound of a sharp bark inside, as Eppie put the key in the door, modified the donkey's views, and he limped away again without bidding. The sharp bark was the sign of an excited welcome that was awaiting them from a knowing brown terrier, who, after dancing at their legs in a hysterical manner, rushed with a worrying noise at a tortoise-shell kitten under the loom, and then rushed back with a sharp bark again, as much as to say, 'I have done my duty by this feeble creature, you perceive;' while the lady-mother of the kitten sat sunning her white bosom in the window, and looked round with a sleepy air of expecting caresses, though she was not going to take any trouble for them.

The presence of this happy animal life was not the only change which had come over the interior of the stone cottage. There was no bed now in the living-room, and the small space was well filled with decent furniture, all bright and clean enough to satisfy Dolly Winthrop's eye. The oaken table and three-cornered oaken chair were hardly what was likely to be seen in so poor a cottage: they had come, with the beds and other things, from the Red House; for Mr Godfrey Cass, as every one said in the village, did very kindly by the weaver; and it was nothing but right a man should be looked on and helped by those who could afford it, when he had brought up an orphan child, and been father and mother to her—and had lost his money too, so as he had nothing but what he worked for week by week, and when the weaving was going down too—for there was less and less flax spun*—and Master Marner was none so young. Nobody was jealous of the weaver, for he was regarded as an exceptional person, whose claims on neighbourly help were not to be matched in Raveloe. Any superstition that remained concerning him had taken an entirely new colour; and Mr Macey, now a very feeble old man of fourscore and six, never seen except in his chimney-corner or sitting in the sunshine at his door-sill, was of opinion that when a man had done what Silas had done by an orphan child, it was a sign that his money would come to light again, or leastwise that the robber would be made to answer for it—for, as Mr Macey observed of himself, his faculties were as strong as ever.

Silas sat down now and watched Eppie with a satisfied gaze as she spread the clean cloth, and set on it the potato-pie, warmed up slowly in a safe Sunday fashion, by being put into a dry pot over a slowly-dying fire, as the best substitute for an oven. For Silas would not consent to have a grate and oven added to his conveniences: he loved the old brick hearth as he had loved his brown pot—and was it not there when he had found Eppie? The gods of the hearth exist for us still; and let all new faith be tolerant of that fetishism,* lest it bruise its own roots.

Silas ate his dinner more silently than usual, soon laying down his knife and fork, and watching half-abstractedly Eppie's play with Snap and the cat, by which her own dining was made rather a lengthy business. Yet it was a sight that might well arrest wandering thoughts: Eppie, with the rippling radiance of her hair and the whiteness of her rounded chin and throat set off by the dark-blue cotton gown, laughing merrily as the kitten held on with her four claws to one shoulder, like a design for a jug-handle, while Snap on the right hand and Puss on the other put up their paws towards a morsel which she held out of the reach of both—Snap occasionally desisting in order to remonstrate with the cat by a cogent worrying growl on the greediness and futility of her conduct; till Eppie relented, caressed them both, and divided the morsel between them.

But at last Eppie, glancing at the clock, checked the play, and said, 'O daddy, you're wanting to go into the sunshine to smoke your pipe. But I must clear away first, so as the house may be tidy when godmother comes. I'll make haste—I won't be long.'

Silas had taken to smoking a pipe daily during the last two years, having been strongly urged to it by the sages of Raveloe, as a practice 'good for the fits;' and this advice was sanctioned by Dr Kimble, on the ground that it was as well to try what could do no harm—a principle which was made to answer for a great deal of work in that gentleman's medical practice. Silas did not highly enjoy smoking, and often wondered how his neighbours could be so fond of it; but a humble sort of acquiescence in what was held to be good, had become a strong habit of that new self which had been developed in him since he had found Eppie on his hearth: it had been the only clew* his bewildered mind could hold by in cherishing this young life that had been sent to him out of the darkness into which his gold had departed. By seeking what was needful for Eppie, by sharing the effect that everything produced on her, he had himself come to appropriate the forms of custom and belief which were the mould of Raveloe life; and as, with reawakening sensibilities, memory also reawakened, he had begun to ponder over the elements of his old faith, and blend them with his new impressions, till he recovered a consciousness of unity between his past and present. The sense of presiding goodness and the human trust which come with all pure peace and joy, had given him a dim impression that there had been some error, some mistake, which had thrown that dark shadow over the days of his best years; and as it grew more and more easy to him to open his mind to Dolly Winthrop, he gradually communicated to her all he could describe of his early life. The communication was necessarily a slow and difficult process, for Silas's meagre power of explanation was not aided by any readiness of interpretation in Dolly, whose narrow outward experience gave her no key to strange customs, and made every novelty a source of wonder that arrested them at every step of the narrative. It was only by fragments, and at intervals which left Dolly time to revolve what she had heard till it acquired some familiarity for her, that Silas at last arrived at the climax of the sad story—the drawing of lots, and its false testimony concerning him; and this had to be repeated in several interviews, under new questions on her part as to the nature of this plan for detecting the guilty and clearing the innocent.

'And yourn's the same Bible, you're sure o' that, Master Marner—the Bible as you brought wi' you from that country—it's the same as what they've got at church, and what Eppie's a-learning to read in?'

'Yes,' said Silas, 'every bit the same; and there's drawing o' lots in the Bible, mind you,' he added in a lower tone.

'O dear, dear,' said Dolly in a grieved voice, as if she were hearing an unfavourable report of a sick man's case. She was silent for some minutes; at last she said—

'There's wise folks, happen, as know how it all is; the parson knows, I'll be bound; but it takes big words to tell them things, and such as poor folks can't make much out on. I can never rightly know the meaning o' what I hear at church, only a bit here and there, but I know it's good words—I do. But what lies upo' your mind—it's this, Master Marner: as, if Them above had done the right thing by you, They'd never ha' let you be turned out for a wicked thief when you was innicent.'

'Ah!' said Silas, who had now come to understand Dolly's phraseology, 'that was what fell on me like as if it had been red-hot iron; because, you see, there was nobody as cared for me or clave to me above nor below. And him as I'd gone out and in wi' for ten year and more, since when we was lads and went halves—mine own familiar friend in whom I trusted, had lifted up his heel again' me,* and worked to ruin me.'

'Eh, but he was a bad 'un—I can't think as there's another such,' said Dolly. 'But I'm o'ercome, Master Marner; I'm like as if I'd waked and didn't know whether it was night or morning. I feel somehow as sure as I do when I've laid something up though I can't justly put my hand on it, as there was a rights in what happened to you, if one could but make it out; and you'd no call to lose heart as you did. But we'll talk on it again; for sometimes things come into my head when I'm leeching or poulticing, or such, as I could never think on when I was sitting still.'

Dolly was too useful a woman not to have many opportunities of illumination of the kind she alluded to, and she was not long before she recurred to the subject.

'Master Marner,' she said, one day that she came to bring home Eppie's washing, 'I've been sore puzzled for a good bit wi' that trouble o' yourn and the drawing o' lots; and it got twisted back'ards and for'ards, as I didn't know which end to lay hold on. But it come to me all clear like, that night when I was sitting up wi' poor Bessy Fawkes, as is dead and left her children behind, God help 'em—it come to me as clear as daylight; but whether I've got hold on it now, or can any-ways bring it to my tongue's end, that I don't know. For I've often a deal inside me as 'll never come out; and for what you talk o' your folks in your old country niver saying prayers by heart nor saying 'em out of a book, they must be wonderful cliver; for if I didn't know "Our Father,"* and little bits o' good words as I can carry out o' church wi' me, I might down o' my knees every night, but nothing could I say.'

'But you can mostly say something as I can make sense on, Mrs Winthrop,' said Silas.

'Well, then, Master Marner, it come to me summat like this: I can make nothing o' the drawing o' lots and the answer coming wrong; it 'ud mayhap take the parson to tell that, and he could only tell us i' big words. But what come to me as clear as the daylight, it was when I was troubling over poor Bessy Fawkes, and it allays comes into my head when I'm sorry for folks, and feel as I can't do a power to help 'em, not if I was to get up i' the middle o' the night—it comes into my head as Them above has got a deal tenderer heart nor what I've got—for I can't be anyways better nor Them as made me; and if anything looks hard to me, it's because there's things I don't know on; and for the matter o' that, there may be plenty o' things I don't know on, for it's little as I know—that it is. And so, while I was thinking o' that, you come into my mind, Master Marner, and it all come pouring in:—if *I* felt i' my inside what was the right and just thing by you, and them as prayed and drawed the lots, all but that wicked un, if *they*'d ha' done the right thing by you if they could, isn't there Them as was at the making on us, and knows better and has a better will? And that's all as ever I can be sure on, and everything else is a big puzzle to me when I think on it. For there was the fever come and took off them as were full-growed, and left the helpless children; and there's the breaking o' limbs; and them as 'ud do right and be sober have to suffer by them as are contrairy—eh, there's trouble i' this world, and there's things as we can niver make out the rights on. And all as we've got to do is to trusten, Master Marner—to do the right thing as fur as we know, and to trusten. For if us as knows so little can see a bit o' good and rights, we may be sure as there's a good and a rights bigger nor what we can know—I feel it i' my own inside as it must be so. And if you could but ha' gone on trustening, Master Marner, you wouldn't ha' run away from your fellow-creaturs and been so lone.'

'Ah, but that 'ud ha' been hard,' said Silas, in an under-tone; 'it 'ud ha' been hard to trusten then.'

'And so it would,' said Dolly, almost with compunction; 'them things are easier said nor done; and I'm partly ashamed o' talking.'

'Nay, nay,' said Silas, 'you're i' the right, Mrs Winthrop—you're i' the right. There's good i' this world—I've a feeling o' that now; and it makes a man feel as there's a good more nor he can see, i' spite o' the trouble and the wickedness. That drawing o' the lots is dark; but the child was sent to me: there's dealings with us—there's dealings.'

This dialogue took place in Eppie's earlier years, when Silas had to part with her for two hours every day, that she might learn to read at the dame school, after he had vainly tried himself to guide her in that first step to learning. Now that she was grown up, Silas had often been led, in those moments of quiet outpouring which come to people who live together in perfect love, to talk with *her* too of the past, and how and why he had lived a lonely man until she had been sent to him. For it would have been impossible for him to hide from Eppie that she was not his own child: even if the most delicate reticence on the point could have been expected from Raveloe gossips in her presence, her own questions about her mother could not have been parried, as she grew up, without that complete shrouding of the past which would have made a painful barrier between their minds. So Eppie had long known how her mother had died on the snowy ground, and how she herself had been found on the hearth by father Silas, who had taken her golden curls for his lost guineas brought back to him. The tender and peculiar love with which Silas had reared her in almost inseparable companionship with himself, aided by the seclusion of their dwelling, had preserved her from the lowering influences of the village talk and habits, and had kept her mind in that freshness which is sometimes falsely supposed to be an invariable attribute of rusticity. Perfect love has a breath of poetry which can exalt the relations of the least-instructed human beings; and this breath of poetry had surrounded Eppie from the time when she had followed the bright gleam that beckoned her to Silas's hearth; so that it is not surprising if, in other things besides her delicate prettiness, she was not quite a common village maiden, but had a touch of refinement and fervour which came from no other teaching than that of tenderly-nurtured unvitiated feeling. She was too childish and simple for her imagination to rove into questions about her unknown father; for a long while it did not even occur to her that she must have had a father; and the first time that the idea of her mother having had a husband presented itself to her, was when Silas showed her the wedding-ring which had been taken from the wasted finger, and had been carefully preserved by him in a little lackered box shaped like a shoe. He delivered this box into Eppie's charge when she had grown up, and she often opened it to look at the ring: but still she thought hardly at all about the father of whom it was the symbol. Had she not a father very close to her, who loved her better than any real fathers in the village seemed to love their daughters? On the contrary, who her mother was, and how she came to die in that forlornness, were questions that often pressed on Eppie's mind. Her knowledge of Mrs Winthrop, who was her nearest friend next to Silas, made her feel that a mother must be very precious; and she had again and again asked Silas to tell her how her mother looked, whom she was like, and how he had found her against the furze bush, led towards it by the little footsteps and the outstretched arms. The furze bush was there still; and this afternoon, when Eppie came out with Silas into the sunshine, it was the first object that arrested her eyes and thoughts.

'Father,' she said, in a tone of gentle gravity, which sometimes came like a sadder, slower cadence across her playfulness, 'we shall take the furze bush into the garden; it'll come into the corner, and just against it I'll put snowdrops and crocuses, 'cause Aaron says they won't die out, but 'll always get more and more.'

'Ah, child,' said Silas, always ready to talk when he had his pipe in his hand, apparently enjoying the pauses more than the puffs, 'it wouldn't do to leave out the furze bush; and there's nothing prettier to my thinking, when it's yallow with flowers. But it's just come into my head what we're to do for a fence—mayhap Aaron can help us to a thought; but a fence we must have, else the donkeys and things 'ull come and trample everything down. And fencing's hard to be got at, by what I can make out.'

'O, I'll tell you, daddy,' said Eppie, clasping her hands suddenly, after a minute's thought. 'There's lots o' loose stones about, some of 'em not big, and we might lay 'em atop of one another, and make a wall. You and me could carry the smallest, and Aaron 'ud carry the rest—I know he would.'

'Eh, my precious un,' said Silas, 'there isn't enough stones to go all round; and as for you carrying, why, wi' your little arms you couldn't carry a stone no bigger than a turnip. You're dillicate made, my dear,' he added, with a tender intonation—'that's what Mrs Winthrop says.'

'O, I'm stronger than you think, daddy,' said Eppie; 'and if there wasn't stones enough to go all round, why they'll go part o' the way, and then it'll be easier to get sticks and things for the rest. See here, round the big pit, what a many stones!'

She skipped forward to the pit, meaning to lift one of the stones and exhibit her strength, but she started back in surprise.

'O, father, just come and look here,' she exclaimed—'come and see how the water's gone down since yesterday. Why, yesterday the pit was ever so full!'

'Well, to be sure,' said Silas, coming to her side. 'Why, that's the draining they've begun on, since harvest, i' Mr Osgood's fields, I reckon. The foreman said to me the other day, when I passed by 'em, "Master Marner," he said, "I shouldn't wonder if we lay your bit o' waste as dry as a bone." It was Mr Godfrey Cass, he said, had gone into the draining: he'd been taking these fields o' Mr Osgood.'

'How odd it'll seem to have the old pit dried up!' said Eppie, turning away, and stooping to lift rather a large stone. 'See, daddy, I can carry this quite well,' she said, going along with much energy for a few steps, but presently letting it fall.

'Ah, you're fine and strong, aren't you?' said Silas, while Eppie shook her aching arms and laughed. 'Come, come, let us go and sit down on the bank against the stile there, and have no more lifting. You might hurt yourself, child. You'd need have somebody to work for you—and my arm isn't overstrong.'

Silas uttered the last sentence slowly, as if it implied more than met the ear; and Eppie, when they sat down on the bank, nestled close to his side, and, taking hold caressingly of the arm that was not over strong, held it on her lap, while Silas puffed again dutifully at the pipe, which occupied his other arm. An ash in the hedgerow behind made a fretted screen from the sun, and threw happy playful shadows all about them.

'Father,' said Eppie, very gently, after they had been sitting in silence a little while, 'if I was to be married, ought I to be married with my mother's ring?'

Silas gave an almost imperceptible start, though the question fell in with the under-current of thought in his own mind, and then said, in a subdued tone, 'Why, Eppie, have you been a-thinking on it?'

'Only this last week, father,' said Eppie, ingenuously, 'since Aaron talked to me about it.'

'And what did he say?' said Silas, still in the same subdued way, as if he were anxious lest he should fall into the slightest tone that was not for Eppie's good.

'He said he should like to be married, because he was a-going in four-and-twenty, and had got a deal of gardening work, now Mr Mott's given up; and he goes twice a-week regular to Mr Cass's, and once to Mr Osgood's, and they're going to take him on at the Rectory.'

'And who is it as he's wanting to marry?' said Silas, with rather a sad smile.

'Why, me, to be sure, daddy,' said Eppie, with dimpling laughter, kissing her father's cheek; 'as if he'd want to marry anybody else!'

'And you mean to have him, do you?' said Silas.

'Yes, some time,' said Eppie, 'I don't know when. Everybody's married some time, Aaron says. But I told him that wasn't true: for, I said, look at father—he's never been married.'

'No, child,' said Silas, 'your father was a lone man till you was sent to him.'

'But you'll never be lone again, father,' said Eppie, tenderly. 'That was what Aaron said—"I could never think o' taking you away from

Master Marner, Eppie." And I said, "It 'ud be no use if you did, Aaron." And he wants us all to live together, so as you needn't work a bit, father, only what's for your own pleasure; and he'd be as good as a son to you—that was what he said.'

'And should you like that, Eppie?' said Silas, looking at her.

'I shouldn't mind it, father,' said Eppie, quite simply. 'And I should like things to be so as you needn't work much. But if it wasn't for that, I'd sooner things didn't change. I'm very happy: I like Aaron to be fond of me, and come and see us often, and behave pretty to you—he always *does* behave pretty to you, doesn't he, father?'

'Yes, child, nobody could behave better,' said Silas, emphatically. 'He's his mother's lad.'

'But I don't want any change,' said Eppie. 'I should like to go on a long, long while, just as we are. Only Aaron does want a change; and he made me cry a bit—only a bit—because he said I didn't care for him, for if I cared for him I should want us to be married, as he did.'

'Eh, my blessed child,' said Silas, laying down his pipe as if it were useless to pretend to smoke any longer, 'you're o'er young to be married. We'll ask Mrs Winthrop—we'll ask Aaron's mother what *she* thinks: if there's a right thing to do, she'll come at it. But there's this to be thought on, Eppie: things *will* change, whether we like it or no; things won't go on for a long while just as they are and no difference. I shall get older and helplesser, and be a burden on you, belike, if I don't go away from you altogether. Not as I mean you'd think me a burden—I know you wouldn't—but it 'ud be hard upon you; and when I look for'ard to that, I like to think as you'd have somebody else besides me—somebody young and strong, as 'll outlast your own life, and take care on you to the end.' Silas paused, and, resting his wrists on his knees, lifted his hands up and down meditatively as he looked on the ground.

'Then, would you like me to be married, father?' said Eppie, with a little trembling in her voice.

'I'll not be the man to say no, Eppie,' said Silas, emphatically; 'but we'll ask your god-mother. She'll wish the right thing by you and her son too.'

'There they come, then,' said Eppie. 'Let us go and meet 'em. O the pipe! won't you have it lit again, father?' said Eppie, lifting that medicinal appliance from the ground.

'Nay, child,' said Silas, 'I've done enough for to-day. I think, mayhap, a little of it does me more good than so much at once.'

CHAPTER XVII

WHILE Silas and Eppie were seated on the bank discoursing in the fleckered shade of the ash-tree, Miss Priscilla Lammeter was resisting her sister's arguments, that it would be better to take tea at the Red House, and let her father have a long nap, than drive home to the Warrens so soon after dinner. The family party (of four only) were seated round the table in the dark wainscoted parlour, with the Sunday dessert before them, of fresh filberts,* apples, and pears, duly ornamented with leaves by Nancy's own hand before the bells had rung for church.

A great change has come over the dark wainscoted parlour since we saw it in Godfrey's bachelor days, and under the wifeless reign of the old Squire. Now all is polish, on which no yesterday's dust is ever allowed to rest, from the yard's width of oaken boards round the carpet, to the old Squire's gun and whips and walking-sticks, ranged on the stag's antlers above the mantelpiece. All other signs of sporting and outdoor occupation Nancy has removed to another room; but she has brought into the Red House the habit of filial reverence, and preserves sacredly in a place of honour these relics of her husband's departed father. The tankards are on the side-table still, but the bossed silver is undimmed by handling, and there are no dregs to send forth unpleasant suggestions: the only prevailing scent is of the lavender and rose-leaves that fill the vases of Derbyshire spar.* All is purity and order in this once dreary room, for, fifteen years ago, it was entered by a new presiding spirit.

'Now, father,' said Nancy, '*is* there any call for you to go home to tea? Mayn't you just as well stay with us?—such a beautiful evening as it's likely to be.'

The old gentleman had been talking with Godfrey about the increasing poor-rate and the ruinous times,* and had not heard the dialogue between his daughters.

'My dear, you must ask Priscilla,' he said, in the once firm voice, now become rather broken. 'She manages me and the farm too.'

'And reason good as I should manage you, father,' said Priscilla, 'else you'd be giving yourself your death with rheumatism. And as for the farm, if anything turns out wrong, as it can't but do in these times, there's nothing kills a man so soon as having nobody to find fault with but himself. It's a deal the best way o' being master, to let somebody else do the ordering, and keep the blaming in your own hands. It 'ud save many a man a stroke, *I* believe.'

'Well, well, my dear,' said her father, with a quiet laugh, 'I didn't say you don't manage for everybody's good.'

'Then manage so as you may stay tea, Priscilla,' said Nancy, putting her hand on her sister's arm affectionately. 'Come now; and we'll go round the garden while father has his nap.'

'My dear child, he'll have a beautiful nap in the gig, for I shall drive. And as for staying tea, I can't hear of it; for there's this dairy-maid, now she knows she's to be married, turned Michaelmas,* she'd as lief pour the new milk into the pig-trough as into the pans. That's the way with 'em all: it's as if they thought the world 'ud be new-made because they're to be married. So come and let me put my bonnet on, and there'll be time for us to walk round the garden while the horse is being put in.'

When the sisters were treading the neatly-swept garden-walks, between the bright turf that contrasted pleasantly with the dark cones and arches and wall-like hedges of yew, Priscilla said—

'I'm as glad as anything at your husband's making that exchange o' land with cousin Osgood, and beginning the dairying. It's a thousand pities you didn't do it before; for it'll give you something to fill your mind. There's nothing like a dairy if folks want a bit o' worrit to make the days pass. For as for rubbing furniture, when you can once see your face in a table there's nothing else to look for; but there's always something fresh with the dairy; for even in the depths o' winter there's some pleasure in conquering the butter, and making it come whether or no. My dear,' added Priscilla, pressing her sister's hand affectionately as they walked side by side, 'you'll never be low when you've got a dairy.'

'Ah, Priscilla,' said Nancy, returning the pressure with a grateful glance of her clear eyes, 'but it won't make up to Godfrey: a dairy's not so much to a man. And it's only what he cares for that ever makes me low. I'm contented with the blessings we have, if he could be contented.'

'It drives me past patience,' said Priscilla, impetuously, 'that way o' the men—always wanting and wanting, and never easy with what they've got: they can't sit comfortable in their chairs when they've neither ache nor pain, but either they must stick a pipe in their mouths, to make 'em better than well, or else they must be swallowing something strong, though they're forced to make haste before the next meal comes in. But joyful be it spoken, our father was never that sort o' man. And if it had pleased God to make you ugly, like me, so as the men wouldn't ha' run after you, we might have kept to our own family, and had nothing to do with folks as have got uneasy blood in their veins.'

'O don't say so, Priscilla,' said Nancy, repenting that she had called forth this outburst; 'nobody has any occasion to find fault with Godfrey. It's natural he should be disappointed at not having any children: every man likes to have somebody to work for and lay by for, and he always counted so on making a fuss with 'em when they were little. There's many another man 'ud hanker more than he does. He's the best of husbands.'

'O, I know,' said Priscilla, smiling sarcastically, 'I know the way o' wives; they set one on to abuse their husbands, and then they turn round on one and praise 'em as if they wanted to sell 'em. But father 'll be waiting for me; we must turn now.'

The large gig with the steady old grey was at the front door, and Mr Lammeter was already on the stone steps, passing the time in recalling to Godfrey what very fine points Speckle had when his master used to ride him.

'I always *would* have a good horse, you know,' said the old gentleman, not liking that spirited time to be quite effaced from the memory of his juniors.

'Mind you bring Nancy to the Warrens before the week's out, Mr Cass,' was Priscilla's parting injunction, as she took the reins, and shook them gently, by way of friendly incitement to Speckle.

'I shall just take a turn to the fields against the Stone-pits, Nancy, and look at the draining,' said Godfrey.

'You'll be in again by tea-time, dear?'

'O yes, I shall be back in an hour.'

It was Godfrey's custom on a Sunday afternoon to do a little contemplative farming in a leisurely walk. Nancy seldom accompanied him; for the women of her generation—unless, like Priscilla, they took to outdoor management—were not given to much walking beyond their own house and garden, finding sufficient exercise in domestic duties. So, when Priscilla was not with her, she usually sat with Mant's Bible* before her, and after following the text with her eyes for a little while, she would gradually permit them to wander as her thoughts had already insisted on wandering.

But Nancy's Sunday thoughts were rarely quite out of keeping with the devout and reverential intention implied by the book spread open before her. She was not theologically instructed enough to discern very clearly the relation between the sacred documents of the past which she opened without method, and her own obscure, simple life; but the spirit of rectitude, and the sense of responsibility for the effect of her conduct on others, which were strong elements in Nancy's character, had made it a habit with her to scrutinise her past feelings and actions with self-questioning solicitude. Her mind not being courted by a great variety of subjects, she filled the vacant moments by living inwardly, again and again, through all her remembered experience, especially through the fifteen years of her married time, in which her life and its significance had been doubled. She recalled the small details, the words, tones, and looks, in the critical scenes which had opened a new epoch for her by giving her a deeper insight into the relations and trials of life, or which had called on her for some little effort of forbearance, or of painful adherence to an imagined or real duty—asking herself continually whether she had been in any respect blamable. This excessive rumination and self-questioning is perhaps a morbid habit inevitable to a mind of much moral sensibility when shut out from its due share of outward activity and of practical claims on its affections—inevitable to a noble-hearted, childless woman, when her lot is narrow. 'I can do so little—have I done it all well?' is the perpetually recurring thought; and there are no voices calling her away from that soliloquy, no peremptory demands to divert energy from vain regret or superfluous scruple.

There was one main thread of painful experience in Nancy's married life, and on it hung certain deeply-felt scenes, which were the oftenest revived in retrospect. The short dialogue with Priscilla in the garden had determined the current of retrospect in that frequent direction this particular Sunday afternoon. The first wandering of her thought from the text, which she still attempted dutifully to follow with her eyes and silent lips, was into an imaginary enlargement of the defence she had set up for her husband against Priscilla's implied blame. The vindication of the loved object is the best balm affection can find for its wounds:—'A man must have so much on his mind,' is the belief by which a wife often supports a cheerful face under rough answers and unfeeling words. And Nancy's deepest wounds had all come from the perception that the absence of children from their hearth was dwelt on in her husband's mind as a privation to which he could not reconcile himself.

Yet sweet Nancy might have been expected to feel still more keenly the denial of a blessing to which she had looked forward with all the varied expectations and preparations, solemn and prettily trivial, which fill the mind of a loving woman when she expects to become a mother. Was there not a drawer filled with the neat work of her hands, all unworn and untouched, just as she had arranged it there fourteen years ago—just, but for one little dress, which had been made the burial-dress? But under this immediate personal trial Nancy was so firmly unmurmuring, that years ago she had suddenly renounced the habit of visiting this drawer, lest she should in this way be cherishing a longing for what was not given.

Perhaps it was this very severity towards any indulgence of what she held to be sinful regret in herself, that made her shrink from applying her own standard to her husband. 'It is very different—it is much worse for a man to be disappointed in that way: a woman can always be satisfied with devoting herself to her husband, but a man wants something that will make him look forward more—and sitting by the fire is so much duller to him than to a woman.' And always, when Nancy reached this point in her meditations—trying, with predetermined sympathy, to see everything as Godfrey saw it—there came a renewal of self-questioning. *Had* she done everything in her power to lighten Godfrey's privation? Had she really been right in the resistance which had cost her so much pain six years ago, and again four years ago—the resistance to her husband's wish that they should adopt a child? Adoption was more remote from the ideas and habits of that time than of our own;* still Nancy had her opinion on it. It was as necessary to her mind to have an opinion on all topics, not exclusively masculine, that had come under her notice, as for her to have a precisely marked place for every article of her personal property: and her opinions were always principles to be unwaveringly acted on. They were firm, not because of their basis, but because she held them with a tenacity inseparable from her mental action. On all the duties and proprieties of life, from filial behaviour to the arrangements of the evening toilet, pretty Nancy Lammeter, by the time she was three-and-twenty, had her unalterable little code, and had formed every one of her habits in strict accordance with that code. She carried these decided judgments within her in the most unobtrusive way: they rooted themselves in her mind, and grew there as quietly as grass. Years ago, we know, she insisted on dressing like Priscilla, because 'it was right for sisters to dress alike,' and because 'she would do what was right if she wore a gown dyed with cheese-colouring.' That was a trivial but typical instance of the mode in which Nancy's life was regulated.

It was one of those rigid principles, and no petty egoistic feeling, which had been the ground of Nancy's difficult resistance to her husband's wish. To adopt a child, because children of your own had been denied you, was to try and choose your lot in spite of Providence: the adopted child, she was convinced, would never turn out well, and would be a curse to those who had wilfully and rebelliously sought what it was clear that, for some high reason, they were better without. When you saw a thing was not meant to be, said Nancy, it was a bounden duty to leave off so much as wishing for it. And so far, perhaps, the wisest of men could scarcely make more than a verbal improvement in her principle. But the conditions under which she held it apparent that a thing was not meant to be, depended on a more peculiar mode of thinking. She would have given up making a purchase at a particular place if, on three successive times, rain, or some other cause of Heaven's sending, had formed an obstacle; and she would have anticipated a broken limb or other heavy misfortune to any one who persisted in spite of such indications.

'But why should you think the child would turn out ill?' said Godfrey, in his remonstrances. 'She has thriven as well as child can do with the weaver; and *he* adopted her. There isn't such a pretty little girl anywhere else in the parish, or one fitter for the station we could give her. Where can be the likelihood of her being a curse to anybody?'

'Yes, my dear Godfrey,' said Nancy, who was sitting with her hands tightly clasped together, and with yearning, regretful affection in her eyes. 'The child may not turn out ill with the weaver. But, then, he didn't go to seek her, as we should be doing. It will be wrong: I feel sure it will. Don't you remember what that lady we met at the Royston Baths told us about the child her sister adopted? That was the only adopting I ever heard of: and the child was transported* when it was twenty-three. Dear Godfrey, don't ask me to do what I know is wrong: I should never be happy again. I know it's very hard for *you*—it's easier for me—but it's the will of Providence.'

It might seem singular that Nancy—with her religious theory pieced together out of narrow social traditions, fragments of church doctrine imperfectly understood, and girlish reasonings on her small experience—should have arrived by herself at a way of thinking so nearly akin to that of many devout people whose beliefs are held in the shape of a system quite remote from her knowledge: singular, if we did not know that human beliefs, like all other natural growths, elude the barriers of system.

Godfrey had from the first specified Eppie, then about twelve years old, as a child suitable for them to adopt. It had never occurred to him that Silas would rather part with his life than with Eppie. Surely the weaver would wish the best to the child he had taken so much trouble with, and would be glad that such good fortune should happen to her: she would always be very grateful to him, and he would be well provided for to the end of his life—provided for as the excellent part he had done by the child deserved. Was it not an appropriate thing for people in a higher station to take a charge off the hands of a man in a lower? It seemed an eminently appropriate thing to Godfrey, for reasons that were known only to himself; and by a common fallacy, he imagined the measure would be easy because he had private motives for desiring it. This was rather a coarse mode of estimating Silas's relation to Eppie; but we must remember that many of the impressions which Godfrey was likely to gather concerning the labouring people around him would favour the idea that deep affections can hardly go along with callous palms and scant means; and he had not had the opportunity, even if he had had the power, of entering intimately into all that was exceptional in the weaver's experience. It was only the want of adequate knowledge that could have made it possible for Godfrey deliberately to entertain an unfeeling project: his natural kindness had outlived that blighting time of cruel wishes, and Nancy's praise of him as a husband was not founded entirely on a wilful illusion.

'I was right,' she said to herself, when she had recalled all their scenes of discussion—'I feel I was right to say him nay, though it hurt me more than anything; but how good Godfrey has been about it! Many men would have been very angry with me for standing out against their wishes; and they might have thrown out that they'd had ill-luck in marrying me; but Godfrey has never been the man to say me an unkind word. It's only what he can't hide: everything seems so blank to him, I know; and the land—what a difference it 'ud make to him, when he goes to see after things, if he'd children growing up that he was doing it all for! But I won't murmur; and perhaps if he'd married a woman who'd have had children, she'd have vexed him in other ways.'

This possibility was Nancy's chief comfort; and to give it greater strength, she laboured to make it impossible that any other wife should have had more perfect tenderness. She had been *forced* to vex him by that one denial. Godfrey was not insensible to her loving effort, and did Nancy no injustice as to the motives of her obstinacy. It was impossible to have lived with her fifteen years and not be aware that an unselfish clinging to the right, and a sincerity clear as the flower-born dew, were her main characteristics; indeed, Godfrey felt this so strongly, that his own more wavering nature, too averse to facing difficulty to be unvaryingly simple and truthful, was kept in a certain awe of this gentle wife who watched his looks with a yearning to obey them. It seemed to him impossible that he should ever confess to her the truth about Eppie: she would never recover from the repulsion the story of his earlier marriage would create, told to her now, after that long concealment. And the child, too, he thought, must become an object of repulsion: the very sight of her would be painful. The shock to Nancy's mingled pride and ignorance of the world's evil might even be too much for her delicate frame. Since he had married her with that secret on his heart, he must keep it there to the last. Whatever else he did, he could not make an irreparable breach between himself and this long-loved wife.

Meanwhile, why could he not make up his mind to the absence of children from a hearth brightened by such a wife? Why did his mind fly uneasily to that void, as if it were the sole reason why life was not thoroughly joyous to him? I suppose it is the way with all men and women who reach middle age without the clear perception that life never *can* be thoroughly joyous: under the vague dullness of the grey hours, dissatisfaction seeks a definite object, and finds it in the privation of an untried good. Dissatisfaction seated musingly on a childless hearth, thinks with envy of the father whose return is greeted by young voices—seated at the meal where the little heads rise one above another like nursery plants, it sees a black care hovering behind every one of them, and thinks the impulses by which men abandon freedom, and seek for ties, are surely nothing but a brief madness. In Godfrey's case there were further reasons why his thoughts should be continually solicited by this one point in his lot: his conscience, never thoroughly easy about Eppie, now gave his childless home the aspect of a retribution; and as the time passed on, under Nancy's refusal to adopt her, any retrieval of his error became more and more difficult.

On this Sunday afternoon it was already four years since there had been any allusion to the subject between them, and Nancy supposed that it was for ever buried.

'I wonder if he'll mind it less or more as he gets older,' she thought; 'I'm afraid more. Aged people feel the miss of children: what would father do without Priscilla? And if I die, Godfrey will be very lonely—not holding together with his brothers much. But I won't be over-anxious, and trying to make things out beforehand: I must do my best for the present.'

With that last thought Nancy roused herself from her reverie, and turned her eyes again towards the forsaken page. It had been forsaken longer than she imagined, for she was presently surprised by the appearance of the servant with the tea-things. It was, in fact, a little before the usual time for tea; but Jane had her reasons.

'Is your master come into the yard, Jane?'

'No 'm, he isn't,' said Jane, with a slight emphasis, of which, however, her mistress took no notice.

'I don't know whether you've seen 'em, 'm,' continued Jane, after a pause, 'but there's folks making haste all one way, afore the front window. I doubt something's happened. There's niver a man to be seen i' the yard, else I'd send and see. I've been up into the top attic, but there's no seeing anything for trees. I hope nobody's hurt, that's all.'

'O, no, I daresay there's nothing much the matter,' said Nancy. 'It's perhaps Mr Snell's bull got out again, as he did before.'

'I wish he mayn't gore anybody then, that's all,' said Jane, not altogether despising a hypothesis which covered a few imaginary calamities.

'That girl is always terrifying me,' thought Nancy; 'I wish Godfrey would come in.'

She went to the front window and looked as far as she could see along the road, with an uneasiness which she felt to be childish, for there were now no such signs of excitement as Jane had spoken of, and Godfrey would not be likely to return by the village road, but by the fields. She continued to stand, however, looking at the placid churchyard with the long shadows of the gravestones across the bright green hillocks, and at the glowing autumn colours of the Rectory trees beyond. Before such calm external beauty the presence of a vague fear is more distinctly felt—like a raven flapping its slow wing across the sunny air. Nancy wished more and more that Godfrey would come in.

CHAPTER XVIII

Some one opened the door at the other end of the room, and Nancy felt that it was her husband. She turned from the window with gladness in her eyes, for the wife's chief dread was stilled.

'Dear, I'm so thankful you're come,' she said, going towards him. 'I began to get . . .'

She paused abruptly, for Godfrey was laying down his hat with trembling hands, and turned towards her with a pale face and a strange unanswering glance, as if he saw her indeed, but saw her as part of a scene invisible to herself. She laid her hand on his arm, not daring to speak again; but he left the touch unnoticed, and threw himself into his chair.

Jane was already at the door with the hissing urn. 'Tell her to keep away, will you?' said Godfrey; and when the door was closed again he exerted himself to speak more distinctly.

'Sit down, Nancy—there,' he said, pointing to a chair opposite him. 'I came back as soon as I could, to hinder anybody's telling you but me. I've had a great shock—but I care most about the shock it'll be to you.'

'It isn't father and Priscilla?' said Nancy, with quivering lips, clasping her hands together tightly on her lap.

'No, it's nobody living,' said Godfrey, unequal to the considerate skill with which he would have wished to make his revelation. 'It's Dunstan—my brother Dunstan, that we lost sight of sixteen years ago. We've found him—found his body—his skeleton.'

The deep dread Godfrey's look had created in Nancy made her feel these words a relief. She sat in comparative calmness to hear what else he had to tell. He went on:

'The Stone-pit has gone dry suddenly—from the draining, I suppose; and there he lies—has lain for sixteen years, wedged between two great stones. There's his watch and seals, and there's my gold-handled hunting-whip, with my name on: he took it away, without my knowing, the day he went hunting on Wildfire, the last time he was seen.'

Godfrey paused: it was not so easy to say what came next. 'Do you think he drowned himself?' said Nancy, almost wondering that her husband should be so deeply shaken by what had happened all those years ago to an unloved brother, of whom worse things had been augured.

'No, he fell in,' said Godfrey, in a low but distinct voice, as if he felt some deep meaning in the fact. Presently he added: 'Dunstan was the man that robbed Silas Marner.'

The blood rushed to Nancy's face and neck at this surprise and shame, for she had been bred up to regard even a distant kinship with crime as a dishonour.

'O Godfrey!' she said, with compassion in her tone, for she had immediately reflected that the dishonour must be felt still more keenly by her husband.

'There was the money in the pit,' he continued—'all the weaver's money. Everything's been gathered up, and they're taking the skeleton to the Rainbow. But I came back to tell you: there was no hindering it; you must know.'

He was silent, looking on the ground for two long minutes. Nancy would have said some words of comfort under this disgrace, but she refrained, from an instinctive sense that there was something behind—that Godfrey had something else to tell her. Presently he lifted his eyes to her face, and kept them fixed on her, as he said—

'Everything comes to light, Nancy, sooner or later. When God Almighty wills it, our secrets are found out. I've lived with a secret on my mind, but I'll keep it from you no longer. I wouldn't have you know it by somebody else, and not by me—I wouldn't have you find it out after I'm dead. I'll tell you now. It's been "I will" and "I won't" with me all my life—I'll make sure of myself now.'

Nancy's utmost dread had returned. The eyes of the husband and wife met with awe in them, as at a crisis which suspended affection.

'Nancy,' said Godfrey, slowly, 'when I married you, I hid something from you—something I ought to have told you. That woman Marner found dead in the snow—Eppie's mother—that wretched woman—was my wife: Eppie is my child.'

He paused, dreading the effect of his confession. But Nancy sat quite still, only that her eyes dropped and ceased to meet his. She was pale and quiet as a meditative statue, clasping her hands on her lap.

'You'll never think the same of me again,' said Godfrey, after a little while, with some tremor in his voice.

She was silent.

'I oughtn't to have left the child unowned: I oughtn't to have kept it from you. But I couldn't bear to give you up, Nancy. I was led away into marrying her—I suffered for it.'

Still Nancy was silent, looking down; and he almost expected that she would presently get up and say she would go to her father's. How could she have any mercy for faults that must seem so black to her, with her simple severe notions?

But at last she lifted up her eyes to his again and spoke. There was no indignation in her voice—only deep regret.

'Godfrey, if you had but told me this six years ago, we could have done some of our duty by the child. Do you think I'd have refused to take her in, if I'd known she was yours?'

At that moment Godfrey felt all the bitterness of an error that was not simply futile, but had defeated its own end. He had not measured this wife with whom he had lived so long. But she spoke again, with more agitation.

'And—O, Godfrey—if we'd had her from the first, if you'd taken to her as you ought, she'd have loved me for her mother—and you'd have been happier with me: I could better have bore my little baby dying, and our life might have been more like what we used to think it 'ud be.'

The tears fell, and Nancy ceased to speak.

'But you wouldn't have married me then, Nancy, if I'd told you,' said Godfrey, urged, in the bitterness of his self-reproach, to prove to himself that his conduct had not been utter folly. 'You may think you would now, but you wouldn't then. With your pride and your father's, you'd have hated having anything to do with me after the talk there'd have been.'

'I can't say what I should have done about that, Godfrey. I should never have married anybody else. But I wasn't worth doing wrong for—nothing is in this world. Nothing is so good as it seems beforehand—not even our marrying wasn't, you see.' There was a faint sad smile on Nancy's face as she said the last words.

'I'm a worse man than you thought I was, Nancy,' said Godfrey, rather tremulously. 'Can you forgive me ever?'

'The wrong to me is but little, Godfrey: you've made it up to me—you've been good to me for fifteen years. It's another you did the wrong to; and I doubt it can never be all made up for.'

'But we can take Eppie now,' said Godfrey. 'I won't mind the world knowing at last. I'll be plain and open for the rest o' my life.'

'It'll be different coming to us, now she's grown up,' said Nancy, shaking her head sadly. 'But it's your duty to acknowledge her and provide for her; and I'll do my part by her, and pray to God Almighty to make her love me.'

'Then we'll go together to Silas Marner's this very night, as soon as everything's quiet at the Stone-pits.'

CHAPTER XIX

BETWEEN eight and nine o'clock that evening, Eppie and Silas were seated alone in the cottage. After the great excitement the weaver had undergone from the events of the afternoon, he had felt a longing for this quietude, and had even begged Mrs Winthrop and Aaron, who had naturally lingered behind every one else, to leave him alone with his child. The excitement had not passed away: it had only reached that stage when the keenness of the susceptibility makes external stimulus intolerable—when there is no sense of weariness, but rather an intensity of inward life, under which sleep is an impossibility. Any one who has watched such moments in other men remembers the brightness of the eyes and the strange definiteness that comes over coarse features from that transient influence. It is as if a new fineness of ear for all spiritual voices had sent wonder-working vibrations through the heavy mortal frame—as if 'beauty born of murmuring sound'* had passed into the face of the listener.

Silas's face showed that sort of transfiguration, as he sat in his arm-chair and looked at Eppie. She had drawn her own chair towards his knees, and leaned forward, holding both his hands, while she looked up at him. On the table near them, lit by a candle, lay the recovered gold—the old long-loved gold, ranged in orderly heaps, as Silas used to range it in the days when it was his only joy. He had been telling her how he used to count it every night, and how his soul was utterly desolate till she was sent to him.

'At first, I'd a sort o' feeling come across me now and then,' he was saying in a subdued tone, 'as if you might be changed into the gold again; for sometimes, turn my head which way I would, I seemed to see the gold; and I thought I should be glad if I could feel it, and find it was come back. But that didn't last long. After a bit, I should have thought it was a curse come again, if it had drove you from me, for I'd got to feel the need o' your looks and your voice and the touch o' your little fingers. You didn't know then, Eppie, when you were such a little un—you didn't know what your old father Silas felt for you.'

'But I know now, father,' said Eppie. 'If it hadn't been for you, they'd have taken me to the workhouse, and there'd have been nobody to love me.'

'Eh, my precious child, the blessing was mine. If you hadn't been sent to save me, I should ha' gone to the grave in my misery. The money was taken away from me in time; and you see it's been kept—kept till it was wanted for you. It's wonderful—our life is wonderful.'

Silas sat in silence a few minutes, looking at the money. 'It takes no hold of me now,' he said, ponderingly—'the money doesn't. I wonder if it ever could again—I doubt it might, if I lost you, Eppie. I might come to think I was forsaken again, and lose the feeling that God was good to me.'

At that moment there was a knocking at the door; and Eppie was obliged to rise without answering Silas. Beautiful she looked, with the tenderness of gathering tears in her eyes and a slight flush on her cheeks, as she stepped to open the door. The flush deepened when she saw Mr and Mrs Godfrey Cass. She made her little rustic curtsy, and held the door wide for them to enter.

'We're disturbing you very late, my dear,' said Mrs Cass, taking Eppie's hand, and looking in her face with an expression of anxious interest and admiration. Nancy herself was pale and tremulous.

Eppie, after placing chairs for Mr and Mrs Cass, went to stand against Silas, opposite to them.

'Well, Marner,' said Godfrey, trying to speak with perfect firmness, 'it's a great comfort to me to see you with your money again, that you've been deprived of so many years. It was one of my family did you the wrong—the more grief to me—and I feel bound to make up to you for it in every way. Whatever I can do for you will be nothing but paying a debt, even if I looked no further than the robbery. But there are other things I'm beholden—shall be beholden to you for, Marner.'

Godfrey checked himself. It had been agreed between him and his wife that the subject of his fatherhood should be approached very carefully, and that, if possible, the disclosure should be reserved for the future, so that it might be made to Eppie gradually. Nancy had urged this, because she felt strongly the painful light in which Eppie must inevitably see the relation between her father and mother.

Silas, always ill at ease when he was being spoken to by 'betters,' such as Mr Cass—tall, powerful, florid men, seen chiefly on horseback—answered with some constraint—

'Sir, I've a deal to thank you for a'ready. As for the robbery, I count it no loss to me. And if I did, you couldn't help it: you aren't answerable for it.'

'You may look at it in that way, Marner, but I never can; and I hope you'll let me act according to my own feeling of what's just. I know you're easily contented: you've been a hard-working man all your life.'

'Yes, sir, yes,' said Marner, meditatively. 'I should ha' been bad off without my work: it was what I held by when everything else was gone from me.'

'Ah,' said Godfrey, applying Marner's words simply to his bodily wants, 'it was a good trade for you in this country, because there's been a great deal of linen-weaving to be done. But you're getting rather past such close work, Marner: it's time you laid by and had some rest. You look a good deal pulled down, though you're not an old man, *are* you?'

'Fifty-five, as near as I can say, sir,' said Silas.

'O, why, you may live thirty years longer—look at old Macey! And that money on the table, after all, is but little. It won't go far either way—whether it's put out to interest, or you were to live on it as long as it would last: it wouldn't go far if you'd nobody to keep but yourself, and you've had two to keep for a good many years now.'

'Eh, sir,' said Silas, unaffected by anything Godfrey was saying, 'I'm in no fear o' want. We shall do very well—Eppie and me 'ull do well enough. There's few working-folks have got so much laid by as that. I don't know what it is to gentlefolks, but I look upon it as a deal—almost too much. And as for us, it's little we want.'

'Only the garden, father,' said Eppie, blushing up to the ears the moment after.

'You love a garden, do you, my dear?' said Nancy, thinking that this turn in the point of view might help her husband. 'We should agree in that: I give a deal of time to the garden.'

'Ah, there's plenty of gardening at the Red House,' said Godfrey, surprised at the difficulty he found in approaching a proposition which had seemed so easy to him in the distance. 'You've done a good part by Eppie, Marner, for sixteen years. It 'ud be a great comfort to you to see her well provided for, wouldn't it? She looks blooming and healthy, but not fit for any hardships: she doesn't look like a strapping girl come of working parents. You'd like to see her taken care of by those who can leave her well off, and make a lady of her; she's more fit for it than for a rough life, such as she might come to have in a few years' time.'

A slight flush came over Marner's face, and disappeared, like a passing gleam. Eppie was simply wondering Mr Cass should talk so about things that seemed to have nothing to do with reality; but Silas was hurt and uneasy.

'I don't take your meaning, sir,' he answered, not having words at command to express the mingled feelings with which he had heard Mr Cass's words.

'Well, my meaning is this, Marner,' said Godfrey, determined to come to the point. 'Mrs Cass and I, you know, have no children—nobody to be the better for our good home and everything else we have—more than enough for ourselves. And we should like to have somebody in the place of a daughter to us—we should like to have Eppie, and treat her in every way as our own child. It u'd be a great comfort to you in your old age, I hope, to see her fortune made in that way, after you've been at the trouble of bringing her up so well. And it's right you should have every reward for that. And Eppie, I'm sure, will always love you and be grateful to you: she'd come and see you very often, and we should all be on the look-out to do everything we could towards making you comfortable.'

A plain man like Godfrey Cass, speaking under some embarrassment, necessarily blunders on words that are coarser than his intentions, and that are likely to fall gratingly on susceptible feelings. While he had been speaking, Eppie had quietly passed her arm behind Silas's head, and let her hand rest against it caressingly: she felt him trembling violently. He was silent for some moments when Mr Cass had ended—powerless under the conflict of emotions, all alike painful. Eppie's heart was swelling at the sense that her father was in distress; and she was just going to lean down and speak to him, when one struggling dread at last gained the mastery over every other in Silas, and he said, faintly—

'Eppie, my child, speak. I won't stand in your way. Thank Mr and Mrs Cass.'

Eppie took her hand from her father's head, and came forward a step. Her cheeks were flushed, but not with shyness this time: the sense that her father was in doubt and suffering banished that sort of self-consciousness. She dropped a low curtsy, first to Mrs Cass and then to Mr Cass, and said—

'Thank you, ma'am—thank you, sir. But I can't leave my father, nor own anybody nearer than him. And I don't want to be a lady—thank you all the same' (here Eppie dropped another curtsy). 'I couldn't give up the folks I've been used to.'

Eppie's lips began to tremble a little at the last words. She retreated to her father's chair again, and held him round the neck: while Silas, with a subdued sob, put up his hand to grasp hers.

The tears were in Nancy's eyes, but her sympathy with Eppie was, naturally, divided with distress on her husband's account. She dared not speak, wondering what was going on in her husband's mind.

Godfrey felt an irritation inevitable to almost all of us when we encounter an unexpected obstacle. He had been full of his own penitence and resolution to retrieve his error as far as the time was left to him; he was possessed with all-important feelings, that were to lead to a predetermined course of action which he had fixed on as the right, and he was not prepared to enter with lively appreciation into other people's feelings counteracting his virtuous resolves. The agitation with which he spoke again was not quite unmixed with anger.

'But I've a claim on you, Eppie—the strongest of all claims. It's my duty, Marner, to own Eppie as my child, and provide for her. She's my own child: her mother was my wife. I've a natural claim on her that must stand before every other.'

Eppie had given a violent start, and turned quite pale. Silas, on the contrary, who had been relieved, by Eppie's answer, from the dread lest his mind should be in opposition to hers, felt the spirit of resistance in him set free, not without a touch of parental fierceness. 'Then, sir,' he answered, with an accent of bitterness that had been silent in him since the memorable day when his youthful hope had perished—'then, sir, why didn't you say so sixteen year ago, and claim her before I'd come to love her, i'stead o' coming to take her from me now, when you might as well take the heart out o' my body? God gave her to me because you turned your back upon her, and He looks upon her as mine: you've no right to her! When a man turns a blessing from his door, it falls to them as take it in.'

'I know that, Marner. I was wrong. I've repented of my conduct in that matter,' said Godfrey, who could not help feeling the edge of Silas's words.

'I'm glad to hear it, sir,' said Marner, with gathering excitement; 'but repentance doesn't alter what's been going on for sixteen year. Your coming now and saying "I'm her father" doesn't alter the feelings inside us. It's me she's been calling her father ever since she could say the word.'

'But I think you might look at the thing more reasonably, Marner,' said Godfrey, unexpectedly awed by the weaver's direct truth-speaking. 'It isn't as if she was to be taken quite away from you, so that you'd never see her again. She'll be very near you, and come to see you very often. She'll feel just the same towards you.'

'Just the same?' said Marner, more bitterly than ever. 'How'll she feel just the same for me as she does now, when we eat o' the same bit, and drink o' the same cup,* and think o' the same things from one day's end to another? Just the same? that's idle talk. You'd cut us i' two.'

Godfrey, unqualified by experience to discern the pregnancy of Marner's simple words, felt rather angry again. It seemed to him that the weaver was very selfish (a judgment readily passed by those who have never tested their own power of sacrifice) to oppose what was undoubtedly for Eppie's welfare; and he felt himself called upon, for her sake, to assert his authority.

'I should have thought, Marner,' he said, severely—'I should have thought your affection for Eppie would make you rejoice in what was for her good, even if it did call upon you to give up something. You ought to remember your own life's uncertain, and she's at an age now when her lot may soon be fixed in a way very different from what it would be in her father's home: she may marry some low working-man, and then, whatever I might do for her, I couldn't make her well-off. You're putting yourself in the way of her welfare; and though I'm sorry to hurt you after what you've done, and what I've left undone, I feel now it's my duty to insist on taking care of my own daughter. I want to do my duty.'

It would be difficult to say whether it were Silas or Eppie that was more deeply stirred by this last speech of Godfrey's. Thought had been very busy in Eppie as she listened to the contest between her old long-loved father and this new unfamiliar father who had suddenly come to fill the place of that black featureless shadow which had held the ring and placed it on her mother's finger. Her imagination had darted backward in conjectures, and forward in previsions, of what this revealed fatherhood implied; and there were words in Godfrey's last speech which helped to make the previsions especially definite. Not that these thoughts, either of past or future, determined her resolution—*that* was determined by the feelings which vibrated to every word Silas had uttered; but they raised, even apart from these feelings, a repulsion towards the offered lot and the newly-revealed father.

Silas, on the other hand, was again stricken in conscience, and alarmed lest Godfrey's accusation should be true—lest he should be raising his own will as an obstacle to Eppie's good. For many moments he was mute, struggling for the self-conquest necessary to the uttering of the difficult words. They came out tremulously.

'I'll say no more. Let it be as you will. Speak to the child. I'll hinder nothing.'

Even Nancy, with all the acute sensibility of her own affections, shared her husband's view, that Marner was not justifiable in his wish to retain Eppie, after her real father had avowed himself. She felt that it was a very hard trial for the poor weaver, but her code allowed no question that a father by blood must have a claim above that of any foster-father. Besides, Nancy, used all her life to plenteous circumstances and the privileges of 'respectability,' could not enter into the pleasures which early nurture and habit connect with all the little aims and efforts of the poor who are born poor: to her mind, Eppie, in being restored to her birthright, was entering on a too long withheld but unquestionable good. Hence she heard Silas's last words with relief, and thought, as Godfrey did, that their wish was achieved.

'Eppie, my dear,' said Godfrey, looking at his daughter, not without some embarrassment, under the sense that she was old enough to judge him, 'it'll always be our wish that you should show your love and gratitude to one who's been a father to you so many years, and we shall want to help you to make him comfortable in every way. But we hope you'll come to love us as well; and though I haven't been what a father should ha' been to you all these years, I wish to do the utmost in my power for you for the rest of my life, and provide for you as my only child. And you'll have the best of mothers in my wife—that'll be a blessing you haven't known since you were old enough to know it.'

'My dear, you'll be a treasure to me,' said Nancy, in her gentle voice. 'We shall want for nothing when we have our daughter.'

Eppie did not come forward and curtsy, as she had done before. She held Silas's hand in hers, and grasped it firmly—it was a weaver's hand, with a palm and finger-tips that were sensitive to such pressure—while she spoke with colder decision than before.

'Thank you, ma'am—thank you, sir, for your offers—they're very great, and far above my wish. For I should have no delight i' life any more if I was forced to go away from my father, and knew he was sitting at home, a-thinking of me and feeling lone. We've been used to be happy together every day, and I can't think o' no happiness without him. And he says he'd nobody i' the world till I was sent to him, and he'd have nothing when I was gone. And he's took care of me and loved me from the first, and I'll cleave to him as long as he lives, and nobody shall ever come between him and me.'

'But you must make sure, Eppie,' said Silas, in a low voice—'you must make sure as you won't ever be sorry, because you've made your choice to stay among poor folks, and with poor clothes and things, when you might ha' had everything o' the best.'

His sensitiveness on this point had increased as he listened to Eppie's words of faithful affection.

'I can never be sorry, father,' said Eppie. 'I shouldn't know what to think on or to wish for with fine things about me, as I haven't been used to. And it 'ud be poor work for me to put on things, and ride in a gig, and sit in a place at church, as 'ud make them as I'm fond of think me unfitting company for 'em. What could *I* care for then?'

Nancy looked at Godfrey with a pained questioning glance. But his eyes were fixed on the floor, where he was moving the end of his stick, as if he were pondering on something absently. She thought there was a word which might perhaps come better from her lips than from his.

'What you say is natural, my dear child—it's natural you should cling to those who've brought you up,' she said, mildly; 'but there's a duty you owe to your lawful father. There's perhaps something to be given up on more sides than one. When your father opens his home to you, I think it's right you shouldn't turn your back on it.'

'I can't feel as I've got any father but one,' said Eppie, impetuously, while the tears gathered. 'I've always thought of a little home where he'd sit i' the corner, and I should fend and do everything for him: I can't think o' no other home. I wasn't brought up to be a lady, and I can't turn my mind to it. I like the working-folks, and their victuals, and their ways. And,' she ended passionately, while the tears fell, 'I'm promised to marry a working-man, as 'll live with father, and help me to take care of him.'

Godfrey looked up at Nancy with a flushed face and smarting dilated eyes. This frustration of a purpose towards which he had set out under the exalted consciousness that he was about to compensate in some degree for the greatest demerit of his life, made him feel the air of the room stifling.

'Let us go,' he said, in an under-tone.

'We won't talk of this any longer now,' said Nancy, rising. 'We're your well-wishers, my dear—and yours too, Marner. We shall come and see you again. It's getting late now.'

In this way she covered her husband's abrupt departure, for Godfrey had gone straight to the door, unable to say more.

CHAPTER XX

NANCY and Godfrey walked home under the starlight in silence. When they entered the oaken parlour, Godfrey threw himself into his chair, while Nancy laid down her bonnet and shawl, and stood on the hearth near her husband, unwilling to leave him even for a few minutes, and yet fearing to utter any word lest it might jar on his feeling. At last Godfrey turned his head towards her, and their eyes met, dwelling in that meeting without any movement on either side. That quiet mutual gaze of a trusting husband and wife is like the first moment of rest or refuge from a great weariness or a great danger—not to be interfered with by speech or action which would distract the sensations from the fresh enjoyment of repose.

But presently he put out his hand, and as Nancy placed hers within it, he drew her towards him, and said—

'That's ended!'

She bent to kiss him, and then said, as she stood by his side, 'Yes, I'm afraid we must give up the hope of having her for a daughter. It wouldn't be right to want to force her to come to us against her will. We can't alter her bringing up and what's come of it.'

'No,' said Godfrey, with a keen decisiveness of tone, in contrast with his usually careless and unemphatic speech—'there's debts we can't pay like money debts, by paying extra for the years that have slipped by. While I've been putting off and putting off, the trees have been growing—it's too late now. Marner was in the right in what he said about a man's turning away a blessing from his door: it falls to somebody else. I wanted to pass for childless once, Nancy—I shall pass for childless now against my wish.'

Nancy did not speak immediately, but after a little while she asked—'You won't make it known, then, about Eppie's being your daughter?'

'No: where would be the good to anybody?—only harm. I must do what I can for her in the state of life she chooses. I must see who it is she's thinking of marrying.'

'If it won't do any good to make the thing known,' said Nancy, who thought she might now allow herself the relief of entertaining a feeling which she had tried to silence before, 'I should be very thankful for father and Priscilla never to be troubled with knowing what was done in the past, more than about Dunsey: it can't be helped, their knowing that.'

'I shall put it in my will—I think I shall put it in my will. I shouldn't like to leave anything to be found out, like this about Dunsey,' said Godfrey, meditatively. 'But I can't see anything but difficulties that 'ud come from telling it now. I must do what I can to make her happy in her own way. I've a notion,' he added, after a moment's pause, 'it's Aaron Winthrop she meant she was engaged to. I remember seeing him with her and Marner going away from church.'

'Well, he's very sober and industrious,' said Nancy, trying to view the matter as cheerfully as possible.

Godfrey fell into thoughtfulness again. Presently he looked up at Nancy sorrowfully, and said—

'She's a very pretty, nice girl, isn't she, Nancy?'

'Yes, dear; and with just your hair and eyes: I wondered it had never struck me before.'

'I think she took a dislike to me at the thought of my being her father: I could see a change in her manner after that.'

'She couldn't bear to think of not looking on Marner as her father,' said Nancy, not wishing to confirm her husband's painful impression.

'She thinks I did wrong by her mother as well as by her. She thinks me worse than I am. But she *must* think it: she can never know all. It's part of my punishment, Nancy, for my daughter to dislike me. I should never have got into that trouble if I'd been true to you—if I hadn't been a fool. I'd no right to expect anything but evil could come of that marriage—and when I shirked doing a father's part too.'

Nancy was silent: her spirit of rectitude would not let her try to soften the edge of what she felt to be a just compunction. He spoke again after a little while, but the tone was rather changed: there was tenderness mingled with the previous self-reproach.

'And I got *you*, Nancy, in spite of all; and yet I've been grumbling and uneasy because I hadn't something else—as if I deserved it.'

'You've never been wanting to me, Godfrey,' said Nancy, with quiet sincerity. 'My only trouble would be gone if you resigned yourself to the lot that's been given us.'

'Well, perhaps it isn't too late to mend a bit there. Though it *is* too late to mend some things, say what they will.'

CHAPTER XXI

THE next morning, when Silas and Eppie were seated at their breakfast, he said to her—

'Eppie, there's a thing I've had on my mind to do this two year, and now the money's been brought back to us, we can do it. I've been turning it over and over in the night, and I think we'll set out to-morrow, while the fine days last. We'll leave the house and everything for your godmother to take care on, and we'll make a little bundle o' things and set out.'

'Where to go, daddy?' said Eppie, in much surprise.

'To my old country—to the town where I was born—up Lantern Yard. I want to see Mr Paston, the minister: something may ha' come out to make 'em know I was innicent o' the robbery. And Mr Paston was a man with a deal o' light—I want to speak to him about the drawing o' the lots. And I should like to talk to him about the religion o' this country-side, for I partly think he doesn't know on it.'

Eppie was very joyful, for there was the prospect not only of wonder and delight at seeing a strange country, but also of coming back to tell Aaron all about it. Aaron was so much wiser than she was about most things—it would be rather pleasant to have this little advantage over him. Mrs Winthrop, though possessed with a dim fear of dangers attendant on so long a journey, and requiring many assurances that it would not take them out of the region of carriers' carts and slow waggons, was nevertheless well pleased that Silas should revisit his own country, and find out if he had been cleared from that false accusation.

'You'd be easier in your mind for the rest o' your life, Master Marner,' said Dolly—'that you would. And if there's any light to be got up the yard as you talk on, we've need of it i' this world, and I'd be glad on it myself, if you could bring it back.'

So on the fourth day from that time, Silas and Eppie, in their Sunday clothes, with a small bundle tied in a blue linen handkerchief, were making their way through the streets of a great manufacturing town. Silas, bewildered by the changes thirty years had brought over his native place, had stopped several persons in succession to ask them the name of this town, that he might be sure he was not under a mistake about it.

'Ask for Lantern Yard, father—ask this gentleman with the tassels on his shoulders a-standing at the shop door; he isn't in a hurry like the rest,' said Eppie, in some distress at her father's bewilderment, and ill at ease, besides, amidst the noise, the movement, and the multitude of strange indifferent faces.

'Eh, my child, he won't know anything about it,' said Silas; 'gentlefolks didn't ever go up the Yard. But happen somebody can tell me which is the way to Prison Street, where the jail is. I know the way out o' that as if I'd seen it yesterday.'

With some difficulty, after many turnings and new inquiries, they reached Prison Street; and the grim walls of the jail, the first object that answered to any image in Silas's memory, cheered him with the certitude, which no assurance of the town's name had hitherto given him, that he was in his native place.

'Ah,' he said, drawing a long breath, 'there's the jail, Eppie; that's just the same: I aren't afraid now. It's the third turning on the left hand from the jail doors—that's the way we must go.'

'O, what a dark ugly place!' said Eppie. 'How it hides the sky! It's worse than the Workhouse. I'm glad you don't live in this town now, father. Is Lantern Yard like this street?'

'My precious child,' said Silas, smiling, 'it isn't a big street like this. I never was easy i' this street myself, but I was fond o' Lantern Yard. The shops here are all altered, I think—I can't make 'em out; but I shall know the turning, because it's the third.'

'Here it is,' he said, in a tone of satisfaction, as they came to a narrow alley. 'And then we must go to the left again, and then straight for'ard for a bit, up Shoe Lane: and then we shall be at the entry next to the o'erhanging window, where there's the nick in the road for the water to run. Eh, I can see it all.'

'O father, I'm like as if I was stifled,' said Eppie. 'I couldn't ha' thought as any folks lived i' this way, so close together. How pretty the Stone-pits 'ull look when we get back!'

'It looks comical to *me*, child, now—and smells bad. I can't think as it usened to smell so.'

Here and there a sallow, begrimed face looked out from a gloomy doorway at the strangers, and increased Eppie's uneasiness, so that it was a longed-for relief when they issued from the alleys into Shoe Lane, where there was a broader strip of sky.

'Dear heart!' said Silas, 'why, there's people coming out o' the Yard as if they'd been to chapel at this time o' day—a weekday noon!'

Suddenly he started and stood still with a look of distressed amazement, that alarmed Eppie. They were before an opening in front of a large factory, from which men and women were streaming for their mid-day meal.

'Father,' said Eppie, clasping his arm, 'what's the matter?'

But she had to speak again and again before Silas could answer her.

'It's gone, child,' he said, at last, in strong agitation—'Lantern Yard's gone. It must ha' been here, because here's the house with the o'erhanging window—I know that—it's just the same; but they've made this new opening; and see that big factory! It's all gone—chapel and all.'

'Come into that little brush-shop and sit down, father—they'll let you sit down,' said Eppie, always on the watch lest one of her father's strange attacks should come on. 'Perhaps the people can tell you all about it.'

But neither from the brush-maker, who had come to Shoe Lane only ten years ago, when the factory was already built, nor from any other source within his reach, could Silas learn anything of the old Lantern Yard friends, or of Mr Paston the minister.

'The old place is all swep' away,' Silas said to Dolly Winthrop on the night of his return—'the little graveyard and everything. The old home's gone; I've no home but this now. I shall never know whether they got at the truth o' the robbery, nor whether Mr Paston could ha' given me any light about the drawing o' the lots. It's dark to me, Mrs Winthrop, that is; I doubt it'll be dark to the last.'

'Well, yes, Master Marner,' said Dolly, who sat with a placid listening face, now bordered by grey hairs; 'I doubt it may. It's the will o' Them above as a many things should be dark to us; but there's some things as I've never felt i' the dark about, and they're mostly what comes i' the day's work. You were hard done by that once, Master Marner, and it seems as you'll never know the rights of it; but that doesn't hinder there *being* a rights, Master Marner, for all it's dark to you and me.'

'No,' said Silas, 'no; that doesn't hinder. Since the time the child was sent to me and I've come to love her as myself, I've had light enough to trusten by; and now she says she'll never leave me, I think I shall trusten till I die.'

CONCLUSION

THERE was one time of the year which was held in Raveloe to be especially suitable for a wedding. It was when the great lilacs and laburnums in the old-fashioned gardens showed their golden and purple wealth above the lichen-tinted walls, and when there were calves still young enough to want bucketfuls of fragrant milk. People were not so busy then as they must become when the full cheese-making and the mowing had set in; and besides, it was a time when a light bridal dress could be worn with comfort and seen to advantage.

Happily the sunshine fell more warmly than usual on the lilac tufts the morning that Eppie was married, for her dress was a very light one. She had often thought, though with a feeling of renunciation, that the perfection of a wedding-dress would be a white cotton, with the tiniest pink sprig at wide intervals; so that when Mrs Godfrey Cass begged to provide one, and asked Eppie to choose what it should be, previous meditation had enabled her to give a decided answer at once.

Seen at a little distance as she walked across the churchyard and down the village, she seemed to be attired in pure white, and her hair looked like the dash of gold on a lily. One hand was on her husband's arm, and with the other she clasped the hand of her father Silas.

'You won't be giving me away, father,' she had said before they went to church; 'you'll only be taking Aaron to be a son to you.'

Dolly Winthrop walked behind with her husband; and there ended the little bridal procession.

There were many eyes to look at it, and Miss Priscilla Lammeter was glad that she and her father had happened to drive up to the door of the Red House just in time to see this pretty sight. They had come to keep Nancy company to-day, because Mr Cass had had to go away to Lytherley, for special reasons. That seemed to be a pity, for otherwise he might have gone, as Mr Crackenthorp and Mr Osgood certainly would, to look on at the wedding-feast which he had ordered at the Rainbow, naturally feeling a great interest in the weaver who had been wronged by one of his own family.

'I could ha' wished Nancy had had the luck to find a child like that and bring her up,' said Priscilla to her father, as they sat in the gig; 'I should ha' had something young to think of then, besides the lambs and the calves.'

'Yes, my dear, yes,' said Mr Lammeter; 'one feels that as one gets older. Things look dim to old folks: they'd need have some young eyes about 'em, to let 'em know the world's the same as it used to be.'

Nancy came out now to welcome her father and sister; and the wedding group had passed on beyond the Red House to the humbler part of the village.

Dolly Winthrop was the first to divine that old Mr Macey, who had been set in his arm-chair outside his own door, would expect some special notice as they passed, since he was too old to be at the wedding-feast.

'Mr Macey's looking for a word from us,' said Dolly; 'he'll be hurt if we pass him and say nothing—and him so racked with rheumatiz.'

So they turned aside to shake hands with the old man. He had looked forward to the occasion, and had his premeditated speech.

'Well, Master Marner,' he said, in a voice that quavered a good deal, 'I've lived to see my words come true. I was the first to say there was no harm in you, though your looks might be again' you; and I was the first to say you'd get your money back. And it's nothing but rightful as you should. And I'd ha' said the "Amens," and willing, at the holy matrimony; but Tookey's done it a good while now, and I hope you'll have none the worse luck.'

In the open yard before the Rainbow the party of guests were already assembled, though it was still nearly an hour before the appointed feast-time. But by this means they could not only enjoy the slow advent of their pleasure; they had also ample leisure to talk of Silas Marner's strange history, and arrive by due degrees at the conclusion that he had brought a blessing on himself by acting like a father to a lone motherless child. Even the farrier did not negative this sentiment: on the contrary, he took it up as peculiarly his own, and invited any hardy person present to contradict him. But he met with no contradiction; and all differences among the company were merged in a general agreement with Mr Snell's sentiment, that when a man had deserved his good luck, it was the part of his neighbours to wish him joy.

As the bridal group approached, a hearty cheer was raised in the Rainbow yard; and Ben Winthrop, whose jokes had retained their acceptable flavour, found it agreeable to turn in there and receive congratulations; not requiring the proposed interval of quiet at the Stone-pits before joining the company.

Eppie had a larger garden than she had ever expected there now; and in other ways there had been alterations at the expense of Mr Cass, the landlord, to suit Silas's larger family. For he and Eppie had declared that they would rather stay at the Stone-pits than go to any new home. The garden was fenced with stones on two sides, but in front there was an open fence, through which the flowers shone with answering gladness, as the four united people came within sight of them.

'O father,' said Eppie, 'what a pretty home ours is! I think nobody could be happier than we are.'

END OF SILAS MARNER.

SELECTED VARIANTS

THE following draws attention to some of the more significant differences between the manuscript of *Silas Marner* and the printed editions. The list does not include minor changes or the large number of corrections to the punctuation that Eliot made for the different editions. (For the 1878 edition in particular, Eliot decided to remove a large number of commas.) Instead, the selection seeks to highlight sentences that were extensively reworked, noteworthy modifications of style and plot/character, and smaller changes that shed an interesting light on the novel's preoccupations and Eliot's working methods.

While the manuscript kept in the British Library is, on the whole, highly legible, deletions were often made in such a manner as to make the words beneath hard to decipher. In addition to the manuscript itself, the insights of Jonathan R. Quick's 'A Critical Edition of George Eliot's *Silas Marner*' (unpublished PhD dissertation, Yale University, 1968) and David Carroll's 1996 Penguin edition have been invaluable in compiling the selected variants below.

References are to page and line number in the current edition. Insertions in the manuscript are indicated by < >. *Poss.* indicates possible readings, mostly of heavily obscured deletions. Crossed-out words indicate deletions in the manuscript.

1 Silas Marner: The Weaver of Raveloe] *the title page of the MS held in the British Library reads* Silas Marner: The Weaver of Raveloe. A Story by George Eliot. *On 28 February 1861, in response to Blackwood's enquiry about how to advertise the novel, Eliot wrote: 'The advertisement, I think, should be headed, 'New Work by George Eliot.' Then, I would simply put 'Silas Marner, the Weaver of Raveloe. In 1 volume'—avoiding the word story' (*The George Eliot Letters, *ed. Gordon S. Haight (New Haven: Yale University Press, 1954–78), iii. 384).*

3.32 as knowing the signs of the weather] *the novel subtly explores experiences that seem both magical and everyday, as in this change in the MS:* as ~~foretelling~~ <knowing the signs of> the weather

4.39 illuminated by any enthusiastic religious faith. To them] illuminated by <any enthusiastic> religious faith. ~~which would make it appear a heavenward pathway instead of a plain along which they plod to the 'parish' and the churchyard~~. To them *MS*

6.3 he would never urge one of them to accept him against her will] he would never urge one of them to ~~marry~~ <accept> him against her will *MS*

6.7 unexampled eyes] ~~unparalleled~~ <unexampled> eyes *MS*

6.12 and he spoke to him, and shook him, and his limbs were stiff] and he <spoke to him, and> shook him ~~and his~~ and his limbs were stiff *MS*

6.37 cure more folks] ~~help poor folks~~ <cure> more <folks> *MS*

7.30 Lantern Yard] *in the MS, this is spelled throughout as Lanthorn Yard. The less archaic spelling that appears in print adds to the allegorical quality of place names in the novel, including the 'Rainbow' and 'Prison Street'.*

8.3 A less truthful man] a less truthful ~~or less sane~~ man *MS*

8.17 Among the members of his church] *no paragraph break in MS.*

8.20 William Dane] *in the MS he was first named William Wake, which was then corrected throughout to William Waif. The name appears as William Dane in all editions. Waif, suggesting an outcast or unowned child, was a curious first choice, given the trajectories of Silas and Eppie. Q. D. Leavis suggests that 'Dane', evocative of 'a heathen savage' is more appropriate (Penguin (1967), 251).*

8.30 self-complacent suppression of inward triumph] self-complacent ~~expression~~ suppression of inward triumph *MS*

9.3 It had seemed to the unsuspecting Silas] *no paragraph break in MS.*

9.20 an effort at an increased manifestation of regard] an effort at ~~additional signs~~ <an increased manifestation> of regard *MS*

9.25 that would be sanctioned by the feeling of the community] that would be ~~justified~~ <sanctioned> by the feeling of the community *MS*

9.31 when one night Silas] when one ~~Saturday~~ <night> *MS*

10.29 'I must have slept,' said Silas] *Eliot usually began direct speech with a new paragraph, but in the MS she kept the exchange within a single paragraph, until 'Silas was still looking'.*

11.13 further deliberation. Any resort to legal measures for ascertaining the culprit was contrary to the principles of the church in Lantern Yard, according to which prosecution was forbidden to Christians, even had the case held less scandal to the community. But the members were bound] further deliberation: any resort to legal measures for ascertaining the culprit was contrary to the principles of the church; prosecution was held by them to be forbidden to Christians, even if it had been a case in which there was no scandal to the community. But they were bound *MS*

further deliberation. Any resort to legal measures for ascertaining the culprit was contrary to the principles of the Church: prosecution was held by them to be forbidden to Christians, even if it had been a case in which there was no scandal to the community. But they were bound *Pre-1878 editions*

11.24 trust in man had been cruelly bruised. The lots declared] trust in man had been cruelly bruised. They rose from their knees and the lots were drawn. The lots declared *MS*

11.33 you have woven a plot to lay the sin] *in the MS, Eliot originally wrote* you have ~~laid~~ <woven> a plot to lay the sin. *This may have been to avoid the repetition with 'lay', but the replacement of 'laid' with 'woven' also builds on the language of weaving that runs throughout.*

12.17 for which no man is culpable] *the MS adds the following, struck-through, passage:* ¶ For two days Marner sat alone, stunned by pain, without hope enough to create the impulse to go to Sarah; and on the third, the minister and a deacon came to him charged with the message

13.15 where well-known figures entered with a subdued rustling] where well-known faces ~~were upturned~~ <figures entered with a subdued rustling> *MS*

13.24 they were Christianity and God's kingdom upon earth] they were Christianity ~~to him, and the seed of~~ God's kingdom upon earth *MS*

13.29 And what could be more unlike that Lantern Yard world] *no paragraph break in MS.*

14.10 The little light he possessed spread its beams] *Eliot deleted in the MS one of the narrator's rare direct addresses to the reader (see, for example, p. 119):* ~~You see~~, the little light he ~~had~~ <possessed> spread its beams

14.34 But at last Mrs Osgood's] But at last Mistress Osgood's *MS*

14.38 he had five bright guineas] *Eliot thought carefully throughout about the precise amounts earned and saved by Silas, as in this MS change:* he had ~~four~~ five bright guineas

15.2 to him who saw no vista beyond countless days of weaving? It was needless for him] to him, who saw no ~~object in life, beyond endless~~ <vista beyond countless days of> weaving? ~~There was no need~~ <It was needless> for him *MS*

15.5 and the satisfaction of hunger, subsisting quite aloof from the life of belief and love from which he had been cut off. The weaver's hand had known the touch of hard-won money even before the palm had grown to its full breadth] and the satisfaction of hunger, ~~lying standing~~ <subsisting> quite aloof from the life of belief and love from which he had been cut off. The <weaver's> hand had known the touch of hard-worn money even before the ~~fingers~~ <palm> had grown to ~~their~~ <its> full breadth *MS*

15.14 made a loam that was deep enough for the seeds of desire; and] made a loam ~~of habit~~ that was deep enough for <the seeds of> desire ~~to plant itself there:~~ and *MS*

15.17 which seemed to open a possibility of some fellowship] which seemed to ~~promise~~ <open> a possibility of some fellowship *MS*

15.26 Silas felt, for the first time] Silas ~~recovered~~ <felt>, for the first time *MS*

15.32 When Doctor Kimble gave physic] *The MS suggests that Kimble was not initially introduced so quickly:* When ~~the~~ doctor <Kimble> gave physic

16.7 Silas Marner could very likely do as much, and more] Silas Marner could very likely do as much, and more ~~than the Wise Woman~~ *MS*

16.17 the applicants brought silver in their palms] *in a novel saturated with the language of hands, Eliot gave careful thought to her choice of words. As with the variant on page 15, in the MS Eliot again changed a word in favour of 'palm':* the applicants brought silver in their ~~hands~~ <palms>

17.2 by repeating some trivial movement or sound, until the repetition has bred a want, which] by repeating some trivial movement or ~~sensation~~ <sound>, until the repetition has bred a ~~desire~~ want which *MS*

17.22 contained his guineas and silver coins, covering] contained his guineas, <and silver coins> covering *MS*

17.35 that had no relation to any other being] *the MS includes the following, struck-through, passage:* The same reduction of a human life to a simple function without the consciousness of any higher end to which the function is subservient must happen to ever man who has been cut off from sympathy—cut off even from that lowest egoistic interest in his fellow-men which makes their

17.39 cut off from faith and love] cut off from <faith and> love *MS*

18.29 until the fifteenth year after he came to Raveloe. The] *the MS deletes 'fifteenth', then deletes the insertion 'twelfth', then underlines 'fifteenth' again. See, also, the correction from 'twelfth' to 'fifteenth', p. 36. The MS also follows this sentence with the following passage:* ~~But in the Christmas tide of this year, his weaving~~ The

18.37 two thick leather bags] two <thick> leather bags *MS*

19.2 pieces of linen which] pieces of ~~cloth~~ <linen> which *MS*

19.5 he would not change the silver] he would not ~~part with~~ <change> the silver *MS*

20.16 the unctuous liquor in which they were boiled] the unctuous ~~water~~ <liquor> in which they were boiled *MS*

21.25 open as he used to do. At one time everybody was saying, What a handsome couple he and] open as he used to do. <At one time> Everybody ~~used to say~~ <was saying> what a ~~fine match~~ <handsome couple> he and *MS*

21.30 according to his place] according to his ~~station~~ <place> *MS*

23.4 hundred pounds] hundred ~~and twenty~~ pounds *MS*

25.4 no future for himself on the other side of confession] no future for himself ~~beyond~~ <on the other side of> confession *MS*

25.37 flog him] ~~beat~~ <flog> him *MS*

25.38 and no bodily fear could have deterred him] and no fear of kicks and bruises could have deterred him *MS*

28.2 where the daily habits] where the <daily> habits *MS*

28.18 Still, there was one position worse than the present] *no paragraph break in MS.*

28.32 far-off bright-winged prize] far-off <bright-winged> prize *MS*

29.14 perhaps because she saw no other career open to her.] perhaps because she saw no other career open to her; it being the opinion of some philosophers that the absence of an alternative has a great deal to do with the faithfulness of spaniels. *MS*

30.10 as Dunstan was quite sure they would be] *Dunstan's excessive confidence in his good luck was stressed in the MS:* as ~~he expected~~ Dunstan was quite sure they would be

30.38 Keating rode up now] Keating came up now *MS*

31.9 Dunstan, however, took one fence too many, and got his horse pierced with a hedge-stake]

Dunstan, <however>, took one fence too many, and 'staked' his horse *MS*

Dunstan, however, took one fence too many, and 'staked' his horse *Pre-1878 editions*

31.15 thrown him in the rear of the hunt near the moment of glory, and under] thrown him ~~behind~~ in the rear of the hunt <near the moment of glory>, and under *MS*

31.37 Dunstan felt sure he could worry Godfrey into anything. The] Dunstan felt quite sure he could ~~bully~~ <worry> Godfrey into anything ~~in the long run~~. The *MS*

32.1 the prospect of having to make his appearance with the muddy boots] the ~~possible unpleasantness~~ <prospect> of having to make his appearance with <the> muddy boots *MS*

32.8 the stable-keeper] *in MS and pre-1878 editions, this reads 'Jennings'. Jennings returned to anonymity for the 1878 Cabinet Edition.*

32.29 gold handle] *in the MS, Godfrey's whip has a silver handle.*

34.1 Nothing at that moment could be much more inviting] *no paragraph break in MS.*

34.13 on such an evening, leaving his supper in this stage of preparation] on such ~~a night as this~~ <an evening>, leaving his supper in this stage <of preparation> *MS*

35.1 found that they were loose] found that they were ~~movable~~ <loose> *MS*

35.38 it is often observable] it is <often> observable *MS*

36.31 fifteen years before] twelve years *MS and first edition*

37.31 shook so violently that] shook so <violently>, that *MS*

38.7 because it is capable of being dissipated] because it is <capable of being> dissipated *MS*

39.1 about the weaver's money] about ~~the money~~ the weaver's money *MS*

39.6 like a forlorn traveller] like a ~~deserted~~ <forlorn> traveller *MS*

39.13 He ran swiftly, till] He ran <swiftly> till *MS*

39.16 The Rainbow, in Marner's view] *no new paragraph in MS*

39.32 in company that called for beer] *the MS then deletes four lines beginning 'The long pipes', fragments of which appear close to the beginning of Chapter VII. David Carroll argues that this suggests that Chapter VI, and the famous Rainbow conversations, may have been added as 'a second thought' (Penguin (1996), 187).*

40.10 his cousin the butcher] *in the MS, this reads 'Snell, the butcher'. The butcher is later named as Master Lundy (p. 47), but in the MS this originally read 'Master Snell'.*

43.7 some contempt at this trivial discussion] some contempt at this <trivial> discussion *MS*

43.24 Ay, you remember when first Mr Lammeter's father come into these parts] *the first edition changed 'come' to 'came'; later editions reverted to the more colloquial 'come'.*

43.27 that complimentary process] that <complimentary> process *MS*

44.9 Mr Drumlow] *referred to throughout the MS as Mr Drummlow.*

44.20 to be married in, for it isn't like a christening or a burying, as you can't help; and] to be married in, <for it isn't like a christening or a burying as you can't help>; and *MS*

45.18 lasses was growed up] *the MS and pre-1878 editions read 'lasses were growed up'; Eliot chose to accentuate the colloquialism for the 1878 Cabinet Edition.*

46.15 he got queerer nor ever] *Eliot's MS correction did not appear in the first edition*: he got queerer ~~than ever~~ <nor iver>

46.29 and then make believe, if you like] and then ~~pretend~~ <make believe>, if you like *MS*

46.38 who was swelling with impatience for his cue] who was swelling <with impatience> for his cue *MS*

47.39 candour and tolerance] *Eliot's MS revision favours a word that suggests a more actively moral stance:* candour and ~~moderation~~ <tolerance>

49.25 I'll let you have a guinea] *Marner's miserly impulse was initially stressed in the MS:* I'll let you have a guinea—one guinea

50.22 there have been many circulations of the sap] there have been many pulsations of the sap *MS*

50.26 it was impossible for the neighbours to doubt] it was impossible to <the neighbours to> doubt *MS*

50.30 as poor Silas was. Rather, from the strange fact that] *the change from 'probable conclusion' to strangeness adds to the novel's preoccupation with matters that appear both mysterious and commonplace. MS:* as poor Silas was. ~~But the <most probable> conclusion was that~~ Rather, from the strange fact that

51.22 where my guineas can be] where my money can be *MS and pre-1878 editions.*

51.27 two hundred and seventy-two pounds, twelve and sixpence] *Eliot clearly thought carefully about the amount, which diminished with each revision. The smaller amount in the printed editions tallies with the farrier's opinion that the money wouldn't be heavy to carry, and Godfrey's later comment that the sum is in fact a small one: 'And that money on the table, after all, is but little' (p. 148). MS:* ~~Three~~ <Four> hundred and ~~seventy~~ two pounds, twelve and sixpence

54.28 memory, when duly impregnated with ascertained facts] memory, when duly impregnated with accomplished facts *MS*

55.16 glazier's wife] *in the MS, this is the 'wheelwright's wife'. As this is Dolly Winthrop, Eliot presumably decided against having Silas's closest friend add to the wild speculations. A further reference to Dolly's interference was removed; see variant for p. 71.*

56.8 men of that sort, with rings in their ears, had been known for murderers] men of that sort ~~had been known for murderers~~, <with rings in their ears, had been known> for murderers *MS*

57.1 a face that implied something disagreeable] a face that ~~heralded unpleasant tidings~~ implied something disagreeable *MS*

58.15 and, finding that he must bear the brunt of his father's anger, would tell] and, <finding that he would bear the brunt of his father anger, would> tell *MS*

58.36 The old Squire . . . for remark.] *in the MS, the entire sentence was added on the otherwise blank verso.*

59.11 he allowed evils to grow] he ~~was heedless of~~ <allowed evils to grow> *MS*

59.26 ten miles round] ~~six~~ ten miles round *MS*. *In the MS, a version of this sentence was initially placed earlier in the paragraph, following: 'before he told him the fact,' and had been struck through.*

60.6 might blow over] *in the MS, there was originally no chapter break here. The break was added, in the MS, later.*

61.12 Fleet, the deer-hound] *the deer-hound is called 'Flint' in the MS.*

61.16 said the Squire, after taking a draught of ale] said the Squire ~~inclined to take things more good humouredly now he had had his draught of ale~~ <after taking a draught of ale> *MS*

62.9 guess as to what could have caused so strange an inversion] guess as ~~to the~~ <to what could have> caused ~~of this sudden~~ <so strange an> inversion *MS*

62.12 'The truth is, sir] 'The ~~fact~~ truth is, Sir *MS*

65.23 manifesting its prudence. ¶ In this point of trusting to some throw of fortune's dice, Godfrey can hardly be called old-fashioned. Favourable Chance is the god of all men] manifesting its prudence. And in this point of trusting to some throw of fortune's dice, Godfrey can hardly be called specially old-fashioned. Favourable Chance, I fancy, is the god of all men *MS and pre-1878 editions*

66.22 equally expected this issue] equally expected this ~~result~~ <issue> *MS*

67.9 When the robbery was talked of at the Rainbow] *no paragraph break in MS.*

67.21 some true opinions] some <true> opinions *MS*

68.20 and that avoidance of his neighbours, which had before] and <that avoidance of his neighbours which> had before *MS*

68.23 This change to a kindlier feeling] *no paragraph break in MS.*

70.6 but Marner remained silent] but ~~Silas~~ <Marner> remained silent *MS*

70.9 he had no heart to taste it, and felt that it was very far off him] he had no heart to taste it, <and felt that it was very far off him.> *MS*

70.26 Here Mr Macey paused, perhaps expecting some sign of emotion in his hearer; but not observing any, he went on.] *this sentence does not appear in the MS.*

71.1 This was Mrs Winthrop, the wheelwright's wife. The inhabitants] This was Mrs Winthrop, the wheelwright's wife, the same exemplary woman who had described the pedlar's earrings with graphic particularity. The inhabitants *MS*

71.7 that would have implied a] that would have ~~argued~~ <implied> a *MS*

71.10 all who were not household servants, or young men, to take the sacrament] all who were not household servants ~~and who could not be spared~~ to take the sacrament *MS*

74.12 prevail on a sick man to take his medicine, or a basin of gruel for which he had no appetite] prevail on a sick man to take his medicine, or a ~~dinner~~ basin of gruel for which he had no appetite *MS*

75.10 But now, little Aaron] *no paragraph break in MS.*

76.11 And you may judge what it is at church] And you may ~~think~~ <judge> what it is at church *MS*

77.2 The fountains of human love and of faith in a divine love] *Eliot chose to underscore the notion of love for the Cabinet Edition. The MS and earlier editions read:* The fountains of human love and divine faith

77.17 Nobody in this world but himself] *no paragraph break in MS.*

80.5 All these thoughts rushed through Miss Nancy's mind] *no paragraph break in MS.*

80.19 There was a buzz of voices through the house] *no paragraph break in MS.*

80.23 who did the honours at the Red House on these great occasions] who did the honours <at the Red House> on these great occasions *MS*

80.31 There was hardly a bedroom in the house] *no paragraph break in MS.*

81.6 her turban] her ~~cape~~ <turban> *MS*

81.9 But Miss Nancy had no sooner] *no paragraph break in MS.*

82.22 her light-brown hair was cropped] her <light brown> hair was cropped *MS*

82.27 and coral ear-drops] and <coral> ear-drops *MS*

82.34 and as she concluded this judicious remark, she] and as she ~~made~~ <concluded> this judicious ~~observation~~ <remark> *MS*

88.4 'Miss Nancy's wonderful . . . might one day] *Eliot had originally struck through this entire section, before indicating in the margin ('stet') that it should be kept as it was. In the MS, there is no paragraph break beginning 'But Doctor Kimble'.*

89.7 nodded, and amiably intended to smile, but the intention lost itself in small twitchings and noises] *Eliot returned to this sentence:*

nodded, and seemed to intend a smile, that, by the correlation of forces, went off in small twitchings and noises. *MS*

nodded, and seemed to intend to smile, which, by the correlation of forces, went off in small twitchings *Pre-1878 editions*

89.36 in a cold tone] in a ~~low voice~~ cold tone *MS*

90.26 he bowed again to the Squire and the Rector, and] he bowed again to the Squire and ~~Mr. Crackenthorp~~ <the Rector, and> *MS*

93.14 a pot o' good ale] a pot o' good ~~beer~~ ale *MS*

94.2 caught under the stately stamp of the Squire's foot] caught ~~in its slight whirl~~ <under the stately stamp> of the Squire's foot *MS*

94.18 'O no, thank you,' said Nancy, coldly, as soon as she perceived where he was going] 'O <no> thank you,' said Nancy, coldly, as soon as she perceived where ~~Godfrey~~ <he> was going *MS*

95.2 her instinctive dignity and repugnance to any show of emotion] her instinctive dignity and ~~dislike~~ repugnance to any show of emotion *MS*

95.8 would you never think the present made amends for the past?] would you never ~~let~~ <think> the present made amends for the past? *MS*

95.13 had driven him beside himself; but blind feeling] had ~~thrown~~ <driven> him beside himself; but <blind> feeling *MS*

95.14 Nancy really felt much agitated by the possibility Godfrey's words suggested, but this very pressure of emotion that she was in danger of finding too strong for her roused all her power of self-command.] Nancy really felt much agitated by the possibility Godfrey's words suggested but her supreme dread of ~~saying anything~~ <behaving in a way> that she would be unable to approve in herself ~~on~~ in after-moments, roused <all> her ~~utmost~~ power of self-command. *MS*

95.39 said Godfrey, with a reckless determination] said Godfrey ~~seating himself on a chair opposite her~~ with a reckless determination *MS*

97.20 Slowly the demon was working his will] *no paragraph break in MS.*

97.26 She sank down against] She sank down ~~at last~~ against *MS*

97.32 But the complete torpor] *no paragraph break in MS.*

98.15 gurgling and making many inarticulate communications] gurgling ~~and chattering~~ and making many inarticulate communications *MS*

98.17 But presently the warmth] But presently the ~~soothing~~ warmth *MS*

98.19 the blue eyes were veiled by] the blue eyes were ~~closed~~ veiled by *MS*

98.21 this strange visitor] *in the MS, Eppie is described as 'this stranger visitor'; in the first edition it is hyphenated as 'this stranger-visitor', and it became 'strange visitor' for the 1863 and subsequent editions.*

98.23 he had contracted the habit of opening his door and looking out from time to time, as if he thought that] he had contracted the habit of ~~looking~~ opening his door and looking out from time to time, ~~with a vague~~ as if the thought that *MS*

98.31 a bewildering separation from a supremely loved object] a bewildering separation from a ~~beloved~~ <supremely> loved object *MS*

99.29 the familiar resisting outline] the familiar ~~rounded~~ <resisting> outline *MS*

99.31 it was a sleeping child] it was a ~~tiny~~ sleeping child *MS*

100.1 and its shabby clothing] and its shabby ~~dingy~~ clothing *MS*

100.10 he had a dreamy feeling] *Eliot once again underscored the novel's pervasive feeling of dreaminess and mystery in the MS:* he had a ~~strong impression~~ <dreamy feeling>

100.12 old quiverings of tenderness—old impressions of awe at the presentiment of some Power presiding over his life; for his imagination] *Eliot indicated in the MS that the clauses she had originally written should be rearranged as they are in printed editions. MS:* old impressions of awe at the presentiment of some power presiding over his life, old quiverings of tenderness. For his imagination

100.18 the child had awaked, and Marner stooped to lift it on his knee] the child <had> awaked and Marner stooped to lift it <on his knee> *MS*

100.24 cool by the dying fire] cool by the dying ~~embers~~ <fire> *MS*

100.26 He had plenty to do through the next hour] *no paragraph break in MS.*

100.38 and baby was at once happily occupied with] and Baby was ~~happy~~ at once ~~in studying~~ <happily occupied> with *MS*

101.4 Under the prompting] *Eliot indicated that this should begin a new paragraph, but the instruction was not followed in print.*

101.26 had advanced to this pitch of freedom] had ~~brought~~ <advanced to> this pitch of freedom *MS*

101.34 only the upper doorway was left free. Bob Cass] only the upper doorway was left free, ~~open for the sake of air~~. Bob Cass *MS*

101.35 whom he repeatedly declared to be just like himself in his young days in a tone that implied this to be the very highest stamp] whom he repeatedly ~~and loudly~~ declared to be just like himself in his young days, ~~as if that were~~ <in a tone that implied this to be> the very highest stamp *MS*

102.6 He stood aloof, because he wished to avoid suggesting himself as a subject for the Squire's fatherly jokes in connection with matrimony] He ~~kept a little~~ <stood> aloof because <he wished> to avoid ~~*illegible deletion*~~ <suggesting himself as a subject> for the Squire's fatherly jokes ~~about~~ <in connection with> matrimony *MS*

102.20 for months past] for ~~three~~ months past *MS*

102.35 dead in the snow at the Stone-pits] dead in the snow ~~against my house~~ <at the Stone Pits> *MS*

102.38 That was an evil terror] That was an ~~wicked~~ <evil> terror *MS*

103.2 a man whose happiness hangs on duplicity] a man whose happiness hangs on ~~concealment~~ duplicity *MS*

103.21 'Why, you'd better leave the child here, then, Master Marner,' said good-natured Mrs Kimble, hesitating, however, to] 'Why, you'd better leave the child here, then, <Master> Marner,' said good-natured Mrs Kimble, hesitating ~~a little~~, however, to *MS*

103.26 It's come to me—I've a right to keep it.' ¶ The proposition to take the child from him had come] It's ~~been sent~~ come to me—I've a right to keep it ~~if I like~~.' ¶ The proposition <to take the child from him> had <come> *MS*

104.13 clinging to Marner, who had apparently won] clinging to Marner ~~as if he~~ <who> had, <apparently> won *MS*

104.28 encountering cold and snow] encountering cold and ~~wet~~ <snow> *MS*

104.33 so good as tell my husband to come, on your way back—he's at the Rainbow, I doubt—if you found him anyway sober enough to be o' use. Or else, there's] so good as tell ~~*poss.* to ask~~ my husband to come, on your way back, <—he's at the Rainbow, I doubt—> if you found him anyways sober enough, to be o' use. ~~And if you didn't~~ <Or else>, there's *MS*

106.14 that little heart had no response for the half-jealous yearning in his own, when the blue eyes turned away from him slowly, and fixed themselves on the weaver's queer face, which was bent low down to look at them, while the small hand began to pull Marner's withered cheek with loving disfiguration] *this passage caused Eliot an unusual amount of trouble in the MS:* that little heart had [~~*poss.* not been taught to respond to~~] <no> response for ~~him~~ the half-jealous yearning in his own ~~as~~ <when> the blue eyes turned away from him slowly and fix~~ing~~<ed> themselves on ~~Marner's withered~~ <the weaver's queer> face <which was> bent ~~*illegible deletion*~~ low down to look at them, while the small ~~finger~~ hand began to pull ~~*illegible deletion*~~ Marner's withered cheek <with> ~~tender~~ loving disfiguration

107.14 as a great artist] as a great ~~painter~~ <artist> *MS*

107.15 his own, are worn as lightly as mere trimmings when once the actions have become a lie] his own, are worn as lightly as mere trimmings [~~*poss.* by men~~] <when <once> the actions have become a lie.> *MS*

108.13 That softening of feeling towards him which dated from his misfortune, that merging of suspicion and dislike in a rather contemptuous pity for him as lone and crazy, was now accompanied] *the clauses were initially arranged differently, and Eliot indicated in the MS that they should appear as they do in print. MS:* That softening of feeling towards him, that merging of suspicion and dislike in a rather contemptuous pity for him as lone and crazy, which dated from his misfortune, was now accompanied

109.25 the sleeping and the waking, and the rain and the harvest—one goes] the sleeping and the waking, and <the rain and the harvest>, and one goes *MS*

109.31 You'll happen be a bit moithered with it] You'll ~~belike~~ <happen> be a bit moithered with it *MS*

110.10 docilely, bringing his eyes very close] *Eliot chose to stress Silas's short-sightedness in the MS:* docilely, ~~putting~~ <bringing> his ~~head~~ <eyes> very close

110.12 with both her small arms] with both her ~~fat~~ <small> arms *MS*

110.28 high hearth] open hearth *in the MS. Given Dolly's description of it as safer for Eppie, 'high' makes more sense.*

110.36 nor the lads. I know what the lads are] nor the ~~boys~~ <lads>. I know what the boys <lads> are *MS*

111.5 I can teach 'em this little un, Master Marner] *Eliot chose to have Marner, in his reply, insist on his ownership of Eppie.* I can teach 'em ~~your~~ <this> little un, Master Marner—*MS*

113.19 same blank limit] same blank ~~goal~~ <limit> *MS*

114.9 As the child's mind was growing into knowledge] *no paragraph break in MS.*

114.14 the tones that stirred] the ~~sounds~~ <tones> that stirred *MS*

114.23 a little in soft and safe places now and then] a little in soft <and safe> places now and then *MS*

114.33 she'll get so masterful, there'll be no holding her] she'll get so masterful ~~it'll be the ruin of her~~ <there'll be> no holding her *MS*

115.8 round her waist, and was long enough to allow of her reaching] round her waist and ~~defied her cleverness in tearing~~ <was long enough to allow> of her reaching *MS*

115.20 she stole quietly from her corner] she stole quietly from ~~the bed her place~~ <her corner> *MS*

117.18 So Eppie was reared without punishment, the burden] So Eppie was reared without punishment ~~except any evil consequences~~, the burden *MS*

118.17 to link him] to ~~bind~~ link him *MS*

119.5 and the hand may be a little child's] *in the MS, the next paragraph, beginning 'There was one person', follows on from this with a paragraph break, but not a new chapter. The MS draws a line under 'child's', and 'Chap. XV' appears in the margin in different ink, suggesting that Eliot had not originally intended the existing Chapter XV to stand alone.*

121.15 a loss which is marked even when the eye is undulled] a loss which is ~~felt~~ <marked> even when the eye is undulled *MS*

121.30 Mr and Mrs Godfrey Cass] Mr and Mrs <Godfrey> Cass *MS*

121–2.32 turned round to look for the tall aged man] turned round to ~~wait~~ [~~*poss.* a moment~~] <look> for the tall aged man *MS*

122.6 not likely to be handsomely clad] not likely to be handsomely ~~dressed~~ <clad>

122.12 answering gaze] answering look *MS and pre-1878 editions*

122.26 That good-looking young fellow] *no paragraph break in MS.*

123.9 by Eppie's side, entering into the conversation without the trouble of formalities. 'It'll be play to me after I've done my day's work, or any odd bits o' time when the work's slack. And I'll bring you some soil from Mr Cass's garden] *Eliot made a number of changes to the passage:*

by Eppie's side, ~~and entered~~ <intruding> into the conversation with an absence of formalities that must shock all polite minds. 'It'll be play to me after I've done ~~shepherding~~ <my day's work>, or any odd bits o' time when the work's slack. And I'll bring you some soil from [~~*poss.* the country~~] <Mr. Cass's> garden *MS*

by Eppie's side, and intruding into the conversation without the trouble of formalities. *First edition (rest as in Cabinet Edition)*

123.22 she added, half-bashfully, half-roguishly, 'only] she added, <half-bashfully, half-roguishly>, 'only *MS*

124.11 It sets one thinking o' that—gardening does] It sets one thinking <o' that>—gardening does *MS*

124.25 with the mild passive happiness of love-crowned age] with the ~~gentle~~ <mild> passive happiness of love-crowned age *MS*

124.35 gratify him with her usual notice] gratify him with her usual ~~attention~~ <notice> *MS*

125.6 the lady-mother of the kitten sat sunning her white bosom] the lady-mother of the kitten sat sunning ~~herself~~ <her white bosom> *MS*

125.10 The presence of this happy animal life] *no paragraph break in MS.*

125.12 the small space was well filled with decent furniture] the small space was well filled with decent ~~cottage~~ furniture *MS*

125.22 Master Marner was none so young] Master Marner was ~~<old for his years>~~ none so young *MS*

126.4 more silently than usual, soon laying down his knife and fork, and watching] more silently than usual, <soon laying down his knife and fork, and> watching *MS*

127.33 'Ah!' said Silas, who] 'Ah!' said Marner, who *MS*

129.24 I've a feeling o' that now, and it makes a man feel as there's a good more nor he can see] I feel that now—and, as you say, it makes one feel there's a good we can't see *MS*

129.37 her own questions about her mother could not have been parried, as she grew up] *the order of the clauses had originally been different, and Eliot indicated in the MS that they should be arranged as they appeared in print:* her own questions about her mother as she grew up could not have been parried *MS*

130.29 were questions that often pressed on Eppie's mind] were ~~thoughts~~ <questions> that often pressed on Eppie's mind *MS*

131.11 said Eppie, clasping her hands suddenly] said Eppie, ~~clapping~~ <clasping> her hands suddenly *MS*

131.19 he added, with a tender intonation—'that's] he added, <with a tender intonation>—that's *MS*

132.16 Silas gave an almost imperceptible start, though the question fell in with the under-current of thought in his own mind, and then said] Silas gave an almost imperceptible start, <though the question fell in with the undercurrent of thought in his own mind,> and then said *MS*

133.25 and when I look for'ard to that] and when I ~~think on~~ <look forward to> that *MS*

134.3 it would be better to take tea] it would be better to stay tea *MS and pre-1878 editions*

134.12 no yesterday's dust is allowed to rest] no yesterday's dust is allowed to settle *MS and first edition*

134.22 All is purity and order in this once dreary room] ~~There is a presiding spirit of~~ <All is> purity and order in this once dreary room *MS*

135.18 wall-like hedges of yew, Priscilla] wall-like hedges of yew, ~~on their way towards Nancy's particular bed of chrysanthemums~~, Priscilla *MS*

137.13 She recalled the small details, the words, tones, and looks] She recalled ~~every~~ <the small> details, ~~every~~ <the> words, <tones>, and looks *MS*

137.17 adherence to an imagined or real duty] adherence to an imagined <or real> duty *MS*

138.3 Yet sweet Nancy might have been expected] *no paragraph break in MS.*

138.14 Perhaps it was this] *no new paragraph in MS.*

138.16 'It is very different—it is much worse for a man to be disappointed in that way: a woman can always be satisfied with devoting herself to her husband, but a man wants something that will make him look forward more—and sitting by the fire is so much duller to him than to a woman.']

'It was very different—it was much worse for a man to be disappointed in that way: a woman can always be satisfied with devoting herself to her husband, but a man wants something that will make him look forward more—and sitting by the fire ~~is~~ <was> so much duller to him than to a woman.' *MS*

'It was very different—it was much worse for a man to be disappointed in that way: a woman could always be satisfied with devoting herself to her husband, but a man wanted something that would make him look forward more— and sitting by the fire was so much duller to him than to a woman.' *Pre-1878 editions*

138.24 Had she really been right in the resistance which] Had she really been right in the ~~refusal in~~ <resistance> which *MS*

138.29 an opinion on all topics, not exclusively masculine, that had come under her notice] an opinion on all topics, <not exclusively masculine>, that had come under her notice *MS*

138.32 her opinions were always principles to be unwaveringly acted on] her opinions ~~had the rigidity of principles~~ <were always> principles <to be unwaveringly acted on> *MS*

140.9 Godfrey from the first specified Eppie, then about twelve years old, as a child suitable for them to adopt. It had never occurred to him that Silas would rather part with his life than with Eppie] *in the MS, a version of this sentence originally came after 'likelihood of her being a curse to anybody?', and was struck through:* Godfrey had specified Eppie, then about ~~twelve ten~~ <twelve> years old, as a child suitable for them to adopt. It had never occurred to him that Silas would rather have parted with his life than with Eppie. Surely the weaver

141.17 told to her now, after that long concealment. And the child, too, he thought, must become an object of repulsion: the very sight of her would be painful. The shock to Nancy's mind] told to her now ~~for the first time~~ after that long concealment. And the child, <too>, he thought ~~would be~~ <must become> an object of ~~that~~ repulsion: the <very> sight of her would ~~become~~ <be> painful. The shock to ~~her~~ <Nancy's> mind *MS*

141.25 Meanwhile, why could he not make up his mind] Meanwhile, why could he not ~~be contented~~ <make up his> mind *MS*

141.31 privation of an untried good] *in the MS, this was immediately followed by the sentence beginning 'In Godfrey's case'. On the verso, Eliot wrote the sentence 'Dissatisfaction*[...]*brief madness', and instructed that it should be inserted into the paragraph.*

143.10 a strange unanswering glance] a strange <unanswering> glance *MS*

146.9 Between eight and nine o'clock that evening] ~~At eight~~ <Between eight and nine> o'clock that evening *MS*

146.17 an intensity of inward life, under which sleep is an impossibility] an intensity of inward life ~~which would make sleep impossible~~ <under which sleep is an impossibility> *MS*

148.17 because there's been a great deal of linen-weaving to be done] because ~~linen weaving was wanted~~. <there's been a great deal of> linen-weaving <to be done> *MS*

148.30 There's few working-folks] there's few ~~poor~~ working-folks *MS*

148.38 at the Red House,' said Godfrey] *in the MS, Eliot inserted 'surprised at' after this, and instructed that additional lines composed on the verso should be added:* at the difficulty he found in approaching a proposition which had seemed so easy to him in the distance

149.4 she doesn't look like a strapping girl come of working parents] she ~~isn't~~ <doesn't look> like the strapping girls ~~in the village~~ <come of> working parents *MS*

149.17 nobody to be the better for our good home] nobody to benefit by our good home *MS and pre-1878 editions*

149.20 It u'd be] *for the Cabinet Edition, Eliot made a number of changes to Godfrey's speech which had the effect of diminishing the gap between his formal speech and Silas's more colloquial language. In the MS and pre-1878 editions, Godfrey says:* It would be

150.19 he was possessed with all-important feelings that were to lead to a predetermined course of action] he was ~~not prepared~~ <possessed> with all-important feelings that were to lead to ~~a certain~~ a predetermined course of action *MS*

150.21 appreciation into other people's feelings counteracting his] appreciation into <other people's> feelings ~~which~~ counteracting his *MS*

151.26 You ought to remember your own life's uncertain, and she's at an age] *in the MS and pre-1878 editions, Godfrey says:* You ought to remember that your own life is uncertain, and that she's at an age

151.38 this new unfamiliar father] this new <unfamiliar> father *MS*

152.22 privileges of 'respectability'] the ~~luxuries~~ <privileges> of 'respectability' *MS*

152.33 what a father should ha' been to you] what a father should have been to you *MS and pre-1878 editions*

152.38 'My dear, you'll be a treasure to me,' said Nancy, in her gentle voice] 'My dear, you'll be a treasure to me,' <said Nancy, in her gentle voice> *MS*

153.3 finger-tips that were sensitive to such pressure] finger-tips that were ~~capable of~~ <sensitive to> such pressure *MS*

153.38 I like the working-folks, and their victuals, and their ways] *Eliot changed this twice, and ultimately decided to stress the novel's concern with food:*

I like the working-folks—and their houses—and their ways *MS*

I like the working-folks, and their houses, and their ways *First edition*

154.3 smarting dilated eyes] smarting dilation of the eyes *MS and pre-1878 editions*

154.23 action which would distract the sensations] actions which would ~~interfere~~ distract the sensations *MS*

155.3 I shall pass for childless now against my wish] I shall pass for childless now against my will *[poss] MS*

156.7 And I got *you*, Nancy] And I got you, Nancy *MS*

157.26 which no assurance of the town's name had hitherto given him] which no assurance <of the <town's> name> had hitherto given him *MS*

159.10 love her as myself, I've had light enough to trusten by] love ~~it~~ <her> as myself, I've had light enough to ~~live by~~ <trusten by> *MS*

160.22 since he was too old to be at the wedding-feast] *in the MS, the words* So they turned aside to shake hands with the old man. He had looked *originally followed, and were deleted and inserted after Dolly's speech.*

161.4 a general agreement with Mr Snell's sentiment] a general agreement with ~~the landlord's~~ <Mr Snell's> sentiment *MS*

EXPLANATORY NOTES

I AM greatly indebted to earlier editions of *Silas Marner*, and in particular Q. D. Leavis's 1967 Penguin edition, David Carroll's 1996 Penguin edition, and Terence Cave's 1996 Oxford World's Classics edition. Quotations from the Bible are from the 1611 King James version; definitions from the *Oxford English Dictionary* (*OED*) are from the online version at www.oed.com.

2 *'A child . . . thoughts.'—Wordsworth*: these lines are taken from William Wordsworth's poem 'Michael, a Pastoral Poem', published in the 1800 edition of the *Lyrical Ballads.* The poem depicts the elderly shepherd Michael and his younger wife Isabel, to whom a son is born when Michael has 'one foot in the grave'. 'Michael' describes the strong 'domestic affections, as I know they exist among a class of men who are now almost confined to the North of England' (Wordsworth to Charles James Fox, January 1801, in *The Letters of William and Dorothy Wordsworth*, ed. Ernest de Selincourt and Chester L. Shaver, 8 vols. (Oxford: Oxford University Press, 1967–93), i. 314). When faced with the loss of money, and therefore the possible loss of his land, Michael sends his son Luke to earn money in the city, but there Luke gives himself 'to evil courses', and eventually hides abroad, causing his father's heartbreak. Beyond the theme of the child regenerating the man, there are many echoes of 'Michael' in Eliot's novel, which is set around the same time as Wordsworth's poem: Wordsworth depicts the relentless industry inside the cottage which, like Silas's, is a source of light amidst the countryside. Like Silas, there is a feminine quality to Michael's fatherly care: while Luke 'was a babe in arms' he 'had done him female service' and had rocked his cradle 'as with a woman's gentle hand'. In a letter to John Blackwood, Eliot wrote of *Silas Marner*: 'I should not have believed that any one would have been interested in it but myself (since William Wordsworth is dead)' (24 February 1861, *George Eliot Letters*, ed. Gordon Haight, 9 vols. (New Haven: Yale University Press, 1954–78), iii. 382). Eliot's first novel, *Adam Bede* (1859), also includes an epigraph from Wordsworth on its title page; as Stephen Gill notes, Wordsworth was, after Shakespeare, the writer from whom she took the most epigraphs ('Wordsworth, William', in John Rignall (ed.), *Oxford Reader's Companion to George Eliot* (Oxford: Oxford University Press, 2000), 473).

3 *thread-lace*: lace made from the thread of either flax or linen, rather than silk, silver, or gold. In the early nineteenth century, thread-lace could also be made from cotton thread. Nancy Lammeter wears both lace and silk: she later stands 'in her silvery twilled silk, her lace tucker, her coral necklace, and coral ear-drops' (p. 82).

alien-looking men: John Blackwood wrote to his wife Julia in 1861 that '"Silas Marner" sprang from her childish recollection of a man with a stoop and expression of face that led her to think that he was an alien from his fellows' ([15] June 1861, *George Eliot Letters*, iii. 427).

4 *In the early years of this century*: there remains some ambiguity concerning the precise chronology of the novel. Q. D. Leavis proposes that Silas leaves Lantern Yard and settles in Raveloe in the late 1780s, Patrick Swinden suggests the approximate date of 1790, and Terence Cave argues that this incident takes place as late as 1797. By common consent, Part Two takes place sometime in the 1820s.

Raveloe: Eliot keeps the location of this fictional village vague, which contributes to the legendary qualities of the story. In 1872, she wrote to the philologist Walter William Skeat that 'the district imagined as the scene of *Silas Marner* is in N. Warwickshire' (*George Eliot Letters*, ix. 39).

loom . . . winnowing-machine . . . flail: Silas uses a handloom, a large wooden structure inside which he would have sat, with his feet on peddles. The winnowing machine was invented by James Sharp in 1777, and was used by farmers to separate grain from chaff. The flail was a wooden tool used to separate grain from husks—a threshing machine was invented for the same purpose in the 1780s, but had apparently not yet reached Raveloe. Philip Gaskell's *The Manufacturing Population of England* (London: Baldwin and Cradock, 1833) described how, in the second half of the eighteenth century, 'the cottage every where resounded with the clack of the hand-loom' (p. 16). He added that

> These were, undoubtedly, the golden times of manufactures, considered in reference to the character of the labourers. By all the processes being carried on under a man's own roof, he retained his individual respectability; he was kept apart from associations that might injure his moral worth,—whilst he generally earned wages which were sufficient not only to live comfortably upon, but which enabled him to rent a few acres of land [. . .] A garden was likewise an invariable adjunct to the cottage of the hand-loom weaver; and in no part of the kingdom were the floral tribes, fruits, and edible roots, more zealously or more successfully cultivated. (pp. 16–17)

rickets, or a wry mouth: rickets is a disease (usually suffered by children) caused by a lack of vitamin D, leading to bone deformities including, often, bow legs; a wry mouth is a distortion of the mouth.

5 *tithes*: a tax paid to the parish rector consisting of a tenth of a farmer's produce; payment through produce such as crops was later often replaced by money, a practice that the Tithe Commutation Act standardized in 1836.

war times: England and France were at war between 1793 and 1815, first during the French Revolutionary Wars, then the Napoleonic Wars. Farmers benefited from the wars since corn could no longer be imported from France, which in turn inflated the price of home-grown produce. Following the end of the wars, the increasingly controversial Corn Laws kept the price of domestic grain high until their repeal in 1846.

5 *Whitsun*: the seventh weekend after Easter, also known as Pentecost, and which marks the Holy Ghost's descent among Jesus's disciples (Acts 2:1–2).

6 *wheelwright's*: manufacturer of wheels. Appropriately, when Silas starts to forge connections with Raveloe's inhabitants, it is primarily through the wheelwright's wife, Dolly.

unexampled: unparalleled—as Eliot first wrote in the manuscript.

with a heavy bag on his back: George Eliot often referred to John Bunyan's *The Pilgrim's Progress* (1678–84). Her image echoes Bunyan's opening sentence in which the narrator, in a dream, sees '*a man cloathed with Raggs, standing in a certain place, with his face from his own House, a Book in his hand, and a great burden upon his back*' (ed. W. R. Owens (Oxford World's Classics), 10). See also note to p. 119. The image also has more personal echoes: Eliot wrote to Blackwood that the story 'came to me first of all, quite suddenly, as a sort of legendary tale, suggested by my recollection of having once, in early childhood, seen a linen-weaver with a bag on his back' (24 February 1861, *George Eliot Letters*, iii. 382).

'fit': Silas suffers from a form of catalepsy (see note to p. 9). To some observers in Raveloe, it appears as a supernatural manifestation; to Silas's companions in Lantern Yard, it is interpreted as a sign of God's favour as well as, conversely, his disfavour.

throw him on the parish: receive financial support from the parish, under the terms of the Poor Law. As Silas's Raveloe neighbours later inform him, 'if you was to be crippled, the parish 'ud give you a 'lowance' (p. 68). See also note to p. 134.

7 *tale*: amount.

a narrow religious sect: Eliot does not specify to which branch of Nonconformism Silas belongs. Nonconformists dissented from the beliefs and practices of the Church of England (or Anglicanism) and included Baptists, Methodists, Presbyterians, and Congregationalists. *Adam Bede* (1859) had offered a sympathetic portrait of Methodism through the character of Dinah Morris. Aspects of Silas's religious experience evoke Baptism (he is only aware of adult baptism), as well as Congregationalism (Dolly talks to Silas of 'folks in your old country niver saying prayers by heart nor saying 'em out of a book', p. 128), as well as other Dissident practices. In her 1855 essay on the Evangelical preacher Dr John Cumming (1807–81), Eliot wrote that 'it is commonly seen that, in proportion as religious sects believe themselves to be guided by direct inspiration rather than by a spontaneous exertion of their faculties, their sense of truthfulness is misty and confused' (*Selected Critical Writings*, ed. Rosemary Ashton (Oxford World's Classics), 145). Although her account of the Lantern Yard religious community is largely a negative one, Eliot also underscores its attractions: the sect's lack of recourse to priests to interpret the Bible makes for a more democratic environment in which 'the poorest layman' has a voice (p. 7). See also notes to pp. 8, 11, and 111.

8 *David and Jonathan*: this biblical friendship is depicted in 1 Samuel 18. Jonathan was King Saul's eldest son and the heir to the throne of Israel; David was the youngest son of a shepherd, and became Saul's armour bearer as well as Jonathan's brother-in-law. As the future King David became increasingly popular, Saul's jealousy grew. Jonathan repeatedly sought to protect David from his father's murderous designs; 'Jonathan and David made a covenant, because he loved him as his own soul' (1 Samuel 18:3). David and Jonathan are also the names of characters in Eliot's 'Brother Jacob', written in 1860: Jonathan comes to despise his brother David after the latter steals his mother's guineas and flees.

Assurance of salvation: Silas belongs to the kind of Calvinist sect which believed in original sin, 'a state of corruption or sinfulness, or a tendency to evil, supposedly innate in all human beings and held to be inherited from Adam as a consequence of the Fall' (*OED*). Select individuals, however, had been predestined by God to be saved. Some Dissenters thought that this divine grace was unconditional, whatever the actions of the elect, a belief vividly explored in James Hogg's *The Private Memoirs and Confessions of a Justified Sinner* (1824).

'calling and election sure': members of certain Dissenting faiths looked for signs that they were amongst the elect. The phrase is taken from 2 Peter 1:10: 'Wherefore the rather, brethren, give diligence to make your calling and election sure: for if ye do these things, ye shall never fall.' On 26 December 1860, Eliot wrote to her friend Barbara Bodichon that although she was sympathetic to those who turned to "forms and ceremonies" for comfort, 'the highest "calling and election" is to *do without opium* and live through all our pain with conscious, clear-eyed endurance' (*George Eliot Letters*, iii. 366).

9 *in order to their marriage*: in preparation for their marriage.

cataleptic fit: catalepsy is defined by the *OED* as 'a disease characterized by a seizure or trance, lasting for hours or days, with suspension of sensation and consciousness'. As Martin Willis has investigated ('*Silas Marner*, Catalepsy, and Mid-Victorian Medicine: George Eliot's Ethics of Care', *Journal of Victorian Culture*, 20/3 (2015): 326–40), contemporary doctors often classed catalepsy alongside hysteria and epilepsy. George Henry Lewes's library included medical texts discussing such conditions, such as Charles Edouard Brown-Sequard's *Course of Lectures on the Physiology and Pathology of the Nervous Systems* (1860).

senior deacon: in Dissident circles, an officer elected to administer the Church.

10 *not in the body, but out of the body*: St Paul evokes religious ecstasy in 2 Corinthians 12:3 in similar terms: 'And I knew such a man, (whether in the body, or out of the body, I cannot tell: God knoweth;)'.

11 *prosecution was forbidden to Christians*: some Calvinist sects believed in the separation of Church and State, and enforced the law within their own religious communities.

11 *drawing lots*: settling disputes in this manner was unusual amongst Dissident religious groups, suggesting that Silas belongs to a particularly rigid branch. Biblical justification for the practice could be found in a number of places. In the Old Testament, for example, Saul places a curse on anyone in the army who eats before evening, but his son Jonathan eats some honey. Lots are drawn to identify who has broken the oath, fingering Jonathan (1 Samuel 14:41–2). In the book of Jonah, mariners cast lots to identify the cause of a dangerous tempest, and 'the lot fell upon Jonah' (Jonah 1:7).

12 *made various by learning*: made varied or, as Terence Cave suggests, 'enriched, opened to many possibilities' (Oxford World's Classics, 182).

13 *Lethean*: Lethe was one of the five rivers in the Greek underworld; drinking from it caused forgetfulness.

petition: prayer, entreaty.

amulet: charm offering protection against evil or disease.

In the early ages . . . divinities: the sentence points to the novel's anthropological interest in religion and myth. See also note to p. 126 on the influence of Comte.

14 *five bright guineas put into his hand*: the guinea coin was minted between 1663 and 1813, and its value from the early eighteenth century was fixed at 21 shillings; sovereigns replaced guinea coins in 1817. In *Middlemarch*, the narrator comments that 'Municipal town and rural parish gradually made fresh threads of connexion—gradually, as the old stocking gave way to the savings-bank, and the worship of the solar guinea became extinct' (ed. David Carroll (Oxford World's Classics), 94). Not only were the specific amounts earned by Silas important to Eliot (see Selected Variants, pp. 14 and 51) but so was the physical nature of the money. As she wrote to Blackwood, 'There can be no great painting of misers under the present system of paper money—cheques bills scrip and the like: nobody can handle that dull property as men handled the glittering gold' (5 May 1861, *George Eliot Letters*, iii. 411).

15 *loam*: a fertile soil.

dropsy: 'A morbid condition characterized by the accumulation of watery fluid in the serous cavities or the connective tissues of the body' (*OED*). Dropsy recurs in Eliot's novels: doctor Pilgrim in 'Janet's Repentance' (1857) is interested in the condition ('a lingering dropsy dissolved him into charity', *Scenes of Clerical Life*, ed. Thomas A. Noble (Oxford World's Classics), 97), Maggie's aunt Pullet cries over the death of an acquaintance who suffered from dropsy in *The Mill on the Floss* (1860), and the miser Featherstone in *Middlemarch* shares the complaint.

16 *water in the head*: in other words hydrocephalus, 'a disease of the brain especially incident to young children, consisting in an accumulation of serous fluid in the cavity of the cranium, resulting in a gradual expansion of the skull' (*OED*).

17 *flock-beds*: a bed filled with wool or cloth.

King Alfred: also known as Alfred the Great (848/9–99), monarch who reigned over Wessex from 871 until his death.

a balloon journey: such a journey would indeed have been a novel idea in the late eighteenth century: the first flight in a hot air balloon, designed by the Montgolfier brothers, took place in Paris in 1783.

18 *his most precious utensil*: the focus on the pot recalls the similar focus on the lamp, 'an aged utensil', in Wordsworth's poem 'Michael'. Silas's pot is a 'companion'; Michael's lamp is a 'comrade'. See also note to p. 2.

19 *title of Squire*: 'employed as a title and prefixed to the surname of a country gentleman' (*OED*).

20 *yeomen*: yeomen owned and cultivated small landed estates, and were socially beneath the rank of gentlemen.

orts: leftover food, scraps.

top-knots . . . pillions: topknots were hair bows, or could take the form of decorated lace caps; a pillion was either a 'light saddle used by women' or 'a pad or cushion attached behind a saddle, on which a second person may ride, or to which luggage may be fastened' (*OED*).

standing dishes: the *OED* defines these as dishes that appear every day, or at every meal.

chines uncut: the chine is a cut of meat that includes the backbone. In chapter 20 of *Adam Bede* (1859), much attention is given to Mrs Poyser's tempting 'stuffed chines', served in slices (ed. Carol A. Martin (Oxford World's Classics), 199–200).

spun butter: ornamental butter worked into shapes.

21 *King George*: King George III (1738–1820), whose reign began in 1760. See notes to pp. 54 and 87.

22 *foxes' brushes*: foxes' tails.

distrain: force him to meet his obligations by seizing his property, or through other legal means.

24 *laudanum*: liquid opium, easily obtainable and used at the time to treat a wide range of ailments. See note to p. 96.

to dig and to beg: in Luke 16:1–3, a rich man's steward is accused of having 'wasted his goods' and, having been relieved of his duties, complains: 'I cannot dig; to beg I am ashamed.'

25 *''listing for a soldier'*: enlisted soldiers were beneath the rank of commissioned officers, which would be a more appropriate position for someone of Godfrey's social status.

26 *trumps*: a playing card which ranks above others.

crooked sixpence: bent coins were often bestowed as good luck charms.

27 *rioting*: dissoluteness or, less pejoratively, revelry.

27 *pierced by the reeds they leaned on*: in Isaiah 36:6, faith in the Pharaoh of Egypt is presented as unreliable, as opposed to faith in the Lord: 'Lo, thou trustest in the staff of this broken reed, on Egypt; whereon if a man lean, it will go into his hand, and pierce it: so *is* Pharaoh king of Egypt to all that trust in him.'

29 *cruel wishes . . . home*: Luke 11:24–6 and Matthew 12:43–5 contain passages with almost identical wording. That from Luke reads: 'When the unclean spirit is gone out of a man, he walketh through dry places, seeking rest; and finding none, he saith, I will return unto my house whence I came out. And when he cometh, he findeth *it* swept and garnished. Then goeth he, and taketh *to him* seven other spirits more wicked than himself; and they enter in, and dwell there: and the last *state* of that man is worse than the first.'

cock-fighting: gambling on which of two cocks would vanquish the other underscores the novel's preoccupation with luck. The practice was banned in 1835 as part of the Cruelty to Animals Act.

ride to cover: in hunting terms, the cover consists of the 'woods, undergrowth, and bushes, that serve to shelter or conceal wild animals and game' (*OED*). The emptying of the Cass stables means that Dunstan has to ride on the same horse he'll be using to hunt; a wealthier man would have opted for an ordinary riding horse to reach the cover. In *Middlemarch*, Eliot portrays Fred Vincy, another young man whose attempt at trading a horse ends badly. Fred had hoped to 'hunt in pink, have a first-rate hunter, ride to cover on a fine hack, be generally respected for doing so' (ed. Carroll (Oxford World's Classics), 342). Like Dunstan, he is disappointed in his expectations.

31 *pocket-pistol*: flask.

34 *jacks*: the *OED* defines a jack as 'a machine for turning the spit in roasting meat; either wound up like a clock or actuated by the draught of heated air up the chimney'.

the treddles of the loom: more commonly called treadles; in other words the levers, or peddles.

35 *horn lantern*: animal horns were often used to make lanterns.

40 *fustian jackets and smock-frocks*: clothes often worn by peasants and other rural workers. Fustian was 'a kind of coarse cloth made of cotton and flax' (*OED*), while a smock-frock was a 'looser outer garment' or 'overall' (*OED*).

red Durham: a variety of Shorthorn cattle, bred in the late eighteenth century in north-east England.

farrier: farriers shod horses, but also treated their diseases.

drenching: giving a dose of medicine to an animal.

41 *'I know . . . what I know'*: this is taken from Psalm 106 in Nahum Tate and Nicholas Brady's *New Versions of the Psalms of David* (1696). The third quatrain reads:

Happy are they, and only they,
Who from thy judgments never stray:
Who know what's right, not only so,
But always practice what they know.

The work was known as the 'New Version', and gradually superseded the sixteenth-century 'Old Version' of Thomas Sternhold and John Hopkins. The choice of psalms remained controversial in the early nineteenth century: the 'New Version' was considered by some High Churchmen to be unauthorized. In 'The Sad Fortunes of the Reverend Amos Barton', first published in 1857, the narrator describes the old-fashioned Shepperton Church, where 'the New Version was regarded with a sort of melancholy tolerance, as part of the common degeneracy [. . .] for the lyrical taste of the best heads in Shepperton had been formed on Sternhold and Hopkins' (*Scenes of Clerical Life*, ed. Noble (Oxford World's Classics), 5).

42 *the 'bassoon' and the 'key-bugle'*: a key-bugle was 'a bugle fitted with keys to increase the range of sounds it can produce' (*OED*). Ben Winthrop appears to be suggesting that the pair sing bass and tenor respectively. However, it is possible that they also play these instruments: church singing was often accompanied by village bands, as Dolly indicates by praising Raveloe's Christmas carols, 'with the bassoon and the voices' (p. 76).

'Red Rovier': this song has not been identified.

43 *liver and lights*: offal; 'lights' referred to lungs.

45 *'cute*: acute.

46 *Old Harry*: the devil.

Queen's heads went out on the shillings: Queen Anne reigned between 1702 and 1714.

47 *as lief*: as soon.

'bate: abate, or reduce.

48 *pike-staff*: staff or walking stick.

49 *Justice*: the Justice of the Peace (JP) was tasked with keeping the peace. A civil public officer, or magistrate, he had the power to hear civil matters and deal with minor criminal ones.

50 *mushed*: dejected, crushed.

52 *nolo episcopari*: (Latin) 'I do not wish to be made bishop.' Bishops supposedly refused the nomination twice before accepting, as a demonstration of humility. The phrase came to signify the rejection of something that is in fact wanted.

53 *'watch for the morning'*: from Psalm 130:6. The full verse reads: 'My soul *waiteth* for the Lord more than they that watch for the morning: *I say, more than* they that watch for the morning.'

54 *justices and constables . . . King George's making*: justices and constables existed long before the reign of King George III, when *Silas Marner* takes place—the local powers of constables and Justices of the Peace derived to

a large extent from an Act passed in 1673. During George III's reign, however, law and order were becoming increasingly professionalized.

55 *take the sacrament*: to receive Holy Communion, or the Eucharist.

56 *'sizes*: assizes. These were the 'sessions held periodically in each county of England, for the purpose of administering civil and criminal justice, by judges acting under certain special commissions' (*OED*).

57 *swinging*: slang or dialect for large, immense.

60 *managing-man*: like George Eliot's father, Robert Evans, who managed a far more impressive estate than that of the Cass family.

61 *unstring*: to undo the strings of his purse.

62 *collogue*: 'to have a private understanding with; to intrigue, collude, conspire' (*OED*).

entail: an entail meant that an estate could not be passed on to whomever the owner wanted. Property settlements and the law of entail play a key role in Eliot's novel *Felix Holt* (1866).

64 *shilly-shally*: undecided, vacillating.

66 *seed . . . kind*: biblical language evocative of Genesis 1:12, 'And the earth brought forth grass, *and* herb yielding seed after his kind, and the tree yielding fruit, whose seed *was* in itself, after his kind: and God saw that *it was good*.'

Commission of the Peace: the collective Justices of the Peace of an area, or jurisdiction. Members appointed to the Commission of the Peace were often landowners or men of similarly elevated social rank.

67 *mural monument*: members of the gentry often had family memorials, sometimes made of stone and either mounted on the wall or placed as floor slabs, built inside their local church.

brawn: at this time, a reference to head meat, often from a boar or pig, that was salted and seasoned, boiled and pickled. In 'Brother Jacob', scheming David Faux manages to get invited to the home of his would-be wife by asking her mother, Mrs Palfrey, for her recipe for brawn, 'hers being pronounced on all hands to be superior to his own' (*The Lifted Veil* and *Brother Jacob*, ed. Helen Small (Oxford World's Classics), 72).

skimming-dishes: a shallow dish, usually employed to skim milk or make cheese.

68 *pigs' pettitoes*: pigs' trotters.

69 *cussing of a Ash Wednesday*: Ash Wednesday is the first day of Lent, six weeks before Easter. The Book of Common Prayer includes 'A Commination, or Denouncing of God's Anger and Judgements Against Sinners', which the priest would recite.

70 *give you trust*: would not demand immediate payment.

Silas's comforters: in his unsigned review for *The Times* on 29 April 1861, E. S. Dallas pointed towards a parallel between Silas and Job: 'He is surrounded with comforters, most of whom are even less sympathizing than the comforters of Job, and he sinks into a deeper despair than that of the most patient of men, for, as we have said, he cursed and denied God in his affliction' (David Carroll (ed.), *George Eliot: The Critical Heritage* (London: Routledge and Kegan Paul, 1971; repr. 2000), 185). In Job 16:2, Job declares: 'I have heard many such things: miserable comforters *are* ye all.'

71 *monthly nurse*: a nurse who took care of mother and child after a baby's birth.

72 *lard-cakes*: more commonly known as lardy cake, this is a bread made with lard, flour, spices, sugar, and raisins. Although its origins are hard to pinpoint, it is often associated with Wiltshire, in the south Midlands.

73 *I. H. S.*: the letters designate the name Jesus Christ, and are a Latin version of the first three letters of the name Jesus in Greek, ΙΗΣ. The letters are also sometimes interpreted as 'Iesus Hominum Salvator', namely 'Jesus, Saviour of Men'.

bakehus: for a modest sum, food could be baked in a communal oven.

74 *I went to chapel*: Dissenters marked their separation from the Church of England through this term.

76 *'God rest you . . . Christmas-day'*: Christmas carol, versions of which reach back to the sixteenth century. In the opening chapter of Dickens's *A Christmas Carol* (1843), a young singer begins to chant 'God bless you, merry gentleman! May nothing you dismay!' at Scrooge's keyhole, before he is scared away (ed. Robert Douglas-Fairhurst (Oxford World's Classics), 15).

"Hark the erol angils sing": Christmas carol evolved from that first published in Charles Wesley's *Hymns and Sacred Poems* (1739).

77 *Athanasian Creed*: the text, which affirms the doctrine and the Trinity and is included in the Book of Common Prayer, was rarely used, and continued to decline in the nineteenth century, often confined to Trinity Sunday. The text was not written by Athanasius (AD 293–373), as its name seems to imply.

79 *a drab joseph*: a long, buttoned women's riding cloak, made of dull brown cloth.

horse-block: a stone or wooden platform with steps used for mounting and dismounting horses.

81 *skullcap and front, with her turban*: Mrs Ladbrook is sporting a close-fitting cap and a band of false hair; turbans, often made of silk, were all the rage in the early 1800s.

mob-cap: Nancy's elderly aunt is wearing an appropriately old-fashioned item: a loose, indoor cap with a frilly border, occasionally tied under the chin with a ribbon. The mob-cap was associated for George Eliot with the realism of seventeenth-century Dutch painters. In *Adam Bede* (1859), she praises their ability to depict subjects such as 'an old woman bending over her flower-pot, or eating her solitary dinner, while the noonday light, softened perhaps by a screen of leaves, falls on her mob-cap, and just touches the rim of her spinning-wheel, and her stone jug' (ed. Martin (Oxford World's Classics), 161).

82 *nattiness*: neatness.

her twilled silk, her lace tucker: the silk has been woven in diagonal lines, and Nancy is also wearing a piece of lace around the top of her bodice.

and even still coarser work: in her biography of George Eliot, Mathilde Blind writes that Mary Ann Evans once remarked to a friend of her hands that 'one of them was broader across than the other, saying with some pride, that it was due to the quantity of butter and cheese she had made during her house-keeping days at Griff' (*George Eliot* (London: W. H. Allen & Co., 1883), 20). This remains a source of debate.

83 *Dame Tedman's*: dame schools were run by older women in their own homes. See also p. 129. Eliot's first school was a dame school; Dame Moore's cottage was located outside Griff House.

84 *hogsheads*: large casks for holding liquids.

a scrag or a knuckle: 'the lean and inferior end of a neck of mutton (or veal)' and 'the end of a bone at a joint' (*OED*).

mawkin: term that could refer to an untidy woman (especially a servant or country girl) as well as a scarecrow.

85 *addled egg*: an egg that has rotted, or failed to produce a chick—a description that gains additional poignancy in the light of Nancy's future.

ear-droppers: drop earrings.

86 *complimentary personalities*: personal remarks, compliments.

87 *since the old king fell ill*: from 1788, King George III suffered from a severe illness, the symptoms of which led to fears that he was insane. His condition worsened to such an extent in 1810 that, the following year, the Regency Act handed power over to the Prince of Wales.

88 *country apothecaries . . . diploma*: this dates the section before 1815, when the Apothecaries Act made training and qualifications compulsory for apothecaries. The professionalization of medicine is one of the themes of *Middlemarch.*

90 *"The flaxen-headed ploughboy"*: a reference to the song 'The Plough Boy', which appears in the popular opera *The Farmer* (1787), written by John O'Keefe and put to music by William Shield, music director of Covent Garden.

"Over the hills and far away": a line included in many eighteenth-century songs. One popular version was an army recruiting song, included for example in George Farquhar's 1706 comedy *The Recruiting Officer* ('Over the Hills, and o'er the Main, | To Flanders, Portugal, or Spain: | The Queen commands, and we'll obey, | Over the Hills, and far away'). It also took the form of a love song, as in 'Jockey's Lamentation', published in *Songs Compleat, Pleasant and Divertive; set to Musick. Volume V* (London: printed by W. Pearson, 1719), which begins (p. 317):

Jockey met with *Jenny* fair
Betwixt the dawning and the Day,
And *Jockey* now is full of Care,
For *Jenny* stole his Heart away:
Altho' she promis'd to be true,
Yet she, alas, has prov'd unkind,
That which do make poor *Jenny* rue,
For *Jenny's* fickle as the Wind:
And, *'Tis o'er the Hills, and far away,*
'Tis o'er the Hills, and far away,
'Tis o'er the Hills, and far away,
The Wind has blown my Plad away.

91 *'Sir Roger de Covereley'*: a traditional country dance. Like the carol 'God rest you, merry gentlemen' (see note to p. 76), this is also mentioned in Dickens's *A Christmas Carol,* during Scrooge's visitation by the Ghost of Christmas Past: 'But the great effect of the evening came after the Roast and Boiled, when the fiddler [. . .] struck up "Sir Roger de Coverley" ' (ed. Douglas-Fairhurst (Oxford World's Classics), 36).

92 *tithe in kind*: see note to p. 5. Here, the clergyman is paid in agricultural goods.

springe: 'active, agile' (*OED*). The only instances in the *OED* of the word 'springe' and 'springest', in all likelihood Midlands dialect, are from the novels of George Eliot: 'springest' appears in *Adam Bede.*

sodger: soldier.

93 *piert*: lively, cheerful; dialect for 'pert'.

slack-baked pie: 'imperfectly or insufficiently baked' (*OED*).

Before I said "sniff" [. . .] *"snaff"*: In his 1863 article 'George Eliot's Novels', Richard Simpson asserted that 'Some of her sayings are simply decanted out of newspapers [. . .] The original of this is to be found in one of the Swinfen trials' (Carroll (ed.), *George Eliot: Critical Heritage*, 234). The trial to settle the disputed will of Samuel Swynfen, or Swinfen, took place between 1856 and 1864.

96 *Opium*: until the 1868 Pharmacy Act, opium was easily available and widely used for medicinal purposes. It often took the form of laudanum, and this black liquid is what Molly consumes. Opium featured increasingly in Eliot's novels: Mr Christian in *Felix Holt* uses it when suffering from 'an access of nervous pains' (ed. Fred C. Thomson (Oxford World's Classics), 120); in *Middlemarch* Lydgate, Will, and Farebrother all try it and it is prescribed to treat Raffles; Hans Meyrick experiments with it in *Daniel Deronda* (1876). The men, however, are largely disappointed by it.

97 *furze bush*: an evergreen shrub with yellow flowers, also known as a gorse.

105 *workhouse*: many workhouses, which developed in the eighteenth century, had on-site burial grounds, where paupers whose families could not pay for a burial were placed in unmarked graves.

106 *parish*: workhouse.

109 *the night . . . the harvest*: as David Carroll notes (Penguin, 191), the speech has strong echoes with Genesis 8:22: 'While the earth remaineth, seedtime and harvest, and cold and heat, and summer and winter, and day and night shall not cease.'

scrat: 'to struggle to make a living or to gain money' (*OED*).

moithered: dialect for confused, overcome.

110 *ringing the pigs*: putting a ring through the nose of each pig, to stop them damaging the fields or their sty with their snout.

111 *the 'I believe . . . deed'*: Church of England catechism in the Book of Common Prayer.

'noculation: inoculation against smallpox. Inoculation was increasingly practised in the eighteenth century, and was gradually replaced by vaccination, following Edward Jenner's experiments in the 1790s.

Dolly's word 'christened' . . . baptism of grown-up men and women: whilst the Anglican Church practised infant baptism, or christenings (see p. 69, when Mr Macey speaks of children having taken 'the water'), Baptists practised adult baptism, which involved complete immersion.

112 *Hephzibah*: in the Old Testament, Hephzibah, whose name means 'my delight is in her', is the wife of King Hezekiah, and mother of King Manasseh (2 Kings 21:1). In Isaiah 62:4, God addresses Israel to offer the nation hope and safety after a period of religious idolatry and military invasion: 'Thou shalt no more be termed Forsaken; neither shall thy land any more be termed Desolate: but thou shalt be called Hephzibah, and thy land Beulah: for the LORD delighteth in thee, and thy land shall be married.'

the haft for the handle: David Carroll defines this as 'mistaking one thing for another' (Penguin, 192).

114 *colly*: dialect, meaning 'to blacken with coal-dust or soot' (*OED*).

Goliath: a giant ('whose height *was* six cubits and a span', 1 Samuel 17:4), killed by the future king of Israel, David.

115 *truckle-bed*: 'a low bed running on truckles or castors, usually pushed beneath a high or "standing" bed when not in use' (*OED*).

119 *city of destruction*: in the opening of Bunyan's *Pilgrim's Progress* (1678–84), Christian, prompted by the Evangelist, leaves his home behind, telling his neighbours they dwell 'in the City of Destruction, the place also where I was born' (ed. Owens (Oxford World's Classics), 13). This in turn echoes Isaiah 19:18: 'In that day shall five cities in the land of Egypt speak the language of Canaan, and swear to the LORD of hosts; one shall be called, The city of destruction.' See also note to p. 6.

famous ring: From Madame Leprince de Beaumont's fairy tale 'Le Prince Chéri' (1785). The Prince is visited by the Fairy Candide who gives him a ring, enjoining him to 'Keep this ring carefully—it is more precious than diamonds. Every time you commit a bad action it will prick your finger' (*Four and Twenty Fairy Tales . . . translated by J. R. Planché* (London: Routledge, 1858), 484).

125 *less and less flax spun*: this section of the novel takes place in the 1820s, when industrialization had an impact on weavers such as Silas. There was a period of recession following the end of the Napoleonic Wars in 1815, and the decrease in the price of cotton affected linen weavers. Edmund Carpenter experimented on mechanical looms in the 1780s, and the spinning of flax was further revolutionized following James Kay's invention of a wet spinning process in 1824. As John Holloway draws attention to in his introduction, the Final Report of the *Royal Commission on the Condition of Handloom Weavers*, produced in 1841, supports Eliot's depiction: in the early Victorian period, 'few weavers but recollect the "good old times" when their labours were four-fold remunerated compared with their present rates of earnings' (p. 39, quoted in John Holloway (ed.), Everyman's Library, x).

126 *The gods of the hearth . . . fetishism*: the Romans in particular worshipped household gods—Janus (god of doorways) and Vesta (goddess of the hearth)—as well as household spirits, including the *lares* (spirits of ancestors) and *penates* (spirits of the larder). Eliot was also interested in the ideas of Auguste Comte (1798–1857), who identified three stages of religious belief. The first was 'fetishism', and entailed the worship of inanimate objects; belief then transitioned from polytheism to monotheism, leading to theologies such as Christianity and Islam. Comte believed that the third, positivist, stage had been reached—what became known as the 'religion of humanity'.

clew: 'a ball of thread, which in various mythological or legendary narratives (esp. that of Theseus in the Cretan Labyrinth) is mentioned as the means of 'threading' a way through a labyrinth or maze' (*OED*).

127 *mine own familiar friend . . . again' me*: an echo of Psalms 41:9: 'Yea, mine own familiar friend, in whom I trusted, which did eat of my bread, hath lifted up *his* heel against me.'

128 *folks in your old country . . . 'Our Father'*: whereas, as a member of the Church of England, Dolly recites the Lord's Prayer, some Dissenters improvised their prayers.

134 *filberts*: hazelnuts.

Derbyshire spar: semi-precious mineral used to make vases and other ornaments.

increasing poor-rate and the ruinous times: parishes levied a property tax used to assist the poor, under the terms of the Old Poor Law (1601), which was soon to be replaced by the Poor Law Amendment Act of 1834. The poor rate had been increasing since the mid-eighteenth century, and the need for poor relief grew after the end of the Napoleonic Wars. In 1825, England also experienced a serious financial crisis.

135 *Michaelmas*: the feast of St Michael, on 29 September, and one of four quarter days, the other three being Lady Day (25 March), Midsummer Day (24 June), and Christmas (25 December).

136 *Mant's Bible*: in 1814, Richard Mant published a commentary on the Bible, written in collaboration with the Revd George D'Oyly, and produced for the Society for Promoting Christian Knowledge. The full title was *The Holy Bible, according to the Authorized Version; with notes, explanatory and practical; taken principally from the most eminent writers of the United Church of England and Ireland; together with appropriate introductions, tables, indexes, maps, and plans.*

138 *Adoption . . . of our own*: although fostering had existed informally for centuries, English common law did not make provisions for official adoption until the Adoption of Children Act of 1926.

139 *transported*: transportation to penal colonies in Australia was an alternative to hanging; it is also evoked in *Adam Bede.*

146 *'beauty born of murmuring sound'*: from Wordsworth's 'Lucy' poem, 'Three years she grew in sun and shower'. The fifth stanza, spoken by Nature, reads:

'The stars of midnight shall be dear
To her, and she shall lean her ear
In many a secret place
Where rivulets dance their wayward round,
And beauty born of murmuring sound
Shall pass into her face.'

(*The Major Works*, ed. Stephen Gill (Oxford World's Classics), 155). See also note to p. 2.

151 *eat . . . cup*: maintains the biblical echoes of Silas's language, this time evoking 2 Samuel 12:3: 'But the poor *man* had nothing, save one little ewe lamb, which he had bought and nourished up: and it grew up together with him, and with his children; it did eat of his own meat, and drank of his own cup, and lay in his bosom, and was unto him as a daughter.'

MORE ABOUT **OXFORD WORLD'S CLASSICS**

American Literature

British and Irish Literature

Children's Literature

Classics and Ancient Literature

Colonial Literature

Eastern Literature

European Literature

Gothic Literature

History

Medieval Literature

Oxford English Drama

Philosophy

Poetry

Politics

Religion

The Oxford Shakespeare

A SELECTION OF **OXFORD WORLD'S CLASSICS**

William Morris	**News from Nowhere**
John Ruskin	**Praeterita**
	Selected Writings
Walter Scott	**Ivanhoe**
	Rob Roy
	Waverley
Mary Shelley	**Frankenstein**
	The Last Man
Robert Louis Stevenson	**Strange Case of Dr Jekyll and Mr Hyde and Other Tales**
	Treasure Island
Bram Stoker	**Dracula**
W. M. Thackeray	**Vanity Fair**
Frances Trollope	**Domestic Manners of the Americans**
Oscar Wilde	**The Importance of Being Earnest and Other Plays**
	The Major Works
	The Picture of Dorian Gray
Ellen Wood	**East Lynne**
Dorothy Wordsworth	**The Grasmere and Alfoxden Journals**
William Wordsworth	**The Major Works**
Wordsworth and Coleridge	**Lyrical Ballads**

TROLLOPE IN **OXFORD WORLD'S CLASSICS**

ANTHONY TROLLOPE

The American Senator
An Autobiography
Barchester Towers
Can You Forgive Her?
Cousin Henry
Doctor Thorne
The Duke's Children
The Eustace Diamonds
Framley Parsonage
He Knew He Was Right
Lady Anna
The Last Chronicle of Barset
Orley Farm
Phineas Finn
Phineas Redux
The Prime Minister
Rachel Ray
The Small House at Allington
The Warden
The Way We Live Now

A SELECTION OF **OXFORD WORLD'S CLASSICS**

HANS CHRISTIAN ANDERSEN	**Fairy Tales**
J. M. BARRIE	**Peter Pan in Kensington Gardens and Peter and Wendy**
L. FRANK BAUM	**The Wonderful Wizard of Oz**
FRANCES HODGSON BURNETT	**The Secret Garden**
LEWIS CARROLL	**Alice's Adventures in Wonderland and Through the Looking-Glass**
CARLO COLLODI	**The Adventures of Pinocchio**
KENNETH GRAHAME	**The Wind in the Willows**
ANTHONY HOPE	**The Prisoner of Zenda**
THOMAS HUGHES	**Tom Brown's Schooldays**
CHARLES PERRAULT	**The Complete Fairy Tales**
ANNA SEWELL	**Black Beauty**
ROBERT LOUIS STEVENSON	**Kidnapped** **Treasure Island**

A SELECTION OF **OXFORD WORLD'S CLASSICS**

ANTON CHEKHOV	**About Love and Other Stories**
	Early Stories
	Five Plays
	The Princess and Other Stories
	The Russian Master and Other Stories
	The Steppe and Other Stories
	Twelve Plays
	Ward Number Six and Other Stories
FYODOR DOSTOEVSKY	**Crime and Punishment**
	Devils
	A Gentle Creature and Other Stories
	The Idiot
	The Karamazov Brothers
	Memoirs from the House of the Dead
	Notes from the Underground and The Gambler
NIKOLAI GOGOL	**Dead Souls**
	Plays and Petersburg Tales
MIKHAIL LERMONTOV	**A Hero of Our Time**
ALEXANDER PUSHKIN	**Boris Godunov**
	Eugene Onegin
	The Queen of Spades and Other Stories
LEO TOLSTOY	**Anna Karenina**
	The Kreutzer Sonata and Other Stories
	The Raid and Other Stories
	Resurrection
	War and Peace
IVAN TURGENEV	**Fathers and Sons**
	First Love and Other Stories
	A Month in the Country

A SELECTION OF **OXFORD WORLD'S CLASSICS**

	French Decadent Tales
	Six French Poets of the Nineteenth Century
Honoré de Balzac	Cousin Bette
	Eugénie Grandet
	Père Goriot
	The Wild Ass's Skin
Charles Baudelaire	The Flowers of Evil
	The Prose Poems and Fanfarlo
Denis Diderot	Jacques the Fatalist
	The Nun
Alexandre Dumas (père)	The Black Tulip
	The Count of Monte Cristo
	Louise de la Vallière
	The Man in the Iron Mask
	La Reine Margot
	The Three Musketeers
	Twenty Years After
	The Vicomte de Bragelonne
Alexandre Dumas (fils)	La Dame aux Camélias
Gustave Flaubert	Madame Bovary
	A Sentimental Education
	Three Tales
Victor Hugo	Notre-Dame de Paris
J.-K. Huysmans	Against Nature
Pierre Choderlos de Laclos	Les Liaisons dangereuses
Mme de Lafayette	The Princesse de Clèves
Guillaume du Lorris and Jean de Meun	The Romance of the Rose

A SELECTION OF **OXFORD WORLD'S CLASSICS**

Guy de Maupassant	**A Day in the Country and Other Stories** **A Life** **Bel-Ami**
Prosper Mérimée	**Carmen and Other Stories**
Molière	**Don Juan and Other Plays** **The Misanthrope, Tartuffe, and Other Plays**
Blaise Pascal	**Pensées and Other Writings**
Abbé Prévost	**Manon Lescaut**
Jean Racine	**Britannicus, Phaedra, and Athaliah**
Arthur Rimbaud	**Collected Poems**
Edmond Rostand	**Cyrano de Bergerac**
Marquis de Sade	**The Crimes of Love** **Justine** **The Misfortunes of Virtue and Other Early Tales**
George Sand	**Indiana**
Mme de Staël	**Corinne**
Stendhal	**The Red and the Black** **The Charterhouse of Parma**
Paul Verlaine	**Selected Poems**
Jules Verne	**Around the World in Eighty Days** **Journey to the Centre of the Earth** **Twenty Thousand Leagues under the Seas**
Voltaire	**Candide and Other Stories** **Letters concerning the English Nation** **A Pocket Philosophical Dictionary**

A SELECTION OF **OXFORD WORLD'S CLASSICS**

ÉMILE ZOLA

L'Assommoir
The Belly of Paris
La Bête humaine
The Conquest of Plassans
The Fortune of the Rougons
Germinal
The Kill
The Ladies' Paradise
The Masterpiece
Money
Nana
Pot Luck
Thérèse Raquin

A SELECTION OF **OXFORD WORLD'S CLASSICS**

THOMAS AQUINAS	**Selected Philosophical Writings**
FRANCIS BACON	**The Major Works**
WALTER BAGEHOT	**The English Constitution**
GEORGE BERKELEY	**Principles of Human Knowledge and Three Dialogues**
EDMUND BURKE	**A Philosophical Enquiry into the Sublime and Beautiful**
	Reflections on the Revolution in France
CONFUCIUS	**The Analects**
RENÉ DESCARTES	**A Discourse on the Method**
	Meditations on First Philosophy
ÉMILE DURKHEIM	**The Elementary Forms of Religious Life**
FRIEDRICH ENGELS	**The Condition of the Working Class in England**
JAMES GEORGE FRAZER	**The Golden Bough**
SIGMUND FREUD	**The Interpretation of Dreams**
G. W. E. HEGEL	**Outlines of the Philosophy of Right**
THOMAS HOBBES	**Human Nature and De Corpore Politico**
	Leviathan
DAVID HUME	**An Enquiry concerning Human Understanding**
	Selected Essays
IMMANUEL KANT	**Critique of Judgement**
SØREN KIERKEGAARD	**Repetition and Philosophical Crumbs**
JOHN LOCKE	**An Essay concerning Human Understanding**

A SELECTION OF **OXFORD WORLD'S CLASSICS**

Niccolò Machiavelli	**The Prince**
Thomas Malthus	**An Essay on the Principle of Population**
Karl Marx	**Capital** **The Communist Manifesto**
J. S. Mill	**On Liberty and Other Essays** **Principles of Political Economy and Chapters on Socialism**
Friedrich Nietzsche	**Beyond Good and Evil** **The Birth of Tragedy** **On the Genealogy of Morals** **Thus Spoke Zarathustra** **Twilight of the Idols**
Thomas Paine	**Rights of Man, Common Sense, and Other Political Writings**
Jean-Jacques Rousseau	**The Social Contract** **Discourse on the Origin of Inequality**
Arthur Schopenhauer	**The Two Fundamental Problems of Ethics**
Adam Smith	**An Inquiry into the Nature and Causes of the Wealth of Nations**
Mary Wollstonecraft	**A Vindication of the Rights of Woman**

A SELECTION OF **OXFORD WORLD'S CLASSICS**

JOHN BUCHAN	**Greenmantle** **Huntingtower** **The Thirty-Nine Steps**
JOSEPH CONRAD	**Chance** **Heart of Darkness and Other Tales** **Lord Jim** **Nostromo** **An Outcast of the Islands** **The Secret Agent** **Typhoon and Other Tales** **Under Western Eyes**
ARTHUR CONAN DOYLE	**The Adventures of Sherlock Holmes** **The Case-Book of Sherlock Holmes** **The Hound of the Baskervilles** **The Lost World** **The Memoirs of Sherlock Holmes** **Sherlock Holmes: Selected Stories** **A Study in Scarlet**
FORD MADOX FORD	**The Good Soldier**
JOHN GALSWORTHY	**The Forsyte Saga**
JEROME K. JEROME	**Three Men in a Boat**
JAMES JOYCE	**A Portrait of the Artist as a Young Man** **Dubliners** **Occasional, Critical, and Political Writing** **Ulysses**
RUDYARD KIPLING	**Captains Courageous** **The Complete Stalky & Co** **The Jungle Books** **Just So Stories** **Kim** **The Man Who Would Be King**